Gypsy Lane

A Love Drama

By

Vernard "Vdor" Dorsey

CLINTON,
   THANKS FOR THE LOVE &
SUPPORT BRO, MISS YOU MY DUDE.

   MUCH LOVE,

   Vdor

By the Author, Buy the Book!

Published by: Amazon Publishing

ISBN: 978-0692788387

Library of Congress Cataloging-in-Publication Data

Vernard Dorsey Gypsy Lane: A Love Drama

Gypsy Lane Credits:

Written by Vernard "Vdor" Dorsey

Edited and Proofed by Lisa Spotwood

Text formation by Vdor

Cover concept and graphics by Vdor

Cover photography by Unknown

Cover enhancement by Danielle Ferreira

Back cover arrangement by Danielle Ferreira

Author Photo by Amira Canty

Printed by Vdor Innovations

First Paperback Edition

Dedicated to the life and legacy of

Colleen J. Evans

February 13, 1982 ~ October 22, 2015

Her life was love, her legacy shall forever live in our

hearts.

"Don't be mean…love!"

Other titles by Vernard "Vdor" Dorsey

Silent Hero: *Another Philadelphia Fable*

Karma: *A Philadelphia Fable (Second Edition Coming 2018)*

The following artists were in constant rotation during the creation of this novel:

Adonye Green, Algebra, Aliza Inez, Aloe Black, Allesia Cara, Anderson .Paak, Anthony David, Anthony Hamilton, Ayah, Bilal, Carmen Rodgers Carol Riddick, Chantae Cann, Choklate, Chrisette Michele, Conya Doss, Daley, D'angelo, Deborah Bond, Debra Debs, Dwele, Ebrahim, Eric Lau, Eric Roberson, The Floacist, The Foreign Exchange, The Fuzz Band, Geno Young, Gretchen Parlato, Goapele, H2O, Hiatus Kaiyote, Havana, INC, India Arie, The Internet, Jazzanova, Jeanne Jolly, Jessie Boykins III, Jill Scott, Jose James, J.Rawls, JSOUL, K'Alyn, Karma Fields, Kendrick Lamar, Kindred Family Soul, Lalah Hathaway, Logic, Liv Warfield, Mali Music, Mark-De-Clive, Marsha Ambrosius, Monica Blaire, Moonchild, Musiq, Nicolay, Schoolboy Q, Snarky Puppy, Quintessence, Ra-Re Valverde, Rhian Benson, Robert Glasper, The Roots, Sohn, Sy Smith, Tank, Teri Tobin, Vikter Duplaix, Vivian Green, Vula, Yahzarah, Yamama'nym, Yolanda, ZO! and many other artists not mentioned.

Thank you for your musical contributions which kept me focused and motivated. To all of you, know that your gift of music extends beyond the reach of the listeners ear. Without your musical influence and creative genius this novel would not have been possible.

Much thanks and appreciation to Choklate, Dwele, J. Tait, Miz Korona, Monica Blaire, Ron Dance, Sy Smith, Tiffany Eaddy, ZO!, and Corren Conway of F12 Films for your interviews and filmography on a great Book Trailer/Documentary for my last novel Silent Hero: Another Philadelphia Fable.

Special thanks to Dwele for inspiring the compelling romantic chapter "Obey" from the song "Obey" of the Greater Than One Album, and Eric Roberson for inspiring the moving chapter "Even Still" from the song "Still" of the Music Fan First Album.

CHAPTERS

Gypsy Lane

A Love Drama

Prepare to be moved...

My Life is Good

"WAIT A MINUTE, WAIT A MINUTE! Since we're on topic here, let's talk about you and your trifling track record, mister 'one-night stand, runnin' man!' How many have you knocked down?" Marty exclaims over the crowd noise as he lines up his cue-ball to knock in the eight ball, but misses the shot.

"WOW! I'm on trial now? I'm on trial?! Okay, let's see...about, two-hundred and twenty-seven different chicks, most of them dime pieces, ninety-two one-night stands and counting, I've had that burning sensation twice, but the package is still intact, ya dig? No kids, no engagements, no alimony, and no exceptions!" A confident Brian avows as he knocks in the game winning bank-shot on the billiards table at *The Fox Sports Bar* in downtown Philadelphia.

"What?! Get the hell 'outta' here! This dude is lying, Marty! Chicks wouldn't even acknowledge this cat in high school." Cortez contests of Brian's statement, who he's known since his ninth-grade year at the High School of Performing Arts.

"I'm still trippin' off the fact that he ain't even ashamed at what he's saying. Like I said...trifling!" Marty instigates.

"Tez, c'mon now! They don't call me the one-night stand runnin' man for nothing, and you know it. Damn, cats love to hate when they lose, don't they? As a matter of fact, Tez, wasn't that your wager on the last game? Exactly! How 'bout you rack'em, then order that next round of drinks, fat boy...and hurry up! I'm almost dry over here!" Brian playfully demands.

"What? Whatever, you fake Morris Chestnut lookin'...broke Stringer Bell dressing...Chef Boyardee cookin'..." Cortez counters to ease the insult directed towards his robust figure.

"Yeah, whatever Biggie! You'll eat anything I cook." Brian fires back.

"Yo, you do be trying to dress like Idris Elba though. You kinda look like him too..." Marty adds.

"C'mon man, you too…?" Brian replies, trying to downplay the comparison.

"Yeah, me too Negro!" Marty laughs.

The guys all joined in laughter at the entertaining moment they were having among themselves like true friends, which was routine every Tuesday and Thursday night after work at *The Fox*. Work was work for these three during the hours of seven to five. But after punching the clock, rest assured it was time for the trio to unwind and have a 'man' moment; reflecting on their personal lives and talk about real-life issues. Somehow the conversations always ended up being a lopsided discussion, considering Marty and Cortez were married, and Brian being Brian, focused on protecting his 'dogism' by all means necessary.

Cortez is a newlywed still trying to find his way around the circle of wedlock, with no strategy on how to sustain it. At twenty-six years old, with a twenty years young mentality, and only five months invested in his newly vowed commitment, Cortez was seeking every avenue necessary to stay in marital bliss and out of the hands of the court system. Especially, with a feisty wife like Brandy who went to the same high school. According to Brian, she might be a few cards short of a full deck. Brian often refers to Cortez as a mutt, because his mother is Spanish and his father is Black.

Marty, on the other hand was a more seasoned veteran in the complicated game of holy matrimony. At forty-two years young and married to his wife Kerry for sixteen of them with a teenage son and a toddler daughter, Marty brings more than enough life experience to his young comrades. Originally from New Orleans, Marty recently retired with a pension from the post office in Philadelphia after twenty-three years. With no major problems at home, the highlight of his week is coming to *The Fox* to listen to his friend's air it out and lend them some much needed mentoring guidance.

As for Brian, ever since his terrible break-up with his 'ex', he's been more interested in investing in tips on reasons to not get married from his presumably doomed friends. Although Brian has it together and is probably the best catch a single woman could hope for at twenty-eight years old, he confidently indulges in this notion by making himself available for any attractive takers willing to go a few rounds with him. At this juncture in life, Brian is more interested in punching as many notches in his belt possible, than to sing the married man's blues. However, outside of being a whore, Brian is focused and very intelligent.

He gained his intelligence from his grandmother 'Grandma Ruth' being raised by her since he was a young boy when he lost his mother to cancer. Although Grandma Ruth is his father's mother, he's never met his father before. His father went to prison right before he was born and died of an accidental overdose on prison medication a short time later. In spite of this, being the grandson of a retired educator, he was raised right destined to make something of his life. Now, with a love for the kitchen, he has an ambition of being a head chef of a restaurant someday, so he attends a culinary school at night and has an internship at Chops restaurant every other Saturday to master the craft of culinary arts.

In the midst of all the laughter, Brian's phone rings as it rests on the pool table. Cortez curiously leans over at the screen to view the caller, since it was within his reach.

"Mallory? Man, I know that 'ain't' Mallory from management, 'B'?" A stunned Cortez inquires as the familiar name illuminating Brian's phone.

Unable to conceal the truth with a straight face, Brian shook his head and laughs in reaction to the question before proceeding to respond.

"First off, it's not like she's our manager. But truthfully I thought you knew?" Brian replies trying to down play the breaking news as he fumbles with the key pendant that dangles from his neck.

"Actually, I never figured you to be the Caucasian type…but damn, Mallory? Really? This Negro is really trying to move up the corporate ladder…he's banging management now!" Marty chimes in.

"Wait, wasn't she messing around with the second shift manager, white boy Frank a while ago?" Cortez inquires, still trying to make since of the situation.

"Yeah, something like that. All I know is that she said he run his mouth too much. When we linked up a while back, she said that she was feeling me because I'm about my business and she liked my style." Brian recalls.

"What's a while back?" Marty quickly probes.

"Hell, I don't know? A while ago…!" Brian carelessly responds.

"Wow! So, I guess you're 'gonna' be head Negro in charge soon, huh?" Marty patronizes Brian as he leans against the table with a beer in hand.

"Whoa, easy playa! Our relationship is strictly 'dickly', nothing business! I just keep her happy during the off-time, so she can come to work happy and make life easy for all of us." Brian clarifies. The fellas shared another round of laughter, as Cortez steps away to fetch another round of drinks.

"So, when are you going to settle down and stop being a 'hoe' Brian? Have some kids? Raise a family? I mean don't get me wrong. I use to put it down just like you back in my hay day, too. But you're creeping up on thirty boss, and time waits for no man. Eventually, at some point in life you're not gonna want to walk alone, brotha." The older, wiser Marty righteously speaks off topic.

"Man listen, no disrespect to you or anyone else's marriage, but marriage is a sucker's bet to me. I'm good being single. A wedding these days 'ain't' nothing more than a dog and pony show. A V.I.P. day for the bride and an expensive, over-rated mingling session slash fashion show for those in attendance." Brian firmly responds.

"Is that right?" Marty mockingly replies.

"Yeah, that's right! The divorce rate is out of control these days and the 'hood' divorce rate is even higher. Why? Because in this day and age, how in the hell can you be married and be broke? Then when it doesn't work out, she walks away with custody of the kids unless she's blind, cripple, or crazy. Meanwhile, I get stuck with the bill, right? Hmph, then she takes me to the cleaners and the only thing I'm entitled to is visitation rights, while my kids are running around calling some other dude, daddy? Naw, I'm cool on that! I'm not trying to be a sucker for love Negro. My life is good as is and I'm legally bounded to no one. And when they leave in the morning, I can put the chain on the door, 'ya' mean?" Brian ardently expresses on a short rant as he takes a swig of his beer and calmly waits for Marty's reply.

"Wowww! That girl really messed your head up, brotha." Marty replies, alluding to Brian's ex-girlfriend Keena Brown a.k.a K.B.

"Hey man, this ain't got nothin' to do with her! I felt this way before I even met her." Brian responds, defending his position.

"Look, I know that's still a pressure point for you. I know you still got some scar tissue left from that wound in your past. But let me share something with you, real quick. It seems to me like you haven't found anyone that's given you 'good reason' to love in your young adult life. Hell,

14

K.B. is probably the closest you've been to love. But you can't give love a try if you keep guarding your heart, playa. I know you've probably seen relationships come and go, and I'm sure that you've had your fair share of trifling women. But trust me, all women aren't like the women you deal with and someday, love is 'gonna' to kick you right in that flat back that you call a butt someday, trust me. Now while you chew that, ask yourself…is it the women you deal with, or is it you that's the problem? By that I mean, out of all the women that you've ran through that wasn't good enough to be 'wifey', who was the common denominator?" Marty replies offering his words of wisdom as Cortez returns with beers and shots of Tequila.

"Look, as far as she's concerned, yeah…there's times when I think about the possibility of what could have been. But I'd like to think we've grown since then. I mean, we're older now, that pain is behind me, and we've both moved on. Honestly, I don't have the energy to toil over the decision she made. I keep it moving!" Brian replies, dismissing the conversation of his 'ex'.

"Uh oh, this sounds like a Keena Brown conversation." Cortez speculates upon return.

"Tez, c'mon man, it's K.B.! We don't say her name, remember?" Marty candidly reminds him.

"Oh yeah, my bad! Wait…you ain't still trippin' on that 'ex' situation, are you?" Cortez asks Brian, testing his concern.

"Naw, I'm good y'all, really! I'm already on to newer and better things in life." Brian assures his friends.

"Well, I see you've already headed in that direction by sleeping with Mallory. Going biracial on us, huh?" Cortez teases.

"Look dawg, I don't discriminate. I have no restriction on who can get it. I'll date them black, white, Latino, Asian, Australian, Italian, Canadian, Cambodian, and every 'Can' you can think of." Brian proudly bolsters.

"Wait a minute, what the hell is a 'Can'?" Cortez asks with a befuddled look.

"You know, Jamaican, Mexican, African, Dominican, Puerto Rican, Haitian…"

"Wait, Haitian isn't a 'Can'." Cortez promptly corrects him.

"I don't care, I'll do them too! Eye crows to camel toes dawg, it don't matter." Brian smartly counters.

"You stupid! You are really stupid!" Marty playfully insults him.

15

"Wait, so you would mess with my Mama too, huh?" Cortez asks measuring Brian's level of triflingness.

"I mean, your mom is fine for an older woman and all, but back in eighty-seven I would have paid to see her naked!" Brian admits as all the fellas laugh at Brian's good humor.

"Yeah, well, you better be careful with those eye crows. Some sixty plus cougar might run up on you and Eartha Kitt your ass. Talkin' 'bout, 'Brian, darling…I don't have any panties on'!" Marty whispers, cautioning his friend.

"Eew…good point!" Brian sneers at the mental image.

"How about one of them Muslim 'sistas', with the garb and all that?" Cortez randomly asks.

"Oh, hell naw! One of those Arab chicks? I'm sorry, but I can't rock with the whole garb thing. Plus, she might get mad at me one day and blow up the spot! I'm just saying…you never know!" Brian replies with sheer sarcasm.

Before Brian could get another word out, Marty nearly spat out the first swig of beer across the room as Cortez held on to the pool table to keep from falling on the floor from Brian's comic relief. With so much animation from his friends, Brian couldn't help but to laugh at his own ignorance.

"Ignorance! That's just plain ignorance! You can't be ignorant all your life, 'B'." Cortez denounces as he shakes his head. Suddenly, Cortez becomes distracted by three attractive women walking into the establishment.

"Damn! Check out these three Nubians that just walked in. Good 'lawd' she's got a fatty!" Cortez declares grabbing the attention of the others.

"Evening sistas." Marty greets as the women walk by.

"Okay, running man, there they go. Let me see where your game really is, playa." Cortez calls Brian out.

"Don't indulge this idiot, 'B'! You ain't got nothing to prove. Those girls are here to have a good time. Just let that one go, dawg! Let'em Breathe!" Marty appeals, trying to discourage Brian.

"Naw Marty, Tez been coming at me pretty hard tonight. I think he needs a reminder of how I used to do it in high school." Brian replies, feeling compelled by his friend's challenge.

"That's bull! You want to go over there, don't you? Look at you, spillin' your drink. You can't even focus, can you? Look at him Tez, over there lookin' like a horny pit bull with that little pink thing hanging out." Marty implies, calling out his friend.

"Relax Marty, I got this. Stick around Tez, you might learn something!" Brian replies as he throws back his shot of Tequila, then taking Cortez's shot and tossing it back before chasing it with a lime slice on the table.

"Naw, 'B'. C'mon! They got nice Mamas, man!" Marty shouts in a desperate attempt to persuade Brian otherwise.

Before making his way over to the women, Brian caught up with one of the waitresses in passing and made reference to where the ladies were sitting, before heading towards them.

"What is this fool up to?" Cortez asks as he and Marty watches from a distance.

"Hold on Tez, just watch. I think I know where he's going with this." Marty replies.

"Excuse me ladies, how are y'all this evening?" Brian opens in a sexy masculine tone.

"Fine, how are you?" The women respond, two of them with arched eyebrows, curious to his motive.

"Not bad. Just enjoying a little after work bonding session with friends, this evening. Umm, but anyway, I apologize if I come off a bit too forward, but, you're sexy!" He tells the cutest, light skinned woman whom he preferred.

"Why thank you. And your name is…" The woman asks.

"Brian…but my friends call me, 'B'." Brian replies with a subtle handshake as he glances at her showy cleavage.

"Well, 'B' this is Kara, this is Adeline, and I'm Cassandra. But my friends call me Cassy." She introduces, acknowledging him with tender eyes.

"Hi Cassy…you know it's too bad you're bad for my therapy." Brian abruptly reveals.

"Excuse me…" She asks, bewildered by the comment.

"Well, my friends over there have me in doggy time out right now. They seem to think that I don't deserve to be acquainted with someone as beautiful as the likes of you. But when you walked in, I had to come over

17

and at least introduce myself, perhaps to prove them wrong?" Brian clarifies, displaying some of his charismatic charm.

"Is that right? So, you're a bad dog, huh?" Cassandra implies, deliberately playing into his trivial game.

"Well, I have been known to be in the doghouse a time or two, so..." A cunning Brian replies.

"Excuse me ladies, three glasses of Moscato wine to start you out and here's a few menus for you to look over, okay...take your time!" The waitress presents the women as she serves each of them a bulb of wine.

"Oh-no! Wait! We didn't order wine." Kara speaks out.

"Actually, the wine is on the gentleman, ladies. Enjoy!" The waitress clarifies, looking over to Brian with a smile before walking off.

"I hope Moscato is okay? That seems to be the lady's choice these days." Brian gracefully addresses the women as he fumbles with his key charm yet again.

"Yes, Moscato is definitely a favorite!" Adeline responds as Kara simply gives Brian a thumbs-up.

"Well, aren't you a gentleman?" Cassandra compliments as she places her glass on a napkin. Brian leans into the table as if he's about to express something important.

"Can I let y'all in on a little secret?" The ladies all nod their heads in agreement.

"Chivalry has never been dead...a lot of men just haven't met him yet." Brian replies, pulling that line on impulse, yet delivering it on point.

She purses her lips to the comment, but is quite impressed by the gesture anyway.

"You ladies enjoy your evening!" Brian concludes with a charming smile.

"Bye...thank you!" The ladies reply, as Brian leaves them with an undeniable lasting impression.

Brian walks back to the fellas, finishing the last of his beer with a swagger as cool as the sweat from his beverage.

"And that my friend's is how it's done. Aaah...that was good!" Brian brags tilting back the last of his beer.

"How what's done? What did you do? You got a phone number? She gave you her panties on consignment? What?" Marty asks eager to know what transpired.

18

"Nope, I just planted the seed?" Brian casually replies.

"Oh, so you went over there and fed them a line of bull, huh? Well, I guess that explains it then?" Marty replies in unenthused fashion.

"Okay, now what really happened?" Cortez asks in a serious tone.

"I mean, I went over and introduced myself, dropped a few lines, and now we wait." Brian nonchalantly replies.

"Wait for what? You didn't do anything! See, I told you Marty! I knew I should have bet you a couple dollars. At least I would have gotten something out of proving him wrong." Cortez declares.

Brian doesn't utter a word. He stands with a grin on his face absorbing his friend's criticism as if he knew the opportunity to make a mockery of their lack of faith was sure to come. As the others turn their attention back to the table, Brian notices the girls standing with their drinks as they walk to a pool table across the room. But while Cassandra's friends walk over to the table, Cassandra walks towards him.

As she approaches, Marty and Cortez take notice and stand by to see what happens.

"Hey, we're heading over to one of the pool tables in the corner, but me and the girls wanted to thank you again for the drinks. And if you'd like to keep in contact, I'll take your number." She states as Marty and Cortez stand behind their pool cues looking dumfounded.

"Oh, no doubt!" Brian replies as she hands him her phone and he adds his information.

"Okay, I'll be in touch." Cassandra smiles as Brian hands her phone back and then she winks before walking off.

"Unbelievable! I can't believe you just pulled that off. Marty said you might have something up your sleeve. But damn, up close...shorty is bad!" Cortez states in disbelief.

"You know what, something just came to me. Yup, that's it...congratulations, dawg! You just earned yourself a new nickname. From now on your alternate ego name is Mojo. I don't even know why, it just seems to fit you. What you think, Tez?" Marty announces flattering his friend's bravado.

"Hmm...Mo' to the 'Jo? Well he's gotta be puttin' some kind of voodoo on these women to pull off stunts like this, so yeah. Mojo sounds about right." Cortez agrees.

19

"Mojo huh? Okay, 'I'ma' let you have that one. I actually kinda like it." Brian replies, embracing his new alias.

"In fact, my bad for doubting you playa! I've got to give you your props!" Marty says giving Brian a pound for calling his own shot.

"You know what, none of this even matters, though. Going back to our earlier conversation, the bottom line is I'm a good dude, and good dudes deserve a good woman in their life. If I ever decide to entertain the idea of going the whole nine yards with a woman, you've 'gotta' convince me that my marriage is not going to end up being a divorce statistic, that's all I'm saying." Brian replies justifying his point.

"Well since you seem to know what's ideal for you, tell us about her. Who is this 'woman' right for Mojo?" Marty mockingly questions, trying to understand exactly what's in Brian's best interest.

"First and foremost, 'wifey' has to be beautiful inside and out, because I'll have to look at and deal with this woman for the rest of my life. Second, she has to be educated or have some kind of skill or goals. I'm don't have time to be rescuing women from their situation like I'm in the Coast Guard or something. Third, I like'em petite or athletic, 'cause it's easier for me to have my way with them in the sack. Umm…let's see, she always has to be on top of her hair and nails game, have a positive attitude, and be a problem resolver that will fight with me as well as for me. I'm not a breast man, so booty and hips are a must. But independence, a cute smile, and loves her man unconditionally, is something I must have as well. And there you have it! That's Mrs. Jones, fellas!" Brian explains, breaking it down to his friends.

"Yo, I like your vision and all, but now let's get real! I want to know what you would settle for, because me and this man will tell you, our wives didn't come in the package we envisioned like a Barbie off the shelf. But we allowed our wives to get close enough to let the love bug bite us in the ass, and now we have families. Remember, the woman that God sends you may not be your woman of choice, but she will be the best woman for you. Aside from that, you got a lot of superficial features going on in your vision. But, whatever happened to what's in the heart?" Marty rationalizes.

"It kind of goes back to that whole 'be careful what you ask for' type deal. God might send you exactly what you want, but she may end up being that woman that you love to hate, 'ya' mean?" Cortez further elaborates.

20

"I mean, if it came down to it, I don't have to have the most beautiful or the most shapely…but I do have standards and having all of her teeth is one of them." Brian replies maintaining his humor. The fellas snicker at each other as Brian continues to explain.

"She's got to be independent, a 'go-getter', have a degree or have a goal of being something! This way I know that she has at least some potential to bring to the table. I'm tired of these bum broads out here with their hands out looking to lean on someone else's blood, sweat and tears to improve their lifestyle! I mean, 'Wifey' and I would have to be a team; it's the only way to get ahead in the game of life, 'ya' mean?" Brian elaborates.

"Hey brotha, I appreciate your honesty and I respect that, Blackman!" Marty replies tapping Brian's beer bottle with his own, yet again.

"Aight y'all, I'm over this conversation. 'Ayo' Brian, not to be off topic, but what's up with them rims you were trying to get a while ago? I saw a car like yours the other day rimmed up and it made me think about yours. I know you've been trying to get them black Gianelle's for a minute now?" Cortez digressed.

"I've been trying to save up for them 'jawns' for months. But every time I stack a little paper, something always comes up!" Brian explains reaching for his jacket from the bar stool preparing to depart.

"Aaw', hell 'naw'! You bouncin', 'dawg'?" Cortez asks, caught off guard by Brian's sudden departing gesture.

"Yeah, man. I have to be up early tomorrow. I'm on the schedule for nine o'clock, but I have to make a few runs before I get to work." Brian explains as he fumbles with his charm again.

"Mmm, Hmm. Let me find out your bolting out the door to run from this conversation?" Marty implies giving Brian a hard time.

"Man, what is it with you and that damn key chain? You've been playing with it the whole night, even when you were talking to the girls earlier. Is it supposed to be the key to your heart or something? Or do you use it to unlock a woman's panties." Cortez asks as Brian continues to play with the charm.

"Not really, I just like when people ask, 'what's that key around your neck for'?" But anyway, we can finish this conversation another time. Isn't it past y'all curfew anyway? And Cortez you know better. You need to get home before Brandy break one off in your ass! 'I'ma' get at y'all tomorrow 'aight', peace!" Brian exclaims, clowning his friends as he chugs the last of another beer, before throwing up a peace sign, and laughing his way out the door.

"You know he ain't going home, right?" Marty says to Cortez after Brian leaves the sports bar.

"Oh, you already know! He's probably going over to Mallory's crib to make our work day better for everyone tomorrow." Cortez replies as they both get a kick out of Brian's relationship with their shift manager.

"I just want to know how, man. How does he do it with these women?" Cortez asks as they watch Brian exit the sports bar.

"Listen, Brian has a quality that women respond to. He's got the look and he's got the swag. From the surface, that's all a woman needs to be satisfied." Marty simplifies for Cortez.

"Hmph, I guess…" Cortez replies before taking another sip from his beer.

As Brian makes his way to his Dodge Magnum SRT 8 he receives a text message from Mallory.

(Text)
Mallory: *If ur coming over, I need a reply. Otherwise the door will be locked. Had a long day, I could use some attention, so I hope you'll be cummin soon! Lol. Ms. DeVito*

Brian chuckles as he reads the text message, and replies back his acceptance. After thumbing through his I-pod to find his Dwele, Glasper, and Zo! playlist collaboration, his mood was set to reflect on the conversation he was having with Marty and Cortez at the sports bar. Although Brian spoke defiantly about his outlook of relationships with his co-workers, he quietly admits to himself that the single life is not always fun as he makes it out to be. He often finds himself bored and alone at times, which is why he spends more time at Mallory's place than at his own. He marvels the beautifully lit downtown skyline while merging onto I-676 on his way to Mallory's apartment in Northeast Philadelphia. Now heading North on I-76 and the illuminated skyline falls smaller in his rearview, the track 'Ah Yeah' by Robert Glasper takes Brian to a relaxed moment of reflection.

"*…So, when you gone to stop being a hoe, Brian? Have some kids? Raise a family? Don't get me wrong, I use to put it down just like you. But* *you're almost thirty and time waits for no man 'B'...Wowww! That girl really messed your head up... Remember, the woman that God sends you may not be the woman you desire, but she will be the best for you..."* Brian reflects as the conversations from *The Fox* play-back in his head.

As Brian moves about the city vibing to the relaxing playlist, the evening moonlight casts an eerie strangeness in the cool night air. Everything in his vision becomes apparent to the idea of either being in love or being married. As he stops at various red lights on Roosevelt Boulevard, he watches as the city seems busy with couples having a night out, even at the eleven o'clock hour, on a chilly autumn evening. Crossing the street before him and walking along side-walks, he observes them holding hands and blissfully enjoying each other's company as if it was an absence in his life. Everywhere he turns there's a bakery displaying gaudy wedding cakes and jewelry stores with mannequin hands displaying engagement rings and wedding sets as if his conscience is speaking a little too loud.

He starts to laugh to himself trying to figure out if he was having a divine epiphany, or a trip through the twilight zone? He even looked up at the moon to determine whether was full or not, which would at least explain why he's tripping, but it was only a crescent. Nonetheless, his conscience was alert and actively poking at his negative judgment towards marriage or even monogamy for that matter, especially since the break-up with his 'ex' girlfriend Keena Brown.

"Hell K.B. is probably the closest you've been to love!" Of all things joked about this evening, this was the one comment that ate at him the most.

It's been nearly four years, yet the pain of yesterday still resonates with him. She was twenty at the time they met and Brian was twenty-four, but she was clearly beyond her years in maturity, which enticed Brian to like her even more. From nearly the first moment he laid eyes on her, it was determined in his mind that this would be the last woman he'd ever share a relationship with, if she would have him. Many of Brian's friends often compared Keena to a young Toni Braxton because of the way she wore her hair and her beautiful baby face. Between Brian's good looks, attractive personality, and infectious smile, he's certainly had his lion's share of women through the years. Yet no one ever moved him quite the way Keena did in his young adult life. She was the only woman capable of curbing his appetite for women. Being the handsome couple they were, Brian and Keena seemed to complete each other and were an inseparable pair.

23

However, Brian was so afraid of being hurt, and so into himself, that he never paused to learn how to love, Keena. He figured two hours of consistent passionate sex, gifts, and movie nights was sufficient enough to secure her happiness. But complacency gave him a false pretense of their relationship. Although he cared for her unconditionally, he could never muster the courage to tell her he loved her. No matter how many times she expressed her love for him, love wasn't a word he just threw around. She never complained or wore the bitterness on her sleeve, because she wanted it to come from him naturally. Nonetheless, it made her feel insignificant. It caused her to question the possibility of sharing her life with someone that couldn't give her the security of knowing she's loved, no matter how strong she felt for him. In his mind, he figured telling her he loved her made him look vulnerable and weakened his manly posture. But, by being young he thought he had time in the world to figure it out. Although the love was there, he chose to keep the words to himself. Even though he knew he was letting her down.

However, fostering this mentality would prove devastating when Keena abandoned him for college when an opportunity opened for her to go to school on the West Coast. She considered going to school to study law at Temple or Villanova to be closer to Brian. But after nearly a year of waiting for Brian to give her a reason not to consider otherwise, a scholarship opportunity at USC confirmed her decision to move on and live with her aunt in California. And just like that, she was gone, which is why Brian struggles till this day to understand how a woman who appeared to be so in love could walk away so easily. But her decision wasn't as vile Brian had assumed. Keena wasn't exactly the emotional type, but the decision to part ways with the man she loved so much didn't come easy. She cried many nights struggling with the decision of an uncertain future with Brian or securing her future in college. Despite the move, they still stayed in contact for a while. But with no desire from Keena to reconsider her decision to move back East, the relationship grew stale. The last he recalls of her, was being shattered by a picture of her and her new beau getting engaged on her social media profile.

Till this day, Brian still has a hard time managing mention or thoughts of her. Marty and Cortez won't even mention her by name because they too were there to witness the pain of that break-up. So, they only refer to her only by her initials the few times she is mentioned. As much as Brian would like to consider the idea of a relationship, the pain of losing Keena was a bit too overwhelming. He felt like she robbed him of the opportunity to know what love truly is. His Grandma Ruth once told him, "you only get three great loves in your life." He felt like Keena was his first love, and all in the name of foolish pride.

Two hundred and twenty-seven women and counting, and only one had ever given him a truly blissful impression. He's never been pressed about seeing a woman, nor has he ever felt empty when leaving them. The adventure of sleeping with as many attractive women he can get his hands on only feeds his confidence and strokes his ego. He finds it exciting and enjoys the thrill of dominating the opposite sex. However, at twenty-eight years old, he does feel a bit of regret with no children, no spouse, and no one to even consider nurturing his first born. The conversation at the sports bar undoubtedly impacted him as it placed him in an evaluative state of mind. Reflecting on his life and accepting his relationship anxiety has only hindered his ability to move forward to be a husband, a father, and a provider, versus being a womanizer.

To no avail, Brian decides to leave his thoughts of monogamy and 'what if's' in the car along with the playlist that flowed with it, and turned his attention to enjoying the meal Mallory made for him, before blessing her with gratitude thereafter as he pulls into a parking spot outside her building. After grabbing his overnight bag from the back seat and getting out, He couldn't help but to notice how quiet and peaceful it is in her neighborhood as he made his way up to the second floor.

Immediately after entering her apartment, the aroma of home cooking fills his nostrils, and diverts him directly to the kitchen instead of the bedroom to drop his bag and greet Mallory.

Mmm…rosemary chicken smothered in white wine and mushroom Alfredo sauce, asparagus spears topped with a hollandaise sauce, and diced redskin, garlic potatoes…nice! He says to himself, admiring another rewarding meal left for him on the countertop.

After placing the plate in the microwave, Brian makes his way towards the bedroom to announce his presence, but to his surprise, barely conscious from her dosing off, Mallory encountered Brian walking towards the bedroom, as she made her way to the bathroom.

"DAMN IT BRIAN! You scared the hell out of me! I forgot that you were even coming!" A startled Mallory yells as she held her chest.

Wearing nothing but a long Flyers jersey, which fell just below the round of her bottom cheeks, Mallory embraces Brian around his neck. With his hormones already preloaded for pleasure, Brian firmly places his hands on the soft round of her bottom and lifts at her intensely.

"Hmph, looks like somebody missed me today?" Mallory says responding to Brian's hasty sexual advances.

"Well, it's something about coming home to a sexy woman wearing nothing but a jersey that I can't resist." Brian explains as they lustfully look into each other's eyes.

"Mmm…how long have you been here?" Mallory asks, thrilled to see Brian finally make it as she pushes her long brunette hair from her face and tucks it behind her left ear.

"Long enough to see that gourmet meal you put together for me. You know, you can cook your butt off for a white girl, right?" Brian jokes about her ethnicity.

"Mmm…? Something like that…!" Mallory replies with no regard to the white girl comment.

Without another word spoken, the two began to playfully peck away at each other's lips. Typical of him, Brian doesn't invest much time in teasing her with foreplay, especially after a long day. He'd much rather pacify her with what she really craves and finish her off with a long kiss goodnight.

As they gaze into each other's eyes, Brian now feeling a bit more aroused, stoops slightly to gain more leverage. He reaches in deeper and feels for her taint before maneuvering his fingers along the sloppy wet of her lips.

"Brian, what about dinner?" Mallory moans as she sighs deeply while Brian fondles her, inserting his middle and index fingers into her moistness.

"I think I'll have my dessert before dinner." Brian softly, whispers.

Unable to contain herself, she surrenders her emotions to the work of his fingers between her legs. As they passionately kiss, she places her left hand behind his head, then grabs for his belt and quickly unfastens his pants with her right. His loosened pants quickly fell to his ankles as she unmasks his stiffness from his underwear and conveniently grips it like a handle bar. Now, fully indulged in the moment, Brian turns Mallory around to put in work. Leaning against the wall for support, Mallory rests her head on her forearm and begins circular massages on her secretion soaked kitten with her free hand, while Brian dons a magnum preparing for penetration.

Brian reaches in, spreads her lips and eases in slowly as she tenses, trying to endure his penetration.

"Uhh…" She whimpers as Brian starts out gently, working her with strong, slow thrusts, knowing from previous encounters that he was a bit large for her to handle from the back position.

"OH, BRIAN…! OH YES! YES BRIAN, YES!" Mallory breathlessly bellows as her voice echo's off the walls of the hallway. With Brian's right hand massaging her breast and the other servicing her clitoris from his reach-around, Mallory is overwhelmed with elation. Brian looks down and watches as himself in and out of her like a well lubricated machine. The sight of him pulling back so far and her reaction to his gyration excited him even more. He couldn't help but to begin hammering away inside her, bottoming out on every stroke. His rapid thrusts were stimulated by every moan and "YES" she cries out.

"Yes! Yes! Yes! Yes! Yes! Yes! Oh my…Oh my…Ooooooooooooh…" She climaxes, reaching for Brian's hand and clinching it like a vice as she releases.

After a few body jolts she begins to loosen her grip and her limp body flops to the floor. Meanwhile, Brian assumes his position and stands over her like a boxer conquering his opponent as she fell to his feet. He chuckles a bit as he went to take up his clothes, then walks to the bathroom to clean up.

"It's not funny Brian!" Mallory mumbles with sarcasm with her face in the carpet, unable to move from her weakened state.

Brian slides the condom off, looks in the mirror and smiles proudly at himself as if to say, *"Yeah…another satisfied customer!"*

A bit later, after enjoying his dinner and putting Mallory to sleep, echoes of the conversation at *The Fox* once again resonates in his mind as he lay silent resting on his back with his hands behind his head in Mallory's bed.

'Hmph', I'm good! Brian thinks as he smiles contently, while looking down at Mallory resting her head on his chest, before quickly fading off to sleep himself.

27

6:00am Brian awakens to the sound of movement and rattling keys as Mallory is on her way out the door and off to work. Brian stretches and yarns with his eyes barely open, as he watches Mallory move about the room. Mallory glances over and pauses as she takes pleasure in watching Brian's well defined, muscular body reach for the heavens on such a beautiful morning. Reminded that this is the same physical frame that broke her down out just hours ago, her inner walls pulsed as she craves him for another stimulating session.

"Umph...if I had twenty more minutes to spare, I'd screw him for twenty-two more!" She lusts.

"Morning! I brought you a muffin and a latte' from D&D. What time do you have to be at work?" Mallory inquired with a straight face, contrary to the dirty thoughts that has her smiling inside.

Struggling to collect himself to the point of coherence he eventually answers. "I got to be in at eight, but I have a few things to do before I go in, so I'll be right behind you." Brian replies as he takes note to how Mallory is dressed, admiring her sexy.

"Okay, I'll see you then. Lock the door on your way out and don't steal anything, alright!" Mallory teases with sarcasm.

"Huh?!" Brian replies with a twisted, befuddled look on his face.

"Uh huh, that's for that white girl comment last night!" Mallory says throwing an ethnic insult back at Brian.

She leans over and kisses Brian on the cheek, before leaving for work. Brian lays content under the cozy thousand thread count sheets thinking about how nice it was to chill with someone so attractive and so caring without any drama, unlike some of the characters he's dealt with in his recent past.

"Hmm...could Mallory be wifey? She is 'badd'...! She does have that good...! Everybody wants her...! She is a good catch...! Hmph...naw, it would never work...! I mean, I work with this chick..., besides, somebody already had her on the job, which would make me look like I'm chasing

sloppy seconds. Plus, she's Italian...her family would never approve of that!" Brian ponders, still plagued by thoughts of monogamy.

After mulling over a game of "what if's" with his conscience, Brian motivated his way out of bed, turns on the wall mounted 50-inch TV and runs his shower. After knocking out his routine eighty push-ups and one-hundred sit-ups, he reaches for his bag, pulls out a fresh set of underclothes, his uniform, and toiletries and hops in the shower. While brushing his teeth, he over hears a news broadcast reporting violence in the Middle-East. Concerned for his little brother who's on an overseas deployment in the Navy, he uses the remote to turn up the volume.

Morning News:
"Today tragedy has once again struck the Middle-East when a suicide bomber detonated an I.E.D. in a crowded market place just outside of Istanbul, Turkey. Turkish authorities have confirmed that there were at least 28 dead and 42 more wounded in the blast. Sources say that the Islamic radical group ISIS may be responsible for the attack and the motive could possibly be linked to the ally relationship that Turkey has with the U.S."

Standing in the doorway of the bathroom with a tooth brush lodged in his mouth and a towel wrapped around his tightly toned waist, Brian shook his head in disgust as video footage of the carnage is displayed on the screen. Brian is very close to his younger brother and even though he chose to joined the Navy verses any other branch of service, he clearly remembers shedding a tear for the 17 sailors lost on the USS Cole years ago and does not take his brother being deployment for granted.

"Animals...dumb, ignorant, cowards is all they are. Damn towel heads!" Brian angrily utters aloud, responding to the news report.

"Lord, please keep Kenny covered and bring him home safe." Brian pleads to God after walking to the window and gazing towards the heavenly sky.

Disheartened by the news report, Brian insisted on not allowing CNN to dampen his morning with the harsh reality of senseless Middle-Eastern violence. Taking his mind off the drama, he changes the channel and starts to get dress. While lacing up his boots in the living room, he looks around the apartment and admires how clean and neat Mallory always keeps her place. Appreciating her cleanliness, he again begins to factor in another idea of being with Mallory, and again, down-plays the idea.

"Hmph, whatever happens, happens...!" He says to himself enjoying his muffin and latte, Brian grabs his overnight bag, and keys, before locking the door on his way out.

While approaching his Dodge Magnum he purchased a few months ago, he unlocks the doors with his key fob. He throws his duffle bag on the passenger seat, when he notices a piece of paper underneath his passenger wiper blade.

"What the hell is this?" Brian says aloud, thinking Mallory may have left him a note when she left. He reaches over the windshield, and grabs the note to read it.

"So, you're a magnum man, huh? Magnums are my fav too...436." Confused, yet amused by the note, he stands puzzled with a strange grin; curious as to know who wrote it, and what 436 meant?

"436? 436? What in the hell does 436 mean?" He inquires.

Completely baffled by the note, Brian is eager to find out who's been watching him and what does she look like, or at least he hopes it's a she. He scans the parking lot looking for anyone who may be watching him at that moment and began looking for anything relating to 436. He started with the license plates on the cars in the lot, but none of them matched. Then he happened to look up at Mallory's building number and saw 440 etched in the concrete above the doorway. So, he began reading off the building numbers within his view to find a match.

"Duh!" He says to himself spotting the numbers 436 on the apartment building directly across from Mallory's building.

He intently looks at each window of the building to see if he could spot anyone watching him, but with no luck he took a mental note, before getting into his car and moving on.

After running a few errands around the city, Brian is finally on his way to work. He strolls in about ten minutes late, which is typically on time for Brian, but he always manages to clock out on time.

"Yo, 'B', what's good?" Cortez yells across the warehouse floor.

Brian acknowledges the loud outburst with a head nod and kept it moving all the way to the break room where he runs into Marty.

"Yo, my main man, Brian! What's the deal, baby?" Marty says delighted to see his friend.

"I can't call it man, just trying to be as wise as you pimpin'!" Brian replies as he walks over to the truck Marty was loading to give him a pound.

"You know Vincent was down here about ten minutes ago looking for you." Marty informs Brian in a more urgent tone.

"What the hell did he want? Looking like a bald, overweight bull mastiff guarding somebody's junkyard?" Brian asks with sarcasm as they both laugh at the insult.

"I have no idea, 'B'. I asked him, but he wouldn't tell me. All he said was to make sure I send you up to see him before you go on route. Oh, and I seen your girl this morning, too!" Marty adds with a slick grin.

"Yeah, and...is she trippin' too?" Brian replies in a sour tone, still agitated about Vincent looking for him.

"Oh-no, she's real cool today. I can definitely tell you tapped it last night. She's been floating around this place all damn morning. Looking like somebody granted her three wishes last night." Marty assumes with a devilish look on his face.

"Actually, it was only one wish. But she got three times her money's worth." Brian confirms, as he walks off to investigate what Vincent wanted.

Brian walks up the long flight of stairs leading to the 'executive suites' as they refer to the offices on the second floor, to see what Vincent wanted before starting his route. Predictably, Vincent happened to be in Mallory's office when Brian found him.

"What's up Vince, you wanted to see me about something?" Brian asks interrupting their conversation. Vincent pauses to look down at his watch before answering.

"Yeah, umm, meet me in my office, Jones. I'll be with you in a minute." Vincent casually replies, before continuing his conversation with Mallory.

"These cats kill me trying to holla at Mallory...I'm already beatin' that dawg! You might want to fall back...its pointless!" Brian arrogantly humors himself, assuming that Vincent was trying to push up on Mallory. Minutes later Vincent enters his adjacent office and closes the door.

"Mr. Jones! How's life treating you, brother...well I hope?" The pudgy, light skinned Vincent asks with a conniving smile on his face.

"I'm good, Vince! What's up?" Brian replies in a concise tone.

"Listen, I'm not going to hold you, I know you have to get out on route. But, it's pay increase time for you soon and amazingly the budget

31

improved by thirty percent this year. So that means Santa may bless you with a little more than coal in your stocking this coming holiday season, which is right around the corner. I'm only telling you this because I see you out hustling everyone on your shift every day. You get nothing but praise from the company's clients, and we really appreciate that. However, I can't justify being extra generous if you can't make it to work on time, my man. In other words, I need you to start setting a better example out there, 'aight'?"

"You got it boss man. It's your world!" Brian reluctantly adheres as he readily turns to leave the office.

"Oh, and one more thing before you go. Umm...I notice that you and Mallory are real tight...

"Oh boy, here we go...!" Brian thinks as Vincent continues.

"...and I was just wondering if she's into brothers like that, or...you know...?" Vincent probes trying to do recon for himself.

"I knew this damn jerk didn't want to talk about me being late. He's just trying to smash Mallory!" Brian thinks to himself before answering.

"You know it's funny that you ask that, because I think she did tell me she was seeing some black dude recently. I heard he was killin' that on the regular, too!" Brian replies, subliminally referring to himself.

"Damn, is that right? She told you all that?" Vincent inquires with a deflated face.

"Man, you'd be surprised of some of the things she tells me." Brian answers enjoying the look on Vincent's face as he turns to walk away. Brian laughs hysterically inside while toying with him.

Brian steps out of the office with a smile of deception on his face as he looks over into Mallory's office, gives her a head nod, and keeps it moving, eager to start his deliveries for the day. Feeling pretty good about himself, Brian leaps into his truck, electronically verifies his inventory and heads off into the cool morning air.

Barely making it out of the truck lot, Brian received a text message from Mallory.

(Text)

Mallory: *Are you trying to ruin your raise? Don't play with Vincent, get here on time Brian. Have a great Apex delivery day. Lol! Smooches!* Brian reads on his phone.

He laughs to himself as he pulls out of the parking lot and heads towards the East Falls/Manyunk section of Philadelphia. Ever since he started this route five years ago, Brian has established a great relationship with the shop owners and resident clients along this route.

Making his usual rounds on Main Street in Manyunk, Brian grabs his routine cookie from the bakery shop when dropping off their supplies. Then he moves on to the other various businesses before making his way into East Falls. After his last delivery on Main Street, he takes a look at the short list of addresses in his electronic clipboard to figure out the best route for the remaining deliveries.

"3911 Gypsy Lane...hmmm...my main man Mr. Batool...I love this block." Brian says to himself looking forward to delivering another round of express mail to one of his proverbial drop-offs.

Ever since Brian started working for *Apex* shipping, Mr. Amir Batool gets a delivery at least twice a week. Although he never really knew what he was delivering, Brian assumed that Mr. Batool was of some importance because he was always draped in a suit and the type of house he lived in obviously blared success. This was clearly one of Brian's favorite drop-offs, because Gypsy Lane was no typical street in the city of Philadelphia. Between Lincoln Drive and Queen Lane, you will find a single stretch of Gypsy Lane with five of the most unique homes in the East Falls area. Aside from being quiet and inconspicuous, the real-estate on this block also carried a heavy price tag. Built on a hill descending from Queen Lane to Lincoln Drive, three of these homes were unconventional, like they belong in the Hollywood hills of California and somehow found their way on this quiet, lavish inner city stretch in Philadelphia. Brian could only imagine owning something so fancy. But it never deterred him from dreaming.

Maneuvering through a series of winding turns on Lincoln Drive, Brian makes his way to his next drop-off. As he passes the old police precinct on his right, Brian makes a right turn onto Gypsy Lane then slowly drives up the incline to Mr. Batool's house near the top of the hill. As he slowly pushes the truck up the block, Brian performs his routine admiration of the magnificent homes to his left. Today was particularly special because behind the homes sat a valley of towing trees that displayed a kaleidoscope of leaves turning to a shade of autumn. Brian studies the detail of each passing home, imagining how nice it must be to live so comfortable. He slows the truck to a stop just past the driveway of 3911 as he always does, scans Mr. Batool's package and walks the cobblestone driveway of the gorgeous home to the front door.

"Cobblestone driveways, fancy cars, bay windows, French doors, nice landscaping...This is what I'm talking about!" Brian aspires as he approached the front door.

"Brian! My friend, please come-in!" Mr. Batool yells from his study as his voice echo's through the door.

Brian opens the door and slowly walks into the marble tiled foyer. Although he'd stood in the foyer many times before, the view from which he stood never ceases to amaze him. The spiraling main staircase to his right and a glimpse of an open floor kitchen with hardwood floors and cherry wood cabinets to his left provoked Brian to marvel for a brief elated moment. His eyes took him to a place of euphoria.

"My friend, how are you?" The short, well dressed, Middle-Eastern accented Mr. Batool asks making his way towards the foyer from his study.

"Not as good as you Mr. Batool." Brian replies looking around the place before greeting Mr. Batool with a firm handshake. Mr. Batool chuckles at the comment as he grabs the electronic clipboard to sign his name.

"This place? Please...my friends have much nicer homes in Conshohocken and Jersey... much, much nicer. You should come with me to watch football this Sunday, my friend. You'll see what I mean." Mr. Batool offers with enthusiasm.

"Naw, Mr. Batool I can't..." Brian modestly declines.

"Please call me Amir, my friend!" Mr. Batool insists as he interrupted Brian.

"I'm sorry...Amir, I appreciate the offer, but I can't contend with you guys. I'm just gone fall back and get some rest this weekend." Brian solemnly replies, intimidated by the offer.

"Oh, come on, get out of your hood for a day and rub elbows with the big dogs." Amir ardently insists.

"Well, maybe next week when Philly plays the Giants? I like New York's chances." Brian playfully defers against the Eagles, yet feeling a bit awkward about being entertained by men who were worth more than their weight in gold.

"Haha…that's so disrespectful! Next Sunday it is then. I will enjoy seeing you upset when Philly sends Tennessee home with a cheese steak up their ass!" Amir sarcastically replies as they make their way outside.

"Here, take my card in case you change your mind this weekend." Amir presents Brian with a business card.

As the men exit the house, a black Yukon Denali pulls softly into the driveway, and parks next to Amir's Mercedes.

"Uh, Oh! The queen of the damned is home!" Amir expresses as the driver opens the door and his daughter emerges from the back seat of the SUV.

"Whoa…excuse me miss, what's your name…?" Brian hymned to himself as the woman instantly seizes his focus.

Frozen in the moment, Brian could only stare as the precious gem that exited the vehicle dressed in a pants suit and black four-inch heels, reaches back into the SUV to grab her attaché case.

"Hello Princess!" Amir exclaims as he stands in the doorway.

"Hello father!" She replies with the softest, most beautiful voice Brian has ever heard.

"Thank you, Carlos. See you tomorrow morning!" She says as she dismisses her driver.

Armed with a Starbucks coffee cup in her left hand, her PDA in the right, and her briefcase and purse on her arm she walks towards the house with a commanding strut responding to a text message. She walks over to her father and greets him with a kiss on the cheek.

"Hello father!" She says as he held her by both arms and kisses her on both cheeks.

She then turns and mentions "hi" to Brian in a passive manner, hiding behind her large Chanel frames.

"Hi, how are you?" Brian replies as she scarcely acknowledges him.

"Wow…" Brian marvels, desperately trying to avoid his lustful eyes from being so obvious.

"حسنا شيء كلّ…اليوم مبكّرة بيتيّ أنت ,(أشيما)؟"

"Ashima, you're home early today…is everything okay?" Amir inquires, speaking in Arabic dialect.

"كلّ اليوم منزل عمل يحضر فقط .جيّد بشكل شيء كلّ ,أب نعم."

"Yes father, everything is fine. I just brought work home today is all." Ashima replies, barely breaking stride as she breezes past her father and made her way to the doorway of the house to slip out of her shoes.

"ولّ فري (ذلك بعد موافقة)!"

"Okay then, very well!"

As he listened to the two speak in their native tongue, Brian is still stunned by how exceptional the young Middle-Eastern woman is. At that very moment, a woman in a pant suit never looked so sexy. Although an Arab woman wasn't exactly his flavor, he was intrigued by the way she carried herself and very interested in finding out more about her.

"Wow, so that's your daughter huh, Mr. Batool...I mean, Amir? I didn't know you had it in you. She must take after her mother or something?" Brian playfully teases as he peeks over Amir's shoulder and notices Ashima removing her shoes in the doorway before walking in with them instead of leaving them at the door with the other pile of shoes.

"My friend, you look like a naked pit bull. Your mother should have changed her mind when she saw you. Get the hell out of here!" Amir laughingly responds, as he playfully pats Brian on his back.

"Aight Amir, I've gotta go, I'll see you later." Brian replies, laughing along with the comical businessman.

"Yes, the alarm will be set, so make sure you knock hard the next time. I have 'AK' in my bedroom!" Amir playfully warns him.

Brian could only laugh as he hurries back to his truck to get back on schedule. While in route to his next destination and throughout the rest of the day, the only thing he could think about was this Arab woman that completely captivated him.

"Damn, she was 'BADD!' Five-foot-four minus the high heels...great posture, nice weight, multi-tasker, nice booty, hella sexy...she is the truth! I need that in my life! Boy, Amir just don't know...!" Brian imagines, amusing himself by thoughts of Amir's daughter.

At the end of his shift, Brian returns to the warehouse early as always and immediately clocked-out. Avoiding the possibility of running into Vincent and ruining his positive mood, he quietly walks to his car and drives off. Brian felt like he was sixteen again with a crush on the girl next door that he knew was out of his league, but he could still fantasize about. On his way home to his apartment in Germantown just off Queen Lane, he traveled his usual way home of I-76 to Lincoln Drive, but today he decided not to bypass Gypsy Lane and instead used it as an alternate route to get home.

As he drove slowly past Amir's house, he was hoping to catch another glimpse of his daughter. To no avail, there wasn't a person in sight. Even the Mercedes-Benz was absent from the driveway.

"Hmph...who in the hell am I kidding? I work for Apex delivery...I make thirty-seven thousand dollars a year...I live in a studio apartment in Germantown...I'm from the hood...I'm not rich and I'm not a damn Punjabi! There's no way she could ever have an interest in me. But it would be nice to have one of them smart Arab chicks on my team though..." Brian thinks as he smiles about his lack of confidence.

At the corner, he makes a left turn onto School House Lane and makes his way home thinking about how nice it would be to actually be in love. As nice as some of the women may have been in his life, none of them have really ever moved him in a way that he could consider building a future with since KB. While zoning out in his moment of pondering, Brian was interrupted by a text message on his phone.

(Text)
Amika: *Hey, wuzzup? R u bringing me dinner 2nite? Would really like 2 c u 2nite!*

"Hmmm. Do I really feel like dealing with this girl tonight? She's a nice one, but she gets on my damn nerves, constantly wearing her success on her sleeve. I mean damn, you're successful...I get it! Then again, she does have a nice body and her chew game is the bomb!"

Brian considers trying to convince himself to chill with Amika tonight. Negotiating the idea of getting sexual with Amika, between the head on his shoulders and the one between his legs, Brian sends his reply.

(Text)
Brian: *What do u have a taste for?* Brian texts back after conceding to his hormones.
Amika: *Can u pick me up a dozen shrimp from Stinger's please?*☺ He reads as his face turns up in disgust.

"Stingers?! See, that's the bull I be talking about! You couldn't ask for a shrimp basket and fries from the Chinese store. I know it 'ain't' the same, but damn...must you be in my pockets for some twenty-five-dollar shrimp? BLACK WOMEN! I could have went to Mals and got dinner, a massage, taboo sex, and breakfast in the morning for free! But nooo! I guess you gone pay for this booty tonight!" Brian rants aloud with a look of dismay on his face. Despite his frustration, he calmly replies to her request.

(Text)
Brian: *U want tartar sauce with that???* Brian replies with utter disdain.
Amika: *Please. Thank you, babe! Smooches! XOXO...*

"Smooches my ass, I'm a get my money's worth or a 'money shot' tonight!" He vents as he throws his phone on the passenger seat.

Blowing off his negative thoughts about Amika, his mind helplessly reverts to thoughts of how beautiful Amir's daughter was while driving to Broad Street to pick up the food. The mere thought of this woman fills his mood with delight and jubilation, and the idea of uncertainty only adds to the thrill of not knowing if he even stands a chance at the Arab princess. But given the opportunity, he would give it his best shot. Suddenly, Brian's phone lights up to another text message.

(Text)
Tez: *What's the deal B? U coming out tonight?* Brian reads after coming off the broad street exit.
Brian: *Got homework 2nite, I need 2 study. I'll take your money on Thursday, chump!* Brian replies blowing off the fellas to answer his booty call.

After picking up the shrimp order and growing even more irritated because he had to pay extra for tartar sauce, Brian made his way to Amika's place at the Presidential apartments on City Line Avenue. Already familiar with the woman at the front desk, Brian gives a casual wave to her as she buzzes him in with all smiles.

"Awe, what did you bring me?" She asks, as the middle-aged, short haired woman with reading glasses always has a kind word for Brian.

"How about you try one of these?" Brian offers as he opens the box and unveils the steaming, succulent, golden platter.

"Uh oh, I see why that girl is in love with you. Let me grab a napkin and I will definitely take one!" The woman baring no shame in accepting Brian's offering of the colossal, butterfly shrimp.

Brian smiles contently as he waves goodbye and proceeds down the passageway to the elevators. On his way to the 14th floor, he begins to contemplate how he's going to seek compensation for his good deed tonight.

"Hmph! Twenty-five bucks, huh? I'm taking twenty-five bucks out of her tonight! Oh yeah, I'm bunny hopping on that tonight. A lil head wop from east knobba...Mmm...Hmm... 'I'ma' sleep good tonight!" Brian assumes as he laughs to himself stepping off the elevator.

After rapping on the door with his signature knock. Amika opens and immediately retreats to the bathroom while drying her hair with one towel and another large towel wrapped around her from breasts to apple bottom.

"Damn, you're a little late, aren't you?" Amika says greeting Brian with a bit of dry humor.

Not entertained by Amika's sorry attempt to amuse him, Brian pauses in his tracks and gives her a blank stare. After not receiving a reply to her comic relief, Amika walks over to Brian as if to try again, only this time with a kiss.

"I'm sorry babe...bad mood?" Amika asks seeking pardon for her poor humor.

"Naw, I'm straight. Just trying to figure out what you're on, that's all." Brian replies in a dry tone, seeming a bit annoyed.

But Brian couldn't stay angry at a woman sporting nothing but a towel just short of covering her lower bottom, and perspiration glistening on her body from the humidity of the hot shower for long. Her thick five-foot, two-inch frame and mocha skin actually gave him a sense of resolve to her lack of appreciation. Already stimulated by the state of her presence, he'd rather take it out on her bent over the kitchen counter with sexual aggression.

"So, how was your day, beautiful?" Brian asks with a more amicable approach.

"My day was fine. I had a few clients cancel on me, but I sold a house today so I can't complain." Amika quickly sums up her day.

"Oh, congrats, congrats!" Brian replies as he taps her bottom as she walks in front of him.

Amika walks over to the kitchen to take a sample of her delicious platter. She opens the box and grabs the salt and pepper to season the food, then grabs one and takes a bite.

"Mmm. These shrimp smell so good?" Amika says, savoring the aroma.

"Mmm. That's not the only thing that smells good over here...!" Brian replies as he presses against her backside and reaches around, underneath her towel to massage the soft moistness between her legs. Amika was content with the idea of having shrimp in front of her and having Brian from behind, until she noticed something disturbing.

"Wait a minute! Wait a minute! There's only eleven shrimp in here, Brian! Did you eat one?" Amika asks in a critical tone.

"Oh yeah, my bad, I gave one of your shrimp to ole' girl at the front desk." Brian replies with laughter.

"Uh no...that's not funny! How you gone just give my food away like that? You knew I was hungry as hell, Brian!" Amika replies adamant and ungrateful. Taking to her level of seriousness, Brian immediately takes offense and naturally reacts.

"Excuse you? Did you pay for these shrimp? Did you even say thank you? You've got some damn nerve!" Brian angrily responds.

"That's not the point, Brian! That's not the point!" She argues.

"You know what...you're right that's not the point...THIS IS THE POINT!" Brian shouts as he reaches for the spring-loaded door, and let it slam freely behind him.

"This chick got some damn nerve..." Brian kept repeating to himself. Fed up and disgusted, Brian puts his phone on vibrate and marches towards the stairwell instead of waiting for the elevator. He heard a door open behind him halfway down the hall, but could care less as to see who it was.

"Damn, that was quick! No mood for romance tonight, huh?" The lady behind the desk asks as Brian moves briskly across the lobby.

"I'll see you around, take care." Brian's expressionless, short reply suggested that this would more than likely be his last time visiting the Presidential Apartments.

Amika's continued tackiness since Brian met her many months ago had finally reached its peak. Brian's tolerance of hood-rats and classless women had just about run its course. Although many of the women he dealt with were a product of his upbringing, he felt like his plan for building a better life for himself would require him to make better choices in women. But he would first have to learn to tame his vice for the club ready vixens he's helplessly attracted to and there lies the challenge.

Special Delivery

♫ *I...don't...want...to...go...to...work...today, I'd rather...stay home...and play...video games...I wanna...chill...! But I gotta get up...! I gotta, gotta, gotta, gotta, gotta, gotta, gotta, gotta, gotta, get up...* ♫

A groggy Brian wakes to his cellular alarm after hitting the snooze button for the third time.

"Time to make the donuts!" Brian blurts out to motivate his way out of bed.

Brian reaches over for his phone on the nightstand after ignoring it the night before and realizes he has twenty-seven missed phone calls and six new voice messages. Twenty-six of which belonged to Amika and one from Mallory. He lays in bed smiling as he listens to his voicemail messages.

(Voicemail)
First new message (7:37pm)
Amika: *Sooo... you're just going to leave like that? How juvenile. You really need to grow up!*
Second new message (7:43pm)
Amika: *You know you really need to grow up! I don't know who pissed you off, but don't bring that crap over here again. Next time you come here, leave your attitude in the lobby, okay?*
Third new message (7:51pm)
Amika: *(Distraught voice) WHO ARE YOU SCREWING, HUH?! WHO YOU SCREWING?! YOU MUST BE SCREWING SOMEBODY, 'CAUSE YOU AIN'T OVER HERE SCREWING ME. YOU AIN'T NO DIFFERENT THAN ANY OTHER TRIFLING NEGRO OUT THERE! YOU WANT TO ACT LIKE A STRAY DOG, STAY OUT THERE WITH THE REST OF THEM FLEA BITTEN MUTTS AND DON'T BRING YOUR FLEAS BACK TO ME!*
Fourth new message (8:12pm)
Mallory: *Hey Brian, was just thinking about you. Give me a call when you get a chance or I'll just see you tomorrow. Smooches!*

"Hmph... 'Smooches...' she kills me with that." Brian laughs as he continues listening to his messages.

Fifth new message (11:43pm)

Amika: *Hey (Sigh), I'm sorry for wilding out on you earlier. I didn't understand why you left at first, but I guess I was being a bitch after I asked you to do 'me' a favor. I'm sure you've heard the other messages I left you by now and I'm sorry for those too. Brian, call me when you get a chance...*

Sixth new message (1:27am)

Amika: *(Sigh...) Click.*

As he paces around the room listening to the last two messages, Brian prepares himself for work. He couldn't help but to laugh at the twenty-six missed calls and five messages Amika left until one o'clock in the a.m.

"My, what kind of respect you get when you ignore ignorance. Later for all that!" Brian says to himself as he grabs his books for school and heads to work.

Brian hurries off to work and arrives ten minutes early, which was enough time to brief Marty and Cortez about yesterday's events and discuss plans for billiards tonight after he gets out of class.

"Awe man, Brian came in early today? I must be hittin' the power ball tonight or something..." Cortez exclaims across the warehouse from the rear of the delivery truck he was loading.

"Yo, hold that thought, dawg! I'm going to clock-in. I've got something crazy to tell you...!" Brian yells back as he scampers to the break room to punch the time clock.

"What up! What up people!" Brian yells out, greeting everyone in the break room while he grabs his timecard. As he pulls his card from the slot, there was a yellow sticky note attached to it.

"See me before you go out today, Vincent!" The note reads.

"Now what?!" Brian sighs as he exits the break room.

Anxious to get back to the warehouse, Brian darts up the stairs to see what type of drama Vincent had in store for him today.

"Vince, what's up man? Listen, I had nothing to do with the truck overturning on I-95 this morning. Sooo...what's good?" Brian facetiously rambles as he walks into Vincent's office with some late morning antics.

"What...?" Vincent replies, not amused by Brian's humor.

"...Anyway, a Mr. Amir Rafiq Batool called this morning requesting a package be delivered to his office at the Mellon Bank Building this morning. Can you do this for me first thing, on your way out?" Vincent politely asks of Brian.

"Sure, I can do it, but isn't that Mark's run. Why not just give it to him?" Brian replies with a bit of confusion.

"Well, the funny thing is, he asked for you in particular and he only trusts you to deliver this package for him. So, you can get this done for me, right?" Vincent asks for assurance.

"Sure, Mr. Batool is my man. No problem!" Brian answers.

"Great, I've got the package right here and some woman named Ashima will be looking for you in the front lobby to receive it. Only Ashima gets this package, okay!" Vincent says with certainty.

"Aight cool..." Brian agrees, relieved that Vincent didn't confront him with more drama.

Hindered by curiosity, Brian couldn't help but to wonder what was in the package, and if Ashima is Amir's lovely daughter he can't stop thinking about. But with no time to waste, if he intends to carry out his unscheduled delivery and finish his route in time for culinary class tonight, he needs to get a move on. So, without delay, Brian rushes back to his truck, to take inventory before heading out.

"Damn, what's the deal, 'B'. I thought you were going to come over to see me about something before you rolled out?" Cortez inquires walking over to Brian's truck to give him a pound.

"Yeah, I was going to tell you about what happened yesterday but I got rerouted by a delivery request for one of my clients. So, I gotta make a run downtown today, but what's good for tonight though? Y'all tryin' to rack'em or what?" Brian asks as he hastily scans his packages.

"I mean, if you want to owe me your check tonight, then sure I'll take your money!" Cortez replies as he watches Brian leave in a haste.

"Bet, I'll see you there then...and please bring cash this time. I have no use for your access card this week." Brian clowns, leaving the warehouse as Cortez extends his middle finger.

Into the thick of the downtown traffic, Brian looks up at the Liberty Tower skyscrapers and the towering Comcast building as he makes his way down Market Street. As he came to a stop at a red light, he gazes at the massive buildings towering above him, watching the scattered clouds race across bright blue sky between the buildings, like the surreal effect of the earth moving at a more rapid pace. He felt right at home imagining how it would be to work as a chef downtown serving gourmet meals for top executives.

As he crosses Seventeenth Street, he pulls to the far-left lane and double parks his *Apex* truck in front of his destination. Unaware of where the front lobby actually is, he grabs Mr. Batool's package and aimlessly passes through the pavilion in front of the building, admiring the likes of sophisticated professionals of all genders and ethnicities. He felt a bit out of place wearing a delivery uniform, while all the other men wore suits and ties and have a special swagger about them.

"One day...one day soon this will be me moving amongst these corporate movers and shakers; watching them make million-dollar deals while enjoying a steak I prepared for them." Brian assures himself as he walks into the building's main lobby area.

"How may I help you, sir?" The receptionist asks sitting behind a vast corporate desk.

"Yes, I have a package for a Mr. Amir Batool of the *Philadelphia Finance and Trust*. I'm supposed to leave it in the care of a Ms. Ashima Batool and I need a signature." Brian explains.

"Okay, one moment please!" The receptionist replies, picking up the phone to notify someone of the delivery.

As he stands at the reception desk awaiting a signature for the package, Brian turns his attention to the vast lobby. There are people everywhere on cell phones, carrying briefcases, and typing away on their company laptops while sipping their Latte's and cappuccino's. Brian nearly gets a sweet tooth from all of the eye candy moving around him. The sound of clacker's echoing the marble floors as beautiful women of all cultures stomp their heels to the beat of an all business rhythm in pant suites and skirts with perfect posture and physique to die for.

"Excuse me, Apex?" A familiar, slightly accented voice calls out from Brian's blind side.

Brian turns to his left to respond and to his surprise, there she stood. The daughter of Amir and the woman whose vision has inundated Brian's thoughts since the moment he first laid eyes on her.

"Whoa...there she is!" Brian says to himself, giving her an unintentional lustful stare.

Frozen in state, the "wow" factor kicked in, as a shockwave of anxiety runs through his body. But instead of searching for the right words to say, he just chose to be himself.

"Don't play yourself, kid! Just be professional and roll with it." Brian coaches himself, trying to calm his uneasiness.

"Hi, I'm Ashima and you're the guy that delivered the package to my house the other day, right?" Ashima recalls with a classy smile.

"Yeah, that was me. It's funny how I saw you for the first time on that day and now twice in one week." Brian replies, unable to resist his admiration of her bold, beautiful eyes and irresistible smile.

"Well, I'm often out of town and always traveling, Mister…Brian, is it?" Ashima asks reading his name tag as she extends to shake his hand.

Brian, gently shakes her hand, and is caught off guard by the firmness of her grip; not manly strong, but professional firmness. He stares into her eyes and blissfully melts from the captivating expression her eyes portray, along with her alluring scent. Even the soft innocence of her voice was compelling and made Brian want to know more about this woman. Meanwhile, Ashima was a bit engaged by Brian's appearance as well. But Brian would never suspect that through her professional façade.

"Hmm…not bad for a delivery guy, I wonder what his story is?" She ponders, taking notice to his strong build and charming smile.

"Oh, okay. When I saw you I couldn't tell who you were? You looked too good to be Amir's daughter, so you must take after your mother?" Brian says as the two share a laugh from Brian's humor.

"Hmph. Cute. But he probably has many children, or was just released from someone's prison with biceps cut that nice? Oh well, too bad!" She assumes with her mind already made up about this man she doesn't even know. After a brief moment of speculation, Ashima hurries things along in order to maintain her professional composure.

"Well if you would excuse me, I must get this to the executive Gods on the 54th floor before they blow a gasket." She explains.

"Oh right! Right! I've gotta get back on schedule myself. So…if I can have you sign here, I'll be on my way." Brian replies, expediting the process to match the importance of his time to the likes of hers.

"Certainly, and thank you for running this over to us this morning…" Ashima replies, once again enchanting Brian with her dazzling stare.

"Oh…! Before you go, umm…I don't mean to get into your business or anything, but I was just wondering what was in the package that was so urgent? You don't have to answer, I'm just asking for my own nosey interest." Brian carefully asks, unsure if he breached a social barrier.

"Oh, it's just more paperwork for me, that's all." Ashima answers nicely without being too disclosing. Brian, quickly getting the hint, didn't inquire any further.

"Oh, okay! Well, good luck with that and it was nice seeing you again." Brian replies, putting on his best departing smile.

"Likewise. Enjoy your day as well." Ashima responds with a tender smirk before turning to walk away, granting Brian one last impression of her curvy, petite frame before disappearing in the elevator corridor.

In a state of disbelief, Brian walks away beaming from ear to ear. *"Wow, I hate to see you go, but I love to watch you leave! Man, this woman is incredible. Hair pinned up, with the sophisticated eyewear… tight body…nice heels…beautiful voice… and that scent? What was that? And what is it about a woman in a pant suit?"* Brian recapped on his way back to his truck.

Meeting Ashima set the tone for Brian's elated mood for the rest of the day. Before, during, and after every delivery, Brian was struck with thoughts of her that opened him up like a gift on Christmas morning. He even ignored several phone calls from his other female interests, including Amika and Mallory, and only replied to text messages in an effort to preserve his mood.

After a full day of trying to stay on schedule and a missed lunch, an exhausted Brian wraps it up around 4:30pm and prepares for his evening classes.

"Mo' to the Jo', what's the deal, baby? Ole' girl came down looking for you about 10 minutes ago. She looked annoyed too dog, is everything good?" Cortez forewarns Brian as he enters the break room to update his inventory and clock out.

"I know, she's been texting and blowing my horn up all day. She probably just needs me to put that thing on her, that's all." Brian passively replies.

"Okay, well handle your scandal, 'Bruh'! I'm off the clock and you know I don't hang around unless I'm gettin' O.T. so…" Cortez replies as he departs with deuce gesture to Brian.

After uploading data from his handheld to the warehouse computer and clocking out as quickly as possible to avoid being spotted, Brian heads to his car in the parking lot, when he spots Mallory leaning against his car waiting for him.

"Damn! I was almost home free!" Brian thinks preparing to deal with Mallory as he walks towards her.

"So, this is what it takes to get your attention?! We work in the same damn building and I can't even get a simple hello in the morning, let alone a reply to my messages?" An agitated Mallory questions as she stands straight up to confront him.

"Well, hello to you too Ms. DeVito…and how has work treated you today?" Brian resorts to a different approach to soften her aggression.

Brian leans over to greet Mallory with a kiss. Mallory responds by stopping him short of landing one on her cheek, turning away and placing her hand firmly on his chest.

"First of all, don't do that! You see where we're at right?" Mallory abruptly reminds him.

"Okay, and you posted up against my car in this wide-open parking lot, doesn't look suspicious?" Brian smartly counters.

"Whatever! Anyway, work was work. But my problem isn't with work, it's with you! I haven't spoken to you since you left my apartment. I mean, I know we're not together and all, but since we're sleeping together, a simple good morning would be nice!"

"Mal-, don't act like that! I texted you today, yesterday, and the day before, so what's the problem?" Brian struggles to understand. Growing annoyed by Brian's response Mallory replies.

"Oh…okay, so when I need to communicate with you we're just using text messages now! That's all I'm worth? No problem! The next time you want me to suck you off, send me a text message and I'll 'sext' you back, okay?!" Taken aback by Mallory's agitated tone, Brian stands froze and speechless holding on to the door of his car.

"This chick is crazy!" Brian thinks as he watches Mallory storm off with a tantrum that matched the likes of a twelve-year-old. Aware that he was short on time, Brian wasn't about to chase Mallory down and have a senseless argument with her that would make him late for class. Instead, he throws his back pack in the car and heads to class with the intent of dealing with the matter later on, minus the drama.

After going over a few measuring equations, sitting through a lecture about French cuisine, wine reductions, and the fall of the Roman Empire, Brian meets with the fellas to unwind, and enjoy a few rounds of beer and billiards and partake in another night of 'man-law' discussions.

As Brian walks in, it looks like a typical night at *The Fox*. A moderate crowd, with lots of business suits and relaxed ties, sophisticated women letting their hair down, having a beer or martini with their colleagues, recapping the day's events. Brian wasn't a fan of advertising his Apex uniform off the clock, so he always made sure he kept it casual for *The Fox*, just in case there was untapped potential to scout. Tonight, he kept it simple with a pair of white Air Force Ones, jeans, and a tight-fitting polo shirt, with a Gortex jacket and Polo beanie to keep him warm. However, he could always tell if the boys got off late, because they would still be dressed in their Apex light blue, pinstripe shirts, and dark blue Dickie work pants. Today was a late one.

"Fellas, fellas, fellas...what's happenin', fellas? Brian asks, announcing his presence in the venue.

"Oh, not a whole lot...just givin' ya boy over here a lesson in physics, that's all." Marty replies with his eyes fixed on a stripe, lining up the next shot.

"Damn Tez, have you played the table yet?" Brian asks taking note to how many solid balls were left on the pool table.

With his beer tilted to sip, Cortez could only deliver a piercing stare in response to Brian's comment until he sucks what's left of his bottle dry.

"Aaaaaaah...that was soooo good! Now, if you're finished talking that nonsense, late man buys the next round. So, if you can get me and Marty a few more beers, you can come back and wait your turn to get spanked too!" Cortez challenges.

"It's all good, 'cause by the end of the night you'll be 'o-fer'. That means you get zero wins tonight, in case you didn't know." Brian replies tossing his jacket across a chair, before back pedaling his way to the bar.

With beers in hand, Brian returns to the table eager to share details of his recent current events. Upon his return, the others were clowning as Brian approached.

"Yo, 'B', Mal was looking good today, Bruh!" Marty says as he takes a beer from Brian.

"Mmph, I concur! She was definitely trying to get your attention today, Buddy. Especially wearin' them booty huggin' jeans and them 'get'em girl stilettos', cleavage was sitting all out, hair all done up, smellin' all good…!

"Yeah, well, when I rolled out to go to class today, Mal was waiting at my car and spazzed out on me out in the parking lot. I don't know what was going on with her, but I think she's getting too attached or something? She really took it there!" Brian says explaining the earlier events.

"Yeah, I saw her standing over there when I was at the loading platform around the time you bounced. Is that what that was all about?" Marty asks.

"Yeah, your girl was really coming at my neck today, talkin' 'bout, 'the next time I want oral action, send her a sext message!' I was like, whoa…okay!" Brian recalls.

"Well, you must have done something, because as the day rolled on I heard her attitude got worse. So, whatever it is that's troubling her, you need to get over there and fix it as soon as possible. You know ain't nothing worse around this warehouse than a pissed off Mallory." Marty implores his friend.

"What?! Man, if I were you, I'd be over her crib sexting right now!" Cortez clowns, as he and Marty give each other dap.

"Now, now…calm down sports fans. Trust me, after I finish putting in work on this table, I'll be at Mallory's putting in some O.T., trust!" Brian assures his friends.

"Yeah, that's if your boy Vince don't get a hold of her first." Marty teases, alluding to Vincent's obvious thirst for Mallory.

"Whewww…your boy be hawkin', don't he?" An animated Brian gestures wiping sweat from his forehead and keying up the others.

"Awe man, dude is crazy with it. One day she was walking the floor and she bent over to pick up a package…man, Vince seen her bent and I promise this dude lost his mind. I know he went to the bathroom to rub one out, 'cause his eyes was so big and he had to wipe his mouth to keep from drooling!" The fellas broke out into an uproar of laughter as Marty told the story and mocked the actions of Vince while explaining.

"Listen, we all know dude is about as thirsty as dry cereal, but even if Mallory wasn't doing me, Vince would have about as much chance to smash as Andrew Jackson jumping off the face of this twenty-dollar bill. But never mind all that! I've got some breaking news to share with y'all that doesn't involve Vince! Brian announces, changing topic.

"Like?" Marty asks after a swig of his beer.

"Like this 'badd jawn' I met during that special delivery downtown today." Brian explains over zealously.

"Oh boy, here we go...! Brian is geeked up about another customer he wants to service outside of his job description!" Cortez taunts of his friend.

"Aight...so, what's good then? Details! I need Details!" Marty demands.

"Well first, let me start by saying that, with regard to the conversation we had the other day about Arab, Middle-Eastern chicks...yeah, you can throw my opinion right out the window because the jawn I met today, awe man...!" Brian pauses and shakes his head dramatizing his thought of the Ashima. "...she was a problem, for real, y'all! She was official!" He finishes with a drink from his beer.

"Okay, but we've heard you describe women like this before, and a few of them didn't quite pan out. So, what sets her apart from any other chick you've dealt with?" Marty questions as he closes in on another shot on the pool table.

"Naw Marty, not like this! This chick was on another level of seriousness. She was, 'thee' perfect verse over a tight beat, kind of serious, ya mean?!" Brian adamantly explains.

"Whoa...! Whoa now...! Watch your mouth Brian Jones. You know that term is not to be utilized loosely. Especially when speakin' on someone you don't even know, c'mon now!" Marty strongly suggests.

"I know, I know! But I'm sayin', this is how serious this situation is." Brian replies.

"So, this isn't a woman we're talking about, this is a situation is what you're saying?" Cortez seeks to confirm.

"Exactly, Tez!" Brian enthusiastically concurs.

"Okay then, let's hear it! Let's hear about this, situation!" Marty demands, pulling up a chair to listen to Brian's entertaining proclamation.

"Aight y'all', think Jessica Alba 'badd'...!" Brian prompts them to visualize.

"Okay?" Marty and Cortez agrees following along.

"Think Zoe Saldana badd!" Brian adds.

"Okay?" The fellas follow.

51

"Now, think Freida Pinto badd!" Brian continues.

"Who?!" The fellas exclaim at once.

"The chick from that Slumdog movie." Brian clarifies.

"Oh…okay! Yeah, she's nice too!" Cortez agrees.

"I mean this girl was gorgeous, with that jet black Indian hair pinned up. Her body was tight like a model. She had that beautiful, flawless skin tone, professionally dressed, and she was wearing some perfume that had me going. Plus, she had good cheekbone structure, a beautiful set of lips, and a cute button nose. She spoke like she had home training and her eyes…man she had these amazing majestic, almond shaped eyes. It was like I was mesmerized or something when she looked at me. Even the sound of her voice almost gave me a woody in my sweats, ya mean? Beautifully human for real!" Brian describes to the fellas.

"Majestic eyes…? Cheekbone structure…? What the hell, you're a cosmetic surgeon now?" Cortez asks, as the men outburst in laughter.

"Naw, man! I'm just saying that's how bad she was." Brian clarifies.

"Uh-huh, I bet if you had the chance you'd lick that 'V' wouldn't you, ya nasty son of a…" Marty asks heckling his friend.

"I aint gone lie, if I had a chance I'd be like, ♫na-na-na-na, la-la, la-la, you get what I'm saying…♫" Brian replies with musical humor and an animated tongue as the fellas break out into a roar of laughter.

"Aight, so did you get a card, a phone number, email address, Facebook name, anything?" Marty inquires trying to get to the point of it all.

"Naw, I couldn't. Her demeanor was strictly about business, and I wasn't about to play myself. I just played the role and made the delivery. But, I know where she works and I know where she lives." Brian assures them.

"What you mean you know where she lives? You stole her mail or something?" Marty comically asks.

"Naw, the first time I ran into her was the other day when I was on my run. Turns out, she happens to be the daughter of one of my favorite drop-offs. Some rich cat that lives off Lincoln Drive." Brian explains.

"Okay, so now what? What's the plan, Mojo? Are you going to try to get at her or what?" Cortez questions.

"I think the real question should actually be, 'can' you get at her? Because it sounds to me like she's a little out of your league, brotha. No disrespect, but, if she's that well-groomed and she's got a rich daddy, I promise you they ain't paying her peanuts up in them skyscrapers. She's about that center city life. Probably on some five-letter shopping for real, and you 'ain't' making enough money to finance that habit, ya dig?" Marty explains before taking another swig of his beer.

"Uh...what's five letter shopping?" Brian asks, bewildered by the expression.

"Dawg, you 'ain't' ever heard of five letter shopping? Gucci, Fendi, Prada, Dolce, Louis?" Marty elaborates.

"Oh, that's hot! I've never heard it put like that before." Brian replies, appreciating the analogy.

"Hell, she might have a man! Most women like that do...a paid one too!" Cortez adds. Brian paused for a moment to process the fellas' point, before giving his assessment.

"Hmm...I see your point. I can attest to that." Brian acknowledges. Marty then raises his bottle for a toast.

"High maintenance...?!" Marty exclaims.

"High maintenance!" The fellas toast across the pool table. The fellas made it their customary practice to toast to every point that they all agree on.

"But...I'm up for the challenge." Brian counters with resilience.

Just as Marty leans in to focus on his game winning shot, he hears Brian's vote of confidence and stands from his shooting stance.

"Is that right?" Marty dubiously replies.

"Yeah, that's right! I mean, the worst thing she can say is no, right? Besides, my stats speak for itself. I think the odds are definitely in my favor on this one." Brian confidently pleads his case.

"Okay then Mr. Mojo, I see you smelling yourself right now. So how 'bout a small motivational wager to help you along your quest?" Marty challenges.

"Hmph, aight! So, what you talking, fifty? A hundred?" Brian confidently replies.

"Nope, one Yankee!" Marty replies with the reasonable wager.

"A Dollar?" Brian replies with a disappointing frown.

"Yup, I'll bet you one dollar that she won't even give you a date, let alone give up that 'hello kitty'! Trust me, I've seen this movie before. I know exactly how this one's 'gonna' end!" Marty assures him.

"Aight bet. It's only for quarters, but a gentleman's bet it is then! And I want my dollar too, Bruh!" Brian replies as he shakes on the bet with all smiles.

"Trust me, this one 'ain't' about the money. It's all about the humility!" Marty explains.

"Ayo, whatever happened to that cute jawn you was messing with on City Line Ave?" Cortez randomly asks Brian.

"Who Amika? Awe man, let me tell y'all about his chick! I had to eighty-six that jawn 'cause she was too clumsy." Brian jokes with a straight face.

"Clumsy? Really?" Cortez responds, surprised by his reply.

"Yeah, man. She was always trippin' over something!" Brian replies as the fellas laugh at the corny punch-line.

"Basically, he's telling you he got bored, Tez. Don't let that negro fool you. This cat changes women like he changes drawls." Marty spells out.

"Naw, seriously! This ungrateful chick copped an attitude with me after I picked up a dozen shrimp from *The Stinger*." An annoyed Brian explains.

"Wow…she bugged out after you bought her a dozen of them expensive damn shrimp? I'd be pissed too!" Cortez supports.

"You couldn't just get her a shrimp basket from a Chinese restaurant and call it a day? You had to spend a percentage of your check on some damn shrimp?" Marty questions.

"My point exactly! She insisted on shrimp from *The Stinger*, then gave me attitude! I'm tired of dealing with these pump fakin', boujee black women." Brian vents with frustration.

"So, now you're going to trade in a boujee 'sista' for a boujee Arab chick?" Marty struggles to understand.

"Look, I know what you're thinking. But, before we get too involved in judging, we don't know a thing about this chick. Besides, according to you, I don't have a chance with her anyway. But, if I do get the opportunity to get close to the young Arab princess, as I said before, I'm up for the challenge!" A poised Brian replies.

"Aight now, you better stop playing with Mallory before she messes around and cheats on you with a basketball player." Marty teases as he gets low for a shot.

"Well, God bless her if she does. Remember she ain't my girl, we just smashin'." Brian reminds Marty, unbothered by the comment.

"Hmph, okay! Well, just be careful. Don't end up getting put down like this eight-ball in the side pocket. Sorry Tez, that's game!" Marty advises as he sinks the game winning shot.

"Mmm, well played!" Brian says before taking another swallow of his beer.

"So, what kind of wild concoction are you cooking up tonight for dinner?" Cortez inquires.

"I don't feel like doing too much tonight, so 'I'ma' just fall back and whip up a single man's special." Brian explains.

"Which is…?" Cortez inquires.

Probably some udon noodles with shrimp, minced garlic, cilantro, cracked pepper and lemon. Maybe throw in some sofrito for added flavor." Brian replies in blasé fashion.

"Wow, and here I was thinking you just add water and the little flavor pack. Maybe get a little fancy with it by adding butter?" Cortez replies, mocking his friend's creativity.

"Anyway, I can't stay too long y'all. I've got assignments due by tomorrow and unless one of y'all can give me a detailed lecture about a cranberry duck fat reduction or the fall of the Roman Empire, I've got to bounce." Brian says, wrapping up his evening with the fellas.

"Damn, you ain't gone get on this table tonight?" Marty asks with concern.

"Awe, c'mon, 'B'! Seriously? I was looking forward to getting another round of free drinks." Cortez pleads.

"Sorry Tez, but, I don't aspire to retire from Apex in twenty years, and don't forget, I've 'gotta' give Mallory some maintenance tonight, ya dig!" Brian smiles with a look of guile.

"I hear you, Bruh. Last night I had to give Kerry some serious maintenance. She was tipsy off that white zinfandel after the kids went to sleep. I had to put that aftershock on her and put that ass right to sleep!" Marty boasts to his friends.

"Aftershock? What the hell is an aftershock?" Brian asks, bewildered by the term.

"See, I knew you two wasn't hittin' it right. Y'all need to take notes from an old pro." Marty

"Okay, so let's hear it Hugh Hefner." Brian jokes as he and Cortez stand attentively like to students preparing for a lesson.

"The aftershock is when you put it down so hard and so long that once she has an orgasm, she can't move until she comes down off that orgasmic climax…" Marty pauses to take a swig of his beer to quench his parched throat.

"That's it? That's the aftershock? Man, I put it down like that all the time, you ain't said nothing impressive!" Cortez replies as he and Brian look at Marty unimpressed.

"Hold on a minute, Mr. Quick Pumper, that's just part of it. The other part of it is the second unexpected orgasm. See, while she's lying there recovering from the first one, her body suddenly convulses like she's having a seizure or something, but she's actually having another orgasm. That my friend's is the aftershock and once you experience it for the first time, it's going to scare the hell out of you because you're going to think she went into shock. But, once you both realize what just happened, you're the man! Remember, it ain't always about the penetration, sometimes it's about the experience, young bucks!" Marty explains with a smile as he takes another swig of his beer.

"Man, that don't sound fun. That sounds scary as hell!" Cortez replies, unsure of how to feel about the aftershock.

"It is fun and it is scary when it happens! Shhh…I almost called 911 the first time it happened to me. But, man…women look at you different when that happens. But, remember this…'cause I can already see that this dude is about to try this on Mallory tonight. All women may not be capable to experience it, the sex has to be really intense, and you've really got to tear her walls down in order for it to happen. You do that and you might be lucky enough to experience it." Marty explains, educating his young apprentices. Brian just smiles curiously of the sexual revelation as if he has accepted this as a new challenge to add to his sexual portfolio.

"Hmph, well on that note 'I'ma' get at y'all tomorrow! Marty, don't worry about me chasing an aftershock tonight, I'm too tired for all that. Tez, don't catch a beat down trying, and I'm out!" Brian replies as he grabs his jacket and tosses his bag over his shoulder, daps up his friends, swallows the last of his beer and chucks up his deuces as he exits the sports bar.

"Aight now…! Don't go out there and hurt something tonight." Marty urges Brian.

56

"C'mon now! It's got to be every man's mission in life to experience the aftershock at least once, right?" Brian replies with a look of guile on his face.

"Brother, at this stage in the game, my only mission in life is to keep my son out of the slammer, keep my daughter off the pole, and keep Kerry out the arms of another man. I ain't got nothing else to prove." Marty casually replies.

"Amen to that!" Cortez concurs.

"Shut up Tez! Your only mission is to keep Brandy's foot out of your ass!" Brian quickly responds.

"Aight black man, go handle your scandal!" Marty encourages as Brian departs.

"Mojo has left the building!" Cortez sounds off in Brian's wake.

"Man, he always does that. Shows up for a few minutes then vanishes like a ghost." Cortez says, expressing his disappointment to Marty.

"Tez, didn't you hear what the man said? He doesn't plan on retiring on the Apex 401K plan. He's in school, where you probably should be unless you plan on retiring with Apex yourself? He's focused, like you need to be on this table right now." Marty rationalizes.

"Can you believe that fool is in school to be a cook? I thought he would have taken up cable installation or auto mechanics or something?" Cortez playfully critiques.

"Yeah, I know. I've never known anyone to go to school to be a cook. But, he's really engaged and he's pretty good at it. So, I hope he gets his own kitchen someday. But, poor Mallory. You know he's going to beat the brakes off her tonight trying to make her an aftershock statistic, right." Cortez speculates.

"Yeah, I think he was the wrong person to tell that too. But, oh, well? If he does do it to Mallory, she'll be wearing a smile to work for like a month. C'mon man, break!" The fellas laugh as Cortez makes his break.

CHAPTER FOUR

The next day is indeed a beautiful one for Brian Jones. After giving Mallory some much needed reconciliation till about 2:30 in the a.m., Brian wakes up in Mallory's bed to a bright sun beaming in his face. The smell of bacon, eggs, and toast fills his nostrils, fueling the rumble of an empty stomach. It's also Friday, which is pay day, and he's expecting a healthy check from some much-needed incentive pay he earned throughout the week. The day couldn't have started any better. But, it certainly became more interesting after Brian walks out to his car to go to work, and discovers another note on his windshield.

"Okay…?" Brian says aloud as he lifts his windshield wiper to read the note from his would-be mysterious admirer.

"No dis to the white girl. But, I think you'd look so much better in something black!" The note reads with a winking smiley face.

Bewildered by the message, Brian is now eager to know who his admirer is and what she looks like.

"Who the hell is this?!" Brian asks himself as he immediately directs his attention to building 436 across the parking lot.

As he did before, Brian focuses on every window of the building and the cars in the parking lot, to see if he can spot anyone watching him leaving for work. Again, he comes up empty. But, just as he prepares to back out of his parking spot, he looks into his rear-view mirror and notices a very attractive woman exiting building 436.

"Hmm…isn't she a tasty, sexy treat! Could she be Ms. Secret admirer?" He ponders as his eyes follow her movements from his rear view.

He watches her until she got into her car to drive off. However, on her way to the car, he notices that she looks twice in his direction. She glances and smiles as she pushes the curls from her beautiful brown face the first time she looks up. Then she glances over again, just before opening her car door. Brian quickly backs up to drive off, timing it to see if he could catch eye contact with her when she pulls away. As she drives past him, he couldn't draw eye contact with her because she hid them behind her curls.

58

The eye contact would have only aided his suspicion. But, Brian was sure that there was a connection with this woman.

Afterwards, Brian hastily enters I-95 south and navigates the early morning traffic to make it to work on time. The sun is so bright he drops the car visors and puts on a cheap pair of shades to block the glare of the sun. On his commute towards Delaware Avenue, he looks to his right and marvels the beautiful view of the Philadelphia skyline that appeared to be more prevalent than ever under the bright burn of the morning sun. It reminded him of how proud he was to be from such a great city and how anxious he was to thrive in it as a chef.

Brian developed a passion for cooking as an adolescent when he was groomed in his grandmother's kitchen during the holidays and special occasions. What started out as just keeping Grandma Ruth company while she slaved over a hot stove, cooking turkeys, hams, sweet potatoes, rutabagas, butternut squash, chitterlings, cornbread, cakes, pies, and other trimmings for a family feast, turned out to actually be his very first lessons as a cook. Under her tutelage he learned how to control his heat, measuring, sifting, mixing, prepping, and his favorite part of all, tasting. His uncles and aunts would help out, but they spent most of their time in the basement entertaining guests, spinning oldies records, drinking, and smoking dope. It wasn't until Grandma Ruth had suffered a recent stroke and became ill, did Brian realize his calling to the kitchen. After she lost her ability to cook for the family, Brian enrolled into culinary school the next school year.

Now he's one semester away from graduating at the top of his class with a bachelor's degree in Culinary Arts and an ambition of heading his own restaurant someday. He also enrolled in a volunteer apprenticeship program sponsored by the school every other weekend at select four-star restaurants throughout the city. Ever since he started the program, Brian has thrived as a natural in the kitchen as a prep cook, line cook, saucier, and assistant sous chef. The professional experience has helped him hone his culinary skill in today's kitchen, with a touch of old school flavor.

Despite the morning rush, Brian shows up for work on time, fully energized and ready to start the day. Before heading out on his run, Brian sees Marty preparing his truck as well.

"So, how'd it go last night?" Marty enquires as he scans the items from his inventory.

(Sigh) "You know, the usual…studying, chillin'… I didn't really get in the kitchen too much last night." Brian casually replies, purposely eluding the real answer to Marty's question.

"Negro please, you know what the hell I'm talkin' about! Did you tighten up Mallory last night or what?" Marty abruptly gets to the point.

"C'mon now, you know I had to handle my business…and, even though I'm really not about that life, I did a little deep-sea diving last night too." Brian shamelessly replies.

"See, that's what I'm talking about! That's why they call you the 'one-night stand running man.' Respect brotha, re-spect!" Marty encourages, giving his friend props with pound and a hug.

"Ayo', check this out, though. Some chick that lives across the street from Mallory is leavin' messages on my window. Talkin' 'bout, 'no dis to the white chick, but I think you look better in black, and you're a magnum man, huh…' referring to my whip of course. But, with dual meaning, ya mean?" Brian paraphrases, explaining his situation with his hands resting on top of his truck.

"So, wait! A girl you don't know is leaving you notes on your windshield?" Marty reiterates for confirmation.

"Yes!" Brian confirms.

"Flirting with, you?" Marty teasingly asks again.

"Yeah, she asked me if I was a magnum man!" Brian replies.

"In front of your girl's crib?" Marty teases with yet another inquiry.

"She's not my girl, but yes!" Brian quickly clarifies.

"Okay and you have no idea how this girl looks?" Marty asks hampering him with another question.

"If it's the same slim, cutie I suspected this morning, she's a certified dime piece." Brian speculates with great expectation.

"Mmm…mmm…mmm…brotha, if this woman does turn out to be the one who wishes to grant you much pleasure, then I've only got five words for you…how-do-you-do-it? I mean, from a married man's perspective, you're like a male whore hero or something? Seriously, you are every married man's hero! I mean, I've got too much invested in my marriage to ever step out on Kerry, so I have to live out my trifling ambitions vicariously through you, and I don't mean that in a trifling way. But, anyway, divide and conquer my brotha, divide and conquer!" A zealous Marty praises as he pumps his fist like a militant revolutionary.

"Divide and conquer?" A confused Brian asks.

"Yeah, brotha! Divide those legs and conquer that God given, ever blessed, sweet nectar known to man!" Marty eloquently breaks down. Brian laughs and gives Marty a fist bump as he reaches for his handheld scanner and starts his own inventory.

"Haha…you always have a way with words, Bruh." Brian points out, grateful for Marty's prolific conversations.

"Like you have a way with women, right?" Marty counters.

"I guess…" Brian modestly replies.

"Speaking of women, are you making a stop at ole girl's crib today, the Arabic chick?" Marty inquires on a more serious note.

"Well, let me see…" Brian replies, quickly searching his hand held to confirm.

"Yup, these two packages right here!" Brian confirms as he holds up the packages to show Marty.

"Aight…aight…since I can clearly see that opportunity will present itself again and again. What's your plan, Bruh? How do you plan on getting to this girl?" Marty asks, realizing that Brian's encounter with Ashima would be inevitable.

"C'mon now! You know how I do. I'm a man apart in my own zone. I always work with a plan." Brian arrogantly replies.

"Okay…I'm listening!" Marty responds waiting for Brian to unveil his crafty scheme.

"Like the old head said in Coming to America, 'you wanna get in good with the girl, you gotta get in good with her father'." Brian quotes from a movie, imitating the voice of the character.

"Okay Mojo, I see you. Play on, playa!" Marty admires as he heads back to his truck.

"Speaking of playa, there goes ya girl, Mal and look whose bringing up the rear!" Marty points out as he spots Mallory heading up the stairs with Vince closely trailing behind.

Mallory looked over at the loading dock and waves to Brian and Marty. Brian reacts with a simple head nod and kept it moving as his face turns foul by the sight of his boss Vincent. Following close behind, Vince just smiles at them like a Cheshire cat up to no good.

Before heading out, Brian sat behind the wheel of his truck momentarily to open his pay statement. He was eager to find out how much was deposited in his account and how much Uncle Sam got over.

"Incentive pay $210.12…hell yeah! That's a good look right there!" Brian says a loud, elated to see the extra income in his check.

It wasn't a whole lot of money, but it was more than what he'd expected and it came on a week where all of his bills were paid. The unexpected incentive only added to Brian's already elated mood as he releases the emergency brake on the truck and heads out.

As Brian made his rounds about the Manayunk/East Falls area, between every stop on his delivery route, the only thing that concerned him was how to get in good with Amir so he could get close enough to his daughter. Although he was unsure if he would ever get close enough to measure his chances against Ashima, he knew of one sure opportunity that he could take advantage of.

After making his perennial delivery to the bakery on Manayunk and leaving with a face full of cookie, Brian made his way over to 3911 Gypsy Lane. As he pulls up to the driveway entrance, he tries to look through the bushes to see who was actually home.

"Hmm…just the Mercedes in the driveway as usual. Damn, this dude 'ain't' ever in the office! I've got to get me a gig like that." Brian thinks to himself checking out the house.

With packages in hand, Brian walks the brick laid driveway to the front door, and rings the bell.

"Oh-no, you again?! Please, stay right here, I'm going to get my bullmastiffs from the back. I'm sure they would love to meet you." Amir jokes after opening the door to greet Brian.

Brian wasn't alarmed by the threat because he's never known this address to have dogs. But, for good measure, his reaction was to look through to the back of the house to spot any evidence of something different.

"Dogs, huh…?" Brian casually replies.

"My friend, I'm just kidding. I have no filthy beasts in my backyard. It's good to see you today! How are you, my friend?" Amir asks in high spirits.

"I'm good Amir, just enjoying another sunny day in Philadelphia." Brian replies, happy to see Amir in a good mood.

"Yes, yes! It looks like we're going to have a pretty good fall. So, what headaches have you brought for me today?"

"Just these two for you today, Amir." Brian replies as he hands Amir the packages and the electronic pad to sign for them.

"Please Allah don't let this be work." Amir pleads as he opens both packages.

"Oh Dear, I guess Allah will not be kind to me today. Oh well, at least they pay well, right?" Amir says playfully hitting Brian with the envelopes.

"Trust me Amir, if my job paid as well as yours, I would never complain about delivering packages." Brian assures him.

"Believe me Buddy you have no idea how dirty these knees have gotten to get where I am today. I say that figuratively of course. I don't go that way, okay Buddy? In fact, your knees look like they could use a little dirt on them too, my friend!" Amir jokes as they laugh together at Amir's dry humor.

"No disrespect, but I think I'm a keep making my money righteously Amir, minus the kneepads." Brian replies as he back pedaled preparing to leave.

Brian enjoys the trade of insults with Amir, simply because he felt like the more comfortable he could make Amir feel, the better his chances were to run into his daughter. Operation 'get in good with Amir' was going as well as he'd planned. Now, it was time to take this plan to the next level if the opportunity presents itself again.

"Fair enough my friend, fair enough. Listen, enjoy your weekend, okay!"

"You too, Amir." Brian kindly replies.

"Oh, don't you worry my friend. I'll be over my friend's house watching the game on Sunday. It's always a good time with these guys." Amir boasts.

Brian didn't want to seem pressed about going, but he was hoping to seize the opportunity to get invited again by Amir to watch the game as a part of his plan. So, he had to think of something to say fast before departing.

"Okay. You're still holding a spot for me, right?"

"Sure Buddy, anytime you want to come just let me know." Amir replies with pleasure.

"Well, if you got room for one more on Sunday, I could probably roll with you then." Brian tentatively replies.

"Oh, what happened? I thought you liked Tennessee's chances next week?" Amir asks teasing Brian.

"Well, they're playing the Giants this week and that should be a good game too." Brian replies.

"Okay then, Buddy. You can roll out with me, my friend. I can show you big pimpin' and guys with lots of bling, bling! Let's go with eleven o'clock on Sunday. You can park your car along the shrubs and we'll head out then." Amir confirms. Brian was taken aback by Amir's urban tongue. But, he also found it to be amusing coming from a man nearly twice his age or older.

"Okay. I'll be here at eleven. Do you need me to bring anything?"

"No, no Buddy, just bring yourself! No worries, okay?" Amir ensures Brian.

"Aight then, I'll see you on Sunday." Brian confirms as he left to return to his truck."

Brian walks back to his truck gleaming with confidence. Not only was his plan to get close to Amir's daughter working, but he's never hung out with a person of Amir's status before. Although he didn't know exactly what he was in for, he knew he was in for a treat.

After finishing his shift, Brian decides to cap off the perfect ending to a productive day by picking up his favorite bacon and mushroom, cheesesteak from Maxx's steaks at Broad and Erie before heading over to Grandma Ruth's to check on her. Since losing his mother to heart failure many years ago, Brian grew even closer to his grandmother to somewhat fill the void. Even at her tender elderly age, she's been the easiest person in his life to talk to and he always made sure she didn't need for anything.

On his way to her house at 29th Street and Allegheny Avenue, Brian makes his way down Erie Avenue with the windows down, stereo blaring, and the aroma of a freshly made cheese steak filling his nostrils. As he approaches Hunting Park, he pulls next to a Dodge Magnum nearly identical to his. But, this car was blinding Brian with the reflection of the sun glaring off the twenty-two-inch rims and glossy low-profile wheels which set it apart from his.

"Damn! That thing is sittin' right. It'll probably take a year to save up for a set of those feet on an Apex salary." Brian says discouragingly as he

looks over at the driver and gives him a head nod, and the driver responds with a nod of his own.

When the light turns green, traffic was held up by several cop cars screeching out of the 39th District Police station, and fire trucks and EMS racing not far behind, responding to a call and heading in his direction down Hunting Park Ave.

"Hmph, the only time cops scramble like that is when somebody gets shot. I pray to God I'm wrong." Brian instinctively speculates, judging from the urgency and the amount of first responders.

After making a left onto Hunting Park Avenue and stopping at another traffic light at Wissahickon Avenue, two more squad cars and a paddy wagon roar past him from different directions.

"Wow, this looks serious!" Brian mutters to himself in awe.

Fully engaged in the blaring activity around him, Brian was curious to know where all the chaos is taking place. He turns his radio all the way down and listened to the ambient noise of sirens bellowing in his proximity. At this point, he knew it was serious judging from the amount of time that passed, and sirens that just kept coming. By the time he made it to Fox Street just past the old Budd plant on his left, two fire engines barreling down Hunting Park Avenue in his rear view were coming fast. Growing up in this neighborhood, it wasn't uncommon to see this kind of activity. But, even this was a little more than what Brian was used to. Now he could only hope that it wasn't someone he knew involved.

After the fire engines nearly made him deaf from their piercing sirens and the earsplitting blast of their horns, he made a left to follow the trucks on Fox Street and find out where they were responding to. Brian could see the trucks turning right onto Alleghany, which meant that the incident was closer to his old neighborhood than he'd originally expected. Once he reaches the intersection of Fox and Alleghany he could see spectators running towards what he could only describe as a scene similar to a war zone.

For as far as he could see from two blocks away, there were cop cars, ambulances, fire engines, and a mob of people at the intersection of 26th and Allegheny. The traffic and the crowd are so thick that the fire truck couldn't get any further than a block from the scene and it was impossible for Brian to drive any closer too.

65

"Oh my God, what is this? What's going on?" Brian anxiously asks as he pulls his car over and put on his hazard lights on to find out what went down.

As he walks up the block he could see women with their hands over their mouths, others shaking their heads, and talking on their cell phones in a distraught manner. Brian literally weaves his way through the crowd before he's finally able to get close enough to notice a large area of the intersection blocked off with yellow tape. Trying to make sense of it all, the scene looks like something from a Hollywood movie. An SUV is sitting on its side on the sidewalk that looks like it knocked over the light pole and a BMW that smashed head on into a route 60 Septa bus with passengers. The light pole fell on a parked Honda, and a man is hanging out of the driver's side of the BMW. The car is riddled with bullet holes, and the windows are shattered. As Brian continues to survey the scene, what actually happened here began to become more apparent.

"Awe, man...this is bad. This is really, really bad! Somebody just got killed here... damn!" Brian realizes as the scene appeared so surreal.

Grown men were crying. Women were acting out hysterically. Little children stood behind the yellow tape trying to process what their innocent eyes were actually seeing, as police and fire radios crackle and helicopters buzzed the sky above. News vans were staging their reporting areas with their huge antennas elevated in the sky. Nearly, everyone in the crowd is taking pictures and video on their phones, documenting the carnage. Caught in the midst of it all was an ice cream truck that came out on this unseasonably warm day, parked in front the United Methodist Church.

The longer he stays at the scene the sadder it became, as he moves in for a closer look, he realizes that the driver of the BMW wasn't the only person in the car. He saw another person slumped over in the passenger seat and two other heads in the back seat. Looking into the car through the open door, he could see the passenger holding a melting ice cream cone in his left hand resting on the center console with blood splattered on it like strawberry topping. He also got a better look at the driver and could see his shirt is soaked with blood. His head resting on the ground in a blood puddle and what appears to be brain matter hanging out the left side of his temple. Brian knew that there had to be four people dead in the car because EMS was on scene, but didn't attempt to treat any of the victims.

66

It seemed as if the entire Philadelphia police force was on hand, processing the crime scene, interviewing people, and maintaining a boundary. Even a few officers appeared to be grief stricken by the horrific scene. You could see the somber expressions on many of their faces. Some even hid their emotions behind sunglasses because it wasn't professional to show their emotion. But, today, even the police weren't police in uniform, they were emotional human beings.

"Yo, what's up, 'B'? I ain't expect to see you 'round here with all this madness going on." A voice rang out from Brian's blind side.

"Kev! What's up man? You talkin' 'bout me…what you doin' down here?" Brian asks giving his childhood friend a pound and a hug.

Kevin has lived next door to Grandma Ruth for many years, and has known Brian ever since he was five years old. He was one of the last childhood friends Brian knew who never left the block.

"Man, this mess is crazy, man. I can't believe this happened. I came down here to get a shrimp and broccoli from the 'Chink Wok.' And while I'm waiting, I happened to hear the ice cream truck down the street. So, I called myself trying to beat the crowd because I know he was only out because it was a nice day, and it was a bunch of kids playing in front of the Chinese store. So, I walked up the street to catch the truck where it's sittin' at right now. And, when I got down here, I saw Jerk and Lacey in front of the line about to leave…" Kevin explains.

"Jerk and Lacey…awe man, I 'ain't' seen them cats in a minute!" Brian interrupts, surprised to hear the names of friends he knew from around the way mentioned.

"Yeah, I know. I ain't seen them dudes since Troy and them ran them out of the neighborhood years ago, after the 'bor' got killed at Whittier Playground. Remember, back in the day them cats was the biggest stick up kids around here." Kevin reminds Brian.

"Yeah, I remember that…then they burnt Troy for that ounce of coke. Troy shot up Lacey mom crib on Bambrey Street behind that. I remember all that. That's why they moved out Southwest. I was still in high school when all that happened." Brian recalls as he watches the crime scene investigators finger print and take pictures of the bodies inside the car.

"Exactly! So, I'm talking to them as they were leaving, and Jerk was telling me that he was doing good, staying out of trouble, got a job with the Water Department three years ago, and how he had a daughter last year, and she changed his life. Then Lacey was just telling me how he doesn't hustle no more and he was trying to move down south. So, I told them that I was glad to see them and all, and after that they got into that BMW and..." Kevin explains before Brian interrupts again.

"Wait a minute! Wait a minute! You tellin' me that Jerk and Lacey are in that car right now?! You saw the whole thing?!" Brian grabs Kevin by the arm and replies with urgent dismay.

"Yeah, that's Jerk's car. He just picked up his little cousin and his cousin's friend around the corner on Bambrey Street. That's them in the back seat. That's all of their family over there crying and going crazy. I think they were on their way to play ball out West Philly, or something? Crazy, man!" Kevin confirms.

"AWE MAN! OH-NO! WHAT HAPPENED, KEV?!" Brian cries out as he put his hand on Kevin's shoulder trying to grasp how personal this tragedy had suddenly become.

"Well, as I was sayin', the car was parked in front of the ice cream truck and when they got in the car that Chevy SUV that crashed over there was speeding down Alleghany Ave. And just as this girl was saying, 'look at this fool driving like he ain't got no sense', the SUV slammed on brakes like it was trying to avoid hitting Jerk's car as he pulled out. But, when he hit the brakes all you heard was BOOM! BOOM! BOOM! BOOM! and a bunch of other shots. Man, everybody in line ducked behind the ice cream truck and I guess the bus must have clipped the SUV when he was trying to turn down 26th Street and it flipped over. Then Jerk ran into the bus head on because he was shot. He opened the door to get out, but he collapsed right there and took his last breath. After the SUV flipped, all three guys that were in it got out and started running. But, one guy tried to run down 26th Street with a shotgun and ran into a beat cop. I think the guy tried to raise up on the cop and the cop popped him like four times. The other two dudes ran down Alleghany. That's why the police helicopter is out here." Kevin explains, recalling the horrific details of the incident.

"So, where is the dude that got shot by the beat cop?" A confused Brian asks.

"He's laying over there behind the cars where the pole fell. But, you can't see him because they tapped it off and put a sheet over him." Kevin replies.

"See Kev, this is the reason why I got the hell up outta here. This crap has been happening ever since we were kids, man. I 'ain't' got the stomach for this no more, man!" Brian vents emotionally, disheartened by the tragic circumstance.

"I hear you, 'B', I hear you." Kevin agrees as he places an arm around Brian's neck to console him.

"I mean, I went elementary and middle school with Jerk and Lacey, man. We were kids, man! Where the hell did we go wrong, Kev?" Brian asks becoming unwound.

"I know man, I was ahead of y'all three years in grade school. I remember. Senseless man…it's just sad." Kevin empathizes.

Brian takes another look at the horrific scene and goes into a surreal-like daze in the midst of hundreds of people. The chaos around him goes silent as he watches the coroner van back up next to the bus. Grown men, women, teens, and children are sobbing and grieving hysterically for their loved ones in front of the church. He watches as people are being taken off the bus by fire fighters and taken to the hospital. The detective behind a smashed Honda Accord lifting the sheet, while CSI takes photos of the crime scene makes it all too real. Then the sight of his childhood classmate as police place a sheet over his lifeless body over takes Brian emotionally. His eyes begin to welt as a Pastor from the Methodist church comes out in his black clergy robe and police escorted him to the car to render last rights and prayer to the deceased under an amber sky as the sun set on another day in North Philadelphia.

"Ayo man, I gotta get out of here, Bruh. I was on my way to check on Grandma Ruth anyway so I'll see you back on the block, aight?" Brian explains, as he becomes overwhelmed by the drama.

"Aight man, I'm a wait for the vigil and give my condolences. Be safe out here too, man! You know those other two knuckleheads are still on the loose somewhere around here." Kevin cautions.

"Man, after all this, I'm not even gone stay long. I'm ready to just go home and try to process what the hell just happened today, Fam. Peace!" Brian replies as he daps Kev before walking back to his car.

As dusk falls and the cool of night begins to set in, the light of day would soon be replaced by the illuminated lights of emergency service vehicles. The flicker of candlelight was already forming throughout the crowd of mourners, even before their bodies were removed from the scene.

Disturbed by the tragedy, Brian is reminded that no matter how normal violence in the streets may seem, he'll never become numb to it. Although he wasn't close his deceased friends as adults, Brian is still touched by the loss of his grade school classmates LaMarcus "Jerk" Taylor and Lacey Porter no matter what they've done or what they were involved in.

"May God rest their souls…Amen!" Brian prays as he sat silent in his car. A tear forms in the corner of his eye as he watches the flicker of lights from emergency vehicles for a while before finally driving off.

Brian parks in front of his Grandmother's house and turns his car off to gather himself and reflect. He looks over at his sandwich, but had no desire to go into the house to warm it up, and no appetite to eat it. He sits in the car melancholy, and quiet, as he people watched from behind his tinted glass windows. As most of the people passed by, the faces that walked the block didn't seem too familiar. Most of the people he knew in his childhood either grew up and moved on, or passed away. It was a bitter sweet experience coming back to Allegheny Avenue. But, talking to Mama Ruth always made it worthwhile. Instead of going inside, he decides to call her just to hear her voice.

"Hello…" Her elderly voice answers.

"Hey Mama, what are you doing?" Brian replies with his spirits lifted a bit.

"Hey Baby, I'm sitting here watching the news, looking at this mess happening around the corner. Did you hear what happened on 26th Street?" Mama Ruth asks prepared to deliver the bad news to Brian.

"Yes Mama, I just came from around there. It was terrible Mama. I had no idea how crazy things were until I seen it with my own eyes." Brian remorsefully explains.

"Yeah, I heard one of them was Agnes' boy. You went to elementary school with him, didn't you?" Mama Ruth replies.

"Yes Mama, I went to school with both guys that were in the front seats." Brian clarifies.

"Mmph…Lord have mercy! Well I guess I'll have to give Agnes a call later on. How are you feeling, baby?" Mama asks with concern for her grandson.

"I'm still in a bit of shock, Mama. 'I'ma' go home and try to sleep this off like it was a bad dream." Brian replies, still struggles to process it all.

"Well, they caught them other two boys they were looking for, so I feel a little bit safer with them off the streets. You just make sure you call me when you get home, ya here me?" Mama Ruth insists.

"Yes Ma'am, I'll call you as soon as I get in." Brian ensures to make Mama Ruth feel better.

"Okay, I love you, ya hear?" Mama Ruth comforts him before hanging up.

"I love you too Mama Ruth!" Brian replies before putting his car in drive and heading home.

As promised, the first thing Brian did was call Mama Ruth as soon as he opens the door to his apartment. What started out as a really great day, turned out to be one of the toughest days he could remember growing up in his old neighborhood. After returning home from a mentally exhausting evening, and with no appetite to enjoy the cheesesteak, the only thing he had left in him is to lay down and catch the rest of today's events on the evening news.

Gameday

Two days after the horrific tragedy, between being consoled by Grandma Ruth and her divine wisdom and going to his cousin's birthday party over the weekend, Brian was able to recover from his anxiety of the incident. But, this morning, Brian had even more reason to feel good since today was the day he would meet with Amir to watch the Eagles game, which he's been anticipating all weekend.

He wakes up all smiles and starts the day by cooking turkey sage sausage, eggs with feta cheese crumbles, diced tomatoes, sazo`n seasoned cheese grits with cilantro, French toast topped with assorted fruit, glazed with raspberry syrup and confection sugar he made for himself and the girl he met at his cousin's party the night before. Although he's reeling from a slight hangover, he still manages to show off his skills in the kitchen to impress his guest. As she lay's comfortably in his bed baring nothing more than a sheet covering her lower half, Brian stands at the edge of his kitchen counter wearing boxer briefs and slippers, admiring her soft, flawless skin, and her golden fair complexion. Although he came home wasted last night and can't remember this woman's name, he clearly remembered her kicking off her heels, slide out of her tightly fitted skirt, and bless him with an incredible birthday suit image that he left paw prints all over just hours before sun up.

"Wow...who needs love when you can have all this when you want it?" Brian randomly suggests, still able to smell her aromatic scent all the way across the room from which he stood in the tiny studio apartment. He takes a sip of orange juice from a glass in one hand, while holding a second glass for her in the other.

"Morning!" Brian calls out in a deep masculine tone, from the edge of the kitchen to his bed.

She moves ever so slightly before opening her eyes to the dark image of a man standing across the room. Suddenly her eyes spring fully open realizing that she was looking at an unfamiliar image. After taking a brief moment to gather herself, her eyes dial into focus to the sight of a pair of boxer briefs tightly conforming to Brian's extraordinary waistline, dips, abs, cute belly button, and of course his bulky package.

"Good morning…" She replies with a grin as she suddenly recalls the activities about last night, in a sweet subtle tone as she reaches to the floor for her cell phone.

Her wavy black hair with auburn highlights, draped in her face was a clear indication that it was indeed a pleasurably, rough night. Brian walks over towards her and offers the glass of orange juice.

"You hungry…? I made you a little something, something this morning." Brian asks as he hands her the glass.

Hair messy and all, the beautiful young woman takes a sip of the orange juice. But, her focus was far more affixed on Brian's hairless, toned chest and flat stomach than the glass of O.J.

"Awe…you're so sweet. Sure, I could go for some breakfast. It smells delicious!" The woman replies as she sits up and wraps herself with the bed sheet before taking another sip.

"Aight. I'll make you a plate while you get yourself together. Oh…I left a fresh towel and washcloth for you on the sink, just in case you wanted to freshen up." Brian asks before fleeing to the kitchen, as she rest on the bed in a princess like posture.

"Thanks. I'm sure I still have a little bit of soap left on me from last night." She cleverly replies.

When she returns from the bathroom, Brian presents her with a garnished plate of good eats. Her stunned facial expression said everything he needed to know about whether she's impressed or not.

"Awe, thank you. I hope you don't mind me wearing your Sixers jersey to breakfast. I needed something to throw on after drying off." The woman mentions. Meanwhile, Brian is admiring how arousing she looks in the jersey.

"Damn, I hope she don't have any panties on underneath that jersey." He says, allowing his hormones to get the best of him.

"Not at all. Actually, I apologize for not offer something to put on before you went into the bathroom, so you're good." Brian regretfully replies.

"Wow, this looks delicious! I love how you put the little fruit on top of the French toast, and the powdered sugar. This looks really good, Mojo." The woman comments as Brian gave his new alias a test spin.

73

"Well, the way you put it on me last night, the least I can do is show you some love in the kitchen." Brian replies as he leans against the counter, and takes a sip from his glass, watching as she samples her first bite.

"Mmm...oh my God! These grits are amazing! What did you put in this, and why are they so orange? That can't be from yellow cheese!" She was open from the first bite. Brian knew that the coriander and annatto in the Sazo`n would tantalize her taste buds.

"Oh, that's just a little Sazo`n I added to give it a little Spanish flavor, nothing major." Brian replies, down playing his culinary skill.

As she samples her way through every taste of the plate, she savors every bite. Her body language told Brian that every morsel was a new mouthwatering experience for her.

"And here I thought you were feeding me that line about being a chef, just to get in my pants last night. But, 'seeing is believing' you can burn, boy!" The woman compliments as she relishes another bite of the sage sausage.

As the two of them enjoy the morning meal sitting on bar stools at the open end of the kitchen countertop, the delectable assortment of flavors not only turns on her taste buds, it also turns on her hormones. Aroused by his good looks, sex appeal, and charm, her kitten begins pulse, having a flashback of how he handled her last night. Presumably done with breakfast, she walks the plate over to Brian with a promiscuous grin as he washes his plate at the sink. He turns to grab her plate as she stands directly in front of him, and sits the plate on the counter behind him.

"Thank you for last night and for the amazing breakfast this morning." She says softly placing her hands on his bare chest and caressing his strong pecks.

"No need to thank me this morning. You thanked me enough last night." Brian replies with a sly smirk.

"Hmm...is that right? Well...let me thank you again." She replies as she reaches up to kiss him, while simultaneously reaching into his briefs.

She kisses him once on the lips and again on his chest. Eventually, she kisses her way down to his stomach, while simultaneously massaging his genitals. Before long she drops down and helps herself to the rise in his briefs. Brian looks down and watches as she handles her business, while enjoying another taste of his O.J. After only allowing her a few moments to have a taste of him, Brian is already primed for something different. So, he rests his glass on the counter, lifts her from her kneeling position and leans her over the counter as he wet his middle and index fingers with saliva, then reaches underneath the jersey to massage her hairless, juicy lips.

"Don't move!" Brian instructs her as he walks to his dresser to grab a magnum.

"Hurry up!" She whimpers with her hormones raging at its peak.

Brian returns to the kitchen and steps out of his underwear fully erected, sliding on his contraception before grabbing her off the counter and turning her to face him. She looks directly in the eyes of her conqueror before he lifts her light five-foot frame with his strong hands and sets her down on his equally strong manhood.

"OH MY GOD!!!" She roars, as he inserts her. Suddenly she realizes that she wasn't drunk like the night before. Under estimating what she was up against, his sobering penetration forces her to brace the countertop as she lifts herself off of him.

She takes a deep exhilarating breath to prepare for him again, wrapping her arms around his neck and her legs around his waist as he inserts her again, then let out a steady sigh as she eases herself onto him until he bottomed out. Biting her bottom lip the entire episode, she endures him until she reaches a point of pleasure.

After giving her another twenty minutes to remember him by and soiling the bottom of his jersey, they both clean up and get dressed. As she cleans herself up at the sink, Brian throws on a pair of jeans, his white number 25 Eagles football jersey, and white Air Force One's to prepare for the day ahead.

"You want me to take you home or...?" Brian asks as she sat on his futon texting with the freak'em dress that attracted him the night before.

"No, I live in Abington. You don't have to take me all the way out there. My cousin that I was with last night lives near Manheim and Wissahickon. If you can drop me off there...?" She replies as she stood to leave with him.

"Damn, I see why I snatched her up last night...you are wearing that dress, baby girl!" Brian thinks as he admires her white button-down blouse, plaid crimson and white skirt, and red heels she wore from the night before.

"Sure, it's no problem. I'll take you anywhere you 'wanna' go." Brian replies, still embarrassed that he doesn't remember the woman's name. On his way to drop her off, she makes a brief phone call.

"Hey girl, it's 'Punkin.' I'm on my way to your house…" The woman says, finally giving Brian a name he could refer to her by.

"Punkin huh?" Brian thinks to himself glancing over with a grin as he continues to listen.

"Oh yeah, girl. I'm good…"

"Hmph, you already know, girl. I'll talk to you when I get there…"

"Okay, bye…!" She concludes.

Shortly after the phone call, Brian pulls to the corner of Manheim and Wissahickon to drop-off his jump-off. Although he likes Pumpkin, he was certain that this would likely be the last time he would see her again.

"This is good right here. My cousin lives down the street." Pumpkin instructs as Brian slows to a stop.

"Are you sure? It's nothing for me to take you to the door, Pumpkin, 'ya' mean?"

"No, I'm okay. 'I'ma' go to the store over there before I go to the house." Pumpkin insists, pointing at the deli across the street before opening her door. "But, thank you for breakfast this morning…and for taking care of me last night. I had a great time!" Brian smiles with confidence at the remark and felt compelled to come up with a clever reply.

"Thanks, I enjoyed you as well…and I told you I can do a little something in the kitchen." Brian humors her maintaining his manly charm.

"Hmph…that ain't the only thing you can do…" She adds leaning in to give Brian a kiss on his cheek. "Whoops sorry…don't want to get anybody jealous." She implies, wiping the kiss off his cheek with her thumb.

Brian smiles as he embraces her soft touch to his cheek before she quietly steps out of his car, leaving him with a seductive lasting impression of her. Pumpkin was a sweet girl, Brian thinks to himself as her sexy physique passes before his bumper while she crossed the street. However, she violated two rules of the man code that Brian couldn't overlook, she slept with him on the first night, and her name was of a food, fruit, or ingredient. These were deal breakers for him. After driving off, Brian does a time check to make sure he's still on schedule.

"Ten-thirty-seven, bet!" He says, knowing it would only take a few minutes to get to Amir's house from where he was. He didn't want his first outing with Amir to be a bad impression, assuming that Amir is the punctual type.

76

By the time he reaches Gypsy Lane, Brian is in full football spirit and ready to get the day started. He pulls into the driveway and parks his car as instructed. When he gets out of his car, he notices that Amir's Mercedes wasn't in the driveway. But, an unattended black Lexus LS was running instead.

As Brian checks out the car, he also took a moment to capture the picturesque surrounding scenery. It was if he was looking at a postcard, or the setting of a commercial. The car sat on the stone paved driveway, in front of the house, and the sun peeking through the thick of the trees behind it serves as a beautiful back drop on the cool of a perfect football morning. Being silly, Brian pauses in his tracks and captures the image with one eye, as he put both hands together to form frame.

"LS 460, huh? F-sport status...damn, that's a nice car!" He says as he walks around the car reading the rear badge.

His excitement grows more intense hoping that Ashima would answer the door. But, no sooner than reaching for the bell, Amir swings the door open and he doesn't look happy.

"My friend, please...have a seat in the car! I need a moment, okay?" Amir asks with an annoyed demeanor and both hands covering his cell phone.

"Oh, aight..." Brian replies in compliance. Amir immediately walks back into the house and yells into his phone in Arabic.

"ماذا أنت تعني إحدى عشرة ثلاثون, أنت قيحةً (تيم وهت) هو يكون؟"

"WHAT DO YOU MEAN ELEVEN THIRTY, DO YOU REALIZE WHAT TIME IT IS?" Amir exclaims as he slams the front door.

Amir's agitated mood starts to bring doubt that the day would happen for Brian. But, having a seat in Amir's Lexus was just what he needed to calm his concern.

"Wow, I bet he paid a couple dollars for this 'thang'!" He thinks before even opening the door.

The black paint is so clean it looks like its wet without the help of the morning dew. If it wasn't for the lights being on, he wouldn't have known that the car was even running. When he opens the door the smell of new immediately rushes his nose.

"Dayum!" Is all he could say as he sinks into the softness of the plush leather seat. The Parchment interior was the perfect contrast to the black

77

glass like exterior. His eyes were in awe as he scans the cockpit, examining the instruments and fine detail.

"What's all that going on in the back seat?" He asks himself, looking at all the buttons on the center console of the rear seats. Even the temperature of the car was pleasant; set at a comfortable 72 degrees as it read on the console display. The radio volume was low, but it was definitely tuned to Middle-Eastern music.

Soon afterwards, Amir comes out of the house and puts a pair of sneakers sitting outside the doorway. He's wearing a jogging suit instead of a football jersey. Judging from Amir's age and ethnic background, Brian just assumes to go with the flow. Amir still has the phone to his ear and ranting as he approaches the car, this time in English.

"Help me understand! Please, help me understand, Aziz!" Amir angrily sounds off as he opens the car door. Once he gets in the car, the car's Bluetooth automatically connects with the phone, and now the conversation could be heard through the car's speakers.

"Amir please, I will replace any capital lost as a result of this incompetence. But, I promise that this was all a misunderstanding." The man pleads in a heavy Middle-Eastern accent, as Amir begins to laugh.

"Aziz…Aziz, please! I don't mean to laugh. But, you're not prepared to replenish 3.5 million dollars in lost capital, okay! Now, listen…it's already Sunday. We will revisit this again tomorrow at the office, okay?" Amir replies growing weary of the conversation.

"You're right Amir, it is Sunday. Please don't despair over this. I will get to the bottom of this tomorrow, okay? Salaam Amir." A much shaken Aziz concludes.

"Salaam Aziz!" Amir responds using the button on the steering wheel to hang up.

"Oh Aziz…you're such a 'yes' man!" Amir voices in frustration, before turning his attention to Brian.

"My friend, how are you today, Buddy? Please, my apologies for this melee. I had to address some discrepancies from the office." He explains as he shakes Brian's hand.

"Oh, it's cool Amir, I understand. You're a busy man. I guess that's how the rich make their millions, right?" Brian empathizes with Amir.

"Brudah, even on Sunday, we never stop printing money, my friend." Amir assures Brian.

"Well there's obviously no doubt about that. Besides, I just spent the last few minutes imagining what it would be like to own a car as nice as this." Brian chuckles, already impressed by looking around the lavish car.

"Oh, yes. The Lexus is a very fine automobile. I think I'm a bit more parcel to it than the companies Mercedes. I saw this one at the car show at the convention center downtown and I couldn't resist. There were many nice ones. My friends have nice ones too. But, this one was fit for an executive with a sporty edge." Amir proudly elaborates.

"And I can see why you went with this one!" Brian concurs.

"Yes, yes my friend! I got tired of utilizing the company car everyday to get to and from work. Always having to call ahead of time to get around, ya know? Plus, the Lexus is far more luxurious. I can sit in the back seat, take my shoes off, recline, and sip on a nice Pinot Grigio after a long day if need be." Amir explains.

"Is that what all of those buttons are for back there?" Brian inquires.

"Oh, yes, my friend, and so much more. Go ahead take a load off my friend, I don't mind." Amir generously offers.

Brian didn't waste any time accepting the offer. He felt compelled to enjoy every moment of this rare experience. Amir, joins him in the back seat to show Brian how to navigate the controls.

"Okay Buddy, so from here I can control the stereo, heated and cooled seats, DVD player, and phone…I can push this button and screens fall from the roof and of course reclining seats, my friend." As Amir explains the features, Brian is open from sitting in the closest thing to a Maybach he has ever encountered. He's only read about cars like this in magazines.

"So, when you push this button here…" Amir pauses to allow Brian to push the button. Suddenly the front passenger chair began moving forward as his seat starts to recline. Brian was amazed at what the back seat of a car could actually do.

"This is crazy, Amir!" Brian declares enjoying the demonstration.

"But, wait my friend, there's more! Now, after a hard day's work, you have to travel to New York for a meeting. But, you just want to enjoy the ride as you sit in traffic on the turnpike. Now you can drop the screen from ceiling, grab your favorite beverage from the chiller behind this wood grain panel, push this button for your rear and side curtains, put on your favorite cinema, and push this button to turn on the chair massager. Now you're 'really' ready for a road trip, my friend! As you say in the hood, 'this is how

I roll, my friend'!" Amir summarizes, explaining the perks of the vehicle as if he was the salesman that sold him his own car.

"Awe, man…this thing is legit, Amir. If you don't mind me asking, how much did something like this set you back?" Brian asks respectfully.

"Upwards of one hundred thirty- thousand after adding a few extras, my friend. But, the money is not what's important, my friend. Quality of life is the only thing that matters." Amir replies emphasizing his point.

"Wow…that's major! By the way, I really appreciate you extending that invitation to me. I knew I was in for a treat today, and this right here was enough to satisfy me." Brian graciously replies.

"Oh please! My friend, we haven't even made it out the driveway yet. I have so much more to show you. Now please relax, my friend. I'll be your chauffer today. I want you to feel what luxury really feels like, okay." Amir requests of his guest.

"Roger that, Amir. Lead the way!" Brian gleefully replies, excited to get the day started.

As Amir slowly pulls away from the house, Brian is overwhelmed with elation, taking in every moment of the ride like a child. He sinks comfortably into the seat, and rides with his feet up like a true executive. He's never been privileged to ride in anything better than a Cadillac, so this was truly a defining moment in his life.

"How are you doing back there Buddy, huh? Nice right?" Amir asks rhetorically.

"Amir, I can't front. I don't even know how to feel right now." Brian replies in a loss for words.

"It's okay, Buddy. Welcome to the finer things!" Just as he says that, Amir pulls to the edge of his driveway, adjusts his mirror so he could see me and turns up the volume on the Arab tune that was playing.

"What the hell is he doing?" Brian thinks to himself as he watches Amir move the cursor on the navigation screen.

Suddenly a familiar Arabic string of tunes over a hip-hop beat begin to drown the premium speakers of the car as Amir speeds off. "♫*It's the Roc in the building…*♫" Amir looks into the rearview and smiles as he begins doing this goofy dance in his seat. Brian is choked up with laughter as he recognizes the song once he hears the voice of Jay-Z on the track.

80

"Haha…Punjabi MC!" They bellow simultaneously as they bob their heads to the beat of the song. Brian is tickled by Amir's dance moves and taste in music. He's shocked that Amir has anything like that in his playlist.

"JAY-Z, RIGHT BUDDY? I LIKE JAY-Z. NOT EVERYDAY, BUT I LIKE ALL MUSIC, MY FRIEND!" Amir exclaims over the blaring music.

But, the shock value of the moment didn't stop there. What happens next was nothing short of a jaw dropping, when Amir began reciting the Arabic verse of the song word for word that no English-speaking American could ever figure out.

"Man, is this dude for real? Is he really dropping a verse on a Jay-Z record? How old is this guy?" Brian asks himself watching Amir recite the lyrics with conviction.

Brian appreciated the idea of Amir being musically grounded and his comic persona despite his affluent status and age. It made the outing with Amir that much more comfortable.

"This is a good tune, right?" Amir asks after turning down the volume.

"Oh yeah, Amir. I love Hov. 'IT'S THE ROC'!" Brian indulges, putting his hands together to form a diamond.

"That's right, Hova! Jay-Z is the man!" Amir agrees.

"Amir, are you sure you don't want me to ride up front?" Brian asks, feeling awkward about communicating with Amir from the back seat.

"No, no worries brudah, you're fine! I just want you sit back and enjoy this experience, okay?" Amir insists!

And that's exactly what Brian did. He sat back and enjoyed one of the finest moments in his young adult life. Not knowing that perhaps the best is yet to come. While Amir excuses himself to take another phone call, this time speaking entirely in Arabic, Brian gazes out his window and zones out. As he rides through the city, he marvels the beautiful colors of the autumn trees as if they were changing before him. He couldn't believe that he was being chauffeured like a VIP of sorts through the crossroads of Philadelphia. The only limo service he'd ever experienced prior to this was in a funeral procession when his grandfather passed away years ago. Brian was all smiles for the entire ride, anxiously looking forward to the rest of his day, and knowing that this would get him that much closer to Amir's daughter.

After a short drive out to City Line Avenue, Brian eventually found himself crossing the beautiful landscapes of Bryn Mawr, PA. He knew from his delivery experience that being a resident in this Zip Code requires a household income of at least a quarter of a million dollars. He used to make deliveries to some of Philadelphia's best professional athletes and executives out here when he first started working for *Apex* some years back.

"My friend, it's very beautiful out here, yes?" Amir asks turning his attention to Brian after his phone call.

"Oh yeah, especially around this time of year when the leaves change color and fall from the trees." Brian agrees.

"Absolutely my friend, out here is where most of my associates live. These guys are spoiled rotten apples. They never had to work hard for anything. They all come from very wealthy parents back East and they come here or Great Britain to get the best education. I've watched these kids grow from young juveniles, ever since they were barely off of their mother's teat. I grew up with their parents back East. Now they are big boys and very westernized. We would like for them to bring back the education back to Egypt. But, in reality, it's much nicer here and they're just much better off here in the states than back home." Amir explains.

"So, how did you end up over here Amir?" Brian asks, curious to know more about Amir's background.

"I came here for the sake of my wife and daughter. Unlike my friends, I didn't come from an oil rich family or wealthy means. My walk-through life was far more humble than that, my friend. I come from a community of very poor families. Most of the parents back home were peddlers, farmers, or sweat shop workers. There was no middle-class like here in the States. You either lived hand to mouth, or you lived like royalty and there is lots of hand to mouth population where I come from. But, there's not enough opportunity for everyone and there is much competition. When I married, I was a very young adolescent. I wasn't experienced enough to seek opportunity elsewhere, until my daughter, Ashima came along when I was just a bit older. Then I knew I had to do something to give her a better life than my own. Fortunately, a childhood friend of mine had very wealthy grandparents. When they passed on to paradise, he was left with the family inheritance. By the grace of Allah, I was able to borrow money from him to travel to the States, get an education, and give my family a better quality of life; especially since he's also Ashima's godfather and the only daughter he

82

could claim. He'll do anything for Ashima. He even funds her accounts. Funny thing is, this man is close to being a billionaire by now, yet he's still the poorest of his peers." Amir further elaborates.

"Wow, Amir. I'm surprised he didn't offer you some of his millions." Brian expresses, entertaining the conversation.

"Who me? Oh, heavens no! I would never take that type of money from him. I am my own man, who makes his own way. I've earned my estate through hard work and education. I've paid him back every dinar he's ever given to me, and what does he do...he turns right around and puts it in my daughter's account. I believe she may be worth more than I am and she's done nothing more than finish school and take a position on my staff." Amir explains as he shakes his head with misunderstanding.

"Damn! Her Godfather is a billionaire and he's the 'brokest' cat in the clique? That's crazy!" Brian thinks in amazement, as he listens attentively to Amir's revelations.

Amir eventually slows to turn onto a street called Derring Lane. The stretch of brick homes and landscapes on this block took Brian to a place he knew all too well. A time when he made deliveries to streets that looked just like this one, when he was being trained at *Apex*. Growing up poor in North Philadelphia, he didn't experience much in his childhood or young adult life. So, going from seeing row homes in the hood, to seeing homes that were the size of small churches and acres of grass and trees that surrounded them, excited him. There was one street he delivered to in Andorra near the Philly city limits that was so beautiful, he used to park his truck at the end of the block and have lunch imagining what it would be like to tour one of these beautiful homes, let alone actually owning one.

Every home they pass seems to follow the same trend. For every driveway with a Honda, Nissan, or Ford, there was a Mercedes, Audi, or BMW next to it. He also notices that there wasn't a single black person in the neighborhood's demographic. In this neighborhood, you were white, Asian, or Middle-Eastern from what he's seen thus far. But, he wasn't intimidated. It was more uninspiring than anything.

83

Arab Money

"Ok Buddy, we're here! I hope you put your game face on because it's about to get exciting for you, my friend!" Amir pleasurably explains. Brian couldn't figure out if Amir was talking about the people, the game or what? But, whatever it is, he's just going to go with it.

"That's what's up!" An anxiously bewildered Brian replies.

Nearing the end of the block, the street opened up to a wealthy cul-de-sac, with three massive gated estates, sitting several hundred feet away from the road and sheltered by tall standing trees. Amir made a beeline to the gate of the most beautiful house Brian has ever seen in Bryn Mawr, PA. It's huge and it looked like a palace from what little he could see from the back seat.

"Damn, this is where we're going?" Brian belts out, in reaction to only seeing a glimpse of the house that sat at the bottom of the steep hill. Unlike the other homes, this house sat recessed in a small valley from the street level and surrounded by a taller standing fence with slender privacy shrubs obstructing any direct view.

"Yes, yes my friend. This is where we love to meet up for football. My son-in-law Fahad lives here. He's been like a son to me. I've watched him grow from a small boy back home, to a fine young man." Amir proudly explains.

Amir punches the code and enters through the opening gate, before ascending the stone paved driveway where the entire house came into full focus. Brian was stunned.

"Who the hell lives here, Lawrence of Arabia or King Joffrey Joffer?" Brian speculates as the gaudiness of the white and sand colored home was clearly out of sorts for anything in this neighborhood.

For a moment Brian really thought he was a V.I.P. being chauffeured to his own estate. The entry way to the house, which had a balcony above it, is surrounded by two massive tundra's that stretch from the ground to the rooftop.

"Man…what is that statue about? This cat has a statue fountain in his driveway? Crazy!" Brian marvels, at the twenty-foot tall, seven-legged statue with water spinning a ceramic globe atop of it.

Amir looks to park his Lexus right alongside an array of the lavish cars sitting in front of the massive home. The cars were parked around the statue like a photo opportunity for a magazine cover. The view was so picture perfect, Brian was tempted to pull out his phone and take a few pictures to share with Marty and Cortez. But, he refused to play himself and had to act like this wasn't new to him.

"Yo, this is crazy! There isn't a car in this driveway under seventy-five thousand! The new four door BMW 6 with the M package, Mercedes S-Class AMG coupe, the Porsche Panamera GTS, a Maserati…and a statue in the middle of the driveway as the center piece, immaculate crib in the backdrop? C'mon man!" In thought he channels his inner aficionado, reading the model badges of each car as he rides by each of them until they find their spot to park. Brian is so giddy inside, he starts getting goose bumps, and this was only the driveway. He can't wait to get out and get a closer look.

"Now, do you see what I mean by luxury, my friend? These guys keep me on my toes!" Amir proudly explains.

"I'm mad these dudes just buy hundred-thousand dollar cars for recreation and I had to get my Dodge tuned up before I could even drive it." Brian mentally notes as he could only shake his head in awe at the ridiculous display.

Brian gets a closer look at each car as Amir leads him to the back of the house where Fahad would normally host his football Sundays.

"Wow. These dudes really love their toys! That's that Arab money for real!" Brian implies, impressed by the collection of cars.

"An M6, huh?" Brian mentions as they walk past the black beauty with red leather interior.

"Yeah, but, he's a fool. He paid a hundred and thirty-eight thousand for it with all the bells and whistles. I could have gotten it for him for less than one-twenty." Amir boasts paying no regard to the overpriced car.

"A hundred and thirty-eight thousand…? Dayum!" Brian silently repeats.

"Hey Amir, if you don't mind me asking, what type of statue is that in front of the house?"

"That my friend is 'The Pearl' statue of the United Arab Emirates, or the UAE. It's a symbol of seven unified Muslim countries in the Middle East. Abu Dhabi, Dubai, Ajman, Ras al-Khaimah, Fujairah, Umm al-Quwain, and Sharjah, I believe." Amir explains.

From the moment they step out of the car, there is nothing mundane about this house. The windows were tall and leaf inspired at the top, with an Egyptian feel. As they pass-by each window, Brian takes notice through every open curtain in passing and it was nothing short of sheer opulence inside. He was as eager to see the inside as much as getting on a roller coaster for the first time. A cool, light seasonable breeze swept the meticulously manicured landscape. Particularly the vibrant tulips and orchids that lined the path leading to the back entrance of the house. As they enter the backyard, he notices the tranquil sound of water from a natural rock garden flowing. The backyard is arranged even better than the landscape in front of the house. The first thing that caught his eye is a round in ground fire pit flaming over blue crystals, a grill built into a rock foundation, an endless pool that appeared to run off into a rock creek with a palm tree emblem in the center of it, and a few fake palm trees potted around the beautiful landscape which gave it the appearance of a stunning oasis. Everyone there is gathered around a wood and stone slab backyard bar with several mounted flat screens for the game.

"AMIR! Finally, you come. A bit tardy for the party, but, it's okay. I forgive you!" A man shouts as they approached the bar.

"All I know is there better be a beer and a shawarma waiting for me…that's what I know!" Amir playfully demands as he walks over to salute each of the men with a kiss on both cheeks. The men laugh at Amir's comic entry, but, after the greetings the focus quickly shifts to Brian.

"Amir, who's your friend?" One man quickly asks.

"Who him? Oh, he's harmless…he's just some stray I picked up along the way looking for a decent meal is all." The men weren't sure if Amir was kidding, but they certainly weren't amused by the reply as the excitement quickly comes to a calm. Brian stands nervously frozen as if he'd just walked into a Klan convention.

"Relax you pansies, he's with me. This is my delivery guy. He's been bringing me slave work from the company for many years now!" Amir jokes to clean up the awkward moment. He walks Brian around to each

86

person and introduces him. "This is Mahdi, but we call him Manny. Manny this is…Mike, right?" Amir introduces with uncertainty.

"Brian…my name is Brian, pleased to meet you." Brian corrected as he shakes Manny's hand feeling a bit embarrassed that the person who invited him couldn't even get his name right.

"Oh yes, Brian! Duh…! I knew it was something simple. Please forgive me Brian. I've been reading your name tag for years and couldn't remember this one time." Amir pleads, feeling a bit embarrassed himself. "Anyway, this is Halim, but we call him, Shelton. This is Jimmy, we actually call him Jimmy." Again, everyone laughs at Amir's dry humor. "And last, but certainly not least, this handsome devil is the host proprietor of this lovely estate, Fahad."

"Brian, pleased to meet you, my friend. I'm Fahad, this is my place and now it's yours. If you need anything, please don't be afraid to help yourself, okay? We have beer and water in the cooler. There's wine in the chiller under the bar. Over here, we have lamb chops, mutton burgers, chicken and lamb skewers on the grill; grilled curry chicken, fresh gyro on the rotisserie; and chilled shrimp, fresh oysters, humus with pita, and some shrimp concoction the chef put together over basmati rice on the table. So please, help yourself to the whole spread." A very hospitable Fahad offers as he points to each item.

As Brian greets each of the men, being observant, he notices how the men were dressed and how short they were. Manny was the tallest and Brian estimated him to stand close to his height. None of the men sported a football jersey, which made Brian feel underdressed for a sporting occasion. Instead, Manny wore a zippered track jacket with jeans and open toe sandals, Shelton wore a yellow, polo style shirt with a palm tree logo, jeans and open toe sandals. Fahad, who was slightly shorter than all of the men, was wearing a green slim fitted button-down shirt with shoulder lapels and the sleeves rolled up, a pair of jeans and closed toe sandals. The top three buttons of his shirt were open exposing the stringy hairs on his chest like he watched too many episodes of Miami Vice. But, the person, who appeared most noticeable, was Jimmy. He was wearing full Arabic garb from Agal to throbe, with a pair of sandals. He stood out by his religious attire and was very unsociable. He sat distant from everyone else, being observant and not saying much watching a cricket match on a different television. All of the men appeared to be in their late twenties or early thirties. But, didn't appear

87

too hip to the American dress code. Fahad seemed to have some sense of fashion. But, the occasion didn't fit his choice of clothing and the sandals are never a good look for a man regardless.

"Thanks Fahad. Actually, I was wondering if I could use your bathroom, before diving in to this really nice spread you got here." Brian replies.

"Yes, absolutely! Walk in through this door, past the kitchen to your left, or down these stairs and straight back to your right. Just please, remove your shoes before you step into the house, thank you." Fahad instructs him.

"Okay thanks!" Brian acknowledges before reaching down to loosen his sneakers to remove them. Brian was in need of relieving himself, but not as eager as he was to see what the rest of the house had to offer.

"Mutton burgers? What the hell is a mutton burger? I know they ain't serving no dog up in here...what the f...?" Brian questions, alarmed by the mutton term. But, instead of offending someone, he decides to check out the term on his phone in the bathroom, just to be politically correct.

"These cats are killing me with those sandals, but damn! This dude is like Arab money for real! This house is crazy!" Brian observes as he walks into the house from the back patio.

Once Brian disappears from sight, the men immediately transition to Arabic dialogue as they speak among themselves. From the outside, Brian is so taken aback by how neat and clean the house is, he was hesitant to even walking across the glossy hardwood floor. Once he enters the home he immediately notices that everything is stainless in the gourmet style kitchen he had to pass through to get to the bathroom. A chef is staged in the kitchen, preparing a tray of spiny lobster and mantis prawns for the grill with a gourmet hat, chef whites and all.

"Good Morning chef!" Brian acknowledges as the chef notices Brian moving through his kitchen while separating a lobster's tail from its carapace. The chef returned his greeting with a simple head nod as he continues his food prep.

"I know this isn't how this dude gets down every Sunday?" Brian speculates pausing for a moment before moving on, through the spacious galley.

This is a kitchen after Brian's own heart. As he casually passes through, he couldn't help but to notice that there was a Viking refrigerator with a glass door that revealed all of its contents, including several different colored bottles of Ace of Spades champagne and Dom Perignon.

"Wow...black, pink, and gold bottles of Ace of Spade and Dom P on tap? Damn! I know how much that costs in the club." He observes with envy as he continues his surveillance of the lavish house.

The counter-tops and vast kitchen island is all made of marble with a knife rack embedded in the island and a pot rack hovering high above it. The stainless industrial style range has eight burners, with a griddle that was also boldly labeled Viking on the lower left corner of the appliance. Brian had never seen anything of this caliber and quality in a person's home before. All the lighting is recessed in the arch shaped vaulted ceiling in the kitchen and the backsplash tiles were engraved with hieroglyphic designs in each sandy colored stone tile. As he continues through the house, he discovers a massive great room to his right, decorated in everything white.

"Damn, that's like nose bleed status right there!" He observes not only the height of ceiling, but two life size white marble giraffes that stood about eighteen feet in the great room as well. Pure white Ferrari pattern leather loveseats and sofa surround the vast white marble column fireplace and a white tiger rug spread out in front of it. The flat screen above the oversized mantle had to be at least eighty inches.

Already in awe of all he'd seen thus far, Brian reaches the bathroom and stands in the doorway eye-balling it before entering. *"Whoa...marble floors and rock slab tile on the walls. A glass bowl basin sitting on a marble slab with a faucet and what the... you can't be serious! Why is there buttons on the damn toilet? C'mon man!"* Brian notions as the complex commode caught his attention.

Brian stands baffled for a moment trying to figure out why there would ever be a need for buttons on a toilet. At the same time, he's trying to figure out how to operate it properly.

"Lid up. Okay, I understand that." Brian utters talking himself through the process.

As he relieves himself he couldn't help but notice the Egyptian Pharaohs painted on the walls staring at him as if they were watching the throne or something? After zipping up, he's still confused about what to push to flush. So, he gambles and pushes the 'bidet on' button. Suddenly a motorized jet appears and began squirting water up from the toilet like a water fountain instead of flushing. Brian simply shakes his head in confusion.

"What is this? Awe man...I hope I didn't break this damn thing. Why in the hell would anyone need a toilet to do that?" He questions as he reaches for another button which actually flushes the toilet.

After getting over the toilet obstacle, he looks in the large vanity mirror surrounded by a halo of soft white light and smiles at his self with silliness. As he places his hands under the automatic soap dispenser and got a palm portion of foam, he realizes that the sink had no knobs. So, he waves his hands under the faucet expecting it to kick on like the soap dispenser, but, nothing happens.

"Man...what the hell?!" Brian exclaims in frustration as he continues waving his hands around trying to figure out how to simply wash them. Suddenly, he balls an aggravated fist full of soap and hammers the faucet head with force. The water instantly kicks on. Relieved, he could finally wash his hands, he repeats the hammer process to turn the water off.

After drying his hands, he pulls out his phone to reference the word 'mutton', to put an end to his curiosity. *"Mutton - A Middle-Eastern term for mature sheep."* He reads from the definition.

"Cool..." he says with relief. Now assured that it wasn't in the Arabic culture to eat the neighbors pet, he was ready to join the others.

However, before leaving, he reaches over to touch the faucet once more for the purpose of being silly. This time he touches it with a lot less aggression just to prove to himself that a simple touch was all he needed. On and off, and on and off again before he was satisfied.

"Man, I can't wait to tell the fellas. This dude has way too much money!" Brian shakes his head as he walks away from the sophisticated lavatory.

As Brian heads, back to join the others, he notices Jimmy lounging on the white furniture, blowing smoke from a tall hookah water pipe, enjoying his televised game of cricket indoors. Amir and the others were still outside engaged in conversation.

"خاصّتي من مشروع محبوبة هو .أمير ,غود برتّي شدادة مثل هو يبدو ,برين صديقتك؟"

"Your friend Brian, he seems like a pretty good guy, Amir. Is he a pet project of yours?" Manny speaks out with belittling intent as the others find humor in the comment.

"رفض, ليس هو مشروع محبوبة. هو ما أحد أنّ يكون سلّمت منزلي لسنون الآن
وقد سأل هو كثير أوقات حول ثقافة إيسلميك وهو يستمتعون كرة قدم. هكذا ما طريق جيّدة أن بيديه,
من أن يحضره خارجا إلى فهد وأعطيته ذوق من كيف نحن نتمّ كرة قدم في يوم الأحد."

"No, he's not a pet project. He's someone that's been delivering to my
house for years now and he's asked many times about Islamic culture and he
enjoys football. So what better way to show him, than to bring him out to
Fahad's and give him a taste of how we enjoy football on Sundays." Amir
explains.

"أه, تسليم فتى؟ إي بئر إي لن ب تخمين هناك كثير أن تلك بووت مع ه, أسد فروم كرة قدم
على الأرجح كنت في رقاقاته على المباشرة؟
ونحن أونصة وفورتي, يستطيع بالتّأكيد أيّ من عدته محراك لعبة نحن كنت سنتلقّى. سيرمي هو"

"Oh, he's a delivery boy? Well I guess there won't be much to talk
about with him, aside from football and a forty ounce, and we can certainly
count him out of any poker game we'll be having. He'll probably be
throwing in his chips on the first hand?" Manny ridicules, while amusing the
others.

"أنا قنيو هو استطاع ساعدت خارجا في المطبخ على المباشرة. أنا سأتلقّى واحدة من
منزر رميته المساعدة."

"I'm sure he could help out in the kitchen as we play. I'll have one of
the help throw him an apron." Shelton adds as the insults were becoming
contagious.

"نعذرة, جيّدا, منّي إعتذاراتي أنّ لا يلتقي ضيفتي موافقتك. ربّما بعد ذلك وقت أنا سوفت
حصلت رضاءك أن يحضر أحد ما إلى منزل فهد."

"Well, excuse me Mahdi, my apologies that my guest doesn't live up
to your standard. Perhaps next time I should get your consent to bring
someone to Fahad's home." Amir becomes angered by the comments.

"أمير جيّدة, بما أنّ أنت فلت ميّال إلى أن يحضر هذا فتى التسليم أسبوع, ربّما أنا سوفت
سألت زوجتي نظام يوغا مدرسة أن يأتي أسبوع تالية؟ هو يبدو أن يكون شدادة برتّي غود بنفسي."

"Well Amir, since you felt inclined to bring the delivery boy this
week, perhaps I should ask my wife's yoga instructor to come next week?
He seems to be a pretty good guy himself." Manny jokes, under minding
Amir's act of kindness.

"يستمع أه إلى أنت منّي, جميعا ياعال عظيمة. أنت تتصرّف أس يف لم يأت أنت من حيّ
من زوجتك. الفقراء كلب مخزون إن بنفسي. أنا لم أعرف أيّ أنا قال أنّ أنت تصبح صيانة عال إفن مور."

"Oh, listen to you Mahdi, all high and mighty! You act as if you
didn't come from slum dog stock yourself. If I didn't know any better, I'd

say that you're becoming even more high maintenance than your wife." Amir fires back at the asinine comment as the conversation suddenly turns personal.

تلقّيت ولا ,الفقراء الحيّ في أسفل إلى يكان أن أنا عمري متوسّط في أبدا أنّ غير ,ربّما" تلقّيت الحقيقيّة الذي كلّ نحن يعرف ,ذلك عن فضلا .كلاب الفقراء لحيّ حالة إحسان يكان وقت أيّ في أنا "؟أمير ,نحن لا يتم ,هنا يكون كلب الفقراء حيّ

"Perhaps, but never in my lifetime have I been down in the slums, nor have I ever been a charity case for slum dogs. Besides, we all know who the real slum dog is here, don't we, Amir?" Manny replies with even more grit.

لم .جيّدة حياة إلى طريقي أنا كسب ,أنت وبخلاف .كلب الفقراء حيّ سابقة ,يصحّ يكون أنّ" هنا شخص هذا كان قد .ي حول هذا ليس أنّ غير .وراثة خلال من ي إلى آخر باتّجاه كان هو يناول "؟نعم ,ذلك بعد هنا يحضره غلطة هو كان ربّما .تقضيه أنت وسابقا دقائق خمسة فقط

"That's right, former slum dog. And unlike you, I earned my way to a better life. It wasn't handed off to me through inheritance. But, this is not about me. This person has been here only five minutes and already you judge him. Perhaps it was a mistake bringing him here then, yes?" Amir stands to his feet fed-up and prepared to leave.

بما عاملته سوفت ونحن ناضيفت برين .يصحّ أمير ,يستمع فلّس !إرجاء أمير يجلس !ارفض" "؟يوافق ,منزلي في جيّدة وقت وأبديته لطف مع قهرته تركتنا .هذا مثل أنّ

"No! Amir please, sit! Fellas listen, Amir is right. Brian is our guest and we should treat him as such. Let us overwhelm him with kindness and show him a good time at my home, agreed?" Fahad candidly speaks, putting an end to the bitterness between them.

".كلّ يكون هنا ينتسب لا هو مثل أشعر فقط أنا .أوافق أنا !دقيقة"

"Fine! I agree. I just feel like he doesn't belong here is all." Manny replies trying to justify his point.

.هو يأتي هنا ,ضيفتنا من يتكلّم .ذلك بعد موافقة ؟حق ,ضيفة يكون هو لما أنّ ,لا هو يتمّ" ".حماقة هذا كلّ مع بكفاية الآن

"Perhaps he doesn't, but that's why he is a guest, right? Okay then. Speaking of our guest, here he comes. So, enough with all this foolishness!" Fahad concludes.

"Hey Buddy, we were starting to worry about you in there." Amir says to Brian, shifting his focus and demeanor.

"Yeah, I had to figure out how to use the toilet. I pushed a button and it squirted water at me." The men erupt in laughter at Brian's dilemma.

"My friend, you were confused about the bidet?" Shelton struggles to ask through his laughter. "He's never seen a bidet before?" Shelton says turning to the others as they all laugh in mockery.

Brian wasn't sure of what the men were laughing about. But, he figured he'd get a good laugh out of it too. So, he timidly joins in the laughter as well. Besides, he was sure that this wouldn't be the only thing that he'd be clueless about today, so he decided to just be a good sport and play along.

"Brian, a bidet is similar to a conventional toilet, only it squirts the water to clean your bottom. Please forgive our ignorance and laughter. It's mainly for female cleanliness and it's very common in our country. Most men don't even use it, unless they're sensitive that way." Amir explains, trying to justify their comic relief.

"It's cool Amir, I thought it was funny too." Brian replies with a snicker of his own.

"Brian please, have some. The chef just brought out some freshly cooked lobster, mantis prawns, chicken and mutton shawarmas." Fahad urges, pointing to the garnished tray of food. As a fan of all things seafood, Brian gladly accepts. After enjoying a plate full of prawns and lobster and sampling a dollop of caviar on pita bread because it was there, he goes in for seconds, this time he tries the mutton.

"So, Brian, Amir tells us that you're a fan of cars parked out front. What type of vehicle do you drive?" Fahad asks making small talk as Brian finishes up his tasty mutton shawarma.

Brian felt uneasy about answering the question, knowing that every person there was driving something way beyond his tax bracket. Nonetheless, it is what it is.

"Well, it ain't nothing like what y'all got going on in the driveway. But, I drive a Dodge Magnum." Brian modestly replies.

"Hmph…okay. Hemi, SRT?" Fahad indulges Brian, giving him the benefit of doubt.

"Yeah, I got the 2006 model Hemi." Brian proudly replies.

"Very nice car, not much luxury, but lots of muscle underneath the hood, right?" Fahad suggests giving Brian a fist bump.

"Well c'mon, please! Let's see what these cars are working with." Fahad asks as he leads Brian back to the front of the house.

"Yes, great idea Fahad, let's get a neutral opinion." Shelton agrees as he and the others follow Fahad's lead.

"So, what do you think?" Fahad asks as they stand among the ransom of luxury cars.

"I think you guys really love your toys is what I think. I mean the best is clearly being represented out here with a Porsche, a Benz, a BMW, and a Quatroporte Masarati?" Brian speculates, looking at the unfamiliar Maserati.

"That's not the Quatro my friend, that's the Ghibli S." Manny quickly corrects Brian's error.

"Okay, I've never even heard of that. But, a Maserati to round out the line-up is just crazy anyway. I mean, are you asking me to choose?" Brian implies to confirm?

"Well, my friends and I were having a debate about choosing the best automobile. We all like saloon style cars, but we also love the power of a coupe. So, we all decided to go with our own taste on luxury and power. So, which would you prefer?" Fahad explains as the others stand-by for a ruling.

"C'mon, Fahad. Brian knows as well as you do that…"

"قرّرت, رجاء هليم تركته ...شه ...شه".

"Shh…shh…Halim, please! Let him decide!" Fahad abruptly interjects, quieting Shelton before Brian figures out who owns which car.

"سيارة نوعية في يفتّش أن ماذا يعرف حتّى هو أنا يشكّ".

"I doubt he even knows what to look for in a quality car." Shelton murmurs in disgust.

As the men speak in Arabic among themselves, Brian is enjoying every moment of being the judge of what he considers a mini car show. Brian takes his time in choosing as he walks around and sits in each car, meticulously looking over every detail from features to comfort.

First, he takes a look at Shelton's Black M6 with vermillion red racing interior. Then he looks over Jimmy's diamond white Mercedes S-class coup with almond interior. Next, he sits in Fahad's silver Porsche Panamera turbo S with cream leather interior. Then he takes another look at Amir's Lexus, before finally assessing Manny's Rosso red Maserati Ghibli with sabbia white interior.

"Well Brian, what do you think?" Fahad asks, anxiously awaiting a verdict.

"To be honest with you, it's a hard sell because they're all great in their own right. But, I couldn't give you a completely honest assessment unless I drove each one of them." The men laugh at Brian's remark, but didn't take him seriously.

"Okay, fair enough. But, which one do you think looks the best?" Amir asks with confidence.

"Overall, although I love the interior of the Lexus, I'd have to go with the Panamera for style and sport." Brian sums up.

"Yes! That's right, brudah! The Porsche is definitely by far the better combination. Amir, I love this guy!" Fahad exclaims with exuberance while the others suck their teeth and speak fowl underneath their breath in Arabic.

"That's okay. I paid much less and will still turn more heads than your four-door imposter of a Porsche." Manny replies with envy.

"Oh, please Manny, you're so defensive. I'm surprised you paid anything at all. Your family owns the dealership." Amir ridicules, responding to Manny's tirade. Manny simply sneers at Amir for his mockery.

"Brian, since you have good taste in cars, I have a real treat to show you, my friend!" Fahad says as he marches them all to the garage on the side of the house.

"Oh yes, Brian. Wait until you see what daddy sent his son for his birthday last summer. This will blow you away!" Amir assures Brian as the garage door begins to open.

Brian had no idea what he was in for, but it might as well be a jet the way these guys seem to have no limit on what they can do with money. As Brian stands fervent, the garage door suddenly reveals something Brian truly didn't expect.

"Whoa...!" To Brian's surprise, what appeared to be a Rolls Ghost at first glance, actually turns out to be the brand-new Rolls coupe.

"Man, I didn't know they made the Ghost in a coupe!" Brian says, stunned by the beautiful display.

"That's because it's not a Ghost, it's actually the new Rolls Wraith. This one in particular was the second one ever made in production when my father ordered it. I believe the rapper Rick Ross bought the first one." Fahad clarifies in a pompous tone.

Even in the garage the car glistens like its show room ready. It's white, it's flawless, and it cost nearly more that all of the other cars put together. It even has the Arab license plate still on the front bumper, so people would know that this was no ordinary U.S. registered car.

"So, how were you so lucky to get it from your father?" Brian curiously asks.

"My father became bored with it, so he bought the Maybach Exelero, just so he can say he owned it before any of his conglomerates. I love this one to take my lady out on the town with on the weekends." Fahad gloats proudly.

"Wow, I'll bet that set him back almost a million huh?" Brian asks frivolously.

"Actually, it set him back about eight million to be exact. It looks like the bat mobile, and happens to be the most expensive car ever built." Fahad corrects him in a posh tone.

"Hmph...!" Was the only reaction Brian could gather at the time. *"Now, why in the hell would anyone spend eight million dollars on a car? I guess when you got it, you got it!"*

"To no avail, I still think my Bentley GT is more luxurious than any Mercedes built machine...you're fortunate I didn't bring it out today." Shelton differs.

"I can't tell. The last time I bought a Bentley, I took it back." Fahad arrogantly replies.

"Fair enough Fahad, fair enough!" Shelton concedes.

"Man, in North Philly we argue about who's got the nicest rims, and the loudest trunk. But, these cats are having differences over Benz's and Bentley's. Ridiculous!" Brian ponders, enjoying the posh argument.

"Well, it's almost game time fellas, shall we venture inside to get comfortable?" Fahad asks everyone.

"Oh yes! I'd like to get comfortable for this plucking of bird feathers." Manny replies who's an avid Giants fan.

"Very well then...Brian, I'll be happy to answer any questions you may have about the estate while we walk to the theater room." Brian responds with a simple head nod.

From the garage, they pass through a set of Palladian glass doors, where they end up in a museum-like hallway. Brian is taken aback by the brick face walls etched with what appears to be hieroglyphic engraved letters on each stone. Every few feet, there was an Egyptian artifact of some sort on display counter sunk in the wall, with a soft light illuminating it. The walkway lights are customized to illuminate the polished hardwood floors. But, what really grabbed Brian's attention are the four Egyptian statues with

96

heads of a dog that stood about seven feet tall on either side of the hallway. They looked as if they were guarding the hallway or the basement in general with their long staffs and aggressive features. The bathrooms in the basement is so unique it was almost as if Fahad took relics from an Egyptian pyramid and furnished them, from ancient trunks to hieroglyphic tapestries, this house had it all.

"Amir, what are these dog-faced statues called?" Brian murmurs as they walk by them.

"These statues are called the Anubis, Egyptian protectors of the dead. Fahad calls them his jackals, hence their jackal faces." Amir explains.

"Okay, well I hope he doesn't have anything mummified down here for them to protect." Brian expresses with silly concern. Amir could hardly control his laughter.

"No, my friend, I promise you the jackals are no more than cool statues to have around the house for people like you who don't understand them. I'm sure they have no symbolism here. Fahad probably got them for cheap somewhere on eBay or someone's flea market." Amir assures Brian.

As they continue to walk the halls, they come across more amazing Egyptian art and fossil like objects before approaching a set of metal framed, frosted glass doors which Fahad entered a code on an electronic key-pad above the door handle. The doors are decorated with an Egyptian like eye etched on the frosted glass at eye level. Curiously, Brian turns to Amir with more inquiry.

"Amir, what's with the Egyptian eyes on the door?" Brian quietly asks to avoid attracting attention from the others for his many questions.

"That, my friend is what we call the Eye of Horus or the Eye of Ra. It's an ancient symbol of royal power, protection and good health…very common to see in Arab culture." Amir explains.

"Yeah, I noticed the symbol in several other places around the house. I've seen it before on smoke shops, restaurants and tattoos. But, I never knew what it stood for." Brian replies with better understanding.

"Yes, yes my friend! Many people wear the eye symbolically for protection and good health…" Amir is suddenly interrupted.

"…But, everyone can't be royalty, right?" Fahad butts in, over hearing Amir's explanation as he holds the door for everyone entering his entertainment room. Brian grins, but wasn't particularly amused.

As Brian walks in, the room opens up to a jaw-dropping man cave on steroids. To his left stood another bar, much like one you would see at a lounge, and to his right were four rows of luxury seats, for the huge theater-like screen. The screen even has its own retractable curtains.

"Dayum! Are you serious?!" Brian thinks bursting with awe.

"Brian, please make yourself at home. Feel free to make yourself a drink. We have cigars and many refreshments." Fahad insists, placing his hand on Brian's shoulder and making him feel welcome.

Brian sits down admiring what feels like a sports bar in someone's basement, while the rest of the men made themselves at home as if they already knew the drill. As he sinks into the plush, burnt orange leather chair, he can't help but notice that there must have been eight flat screen TV's lining the walls around him. The fancy dart boards, brown felt pool table, framed autographed jersey's from every Philadelphia sports team and a United Arab Emirates football jersey on the wall, the fireplace, bar stools, and the ridiculous bar selection made for an incredible moment for the young man from North Philadelphia. Brian felt like he'd won a sweepstakes and the prize was a day in the life of someone rich and famous. It was already a gleeful experience and the game hasn't even started yet.

Every bottle behind the bar is neatly shelved for display on both sides of the showcase, highlighted by white L.E.D. lighting for the cognacs and blue L.E.D.'s for the vodkas. The shelves are stocked with the typical high-end cognacs, vodkas, whiskey, and rum. But, there's also a display case built in the base of the bar with pigeon holes illuminating a unique display of bottled liquor. Recognizing at least one of the bottles being Louis the Thirteenth from working at the restaurant, Brian knew that these bottles were a special selection.

"So, Brian, what will it be? Anything in particular I can make for you?" Fahad asks, after turning on all the entertainment in the room.

"Well, I'm usually a crown and 'cran' kind of guy. But, since I'm a guest at your house, I'll have whatever you recommend?" Brian modestly replies.

"Well, around here my friend, we drink within the traditions of home, meaning Egypt. So, I will make you something Egyptian, yes?" Fahad explains the house rules.

Fahad places a glass for each of his guests on the counter, adds a sphere-shaped ice cube to each glass, pours each glass with a bottle of something with Arabic writing on the label, adds a little water and garnishes the glass with a mint leaf.

"There you are my friends, enjoy!" Fahad announced as everyone reached for their glass and Brian walked over to the bar to join them.

"Hmph, okay...this should be interesting." Brian thought, suspicious of the milky white substance in his glass. He's also intrigued by the solid ball of ice sitting in his glass.

"Fe sahetek!" Fahad exclaims. "...and cheers to you Brian." Fahad expresses as they all raised their glasses in salute and took their first sip.

"Mmm...okay. This is pretty good, Fahad. What do you call this?" Brian asks enjoying his first sip.

"Snake urine." Fahad playfully replies.

Shelton nearly spat out all of his drink as the others burst out in laughter. Brian on the other hand stood bewildered, unsure of what to think.

"I'm joking my friend, I'm joking! Back home we call this Arak, the milk of lions. It's actually a Lebanese beverage that has grown popular throughout the Middle-Eastern community. I'm glad you enjoy it, my friend." Fahad explains.

"Brian, you should have seen the look on your face though, my friend." Shelton says, hardly able to speak from the continuous laughter. Brian smiled as he took another sip of the drink.

"Well, whatever it is, it tastes like really good licorice, and I don't even like licorice." Brian replies.

"Don't love it too much my friend. It's only your first time. This is potent stuff." Amir warns.

"So, what kind of ice is this in this glass? I've never had a ball of ice rolling around in my drink before." Brian asks as he twirls the glass rolling the ice ball in it.

"It's called Glace. It's a luxury ice that lasts longer than typical ice cubes." Fahad explains.

"Hmph...so, how do you make gourmet ice?" A naive Brian asks.

"You don't...you buy it!" Fahad condescendingly replies with arrogant humor.

The men begin to talk among themselves in Arabic dialect, while Brian takes his drink and focuses his attention on the bottles beneath the bar.

"You're familiar with these brands, yes?" Fahad asks yielding his attention to Brian.

"Well, the bottle to the right looks familiar. I've seen that bottle at the bar of the restaurant I work for. Isn't it like Louis the eighth or something?" Brian speculates.

"Thirteenth…Louis Thirteenth." Fahad corrects him.

"Yeah, exactly…that's like a ten thousand-dollar bottle, right?" Brian purposely exaggerates.

"Well, not quite ten. But, it's expensive indeed!" Fahad replies with certainty.

"That one above is a fifty-five-year-old Macallan scotch whisky. I think I paid about twelve-five for it, and the one next to it is a bottle of Dalmore Trinitas 64. It was a gift from a friend two years ago. That bottle goes for about one-forty." Fahad explains before taking another sip of his Arak with his pinky extended. Brian mentally notates the snooty gesture.

"Oh, that's a nice bottle for a hundred and forty bucks!" Brian assumes. Fahad shakes his head and smiles at Brian's clueless assumption.

"Hahaha, try a hundred and forty thousand, my friend! See, we count big faces around here, young money grip!" Fahad candidly replies with a bit of swag.

Feeling slighted by the reply, Brian's eyebrows suddenly buckle and his facial expression tells a less than pleasant story. He quickly turns away to conceal his disapproval.

"What the…? Okay, one minute you're sippin' on your drink with your pinky out, and now you're dropping lines like 'big faces and young money', like you're really 'bout that life? 'I'ma' need you to stay in your lane for real, Iron Sheik!" Brian thinks intensely, as he restrains himself from speaking his criticism aloud. He struggles to hide his disapproval behind a shallow smirk as he quickly remembers that he's a guest. So, he hides behind a tactful façade to maintain his cool.

"I noticed you have a collection of Ace of Spades champagne in the kitchen too…very nice! That's actually the first time I've seen that many different bottles of that brand." Brian compliments to change his annoyed mood.

"You mean they don't do it like that in the club?" Fahad asks with a chuckle.

"None that I've seen…" Brian replies with a slightly confused expression. Unsure if Fahad was taking another shot at him, Brian is about one insult away from taking a shot of his own.

"Yes, I like the Ace of Spades. I try to keep the shelves stocked for good company. If I can only get my fiancée to stop making mimosas of them…but, it doesn't compare to my prized vodka collection you see in my showcase." Fahad points out, ensuring that Brian takes notice.

"You mean your daddy's old collection, Fahad? As your guest, you should at least tell the man the truth." Manny loudly interjects with playful intent.

"Manny please…away with your jealousy!" Fahad replies disregarding the comment.

"Anyway, yes, my father did send me many of the bottles. He wanted me to be more involved in the tastes of fine spirits as he is. So, starting from the left you have the gem studded Iordinov vodka, that's about forty-five hundred U.S. In the middle, you have another beautiful gem studded Oval vodka bottle, that's a seven-thousand-dollar bottle. And next to that you have the handsome Belvedere Belver Bear. That one is designed by Jean-Roch and is priced just a bit over seven thousand. I like that one because the women always want to touch my teddy bear." Fahad proclaims with humor.

"Wow…I can only imagine what your father did to trump that." Brian replies to stroke the arrogant Arab's ego.

"My friend, you have no idea. The Sheik, as we call him, does not like to be out done. He now owns a bottle of Russo-Baltique vodka and a bottle of Henri Fourth Heritage Cognac which is the jewel of his cognac selection. Russo is the second highest priced vodka at over one million, and the Cognac is worth about two million. Very regal stuff indeed, my friend." Amir bolsters chiming in on the conversation.

"Yes, but even the Sheik has his limits. He still doesn't understand why one of his colleagues went out of his way to buy a nearly four-million-dollar bottle of Billionaire Vodka to prove a point." Manny adds.

"It's ego, Manny…it's all ego! A battle among friends on an unthinkable financial level." Fahad answers.

"Yes, but Fahad, what kind of man buys a bottle made with man-made fur and diamonds?" Shelton adds to the conversation.

"Haha, that one is easy…a billionaire!" Fahad replies as they all indulge in a haughty laugh.

As the men enjoy their lazy afternoon of high class refreshments, beverage of choice, and the pre-game show on any screen in the room, they're abruptly interrupted by the sound of clicking heels and heavy movement, and chatter from the floor above them.

"Uh oh, it sounds like the Shahs of Philadelphia have arrived early. Everyone quick, hide your black cards and check books, especially you Fahad." Shelton announces as the women stampede above them.

"Halim, I'm the least person you should be telling to be careful. Ashima won't even accept my money. She's too resilient. You on the other hand, your wife has never worked for a pay check in her life. All she does is wash your dirty undergarments and lay down with you for Gucci hand bags, yes?" Fahad counters with a stiff jab of his own.

"Whoa Fahad, I thought you two were sparring. You took the gloves off on that one." Manny instigated.

"No, no, Manny it's okay. Fahad is feeling a bit backed up these days. Especially, since Ashima would rather sleep with her Gucci handbags, than to lay down with the likes of him." Shelton strikes back with a personal blow.

"Ashima? Did I hear that correctly? That can't be Amir's daughter their talking about? It can't be the same person." Brian desperately tries to deny.

"Uh, oh...this could get dangerous, I need to put an end to this." Amir whispers to Brian.

"كلّ نحن. وسخة مغسلك خارجا هوّيت يكون أن الوقت ليس ذاه !هراء هذا مع كافي
إحسنا ,هنا صديقات"

"Enough with this nonsense! This is not the time to be airing out your dirty laundry. We are all friends here, okay!" Amir insists, speaking adamantly in Arabic.

Amir gives Shelton a stern stare, as if he was embarrassed for Fahad. Brian merely stands-by as a spectator as Amir defuses the hostility.

"صديقتي, إعتذاراتي ,فهد. أمير, يصحّ أنت"

"You're right, Amir. Fahad, my apologies, my friend!" Shelton sincerely expresses as he lifts his glass in a salute to Fahad.

"حسنة شلتون"

"Okay, Halim." Fahad pardons as he toasts Shelton's glass as a gesture of acceptance.

As Shelton turns away to have a seat, Fahad delivers a scornful stare at him while taking another sip of his drink. Fahad was embarrassed by the comment, which served as a bane reminder of his circumstance with

Ashima. He then turns a cold stare to Amir, as if he was responsible for his daughter's actions. Amir was completely caught off guard by the shocking disclosure and took note of his daughter's lack of affection.

As the atmosphere in the room dimmed to an awkward silence, two servers from the kitchen walk in with four hose hookah pipes in each hand.

"Ah yes! The shisha has arrived…perfect timing! Now we can relax. Just in time for kick-off too." An excited Amir announces as he anxiously rubs his hands together.

"Wow, these dudes broke out the hookah pipes for the game? And not just any hookah pipes. These look like the restaurant style 'jawns'." Brian observes as the hookah presentation adds to his already crazy experience with Amir.

"أنت ل نعناع قاوون مفضّلة وك ,دراق ,ليمون ,حامضة تفّاح أنا أعدّ قد اليوم ,سيد
وضيفاتك."

"Sir, today I've prepared a sour apple, lemon, peach, and your favorite melon mint for you and your guests." One Middle-Eastern man explains to Fahad as he sits the pipes on the floor where the men sit on leather sectional and leather chairs.

"شريفّ ,أنت شكرت .علي ,أنت شكرت."

"Thank you, Ali. Thank you, Sharif." Fahad replies in his native dialect to his Arab chef and server.

The hookah flavors are distinguished by the color of their bowls. Therefore, everyone knows where to sit for their preferred tastes. Brian simply sits at random with the intent to try them all.

"Brian, are you familiar with shisha smoke at all?" Amir asks after taking a long pull.

"هناك العداد على ميلدس و الأسود قلته !هو ليس كورس أف ,أمير."

"Amir, of course he isn't familiar! Tell him the Black and Milds are on the counter over there." Manny butts in.

"إكافي !حسنا ,هو ,مهدي يبرد!"

"Mahdi, cool it, alright! Enough!" Amir aggressively replies, waving his hand at Manny.

Brian wasn't sure what the edgy exchange was about, but he starts to feel instinctively uncomfortable because Manny has been avoiding eye-contact with him since he arrived.

"Yeah, I've been to a few places that serve it. But, we don't call it shisha, though. We call it hookah." Brian explains.

"Yes, hookah is the instrument you smoke from. Shisha is the tobacco you actually smoke." Amir helps Brian to understand.

"Roger that! Thanks for clearing that up." Brian replies.

The men all settled down and begin taking pulls on the various flavors of hookah as the football game kicks off. Resting comfortably from the relaxing calm the hookah gave them, the men blow thick clouds of aromatic smoke while snacking on the food prepared for them. This hookah is much smoother than any Brian had before, as he easily fills his lungs with long pulls. He sinks into the comfort of his chair and zones out, looking directly to the ceiling, and noticing the Egyptian cotton drapes that hung from it throughout the lounge area. To him, it felt like it could be Egypt.

"How is it, my friend?" Fahad asks Brian.

"I'm sorry...?" Brian replies, realizing Fahad was addressing him.

"The shisha...how is it?" Fahad reiterates. Brian responds with a head nod and a thumbs-up, unable to respond because of his smoke-filled lungs.

"It's good! Really good flavor!" Brian is finally able to verbalize.

"That's melon mint, my personal favorite." Fahad informs Brian.

"You have a good build and posture. Did you play football in school at all?" Fahad implies making small talk.

"Yeah, I played strong safety in high school." Brian proudly replies.

"Like Brian Dawkins, right?" Fahad replies with excitement.

"Haha, not as good, but, yeah he's my favorite. I even wore his jersey number in high school, number 20." Brian adds.

"I'm sure a man like you can appreciate that autographed Eagles jersey up there, huh?" Fahad asks, pointing to the autographed Brian Dawkins jersey framed on the wall.

"Yeah, I peeped that when we came in. How did you get that signed?" Brian inquires.

"It was just perfect timing. I was having lunch with his attorney and Dawkins happened to stop by when I had the jersey in my car." Fahad casually explains as if it was nothing.

"That's what's up!" Brian replies before taking another hit of the hookah.

As the conversation ends, Brian shifts his focus to the theater side of the room, where he'd only seen a set-up like it on either MTV Cribs or in a magazine. The theater walls were painted an earth color faux and had concrete columns that looked as ancient as the Roman Empire. The theater has fancy wall sconces that illuminates framed movie posters on both sides, with small recessed lighting that gave the theatre area just enough light. Even the aisles are lit-up like a real theater. The ceiling was twinkling with tiny lights that looked like stars and a glowing ring of light that seemed to changed color every minute. There was gold crown molding on the ceiling with gold highlights throughout the room. In back of the last row, there was a high standing table with three bar stools for more spectators and a popcorn cart in the corner.

"Dayum! A man can dream, can't he?" He imagines before turning his attention back to the politics of the lounging area.

"So, Manny what is this I hear, that you're working on your second wife...and how does Crystal feel about that?" Amir insinuates, opening a new topic.

"Yes, that's right. I spoke with Crystal about it, and she didn't like it but, what can she say? She's my wife, and she will adhere to the rules of Sharia Law. It's that simple!" Manny arrogantly replies.

"Yes, she should abide by the rules of Sharia Law, Manny. But, remember, she's a groomed 'American' Muslim. She may know Sharia Law, but she may not be so willing to comply with the traditions of back home." Shelton rationalizes.

"Oh please...she'll be fine. I've already explained to her that my concubine interest lives in Cairo and I have no interest in moving to Cairo." Manny tries to justify.

"In that case, I'm confused. Why do you want to marry this woman again?" Amir questions.

"Convenience and insurance, Amir! You know my work forces me to frequent Cairo several times a month. She's there to pleasure me when I need the affection away from home. And unlike Crystal, she was raised and abides by the old traditions of Sharia Law. So, if Crystal ever wants to divorce, I can make this one my full-time bride." Manny answers, explaining his strategy.

"So, wait, it's legal to have more than one wife where you're from?" Brian interjects with a look of confusion as he centers his attention on the conversation.

"My friend, in most Islamic countries, including Egypt, every man of Islam is allowed to have up to four wives as long as he can provide for them.

105

Here in the states, you call it bigamy or polygamy and it's a crime. But, back east not only is it legal, it's righteous." Manny proclaims.

"Hmph, maybe I need to convert, 'cause I don't see nothing wrong with that." Brian playfully mutters in a relaxed tone as he envisions ways to amplify his doggish nature.

"Someone quick, grab the Koran so we can convert this man." Manny cheerfully plays along as the others laugh.

"Excuse me gentleman, I will be right back." Amir suddenly pops to his feet.

"Amir, where are you headed?" Fahad questions, seeing Amir move about.

"I have to drain the weasel, if you know what I mean? You should come help. I could use a strong hand for lifting." Amir jokes as the men continue to laugh at the comic relief.

After Amir disappears, Shelton looks to Fahad to readdress the earlier quarrel.

"Fahad, I'm truly sorry if I offended you, my friend. I was only trading insults with you, but perhaps we both took it too far." An apologetic Shelton speaks out.

"It's okay my friend. I'm not upset over it. Besides, you don't really think that I'm affected by Ashima's sexual short comings, do you?" Fahad asks bringing his voice down to nearly a whisper. Manny and Fahad look to each other with smirks of subliminal validation.

"No, I would be foolish to believe that." Shelton replies, knowing how promiscuously capable Fahad was.

"Trust me, it was getting so out of hand that I had to stop myself. I used to pull out any vehicle and cruise to anywhere in the city. I found myself bringing one home every night. These women are dehydrated like camels. They're always thirsty for action!" Fahad secretly reveals as Manny shakes his head in agreement.

"Manny, you knew of Fahad getting the royal treatment, too? I guess I'm the last to know." Shelton replies as this is news to him.

"Of course, Manny knew, and Amir has no reason to think otherwise of myself or his daughter. So, this will be the last I hear of this, yes?" Fahad cautiously urges Shelton.

Brian carefully listens to the discussion in disbelief, but played along to secure information about Fahad for his own indulgent interest of Ashima.

"Fahad, I have to ask, since we're all men here...do you not love Ashima?" Shelton asks with caution.

"Love for Ashima? Please...she's a lovely friend at best. Ashima is a trophy. She's been most sought after by so many affluent associates of mine. Most of them are very jealous because I claimed her first. The arrangement between Ashima and I is more important to Amir and my father than it is to us. For Amir, a wedding is to secure his position in the Gabr family. As for the Sheik, he can rightfully claim Ashima as the daughter he never had once we marry." Fahad explains, pausing to take a sip from his glass before he continues. Brian and the others simply remained silent as Fahad carries on.

"She's not much of a lay, anyway. It's like making love to a mannequin...and she won't give me head. But, I get head and anything else I want from Nisa. She's the one who pleasures me most." Fahad praises. Manny is familiar with Fahad's mistress, but Shelton has no idea.

"Fahad, you dirty dog! I didn't know you were sleeping Aman's daughter?" A keyed-up Shelton whispers in awe.

"It's just sex, but its good sex! I've even considered marrying Nisa after I marry Ashima. Since Nisa is embedded in traditional Sharia Law I have no worries about her. But, I don't think Ashima will go for it without being totally committed to Islam." Fahad explains.

Brian inhales another pull of hookah smoke as he continues taking mental notes of how this group of Arab men really moved.

"Good for you, brudah. Yes, I love sluts!" Shelton praises as the fellas are all smiles.

"Checkmate, my camel jockey friend! Checkmate!" Brian smirks as he gives Fahad a shrewd prolonged stare.

"صديق الكافر هذا أقصد أنا الضيوف؟ أمام هذا مثل نتحدث من أنه تعتقد هل فهد"
" .أمير

"Fahad do you think it's wise to talk like this in front of our guest? I mean, this infidel is a friend of Amir's." Manny cautions.

"هنا إلى أحضرت الأليفة للحيوانات ميرمشاريـع من آخر مجرد وهو .ضار وغير ه؟ل الذي"
" .بالألغام المتعلقة للأعمال قلق لا .جيدة بحياة التباهي يمكن أمير حتى

"Who him? He's harmless. He's just another one of Amir's pet projects brought here so Amir can gloat about the good life. He's no concern of mine." Fahad arrogantly replies, taking another sip from his glass. Manny simply shrugs it off and takes a sip from his glass as well.

"My God, you guys all look stoned. The room is so dead. I thought there was a football game on?" Amir blurts out as he re-enters the room.

Amir's observation was with good reason. Between the hookah, food and conversation, there wasn't much of any football being celebrated in the room. Nonetheless, not far behind him was the rumble of heels and female chatter echoing closer.

"Are you kidding me? I would never give them the satisfaction!" One of the women declares with a heavy foreign accent as they approach the door.

The chatter of the conversation ends as three radiantly attractive women began filing into the room. There was a certain air about the way they dressed and the way they moved, as if they were above anything petty. Wearing nothing less than four inch, red bottom heels, large designer eyewear, and bulky designer purses draped on their arms, with earrings and bangle bracelets to complete their attire. The women were very confident as they sip their mimosas from champagne flutes. Their presence is commanding as all of the men in the room stand to their feet to greet them in near simultaneous fashion. Brian follows suit, like a respectable guest adhering to the house rules.

"Wow...Shahs of Philly is right. Dayum! Okay, I see how y'all Arabs get down!" Brian says, surveying their chic appearance.

"كلّ مرحبا..."

"Hello all..." The first woman greets as they usher in boisterously.

"أهلن!"

"Ahlan!" The men all reply.

As the women walk in, one of them is wearing a head garment while the others are stunningly beautiful from head to toe. The women removed their shades to greet each of the men in the room with a kiss on each cheek. Brian doesn't recognize her at first, but with her glasses removed, unveils the beautiful vision he'd been waiting for. Suddenly, Brian is rushed with a sense of nervousness, as his heart rate spikes at the sight of Ashima. His eyes light up as bright as high beams for a woman that hardly even noticed him when coming in the room. Yet it didn't stop him from being ambitious. In fact, none of the women greeted Brian with a kiss on the cheek like they did with the others. Instead, they gave him a simple 'hello' and a casual wave, barely making eye contact. Brian was none the wiser. But, he did notice that Ashima didn't greet Fahad when greeting the other men. She

108

deliberately walks past him to greet her father instead. Fahad stands stupid while tilting his glass to his mouth to hide the shame. The shunned gesture made Brian attentive to Ashima's interaction with Fahad.

"Amir, who are the ladies that walked in? I don't want to offend anybody." Brian whispers, confused by the evasive introductions.

"Oh, my apologies for not introducing you. However, as you can see the women are very engaged in conversation, so I'll just explain who they are from here. The one that looks like she can pass for a Kardashian on the left is Naima, she's from Morocco. The loud one with the sunshades on her head is Crystal, she's from right here in Philadelphia. And, you've already met my lovely daughter Ashima. She's Fahad's fiancée." Amir explains.

"Fiancé? This whack, Arab Punjabi is her fiancé? Man, money can attract anything. Must be nice!" Brian jealously protests.

"Ladies, you're back quite early. How was shopping today? Hopefully all bank accounts are still intact?" Manny suggests as the women corral at the bar to enjoy their mimosas. The women are amused and snicker at Manny's petty concern.

"Oh, Manny please…you know we couldn't blow through your accounts in one afternoon. That would take at least two days." Crystal quickly counters, which set the women off with amusement yet again.

Brian looks over at the women and notices they were wearing some type of hand tattooing on both hands. He finds the hand art creative. But, what really draws his attention is how he caught the women glancing over at him, like the stranger in the room he is. In spite of this, Brian held his focus on the game despite the distractions. Despite, being in a house full of Muslim men, the women's appearance wasn't quite what he'd had in mind for the setting. He was perhaps expecting them to be wearing some type of Islamic garb from head to toe. But, these particular women were very unassuming. The women whisper and giggle among themselves like chatty little school children at play. The behavior peaks Brian's interest and now he's curious to know what all the parody is about.

"Fahad, would you mind if I help myself to some more of that snake urine?" Brian jokes as the men enjoy Brian's sense of humor.

"Not at all, my friend…please, help yourself to whatever you like." Fahad encourages, which is exactly what Brian plans to do.

As Brian boldly walks towards the bar, the women never look up but, knew he was coming towards them.

In a sexy baritone voice, Brian excuses himself. "Excuse my reach, may I just grab this bottle, please?" Brian asks Ashima who sat directly in front of the bottle of Arak.

"Oh, I'm sorry! Am I in your way?" She replies as she scoots to here right.

"You're Amir's daughter, right?" Brian asks reaching for the bottle. As he leans in, he catches a strong captivating whiff of Ashima's fragrance.

"Mmm...I've never smelled that on a woman before. Good gracious!" Brian thinks as he tapes into his inner bliss.

"Yes..." She replies in a less than enthusiastic tone. Taken aback by her short response, Brian quickly follows up with another question to avoid an awkward moment.

"I remember you from downtown and I met you at your house." Brian attempts again for a better response.

"Yes, yes I remember now. Apex, right?" Ashima replies with a patronizing expression. In a defensive posture, the other women avoid eye-contact and remain expressionless like vultures perched on a wire, ready to pick Brian off with any sudden movement.

"Actually, it's Brian. But, yes, I do work for Apex." Brian replies, feeling a bit played by the *Apex* reference, but he just brushes it off.

"Okay...this was probably a bad idea." Brian second guesses as he decides to quit while he was ahead.

"Well, enjoy your drinks ladies." Brian says, dismissing himself from their presence.

"And you the same." Ashima's lone reply rang out.

As Brian returns to his seat, he notices Fahad standing in a corner of the room, quietly observing his interaction with the women. He lifts his glass and gives Brian a head nod, as they establish eye contact. Then he takes a sip from his glass and looks towards the women with a hard stare, before casually making his way towards them.

"Ashima, I hope you didn't help yourself to another bottle of Ace of Spade to make mimosas again?" Fahad questions with suspicion.

"As a matter of fact, I did. The bottle was half empty, Fahad. Furthermore, what's a bottle to you? Just replace it!" Ashima justifies with no regard to Fahad's concern.

"النقطة ليس أنّ, أشيما! أنا اشتريت دوم برينون و موت ل ميميسس ك. نحن يتلقّى نتناقش هذا, أتمّ نحن لا؟"

"That's not the point, Ashima! I bought the Moet for your mimosas. We've already discussed this, have we not?" Fahad replies with agitation in his voice.

"وأنت أيضا يتكلّم إلى ي مع هذا إعتداء, مع ذلك قد بدات أن يتلقّى نحن ويتناقش نسيت, أنّ هوه؟"

"And we've also discussed you speaking to me with such aggression, yet you've seemed to have forgotten that, too!" An animated Ashima lashes back.

"أشيما, أنت هكذا جازمة وعنيدة. أنت سوفت حاولت يكون ثراك سوبميسّيف ومحترمة."

"Ashima, you're so assertive and unruly. You should try being more submissive and respectful." Fahad calmly replies, trying to defuse the angry tone of the conversation.

"أنا فهد آسفة, أراد أنت يحبّ ل ي أن يشتري أنت نو ون, وينبطح في أقدامك في يقدّم هو إلى أنت؟"

"I'm sorry Fahad, would you like for me to gift wrap you a new one, and grovel at your feet in presenting it to you?" The condescending remark amuses the other women, but infuriates Fahad.

"أشيما! قانون شريا! قانون شريا!"

"ASHIMA! SHARIA LAW! SHARIA LAW!" A fiery Fahad demands of her.

"قانون شريا؟ قانون شريا؟ أنا قبطيّة أنت أحمق, أنا لست من!"

"SHARIA LAW?! SHARIA LAW?! I'M COPTIC YOU IDIOT, I'M NOT OF ISLAM!" She abruptly corrects him, elevating her voice to match his.

"أمير!"

"AMIR!" Fahad pleads with fire in his eyes, as he struggles to tame Ashima.

"فهد, أشيما إرجاء! أخذت شؤونك في مكان آخر!"

"FAHAD, ASHIMA PLEASE! TAKE YOUR AFFAIRS ELSEWHERE!" Amir interrupts as the room chatter becomes silent. The only sound remaining was the commentary and the crowd noise of the football game.

Brian wasn't sure if his interaction stirred up the melee. But, he began to feel like the elephant in the room.

Ashima momentarily stands frozen before rolling her eyes and storming off with embarrassment. On her way out of the room, she threw the remaining contents of her glass into the sink behind the bar and slammed the glass on the counter so hard, she breaks the base of the glass. Fahad, follows in her turbulent wake to further address the matter. As everyone else in the room begins to speak amongst themselves in Arabic dialect, Amir came over to Brian to clear the air.

"My apologies, my friend! I'm sorry you had to witness that. Their relationship has not been well lately. Two egos colliding is never good." Amir regretfully explains.

"No worries Amir. Where I come from, I've seen far worse, trust me!" Brian assures Amir. Although Brian was a bit unnerved by the ferocious clash, once the two left the room everyone else carried on as if it was a normal occurrence.

"Naima, what happened to Jasmine? I thought she was with you all?" Shelton inquires from across the room.

"She took off with Jimmy once we got here. I guess there was a problem with that new Maserati truck she's shipping from your friend's dealership in Palmyra." Naima explains.

"The Levante? What problem?" A baffled Shelton frantically asks.

"I don't know Shelton, something about paperwork, I guess?" Naima speculates with a simple shoulder shrug.

"Okay. I will call him." Shelton replies.

"Wow, Maserati has a truck now? Dayum! Everything these people talk about involves money. Amir was right. This day has already been more than I bargained for." Brian makes notion to himself. Brian only takes a moment to mull over that notion before reverting back to the calamity he'd just witnessed between Fahad and Ashima.

He keeps an ear open, to see if he could hear any further commotion from outside the room, while faking like he is fully engaged into the 21-3 beat down Philly was handing New York. When Ashima returns, she enters the room with her arms folded in a defensive posture. The look of disgust on her face could've melted an ice sculpture. Mama Ruth always said that Brian was a good judge of character, and in this instance, there was no denying the obvious. Despite all of the glamour and extravagance that surrounds her, this woman was not in a good place in her life.

112

As the women converse amongst themselves, Brian found an opportunity to interrupt and possibly soften the lady's callous stance towards him.

"Excuse me ladies, I don't mean to be intrusive, but I couldn't help but overhear that you hang at the Red Owl Tavern, downtown?" Brian interjects with his best display of grammar.

"Yeah...?" Ashima replies with an empty, shallow reply. Undaunted by her short, passive response, Brian continues.

"Well...I go there quite a bit myself, and I'm surprised I've never seen you there before." Brian implies, speaking directly to Ashima. Brian has never even been to the Red Owl tavern, but for the sake of getting closer to Ashima, he was willing to stretch the truth. To no avail, Ashima looks him off and gives him no sense of interest.

"Oh, I see...when I met you downtown, it was all smiles and business. But, now that you're around all of your Arab friends, letting your hair down and sipping on mimosas, it's beneath you to even be friendly? Aight, you're smelling yourself right now...roger that!" Brian presumes, feeling a certain type of way about Ashima's actions. Brian was beginning to sense that his pursuit of her is going to be more trouble than she's worth. But, he wasn't convinced that she was genuinely that callous.

"Really? Wow, they have great food there!" An enthused Crystal chimes in.

"Yeah...they're food is really good!" Naima confirms.

"Yeah, happy hour is pretty good. Have y'all ever had the fried fish they serve? That's one of my favorites." Brian implies, hoping there was some type of fish on the menu. He also notices how the women limit their eye contact as they speak to him. He found it distracting, but played along.

"Yes, I love their fried catfish, garlic mashed potatoes, and sautéed spinach!" Crystal replies with excitement.

"With the dill sauce on the fish?" Brian randomly endorses.

"Yes, I love that dish!" Crystal confirms.

"It is really good. I actually had to steal that idea and make it for myself." Brian replies finally able to get comfortable with the women.

"Wow, you must be a good cook. Are you a chef?" Naima asks.

"Yeah, I work at the restaurant in the Comcast building downtown." Brian proudly replies. Still visibly upset from the argument with Fahad, Ashima sat silent and listens as the conversation resumes.

"Wow, that sounds exciting. Maybe you can make a dish for us someday?" Naima proposes.

"Well, I only work every other weekend, but I definitely think I can manage that." Brian accepts her offer with a charming smirk, as he grows excited about the potential rendezvous.

"Well, we look forward to seeing you there, someday." Crystal concludes.

"Well, maybe I'll see y'all this weekend at the Red Owl?" Brian alludes to securing a sooner encounter.

"Yeah, actually we were discussing going there when you walked over. So, maybe you will." Crystal concludes.

"Aight then cool. It was nice speaking with y'all. But, 'I'ma' get back to this game and enjoy this drink." Brian replies, feeling good about his chances of interacting with them again in a different setting.

Meanwhile, Brian joins the other men who appear to be focused on the game. But, as he sits to enjoy the game and smoke more hookah, he couldn't help but notice that every time he'd glance at the bar, he would catch Ashima looking him off as if she found him interesting, or simply taking mental notes. He also notices that Fahad and Manny were having an intent side conversation. Brian could sense the awkward energy in the room from Manny who gives Brian an occasional side eye.

"فهد, أنت أمكن أن أردت قريبا يحافظ على راقبت ,ضيفتك الكافرة. أنا أرى الطريق هو
ينظر في أشيما, ويلاحظ أنا هو يحافظ ينظر طريقه أس يف هو يجده يهمّ أيضا."

"Fahad, you might want to keep close watch on your guest, the infidel. I see the way he looks at Ashima, and I notice she keeps looking his way as if she finds him interesting as well." Manny warns as he sips from his glass.

"مني رجاء, لما تكون أنت لذلك يتعلّق من ه نظرت في ه لإلهة خاطر. كيف استطاع هو من
كلّ الناس, من المحتمل طرحت تهديد. أنا حقّا أفكّر يهيعط أنت بعيدا توو موش إنتباه."

"Manny please, why are you so concerned of him. Look at him for God sake. How could he of all people, possibly pose a threat. I really think you give him far too much attention." Fahad replies downplaying Manny's overzealous concern.

"فهد, ربّما يكون أنت بعيدة أيضا يتفخّر. نظرة! نظرت في ه نظرة! ه في نظرة هو الطريق يكون
غوك في ه!"

"Fahad, perhaps you are being far too arrogant. Look! Look at him! Look at the way he's gawking at her!" Manny observes, eager to gain Fahad's attention.

114

As Brian turns his attention away from the bar, stealing another glance at Ashima, he's confronted this time by Fahad and Manny's focus on him.

"‏كافر هذا أثق لا أنا. فهد أنت أنا قال!‏"

"I told you Fahad. I do not trust this infidel!" Manny vehemently attests.

"Hmph…" Fahad glares as he lifts his glass to Brian with a cold, menacing stare.

Brian could tell he was being given a pass because of his nonreligious affiliation, and that his interaction with the women wasn't exactly warranted. However, he receives the cold stare with a crafty smirk of his own, lifting his glass as if to accept his challenge. Although, Brian didn't measure up to the means of the opulence surrounding him, doesn't mean that he couldn't hate from a distance, which was exactly what he'd planned to do.

"I got you…!"

CHAPTER SEVEN

In a boardroom on the 52nd floor of the Mellon Bank Building in downtown Philadelphia, Ashima is conducting a meeting with staff members regarding fourth quarter earnings currently in the red. Although retired as the Chief Financial Advisor, yet still a chair on the Board of Directors and lobbyist, Amir assigned his daughter (senior financial consultant) the disheartening task of informing the rest of the staff of the budget cuts and looming lay-offs.

"Excuse me, Ms. Batool. But, that call is still holding for you on line one!" Ashima's assistant Samantha interrupts.

"Sam please…no calls for thirty minutes, okay!" Ashima replies in calm yet agitated tone.

"I'm sorry Ms. Batool, but it's your father and he's been holding since your meeting started twenty minutes ago." She reminds her.

Ashima looks at the boardroom clock and sighs heavily as time appeared to be moving faster than she can keep up. "Why yes it has. Okay then, tell him I'm wrapping up now and I will be with him shortly."

"Yes Ma'am, right away!" Samantha complies.

"Thanks Sam." Ashima replies as she returns her attention to the meeting trying to justify the company's aggressive budget cuts.

"Listen people, I don't want to beat this horse to death. But, I can only promise you that things will get better in the foreseeable future. I'm not in the position to prognosticate anyone's future with the company post separation. But, I am trying my best to urge the board to give each of you a premium for those who will be departing the company. I can't guarantee what the figures will be at this time, but my proposal is at least six months base salary. However, there is one certainty; for those who are departing at this time, when I am directed to begin filling positions again, between you and I, everyone in my department shall be the first called back to work." Ashima assures, trying to be a good steward for her staff.

"So, what happens to those who are staying in the department? What about their future?" One staff member speaks out.

116

"For those of us that will be fortunate enough to stay with the company, by that I mean the most senior and the most qualified, it will be a tough road ahead, trying to juggle our own priorities as well as taking on some of the responsibilities of those relieved from their duties. Even Freddy the janitor has to cut back on flirting with all the receptionists because he's losing all but one of his sanitation colleagues." Ashima playfully mentions, trying to instigate a bit of humor despite the tense, solemn tone of the meeting.

"With that said, let's all go back to work and finish up strong for future considerations sake." Ashima concludes, trying to maintain a positive complexion with her staff and inspiring her team to stay motivated.

Ashima leaves the meeting and immediately returns to her office to answer her father's phone call.

"Salaam father…you called?" Ashima answers.

"Yes Princess, are you done with your meeting?" An impatient Amir asks.

"Yes father. I'm preparing to go home. Was there something I can help you with?" Ashima asks as she starts to gather her things.

"Ashima I had something important to pass to you before letting them go and you blow me off?!" A displeased Amir replies.

"Excuse me, father. But, in the midst of handling your dirty work, you call at such a late hour in the workday. I'm trying to get these people home at a descent hour and handing them pink slips out the door." Ashima defensively replies trying to rationalize with Amir.

"Nonsense, you have no pink slips, Ashima. You are only doing as you are told. There's no need to exaggerate." Amir responds, downplaying Ashima's defense.

"So, what was it exactly why you called father?" Ashima responds ready to end the call.

"I wanted you to tell the staff members of your department that the holiday bonuses are suspended, and the tickets to the Holiday Gala are $50.00 this year." Amir stresses to her. Annoyed by her father's response, Ashima resorts to her Arabic dialect in her frustration.

"أخبار من تسليمي يوقف أن أردتني أنت أنت؟ أن تكون حسّاس غير كيف؟ تمزحني أنت يكون" هذا من ماكرة هكذا ···ساخرة هكذا كنت أنت يستطيع كيف نجلت؟ سيّئة أخبارك من أكثر مع سيّئة "وافرة أجورك يبرد أن بشدّة هكذا عمل ف الذي الناس!"

"Are you kidding me? How insensitive are you? You wanted me to interrupt my delivery of bad news with more of your bad news? Father, how can you be so cynical...so insidious of these people who've worked so hard to justify your copious wages!" Ashima angrily replies.

"إأشيما···أبك بعد أنا أشيما إنغمتك أنت يراقب أشيما"

"Ashima, you watch your tone! Ashima, I am still your father...ASHIMA!" Amir lashes back with equal discourse to regain composure of the conversation. His daughter was becoming too liberal for his liking.

"Father, I'm going to hang up now before I say something unbecoming of me, I will see you when I get home, Salaam!" She replies, calming herself back to speaking in English.

"Ashima, I am talking to you...ASHIMA! ASHIMA!" A frustrated Amir exclaims into the empty phone.

Ashima's disappointment of her father topped off what proved to be a trying and exhausting day. Already armed with her attaché case and designer handbag in hand, she grabs her house keys and smart phone, conceals her face with her large designer shades, and makes her way to the ground level to elude her job-related stress. She walks with an authoritative swagger, as the thunderous sound of her red bottom Manolo Blahnik heels echo the corridor of tall glass walls and marble tiled floors. While waiting for the elevator, she calls down to her driver Carlos to inform him she's on her way. After stepping out of the elevator and blending in with the hundreds of others of the evening rush, she sees Carlos pulling in front of the building, among the other drivers.

"Right on time!" Ashima says pleased to see the black Denali pull up to her rescue.

"Buena tarde, Ms. Batool."

"Good evening, Ms. Batool." Carlos greets as he holds the door for her.

"Buena tarde Carlos...hogar por favor."

"Good evening Carlos...home please." She initiates in Spanish as she threw her bags onto the back seat and despairingly climbs into the SUV.

"Si Ma'am!"

"Yes Ma'am!" Carlos acknowledges before driving off.

Ashima sinks into the back seat of the Denali and lets out a sigh of fatigue as she rests her head against the window and look up at the dusk

118

falling sky. As her body finally relents to relaxation, her brief coziness is abruptly interrupted by the sudden ring of her phone.

"Salaam…" She answers.

"Salaam Princess…and how was your day?" Fahad gracefully asks.

"Aside from Amir's usual foolishness, I am well. On my way, home now." She replies.

"At it with daddy again I assume?" Fahad implies, making reference to the perennial disputes between Ashima and her father.

"Yes, well you know how my father can be, especially during these turbulent times. I'm sure you've heard that a few of our international corporate partners went under today, and a domino effect could be imminent." Ashima explains with disappointment.

"Yes, I am aware. There's also talk of a few of the nation's top corporate players here could be next. A very scary plight indeed…but, I'm sure that if Philadelphia Finance and Trust goes under, between your father and I, you should have enough tucked away to maintain." Fahad assures her.

"Fahad, this is part of my reason of disgust for him. He's so worried about how to shore up the executives, and cares nothing for the middle-class. He's no different than the state of our social environment…it's disgusting!" Ashima ardently vents.

"Ashima, we are nothing like the middle-class. We live well and we come from good stock. We must not burden ourselves with the pettiness of our accusers, holding us responsible for this financial calamity." Fahad states ensuring that Ashima understands.

As she listens to Fahad speak, she starts to get very annoyed of his insensitive reasoning as well.

"We also account for some of the blame for this mess, Fahad! Our people, our kind, as you say we are! It is our greed and our conquest that make us predators of the weak! Instead of millions of dollars in bonuses, how about you filter some of that money down to others who work hard to keep making the status quo!" A worked up Ashima expresses.

"Oh, listen to you…you sound like a martyr. Ashima when we marry I will have none of this! You cannot save the world, take care of my home, and raise my children all at once! Your job is to do the ladder. Let me worry about the finances." Fahad boldly stats in an attempt to put Ashima in her place.

With every grain of tolerance, Ashima resists a negative reaction to Fahad's egotism.

"أب ك ل لم ب هو إن !نحن سيزوّج أنّ يفترض أنت جسارة كيف !إشيت ال قطعة أنت"
"!غو لونغ وجهك في أنا سبت ,لغم ومنجم"

"You piece of shit! How dare you assume that we will marry! If it was not for your father and mine, I would have spat in your face long ago!" An enraged Ashima vents her thoughts of Fahad, biting her tongue in Arabic dialect before calmly using a better choice of words.

"Well of course…it's all about you right, Fahad?" Ashima condescendingly yields.

"Ashima, that is not true. It's not about me, but it is tradition in Islam that a woman is obedient to her husband. Of course, you will be well versed in this, once you convert and cleanse your soul of this western religious foolishness, yes?" Fahad arrogantly assumes.

"Of course, how could I forget? Listen, I have a headache from work among other things and I'm going to relax now. So, I'll speak to you later…oh, and before I go remember one thing, I don't have a husband just yet, okay…Salaam!" Ashima hurries off the phone, barely able to stomach a conversation with her alleged 'would be' husband.

After coming home from such a frustrating day, Ashima is in much need of relaxation and was not in the mood to joust with her father about the petty events at work. She removes her shoes in the foyer and carries them through the house, not only because it's house etiquette, but to quietly avoid detection from her father, as if he didn't hear her already from the chime of the alarm system. Before walking up the back stairwell to her room, she paces around the kitchen's open floor space and places her heels on the granite counter-top island. She stands in front of the six-foot tall, glass front, wine chiller that automatically lit up from a motion sensor, and searched for her favorite bottle of Riesling.

"Let's see, Sauvignon Blanc, Pinot Noir, Grigio, Shiraz…ahh, there we go, crisp and fruity Riesling." She recites, reaching for the bottle and shoving it into her Birkin bag.

She then cuts a piece of oozing Brie cheese from the wheel on the counter and places it on a clear plastic plate, along with a piece of Jarlsberg cheese to confuse her taste buds. But, the plate looked naked and needed some contrasting flavor. So, she opens the matching cabinetry sub-zero refrigerator door and grabs a stem of grapes and a few strawberries to complete the edible dish. Now, with a plate and the spaghetti straps of her shoes in her left hand, her bag with the bottle of Riesling on her right shoulder, and a goblet sized wine bulb in her right hand, she was all set to retire to her room for the evening. Once she reaches the top of the spiral staircase, she can hear Amir speaking to someone loudly behind the closed door of his bedroom, which is relieving. Immediately after entering her room, she places the wine and cheese plate on the night stand, and plops face first onto her king size sleigh bed with everything still in hand.

"Wine, cheese, fruit, and a bath...this should be good!" she mutters, lying comfortably as she gazes into her adjacent bathroom with her naturally straight, jet black, Indian hair partially covering her face.

Although, unmotivated to move, she tries to motivate herself back to her feet to prepare a hot, relaxing, bubble sanctuary to unwind. After mustering enough energy to get off the bed, she finally stands to her feet and walks into the bathroom. Using the digital settings on the tub, she set the water temperature to fill the tub at a perfect 112 degrees and adds a stress relieving Eucalyptus Mint bath bomb as a finishing touch. Then she strips down to her petite naked core, and slips on a red and white flower pattern Kimono she grabs from a hook-on bathroom door. Before immersing herself into the large jetted tub, she lights candles to provide a tranquil setting, poured a half bulb of wine, killed the lights, and with her tray of cheese, fruit and smart phone at the edge of the tub, she slowly sinks into the warmth of the soothing bubble bath. Submerged neck deep in sultry relaxation, she's finally content and at peace. She reaches for the remote to her iDock and mellows out to a relaxing playlist. With the flicker of candlelight, wine, and music to set the mood, she lay silent staring out her bathroom window at a bright orange moon through a break in the trees in her backyard.

With complete disregard to the day's drama, she simply let's go. She takes a sip of wine as thoughts of her mother began to play in her head. As much as she misses her mother, Ashima knew that she was too Americanized to live in Cairo where her mother lives as a successful accountant. Moreover, Ashima's parental origin of having an Islamic father and a Coptic Christian mother is considered sacrilegious, and would surely get Ashima killed if it was ever discovered while living in Egypt. However, it's been nearly a year since her mom came back to the states to visit and Ashima was looking forward to their trip to the United Kingdom that they

121

plan every year. But, thoughts of her mother also brought an overcast of resentment for her father because of the circumstances for which her mother left.

The same controlling, traditions of Islamic sexism that drove her mother away are now threatening to impose on Ashima by her consideration of marriage to Fahad. But, the resilience she picked up from four years of private school and another five years of college and graduate studies has fortified her mentality of becoming an independent woman. Not to succumb to the restricted tolerances of Islamic culture. In fact, her only reason for living at home and tolerating her father is because of her promise to her mother to take care of him. Although she was disappointed in her mother's decision to leave for Egypt, she understood her mother's intent to be closer to her Nana, Ashima's fragile grandmother, and leaving Ashima behind to have a better life in the United States. In the midst of her brainstorm, she's suddenly interrupted by a call from her college girlfriend Carolyn.

"Hey girlfriend, what are you up to?" An upbeat Carolyn asks, providing much needed positive energy to Ashima's depressing day.

"Hey Lenny…enjoying a much-needed bath bomb right now." Ashima replies.

"Ooh…I could go for one of those right now! And I hear that soundtrack in the background playing. Is Fahad over there? Do you need me to call you back?" Carolyn asks, implying that Ashima may be having a private moment.

"Fahad? Oh, heavens no! I've got my soundtrack going, my wine and cheese, some fresh fruit, and no Fahad! He's a simple minded 'yes' man for my father, and I want nothing to do with him." Ashima flares up, at the mere mention of Fahad.

"C'mon Shima, all that money he's got, you know you're not going anywhere. I know I wouldn't!" Carolyn teases, but not getting the response, she anticipated.

"Lenny, why do you talk like this…surely you must understand that money isn't everything. You know he can do nothing for me, my father is worth millions and I have access to so much more. Actually, I'm tired of hearing him say what he's going to do for me with his money. All he's got…is all that money with an IQ of a squirrel. He has no personality, he's very demanding, ostentatious, and bossy…he sucks!" Ashima passionately

122

explains as her voice cracks in frustration. Carolyn gasps as the sound of sniffles alerts her of something being wrong with her friend.

"Oh-no! Ashima what's wrong?" She cries out with sincere concern.

Ashima takes a moment to gather herself before speaking. Using both hands, she pushes tears away to regain her composure.

"I'm sorry Lenny. I'm just so worn down from missing my mother, the pressure and demands of my father in my personal life and work, and that pretentious loser he wants me to marry that continue to stress his demands of me." Ashima stresses with frustration.

"You mean, like an arranged marriage?" Carolyn asks.

"Yes, exactly! Lenny, I'm playing this game, pretending to be in love with this man out of respect for my father, because that's the way I was raised. But, the interest of this marriage has absolutely nothing to do with love. It has nothing to do with his 'little Princess' being happy. It's nothing more than a ploy to create a lineage between our families. Fahad's father Shafik and my father have been friends since they were very young. As a child, my grandparents use to take my father to the market place, where Fahad's family worked as merchants. Although my father was very poor and Shafik was raised as what we would consider middle-class, they used to play together and became great friends growing up. Before long, they were off to college together, and well into their studies at American University in Cairo. Things were just fine until my parents were forced to flee Cairo after receiving death threats from Islamic radicals." Ashima explains before Lenny interrupts again.

"Wow! Your parents were 'forced' to leave Egypt?" Lenny asks trying to keep up with the story.

"Yes, my father met my mother during a crisis between Muslims and Coptic Christians in the suburban town of Hausus where they lived. My mother's oldest sibling was killed during a violent night of conflicts and the rest of the family was in grave danger. My father, a devout man of Islam, saw my mother grieving after the tragedy and felt remorse because he thought my mother was too beautiful to be under such duress. Suddenly, he went from a passionate protester to a redeemer, convincing the other activists to set aside their aggression and return to their families. Afterwards, he offered to help my mother and her family. My mother was defiant at first, but my father was persistent and used to come at night to render aid. Eventually my mother would give in to my father's kindness and charm, and was prepared to leave Hausus at any cost. So, she ran off with my father while he attended college in Cairo. However, despite falling in love, my mother was not so willing to convert to Islam to marry my father which was a very dangerous situation. But, she became pregnant and was forced to convert to Islam and marry him anyway for my safety and hers. But, she hated the idea of converting to Islam in Egypt, so she compromised with my father and would only agree to convert and marry him if he moved to the U.S. or the U.K. He made her a promise that he would, but only after he finished his education in Cairo. Eventually, my father had no choice but to move. Sectarian violence grew so much in Cairo, that by the time I was three he had to either move us abroad to start a new life, or stay in Cairo and risk being killed by the radicals. So, here I am!" An uneasy Ashima recollects.

"Killed? What do you mean? They would have killed you and your mother because you were females?" Lenny was horrified by Ashima's revelation.

"No, my father started receiving death threats that said 'the blasphemous child must die.' But, we never found out where the threats came from or how anyone knew of how I was conceived. You see, in Egypt, I am illegitimate to the Islamic culture and the penalty could have been death. So, my parents had to flee Cairo." Ashima replies.

"Oh my God, Shima, we were roommates. I'm surprised you've never told me this before!" Carolyn states in awe.

"I know. It's such an interesting story, but it reminds me of such tyranny and inequality in my native Egypt. I don't remember much as a child at that age. But, I remember vividly the day we were leaving Cairo, there was a man standing at the platform of the train station. My parents were busy talking and didn't notice that the man was staring at them, but I did notice. He was commonly dressed with a brown shirt, khakis, and sandals holding a newspaper as if he was reading it. When the man saw me looking at him, he smiled then looked into his paper. When the train arrived, we boarded, but the man remained standing at the platform still staring at us. It was really creepy. Even when we boarded the train, I took a window seat and saw the man still standing there staring at us on the train. Once he spotted me in the window, I looked directly into the man's eyes. Only this time he wasn't smiling. Staring at me with the most ominous look, he took out a huge shiny knife that reflected the sun off the blade and made a throat

124

slitting gesture towards me, just as the train was departing. I was so terrified I turned away from the window, closed my eyes, and clutched my father with the strongest hug. I was yelling, "Daddy! Daddy!" and my father asked me what was wrong. I was so terrified I couldn't even raise my head to tell him. Eventually, once I looked back, he was gone...and that was my lasting impression of Cairo, Egypt." Ashima painfully recalls.

"My God Ashima, I'm terrified just imagining what that must have been like as an adult, let alone a child! So, how does all of this play into you marrying Fahad?" Carolyn queries further with the conversation.

"Well, Shafik's parents adored my mother and father when they moved to Cairo; so much, that it was their idea for my parents to move to the U.S. for their own safety and better quality of life. But, the only way that would have been possible was for his parents to sponsor my parent's move and their education. In doing so, my father felt completely indebted to them. But, with little to offer, he appointed Shafik as my Godfather, and his parents as my God grandparents. They were so in love with me and the idea, that I was secretly added to the family will. Later, when Shafik's parents passed on, they left him a small fortune, which he's grown to a massive investment and development empire in Cairo and Dubai. Now he is known as 'Sheik Gabr' or 'the Sheik'." Ashima explains.

"Oh my God! Is there more than one Shafik Gabr in Egypt?" Lenny asks with astonishment.

"Well, I'm sure there is...why do you ask?" Ashima replies.

"Because, it says that this guy is worth about three quarters of a billion dollars?" A stunned Carolyn reveals.

"Yes, that's probably him...wait! How do you know that?" Ashima asks bewildered by Carolyn's quick reference.

"I just googled him on my iPad, Shima. This guy is your Godfather? Oh, my goodness! Shima...you're rich, heifer! No wonder, you were never hurting in college. Here I thought your parents were financing your tuition and...you worked through college at the clothing store in the Liberty Place Mall. Hell, you probably could have bought the Liberty Place Mall?" An astounded Lenny exclaims. Flattered by the gesture, Ashima modestly replies.

"Well, my parents have always taught me that one of the most important things to remember in life is humility. Never live life pretentious, and always help those in need, which is exactly why I'm blessed today." Ashima humbly replies.

"Yeah, but being your roommate for four years, never once did you mention that little detail about yourself. That is simply incredible." Carolyn shockingly recalls.

"Yes Lenny, you're right. But, know this, money doesn't change you, it changes the people around you. And I didn't want you to treat me any different than the person you've grown to know. I wanted you to accept me for me, and have the great friendship we've established over the years." Ashima profoundly explains.

"Awe...Shima...that's so sweet! And I'm so glad we're such great friends. Even if you didn't tell me you were rich when we we're eating Ramen noodles for a month to save a buck." Carolyn jokes as the two explode with laughter.

"Awe, I miss those days!" Ashima reminisces.

"Sooo...are sure you don't want to marry into this extraordinary family?" Lenny teases.

"Lenny please!" Ashima replies in an abrupt, revolting tone.

"I know, I know Shima, I'm just teasing. I never liked him anyway. He's just not your type in my opinion. Anyway, what's up for the weekend, are we having lady's night out or what?" Carolyn asks crossing the topic.

"It could be ladies weekend for all I care. I need a vacation, bad! Amir needs someone to travel to London to close an acquisition and I hope he tells me to go. I could really use the break." Ashima replies.

"Well, if he sends you, call me! I'm sure me and the rest of the girls will have no problem altering our schedule to meet your leisurely needs." Lenny jokingly mentions. Ashima laughs with her friend, but her laughter was filled with empty sentiment as she was still hung up on repulsive thoughts of Fahad.

"Okay, I'm getting out of the tub now. But, I will call you tomorrow to figure out what we are doing this weekend." Ashima concludes for a relaxing moment to herself.

"Oh, Shima before you go! Me and a few friends from work are heading to Old City for a few drinks? Are you interested in going?" She asks trying to lift her friend's spirit.

"Hmm...no, I think I'll just save it for the weekend so I can really unwind. I need to focus on some stuff at the office this week anyway." With fear of being tired for work in the morning, Ashima regretfully declines, knowing there was much of Amir's work to be done.

"Well, if you decide to change your mind, call me back so I can tell you where to meet me." Carolyn replies.

"Okay bye..." Ashima hangs up with no intention on joining them this evening.

After retreating from the relaxing, jetted tub, with a large towel covering her body from chest to bottom, and a towel wrapped around her head, Ashima sits at the edge of the tub emotionally vulnerable. She pours herself another taste and sips from her glass reflecting on her life. Her playlist fills the room with another soulful compilation. As she listens to the sounds of subtlety and watches the candlelight flicker, her mood is filled with sadness, living with the idea of never really knowing what it was like to experience love. Under the strict rule of a success driven father, Amir kept her away from any real social life through high school and her undergrad studies. Even as she attended Wharton School of Business at the University of Pennsylvania in pursuit of her MBA. He demanded transparency of all of her activities, so she would stay focused.

On the other hand, her relationship with Fahad in college was pestering at best. Despite knowing him since adolescence, her intimate relationship with him wasn't exactly what she envisioned. What started out as a gentle, pampering Fahad, quickly turned into a pompous, controlling, chauvinist pig that only cares about himself and manipulating the people around him. Yet she continued to date him because of the pressure of her peers and her father. It wasn't until she gave into Fahad's unrelenting determination that she'd ever given herself to anyone, which she recalls as being a vile and unpleasant experience.

Everyone in her social circle is successful and either married or engaged. But, Ashima feels emotionally vacant in her relationship with Fahad, and is indeed looking for someone else to eloquently fill the void. The combination of melancholy and wine softened her sentiment to the point of sending streaming tears of frustration down her face. Her emotions were fed by each song that played as she felt pitiful and at times hopeless. As she moisturized her silky-smooth legs, she reflects on her unpleasant encounter with Fahad on Sunday, and how embarrassing it was in front of her friends, and this time in front of man she doesn't even know. However, there was something gripping about this handsome delivery man that her father suddenly befriended. This man that appeared to be totally out of place, somehow managed to fit into her puzzling, calculated thoughts. Despite slighting him among her friends at Fahad's house, she genuinely found him easy on the eyes. This was confusing to her because from the surface, the obvious contrast in their lifestyles wouldn't normally merit a second look. Being a delivery man for *Apex* didn't exactly qualify him to live up to the likes of a wealthy princess from Egypt. Yet something about him has certainly made him worthy of a second thought.

"I'll bet he doesn't treat 'his' lady-friend like crap!" She speculates taking another sip of wine between thoughts.

Still reeling from a low state of emotion, she holds her glass up to the flicker of the candle and slowly twirls the glowing glass bulb with her fingers as she watches the condensation roll down the sides of the glass like tears. Ashima thought of this as being metaphorically tantamount to her mood.

"Hmph, a crying glass, filled with spirits of misery, in a cold and harsh world...God grant me the serenity...!" She openly voices, leaning on faith to will her the strength to deal with the absence of her mother, the vacancy of love, and life's despair.

Nonetheless, being the resilient woman, she is, not even hampering feelings of despondence couldn't hold her there for long. She picks herself up emotionally, looks over at the vanity mirror and smiled at her unwavering reflection as her faith in God restores her optimism.

Yet just as fast as she lifts herself emotionally, her renewed spirit takes another plummet as she hears her father knocking at her bedroom door.

"Ashima! Ashima!" Amir, calls out.

"Yes father!" She answers in an annoyed tone.

"أشيما، أود أن أتحدث إليكم مرة واحدة!"

"Ashima, I would like to speak to you at once!" An agitated Amir requests, resorting to Arabic dialect.

"حسنا، لحظة واحدة!"

"Okay, one moment!" Ashima responds, mentally preparing her defensive posture.

With a sudden swing in temperament, she's now armed with nothing less than anger and resentment, and was not in the mood for her father's senseless lecturing. Reluctantly, she drops her towel to cover herself in her

Kimono robe, takes in a deep breath, and readies herself for his drama. Knowing her father all too well, she opens the door barely enough to poke her head out in order to disarm his ability to control the conversation.

"يسرّ, أنا يدخل ماي شهر?"

"May I enter, please?" Amir asks, annoyed by the barrier between them.

"ما من يمكن أنت لا, أنا كان حمّمت عندما أنت طرقت وأنا لست كلّيّا هبوط!"

"No, you may not, I was bathing when you knocked and I'm not fully descent!" Ashima quickly denies him.

"فري ولّ, بعد ذلك···"

"Very well, then…"

"··· أشيما, خيّبت أنا كان جدّا مع أنت اليوم. أبدا تلقّيت أنا رفع أنت إلى تصرّف إداريّ
أنت. افتقار الإحترام هذا أتسامح لن أنا. تمرد هذا مع ي إلى أنت يتكلّم ت أند إزدراء هذا مع بنفسي
تفهم?"

"…Ashima, I was very disappointed with you today. Never have I raised you to conduct yourself with such disrespect and yet you speak to me with such insubordination. I will not tolerate this lack of respect. Do you understand?" Amir ardently explains with grave disappointment.

Ashima stands in the doorway with such disgust of her father's arrogance that she couldn't even immediately respond. She takes a moment to digest her father's comments while thinking of how to defend her actions without provoking him further.

"نجلت أنا لا يتمنّى أن يكون قليل احترام عندما يوصل عمل. مهما, أنت يخلق بيئة عدائيّة ل
ي عندما يحاول أن يوصل عمل أس يف أنا لست سابقا تحت بما فيه الكفاية احتجاز أثناء اليوم."

"Father, I do not wish to be disrespectful when conducting business. However, you create a hostile environment for me when trying to conduct business as if I'm not already under enough duress during the day." Ashima yields with a calm demeanor.

"أشيما, أعطيت أنت كان إنذار وافرة حول الموقعة وبيئته يقبل الشغل. أنا مدركة من
هوو موش إجهاد داخل يومك. بعد, عندما أنت المستشارة رئيسيّة ماليّة من حظ 500 مؤسسة,
شركة. يأتي هو بما أنّ من يتيح مهمة ويكون ابنتي لا يجعل أنت معف من الإجهاد من يعمل ل هذا"

"Ashima, you were given ample warning about the position and its environment prior to accepting the job. I am aware of how much stress goes into your day. Yet, when you are the Chief Financial Advisor of a Fortune 500 institution, it comes as no easy task and being my daughter does not make you exempt from the strain of working for this company."

129

"نعم, هذا أنا أفهم أن غير ··· أنّ كابنتك ,لا أنت تستطيع تحدّثت إلى ي في يعزّز, أنغام كريمة,
كفا ال من أنت تقاعدت ,ذلك على علاوة ,ملاكتي من سلطتي يهدّد هو .تابعاتي بحضور خصوصا
إلى فوق يمسك أن يحاول على أنت يلحّ ذلك مع .الآن ماليّة لفيلادلفيا رئيسيّة الضاغطة أنت .موقعة
شغله يتمّ أن سمحته أنت إن كثير هو قدّم يوقن وأنا ,الآن شغل فرنكلين أنّ .سابقة رسمك واجب".

"Yes, I understand this…but as your daughter, can you not talk to me
in elevated, distasteful tones, especially in the presence of my subordinates.
It threatens my authority of my staff. Furthermore, you are retired from the
CFA position. You're the chief lobbyist for Philadelphia Finance now. Yet
you insist on trying to hold on to your former duties. That's Franklin's job
now, and I'm sure he would much appreciate if you would allow him to do
his job." Ashima pleads.

"فرنكلين, يقول أنت! فرنكلين متدربتي. هو بعد يتلقّى ا لوت من يعلم أن قبل هو
الآن, .وصايتي تحت ماليّة أوامر يعالج أن كيف يعلم هو .وحيد مسؤولية على أخذت يستطيع
يمكن يكون أن أنا يحتاج ,يتمّ الشغل يحصل أن أنت أحتاج أنا إن أشيما .أتكلّم أنا كيف وف رغردلسّ
لا ,عدوانيّة وموقف صارمة شغل هذا يتطلّب .هذا من ثقة كثير مع أنت رفعت أنا .أنت على يعدّ أن
هذا حماقة ضعيفة أنت تتكلّم من إن".

"Franklin, you say! Franklin is my apprentice. He still has a lot of
learning to do before he can take on sole responsibility. He learns how to
handle financial matters under my tutelage. Now, regardless of how I speak.
Ashima if I need you to get the job done, I need to be able to count on you. I
raised you with more confidence than this. This job requires stern and
aggressive attitude, not this feeble foolishness you speak of!" Amir replies,
justifying his point.

"هذا يصحّ أب ,علمني أنت أن يكون رجوعيّة وعدوانيّة .مهما ,علمني أنت أيضا أن يحترم
أنّ الذي يحترم أنت .أنت ابنتك ,أنت تستطيع ماذا أتمّت تشعر أنت في يثبت مثال جيّدة .غير أنّ
كمحترفة, لن أنا يتسامح يكون ديسرسبكتد ب أيّ شخص ···ونعم, أنت علمتني أن أيضا!"

"This is true father, you did teach me to be resilient and aggressive.
However, you also taught me to respect those who respect you. So as your
daughter, you can do what you feel in setting a good example. But, as a
professional, I will not tolerate being disrespected by anyone…and yes, you
taught me that as well!" Ashima replies with a condescending flair.
Appalled by his daughter's rebuttal, Amir firmly stands his ground and
interrupts her.

"··· وكأبك أشيما, يحذّر أنا أنت أن يبالي لسانك .أنت تصبح لقمة أكثر لليبر اليّ أنا من عناية
أن أنت على يعدّ أنا أستطيع .اجتماع الجمعة ليوم يتمّ فصليّة التقرير أنا يحتاج غدا ,الآن .يتسامح أن
يتلقّى؟ هذا يتمّ".

130

"…And as your father Ashima, I am warning you to mind your tongue. You are becoming a bit more liberal than I care to tolerate. Now, tomorrow I need the quarterly report completed for Friday's meeting. Can I count on you to have this done?" Amir asks at his tolerance peak.

"هو إن ,الآن. الأربعاء يوم منذ مكتبك على كان قد هو. أب أسبوع متأخّرة يتمّ التقرير كان"
"نهاية بأسبوع ينهي أن العمل لوت ا أتلقّى أنا. ينام أن أنا أحبّ أنت مع حسنة يكون".

"The report was completed last week father. It's been on your desk since Wednesday. Now, if it's okay with you I would like to go to bed. I have a lot of work to finish by week's end." A crafty Ashima replies.

"ذهبت "نعم, رجاء…!"

"Yes, please go…!" Agitated by his daughter's slick demeanor, Amir shoo's her away with a hand gesture.

Ashima rolls her eyes and exhales deeply through her flaring nostrils like a bull seeing red before shutting her door. Shaking her head in dismay, she sits at the edge of her bed to dry her hair. Then she notices a sudden text notification from her cell phone.

(Text)
Lenny: *So, am I picking you up or you're leaving me hanging?*

Despite needing an outlet after the edgy exchange, she just had with her father, Ashima toils over her decision for a moment before responding.
Ashima: *Sorry Lenny, I'm in bed. I'll see you all on Friday.*
Lenny: *C'mon Debby downer, I know Amir is holding you hostage over there* ☺
Ashima: *Zzzz…*
Lenny: *Whatever! I'm calling WA on you in the morning.*
Ashima: *WA?*
Lenny: *Workaholics anonymous!!!* ☹
Ashima: *Lol. Have fun. Make safe choices!* ☺

Fearing a late night with friends and knowing how demanding her father is, Ashima decides to wrap her hair and call it a night.

CHAPTER EIGHT

After a bustling week of meetings, acquisitions, training, stress, non-stop delegation from her father acting as her boss, and tasking from her real boss, Ashima is elated that Friday has finally arrived.

"Have a pleasant weekend, Ms. Batool." A voice rang out from behind the security desk as she briskly made her way through the building lobby.

"Thank you, have a good weekend guys!" Ashima replies with a casual wave.

As she exits the building, as expected, there was Carlos, double parked with his hazard lights blinking awaiting her arrival.

"Good evening Ms. Batool." The middle-aged Carlos greets her while opening the rear passenger door.

"Hola Carlos…!"

"Hello Carlos…!" Ashima replies as she quickly climbs into the tall SUV.

"Chocolates y vino como pediste, Ms. Batool…"

"Chocolates and wine as you requested, Ms. Batool…" Carlos replies, responding in Spanish only if Ashima initiates it.

"Sí, gracias Carlos."

"Yes, thank you Carlos." She inertly replies, while immersed in a text message reply from work on her cell phone.

After sending a reply message to an associate, Ashima immediately let out a deep sigh of relief and kicks off her weekend by enjoying a glass of Cabernet and the gourmet chocolate covered strawberries Carlos picked up for her in route. On the way home, she finally has an opportunity to acknowledge the missed calls and messages she was too busy to address throughout the day.

(Voicemail)
Crystal: *"Happy Friday Shima, it's time to turn up! I can't wait to get off work today. These people are driving me crazy! Anyway, call me when the jockey is done whipping you to the finish line, Ciao'!"*
Lenny: *"Hi Shima, hope your day is going good. Are we meeting at this place tonight, or am I picking you up? Let me know...okay bye!"*
Naima: *"Oh, my God! Guess what day it is? Guess what day it is? It's Friday, Yayyy! I am too excited! Okay, so we really need to party like rock stars tonight. #ladiesnightout. #excited!!!"*

Inspired by the excitement of her friend's voice messages, Ashima is equally excited about unwinding for the weekend, after an exhausting week of headaches in the office. She responds by taking a selfie with her glass of wine in hand and sends the photo to each of them with the caption, *'Cheers ladies! Let the weekend begin!'*

Lenny responds to the text with her own wine glass selfie. The selfie trend triggers the other girls to get involved. So, Jasmine sends her wine glass selfie, and Crystal sends her selfie with a bottle of Cîroc.

(Text)
Ashima: *"Really Crys? Lol..."*
Crystal: *"I'm just saying...forget all of these wine selfies, "LET'S TURN UP!"*
Jasmine: *"Ditto Crys! Its Friday everybody...Whoop! Whoop!"*

Ashima smiles as the messages kept her amused during the tedious rush hour commute.

"Parece alguien listo para el fin de semana."

"Looks like someone's ready for the weekend." Carlos suggests, observing Ashima's body language in his rearview mirror.

"Ha sido una semana muy que intenta, Carlos. Pensé que nunca terminaría. Agradece a dios que debe siempre allí para tomarme lejos de todo el caos."

"It's been a very trying week, Carlos. I thought it would never end. Thank God you're always there to take me away from all the chaos." Ashima graciously replies. Carlos chuckles at the comment.

"Cualquier cosa bueno previsto para el fin de semana, señora del jefe?"

"Anything good planned for the weekend, boss lady?" Carlos inquires as he inches his way through the thick of the five o'clock traffic.

"Nada realmente. Apenas el colgar hacia fuera con los amigos esta noche para desenrollar es todo."

"Nothing really. Just hanging out with friends tonight to unwind is all." Ashima replies, excited to start the weekend.

"Bien, es ciertamente un buen día para él. Ha sido hermoso todo el dia, Ms. Batool."

"Well, it's certainly a good day for it. It's been beautiful all day, Ms. Batool." Carlos informs her.

"Sé, yo estaba tan impaciente por salir de la oficina todo el dia. Pero, este tráfico realmente aspira ahora, y está matando a mi humor!"

"I know, I was so anxious to leave the office all day. But, this traffic really sucks right now, and it's killing my mood!" Ashima digress, becoming spontaneously annoyed by the endless horn blowing and crawling traffic.

"Ningún se preocupa a Ms Batool. ¿Podría bajar en la impulsión del oeste del río del Parkway y del golpe de Ben Franklin si usted quisiera? Nunca hay cualquier tráfico que va esa manera."

"No worries Ms. Batool. I could get off at Ben Franklin Parkway and take West River Drive if you'd like? There's never any traffic going that way." Carlos suggests.

"Sí, eso suena como un plan. Hagamos eso."

"Yes, that sounds like a plan. Let's do that!" Ashima agrees.

"Si Ma'am!"

"Yes Ma'am!" Carlos complies."

As anticipated, once Carlos exits to the Ben Franklin Parkway and ride by the *Philadelphia Art Museum,* there was nothing but open road on West River Drive all the way to Gypsy Lane.

As Carlos turns onto Gypsy Lane, Ashima gathers her things and mentally prepares herself to endure the stress of her father routinely.

"Hmm…Amir is not home?" She observes as Carlos pulls into the driveway of her house.

"Gracias tanto por conseguirme casero de una manera oportuna, Carlos… y tenga un buen fin de semana."

"Thank you so much for getting me home in a timely manner, Carlos…and have a good weekend." She says while handing him a crisp one-hundred-dollar bill for his troubles as he holds the door open for her.

It was unconventional for Ashima to tip Carlos for his services, because her father takes care of the expenses. However, Ashima is known for tipping big when sending her driver to run errands and doesn't mind tipping a little extra to show her appreciation.

"Gracias, Sra. Batool. ¿Espero que tienes un gran fin de semana con tus amigos y si me necesita, por favor no dude en llamar, okay?"

"Thank you, Ms. Batool. I hope you have a great weekend with your friends and if you need me please don't hesitate to call, okay?" Carlos assures her.

"Gracias Carlos. Si fuera necesario, te llevaré esa oferta. Disfruta de tu fin de semana."

"Thank you, Carlos. If need be, I will take you up on that offer. Enjoy your weekend."

Ashima replies as she graciously smiles, pleased to know she can depend on her driver.

After a quick check of the mailbox, Ashima walks in the house and immediately kicks off her shoes. Her friend's lively spirit prompts her to kick it up another notch, so she throws her designer bag on the kitchen counter and grabs a bottle of something festive from the wine chiller. A pink bottle of Ace of Spades champagne becomes the bottle of choice as she snaps a selfie with wearing her bold Channel shades, and sends the photo with the caption, "Let's turn up then!"

Her phone is immediately bombarded with "LOL" and "OMG" replies from her friends, responding to Ashima acting way out of character.

(Text)
Naima: *"Ashima you are too turned up over there!"*
Crystal: *"Blahahaha…U need 2 stop! U know u got that bottle from Fahad. Lmao!"*
Ashima: *"Yup, and I'll take all his other bottles too!"* ☺

Crystal: "Hot mess" ☺
Naima: "I'll be there around 7 to pick you up after I pick up Crystal."
Ashima: "Don't bother, you live too far. My friend Lenny lives closer this way and will hopefully be here before Amir comes. I don't want to be bothered by his BS."
Naima: "Who???"
Ashima: "You'll meet her tonight."
Crystal: "Okay then."

Attempting to maintain her vibrant mood, Ashima pours herself a taste of the premium champagne before placing it back in the chiller. Then she scampers to her room for a quick shower before letting her hair down for a night out. Before getting into her evening outfit, she grabs one of her favorite COCO Chanel fragrances from the dresser and sprays herself with a mist across the chest, another across her abdomen and lastly a quick mist for her privacy. Then she squeezes into a pair of black hugging pants, and a shear white open collared blouse with rolled sleeves. She makes up her face with a light foundation of MAC, before adding a sparkly silver neck accessory and bangle bracelets to match. She completes her ensemble with a BVLGARI watch and a Hermes clutch that matches her black two-inch heeled designer boots. She gives herself a once over in the huge mirror atop of the winding stairwell before waiting for Carolyn to arrive. However, Carolyn couldn't get there fast enough as she would soon be interrupted by Amir entering the front door with his briefcase in hand.

"Oh…off to a night on the town, are we?" Amir questions as he leans in and gives his daughter a kiss on the cheek.

"Yes father, I'm joining friends for a girl's night out." Ashima replies confused of her father's docile behavior this evening.

"Did Benjamin pick up the reports and take them over to the Trade Center today?"

"Yes, father and I gave him the envelope with the sticky note attached." Ashima assures him.

"Okay…that was very important and needed to be done. You look nice tonight, please enjoy yourself!" Amir rambles in a low exhausting tone.

"Father, you look tired. Perhaps you should get some rest?" Ashima urges as Amir looks like he's going to fall over.

136

"Oh-no! I have much too much work to do this evening. I wish I could afford the time to dress up and hang out with friends like you are doing." Amir replies with sly intent. Ashima, undaunted by the remark simply responds with a lofty grin.

"Well, I guess I'll see you tomorrow. Good night father!" Ashima bids him as she spots the headlights of a car pulling into the driveway.

"Okay Princess, have a good evening!" A tired Amir replies before heading up stairs with heavy feet.

Meanwhile, as a busy day at *Apex* comes to a close, Brian, Marty, and Cortez are loitering in the break room preparing to shift gears with plans to hang out at *The Fox* for a round or two of drinks.

"Yo, it's been a crazy week y'all, right? This week had that holiday tempo to it or something, right?" Cortez speaks out, lounging with his foot resting on a bench seat in the break room.

"Yeah, man. I can't believe its November already! Thanksgiving is right around the corner…it's almost time to break out that bubble coat." Brian replies.

"I know, I've hardly had a chance to catch up with y'all all week. Between Brandy whoopin' his ass and you on your non-stop whore tour…damn, what's up fellas? I miss y'all!" Marty candidly jokes.

"Better yet, what's up with the text messages about the collared shirts you sent earlier this week, 'B'?" Cortez questions with concerns about Brian's dress code request.

"Yeah, so is there a special occasion going on at *The Fox* tonight, or are you suddenly trying to fit in with the white-collar yuppies down there?" Marty inquires with equal concern.

"Naw, nothing like that...I just wanted to switch it up a little bit this week. You know…dare to do something different?" Brian explains with laughter.

"Okay, so we're not going to *The Fox* tonight?" Marty implies sensing Brian was up to something.

"Naw!" Brian quickly responds.

"Sooo…what did you have in mind?" Marty replies with a discerning look.

"Well, it's a new spot down at fifth and Chestnut I wanted to check out tonight. I heard they have a pretty good happy hour down there." Brian explains.

"Oh yeah, you're talking about that new spot *The Red Eye* in Society Hill in the hotel across from Independence Hall, right? Brandy told me about that place a few weeks ago. She said it was tight!" Cortez interjects.

"That's what's up! I'm down for something different. But, man, the parking situation is serious down there." Marty adds with concern.

"Exactly, that's why we need to make moves soon, before the after-work crowd gets a jump on us or park somewhere else and take the 'El' train." Brian suggests.

"Aight then, I'll see y'all down there." Cortez hastens, grabbing his bag which motivated the others.

"Yeah, 'I'ma' get up out of here before the break room Nazi, Vincent comes through here with his bull-ish!" Brian agrees.

"Oh, y'all ain't got to worry about Vince. I spoke with that fool this morning, and he told me he was leaving this afternoon to go to corporate in Houston for a conference." Marty informs them.

"Really...!" Brian astoundingly replies.

"Yup! I heard he tried to take your girl with him too. But, she gave him a lame excuse so she wouldn't have to go." Marty explains.

"You know what...I'm glad you said that. Since he's so hard pressed to get at Mal, 'I'ma' let him have exactly what he wants, and I hope he enjoys it." Brian contemplates with vindictive intent.

"I don't even like the way that sounds. What you 'bout to do, 'B'? 'Cause I know you ain't about to pass Mal off like that, especially not to a character like Vincent." Marty inquires, suspicious of his friend.

"Shhh...chill y'all. I'm not gone to do nothin' crazy. Just trust me!" Brian replies with a sneaky expression.

"Well, whatever you plan to do, just make sure it doesn't involve me losing my job, aight?" Cortez strongly urges.

"Trust me, he'll never find out, but you might not want to write home to mom about this one." Brian assures them with a crafty smile.

"Well, look I'm out! I'll see y'all down at the spot, aight!" Cortez concludes.

"Aight, y'all let's be out!" Marty seconds as they all head for the parking lot.

Shortly after 6pm, the fellas find themselves sitting at the bar of the *Red Eye Tavern*, enjoying beer, appetizers, and laughter. The earth-tone hue, contemporary open floor layout with rustic accents and wrap around loft area was vibrantly filled with young ambitious professionals letting their hair down relaxing and neckties open. The soft lighting, brick accented walls and soulful music set the social tone for this attractive and diverse Center City crowd, grateful for happy hour.

"Yo, this place is aight, 'B'. Nice ambiance, good food, good prices…hell, we may have to do this more often!" Cortez credits Brian, appreciating the change of venue.

"I agree Tez…Brian got us down here mingling with high society and all. The crème de la crème! Hmph, aside from circling the block about thirty times to find parking, this is definitely a good change of pace. Not to mention the diversity up in here this evening. Good lawd!" Marty lustfully observes.

"Oh, no doubt! There is definitely some potential in the building tonight, ya dig!" Brian concurs with an exuberant handshake with Marty.

"Uh huh…you got potential…and you got potential…" Cortez randomly utters as he singles out beautiful women with his eyes as they pass by.

"Excuse me guys. Hi, may I interest you guys in a round of our happy hour shots?" The young, flawless Ebony bartender asks with an unusual accent.

"Before I say yes and buy my friends here a round, I've got to tell you that I am in love with your hair and your accent. British, right?" Marty confesses, nearly drooling over the woman's afro-centric, ebony complexion, naturally twisted hair, gorgeous smile, and heavy foreign accent.

"Actually, it's Australian." The woman charmingly corrects him.

"Oh, you're an Aussie, huh? I didn't know they had black people back down under…especially none as fine as you. What brings you here to the states?" Marty asks, attempting to stimulate small talk.

"Well thank you, I'm flattered…and yes, there are actually quite a few black people in Australia. I was actually a military brat that lived there for 12 years. But, this is home, where I was born and my entire family is from." The woman replies with all smiles.

"Well, I know you have a job to do, Miss…?" Marty pauses to get her name.

"Eva, my name is Eva." She tantalizes Marty once again with her divine foreign dialect.

"Well, Miss Eva, I'm Marty and it was definitely a pleasure to meet you!" He replies as gently shaking her hand.

"Likewise, enjoy gentlemen!" After serving each of them house rum shots, Eva moves on to business as usual.

"Oh my God, did y'all see that Australian Goddess? And that ass…I didn't know they make asses like that in Australia! She had the girls all out, looking all sexy!" An overzealous Marty describes.

"Of course, how could we miss the pair of eyes tattooed on her lower back?" Cortez answers.

"Yup, too bad both of y'all got that matrimony disease. I'm proud of you though, Marty. For a minute there, I thought you were going to jump the counter and hump her leg or something…good choice staying tame there tiger." Brian teases as the fellas break out in laughter.

"Yeah, well, if y'all see a little moisture in the front of my pants, that ain't about nothing, aight! Don't judge me!" Marty jokes as he raises his shot glass to initiate a toast.

"Good choices…?!" Marty speaks out.

"Good choices!" They repeat at once, before toasting glasses and downing the shots.

"So, Brian, whatever happened with the Arab cat you were supposed to be hanging out with?" Marty inquires in a mildly inebriated tone.

"Awe man, I didn't tell y'all?! Yo, this weekend was so crazy I don't even know where to begin!" Brian replies with excitement.

"From the top would be a good start. Just keep it simple!" Marty insists.

"Aight, so Friday after we got off, I headed down Allegheny to check on my grandmother before heading to the crib. All of a sudden, I'm hearing cop cars, fire trucks, and ambulance sirens racing through the neighborhood like crazy. So, I called myself being nosey, since I had nothing else better to do, and I followed them to see what was up. Man, by the time I got to Allegheny, it was so many cars and people and cops, that you couldn't even drive down Allegheny Ave. You had to get out and walk to see what was going on. So, I park and walk up on the scene, only to see these cats I knew from back in the day laid out in the middle of 26th and Allegheny. They hit a bus head on and everything." Brian regretfully recalls.

"Yo, I seen that on the news that night. They got shot and had two young bors in the back seat that got killed too, right?" Cortez asks, corroborating the story.

"Yup…Tez, I could have lived the rest of my life without seeing something so violent. I got weak standing there, just imagining it being me or someone close to me. One of them was still holding an ice cream cone from the truck sitting at the corner only a block away." Brian explains.

"Wow, the bodies were still in the car when you got there?" Marty asks looking dumbfounded.

"Yeah, it must have happened less than ten minutes before I got there. The ice cream was just starting to melt. That's how recent it must have happened." Brian explains as the mood of the fellas went from upbeat to somber.

"Anyway, the next day I went out with my cousin for his birthday, and I had to turn on that Mojo 'cause the women were out in force that night. Man, I messed around and bagged this bad jawn at the club. A cute, little light skinned shorty from Abington. I mean, when her song came on, she snatched me up and we must have danced for like five songs straight. The DJ was killing it too! But, she must have been on that molly or something, because when the lights came on, she told her friends she's catching a ride with me. Her friends was on some, 'Naw, you're riding back with us, I don't care if we are six deep in an Altima, you're riding home with us'!" Brian further explains in animated fashion.

"Damn, six deep in an Altima to the club? Where they do that at?" Cortez clowns as the men continue to listen.

"Yeah! I know, right? Anyway, shorty was not having it. She was adamant about not riding on somebody's lap back to the crib. She told them she'd rather catch the bus or call a cab, and she was probably embarrassed explaining the situation in front of me. So, her peoples are looking at me as if I had some kind of control over the situation, and you know 'I'ma' look out 'cause 'I'ma' good dude. So, I explained to them that I'll make sure she gets home safe, blasé blah… you know, still on my Mojo. But, when she got in the car, she was like, 'I don't feel like going to the crib tonight, where do you live?' So, I told her where the spot was, and she said, 'Well, the nights still young, you feeling a night cap?' Mind you, it's damn near three in the morning and the night was not young, plus she don't know me from Adam, so she must have been on one. But, the way she put it on me on that dance floor, I was definitely trying to put her legs where my third eye could see. So, I stopped at the gas station and picked up some magnums, and the rest as they say, is history!" Brian recaps taking another swig of beer.

"Wow, Mojo does his thing, again!" Marty replies, giving Brian dap for his sexual antics.

"Well, that was Saturday. Then Sunday rolls around, and you know your boy, I've got to play host, 'cause I be hostin'! So, I blessed her with the cheese omelet and orange juice in the A.M. before we tussled again. Then I dropped her off on my way to meet with the Arab cat." Brian recalls.

"Whoa, whoa, whoa...you hit her with the cheese omelet, dawg?" Marty asks in disbelief.

"Yeah, I hit her with the cheese omelet, with the feta crumbles, diced tomatoes, cheese grits with cilantro on top, and all that!" Brian boasts with assurance.

"Oh sh...she must have put that thunder cat on him!" Marty proudly responds.

"Well damn, there's just never a dull moment in Mojo's world, huh?" Cortez implies with admiration, while Marty stares at Brian shaking his head.

"My man, Mo' to the 'Jo! So, you must really like this one, huh, 'B'?" Marty assumes.

"Naw, I wouldn't say all that. I mean, don't get me wrong, she's a nice girl and all...but, she wasn't exactly 'wifey' quality, ya mean?" Brian tries to justify.

"Oh, here we go! Aight, so where did this one go wrong?" Cortez blurts out.

"Negro please, when has a woman ever been wifey quality for Brian Jones?" Marty protests.

"Naw, y'all got to hear me out on this one though...just here me out on this one!" Brian pleads over the taunts of his friends.

"Aight, let's hear it then. What did this one do that didn't quite measure up to Mister Brian 'Mojo' Jones' standards? C'mon, give it to me raw, dawg!" Marty demands as he turns his chair backwards to get comfortable.

"Uh...you might not want to go there with him, Marty. This is Mo' to the 'Jo we're talking about. I mean, this dude here is liable to f*ck the crack of dawn. I'm just sayin'...!" Cortez cautions Marty.

142

"Yeah, you might be right on that one, Tez." Marty replies reconsidering his choice of words as he and Cortez gave each other a pound.

"Awe man, whatever! First of all, this ain't even a Mojo thang, this is a guy code thang we talkin' about, aight. Number one, she let me say 'hello' to the kitty on the first night. Now, you know I can't wife a jawn if she gives it up on the first night. If she spread eagle for me, you know she'll do it for the next cat and y'all already know that's a no go in the guy code handbook. Am I right?" Brian explains, seeking confirmation from Marty.

"True dat! I'll give you that one." Marty cosigns. Meanwhile, Cortez momentarily sits silent.

"Tez...?" Brian urged for a reply as he and Marty looked to Cortez for a response.

"Tez...! Brandy gave it up on the first night, didn't she?" Marty speculates in awkwardness.

"Yeah, man. She did, aight! We were young, we were drunk, she was feeling me, I was feeling her, blah, blah, blah...but, you never heard me speak of that, aight! Don't judge me, just love me, 'brothas'." Cortez confesses with added insecurity.

"Naw, no judgment this way, Bruh. It happens...it happens to the best of them. It'll never happen to 'me'! But, you're still my dawg, though." Brian supports. Marty simply nods in agreement.

"Anyway, aside from getting flagged for that, I was so gone off that Patron, I couldn't even remember shorty's name that night. But, I played it cool the next morning, vibin' with her and all, waiting for her to drop a name for me. Finally, makes a phone call on my way to drop her off and she says, 'Hey girl, this is Punkin...not Pumpkin, Punkin! Punkin?' C'mon y'all, we just had that conversation about dating chicks with a nickname of a food, fruit, or ingredient." Marty and Cortez look at each other with matching grins, then immediately busts into an outburst of laughter at Brian's dilemma.

"Dawg, you dismissed the chick because her name was Pumpkin? Man, pull your skirt up, 'B'. I'm about to revoke your hood card, for real!" Cortez teases.

"So, did the pie taste like pumpkin, 'cause I know ate a slice, you pie eating son of a b*tch!" Marty taunts him.

143

"No, it didn't taste like pumpkin…it tasted like pumpkin seeds, but that's beside the point!" Brian replies with a straight face before tipping his bottle to hide his embarrassing smirk.

Cortez nearly spat his beer across the bar trying to prevent from laughing so hard, while Marty was nearly reduced to tears from the antics. Even the bartender, who ear hustled the conversation could only shake his head.

"I'm just sayin', I'm not trying to wife no damn peaches, pumpkins, peanuts, or pomegranates, aight! I just want a nice dime piece to call wifey, that's all!" Brian concludes talking over the roar of laughter.

The laughter is so loud and contagious, it began to attract attention. The bartender passed Cortez a glass of ice water because he thought Cortez would pass out from the comic relief.

"Damn, I kinda liked that one too. But, oh well…" Brian randomly says. Once the excitement died to a reasonable calm, Marty speaks on the matter.

"See, I know what your problem is…you haven't been tested by a woman yet. You need to meet a woman that intimidates you, a strong, no nonsense, independent sista that's never needy and can bring to the table just as much as you can." Marty proclaims through his slurring speech.

"A boss chick!" Cortez co-signs at about the same intoxicated pace.

"A chick that's gone look past the superficial and recognize the true Mojo, I mean Brian Jones." Marty rationalizes, in his inebriated state.

"True dat!" Cortez confirms as he and Marty trade jabs at Brian. Before Brian could muster a response, he notices a few women in the loft that captures his attention.

"Awe man, is that's them?" Brian utters loud enough to be heard by the others.

"Who's them? Some other poor guy's daughter you've recently violated?" Marty sarcastically presumes.

"Naw, somebody else…" He passively replies, as his attention is completely locked in on what appears to be two of Ashima's friends he'd met on Sunday, enjoying martini's and looking over the railing at the crowd below.

His anxiety quickly rises, realizing that if Ashima's friends are here, then she would definitely in attendance as well. No sooner than pondering that notion, Brian notices the women suddenly waving eagerly to draw the attention of someone they spotted in the crowd below. At the same time, Marty reacts to someone or something that just walked in through the turnstyle entrance.

"Oh sh…! Now that's what I'm talking about!" Marty spontaneously exclaims.

"What? What happened?" Brian anxiously asks, as he and Cortez lean back in their chairs to investigate, looking in the direction that many other eyes in the venue followed.

"Fellas, I think I just seen the main attraction walk up in here…the headliner…the featured presentation and her legit Asian sidekick!" Marty exaggerates, lusting the sight of the women.

At first glance, there was nothing to see but a crowd of patrons and staff shuffling around.

"Damn, I lost them in the crowd. Just give it a minute!" Marty declares with frustration.

But, just as he requests their patience, the two stunning women emerge from the crowd, ascending the stairs to the loft area. Almost immediately, Brian identifies Ashima and another attractive friend he didn't meet on Sunday. The women gleefully wave to acknowledge their friends in the loft. Brian, Cortez, and Marty wasn't the only ones to take notice to the pair, as many others in the crowd followed the them up the stairwell as if they were prominent celebrities.

"Are y'all seeing this?" Marty asks, grabbing both of his friends by the neck to brace his self.

"Hello, my Asian persuasion. Yum, yum, dim, sum!" Cortez lustfully observes.

"Mmm…mmm…mmm…I need a drink on that note! Bartender please, Hennessy…on the rocks…no chaser!" An animated Marty requests.

"Dayum! Make that two!" Cortez seconds.

As the other's carry on, Brian sits in quiet awe, thrilled to see Ashima yet again. With even more eye-catching appeal than before, Brian was nearly convinced it wasn't her, until she placed her hand on the railing of the staircase and he notices that same tattoo art he remembered her wearing on Sunday. Captivated by her allure, Brian's eyes helplessly follow her every move as she climbs the stairwell. Suddenly to his surprise, she looks out at the sea of people and immediately single out Brian's fixation on her.

"Oh damn, I'm busted! Oh well, I'm sure she doesn't recognize me outside of an Apex uniform or a football jersey." Brian suggests, assuming his off-white button down with rolled sleeves, brown v-cut sweater vest, pair of tan Khakis, and striped Kangol hat, would conceal his identity. But, after a very brief stare, Ashima looks away and keeps it moving.

"Marty...Tez...that's her!" Brian abruptly announces.

"Who, Pumpkin spice?" Marty facetiously clowns.

"Naw, the Arab chick I was telling y'all about." Brian reminds them.

"Say what? Hold on, let me wipe the fog from these glasses, because I don't think we lookin' at the same girl." Marty insists with disbelief.

"Wait, let me see..." In an exaggerating gesture, Brian grabs Marty's glasses, wipes them clear with the bottom of his shirt, blows them clean, and peers through the lenses to take another look.

"Yup, that's her." Brian confirms with poise.

"Wow. Okay, now it all makes sense now. Switch it up a little, huh? You dragged me and Tez all the way down here to high society to 'holla' at ole girl, didn't you?" Marty confronts Brian revealing Brian's true motive. Unable to hide the truth, Brian avoids eye-contact, smiles, and sips his drink as Marty stares at him with a smile of his own.

"Mmm...hmm...that grin says it all. Well, I hope you brought your 'A' game with you because the girl I'm staring at looks nothing like a Pumpkin, peanut, or pomegranate!" Marty candidly makes clear.

"Yo, 'B', don't you think you're taking this Mojo thing a little too far? I mean, you're my man and all, and I love you like a dog love its mutts, but real-talk...she's a monster and might be a little out of your league!" Cortez asks with genuine concern.

"Not to mention your tax bracket." Marty adds.

"Oh, c'mon now! You've got to have faith, playas." Brian responds, brushing off his friend's lack of faith.

"Yeah, but you know there's a fine line between faith and stupidity, right?" Marty contends.

"Yeah, well I only stand to lose a buck, so I like my odds." Brian dismisses.

"Hell, after seeing what I'm betting against, I'll make it my whole check for a month! I mean, you got your hands full with this one, daddy! As a matter of fact..." Marty vibrantly taps the counter to get the bar tender's attention. "...bartender can you please hit my man off with a shot of liquid courage, 'cause it's gone take more than game and good looks to land that show piece!" Marty dubiously expresses. Brian responds by clapping to Marty's lack of confidence.

"I love it! I love the element of doubt! But, just remember, they don't call me the 'one-night stand running man' for nothing!" Brian boasts raising his glass to salute Marty before taking another sip of his drink.

Meanwhile, after making their grand entrance in the considerably populated venue and make their way through the crowd, Ashima and Carolyn draw the attention of many onlookers, while simply trying to rendezvous with their awaiting friends Naima and Crystal. The ladies weren't provocatively dressed, but the stunning Middle-Eastern and Asian duo even capture the attention of a few other well-kept female patrons who gives them a competitive stare. As they maneuvered their way to the end of the loft, they couldn't help but to notice the many eyes following in their direction. Ashima looks back at Carolyn with an embarrassing smile because at that moment, she realizes they didn't just walk into the venue to meet with friends for drinks, they stole and owned the whole damn moment.

"My goodness, you would think we were celebrities or something the way everyone is gawking at us." Ashima mentions, feeling uncomfortably flattered from the attention.

"Yeah, I know right! I didn't realize wearing a sundress and heels would command so much attention. Hmph, who knew?" Carolyn agrees as she downplays her stylish blue patterned, spaghetti strapped sundress with red open toe heels and red clutch. They both snicker at the attention.

When Ashima looks out to the crowd again, she immediately notices a smartly dressed guy at the bar that wouldn't take his eyes off of her. But, instead of provoking a staring rivalry, she made a mental note of it and turns away. Finally reaching her friends, they greeted her with a shriek of laughter.

"Yayyy...Shimaa...!" Naima calls out over the crowd noise. Ashima responds with equal elation.

"Hi girls, I finally made it!" Ashima replies.

Naima and Crystal greet Ashima with hugs and prissy cheek smooches, and although they didn't know Carolyn, they greeted her with prissy smooches as well. Crystal immediately signals for the waitress to add two more shots to the table because the girls were just in time for a round of lemon drops.

"Ladies, this is Carolyn. She's my best friend from college. But, she goes by her nick name, Lenny. Lenny, these are my crazy friends Crystal and Naima." Ashima introduces.

"Hi, Lenny from college. I'm sure if you're friends with this workaholic, then you must be good people." Crystal presumes.

"Hey now! If you had a father like mine, you'd be a working ball of stress, too." Ashima defends.

"Now see, that's exactly why we had to get you away from that misery so you could enjoy some much-needed downtime with the ladies tonight." Crystal says justifying her point.

"Yes, and there's so many people in here tonight." Ashima observes.

"Yeah, well it is almost seven o'clock, Shima!" Crystal replies reminding her of her tardiness.

"I know I should have come straight from work. But, the shoes I wore today were killing me. Speaking of coming, whatever happened to Jasmine? I haven't heard from her since the texting earlier." Ashima openly asks.

"Please...Shima, you know Jimmy has a choke hold on her. He's a very traditional, controlling Muslim man who's all about dominating her. He wants Jasmine doing nothing more than cleaning their home and bearing his children." Crystal explains.

"I know it's such a shame too. Jasmine is a really nice and fun girl to be around." Ashima agrees.

"That's why I've established a full understanding with Shelton before we get married, there will be no slavery to Islam in our household or there will be no marriage. Shima, you'd best be careful with Fahad too. He's quite capable of being a tyrant who's as idealistic about Islam as Jimmy." Naima warns.

"Well, I don't want to speak of Fahad this evening. That's a conversation for a later time. Tonight, I just want to have a good time, starting with these shots that have just arrived!" Ashima replies dismissing any talk of Fahad just as the waitress returns with the tray of lemon shots.

"Yes ladies, let's turn up!" Crystal exclaims as the girls all grab a shot glass garnished with a fresh lemon peel from the serving tray.

"So, what are we toasting to?" Naima asks as she lifts her glass to lead the women in a toast.

"How about no stress and sandy white beaches...?" Lenny blurts out.

"Yasss! A one-month cruise with no kids, no husband, and an all-male staff with beach bodies!" Crystal follows-up.

"Mmm…how about a rich Saudi Prince with no drama?" Naima adds as the girls waited for Ashima to finish the toast.

But, before she could deliver her response, she was interrupted by her phone ringing in her purse.

"Wait, hold that thought ladies…" Ashima says as she reaches into her purse to see whose calling.

She takes a deep sigh of disappointment as she reads the name, Fahad.

"Hmph, not tonight!" Ashima, says aloud, sending the call to voicemail, then turning her phone off.

The call from Fahad momentarily stole her enthusiasm. But, she refuses to allow her spirit to be broken and proceeds with the toast. Lifting her glass again, she has no regard for white sandy beaches, a trip with no kids, or a Prince as her friends did. At this moment, her desire yearned for something far more unpretentious.

"Umm…to happiness." She replies with strained optimism; picking her head up and lifting her glass significantly higher. Expecting a more exotic answer, the women pause for a moment to understand the reply.

"Hmph, to happiness…! Why not?" Crystal encourages, supporting Ashima's modest reply.

The women all look at each other before busting out with a loud feminine cackle, then toast their glasses before swallowing down the first shots of a great night. Ashima joins in the laughter with her friends, but was genuinely sincere about the toast. She arrived at the venue wearing the façade of happiness. But, was prepared to dissolve all of her displeasure in one night of amusement with her friends.

While the women were in the loft getting loose from what seemed like endless drinks and girl-talk, Brian and his friends were enjoying themselves at the bar below invested in a recap of Brian's Sunday with Amir.

"Look, all I'm saying is, based on everything you've explained, from the house, to the cars, to the half pint, Miami Vice, camel jockey that she's with; that the chips maybe stacked against you a bit, 'B'." Marty explains as the men were amid discussion of Brian's ambition to pursue Ashima.

"I mean, I hear you and all. But, what's the worst that could happen…she tells me no? Okay! I'm good with that. It won't be the first time, and you know my philosophy…next!" An annoyed Brian replies from his friend's lack of confidence.

"Okay then, roger that!" Marty concedes without further comment at the moment.

"Are you guys good? Do you need another round?" The bartender asks checking on the men.

"Yeah, we're good!" Marty and Cortez reply, while Brian has his back turned to the bar with his elbows propped on the counter, sipping his drink.

"How 'bout him?" The bartender asks as Brian never even flinched to acknowledge him.

"Who him? Dude, ain't listening right now. His head has been stuck in that loft since them 'jawns' came in her a minute ago. Just get him another shot of liquid courage so it can build up his immune system for rejection. I don't want my boy to fall too hard." Marty clarifies.

"So, what you gone do, playboy?" Cortez asks, prompting Brian for an answer to his dilemma.

"Hmph…!" Brian sighs, disappointed in his friend's confidence of him. However, he takes his time to acknowledge Cortez as he takes another sip from his glass, perceiving the question as a challenge.

"I'm about to go up in that loft and put a little Mojo on her is what I'm about to do!" Brian confidently replies.

"Whoa…are you serious?" Marty interjects.

"Dead serious! I mean, how will I ever meet my wife, if I never meet my wife?" Brian queries of his friends.

"So, you're telling me she's not going to end up another Mojo statistic?" Marty doubtfully replies.

"I mean, look at her. You're telling me you wouldn't wife that if you had a shot?" Brian asks convincingly.

"I would have probably 'wifed' a lot of the 'jawns' you tossed to the wayside. But, you're Brian Mojo Jones, and monogamy ain't exactly in your vocabulary." Cortez chimes in.

"Wait a minute, who's that up there with her?" Marty inquires as he notices the four beautiful women standing together.

"Oh, that's the other part of the team I seen her with on Sunday." Brian replies.

"Oh my God, there's four of them…?" An astounded Marty blurts out. Brian laughs at his friend's reaction.

"Yeah, I call them the Shahs of Philly." Brian replies as the fellas laugh at his proclamation.

"Yo, seriously though, I don't doubt your ability to get women. But, as bad as she is, that one right there might give you a little trouble." Cortez maintains.

"Yeah, well, I could use some trouble in my life, as a matter of fact..." Brian carelessly replies before tossing back what's left of his liquid courage then finishing his statement.

"...I'm 'bout to get into some trouble tonight!" Brian concludes leaving his finished glass at the bar and walking off.

Marty and Cortez, could only watch as their friend makes his way up to the loft for an uncertain encounter.

"You think we should follow him up to run interference? He looks like he might need some help." Cortez suggests, anxious to introduce himself to the women as well.

"Naw, just chill! I wanna enjoy this." Marty casually replies as he kept a watchful eye on what was about to unfold.

Preparing himself for the worst, Brian moves with a confident swagger as he makes his way towards the women. However, his confidence began to rapidly deflate as anxiety overtook him the closer gets. As he closed within arm's reach of the women, Brian uncharacteristically aborts his direct approach. He adjusts his hat a bit lower over his eyes and pulls out his phone as a diversion to breeze past the women and over to the bar in the loft. He realizes his tactic would have been a bit too direct, and he needed a drink in his hand to give him some since of purpose. Nonetheless, as he walks by he glances over at the women, and engages direct eye contact with Crystal who locks onto him as if his cover is blown.

"Apple Crown and cran please!" Brian exclaims over the volume of blaring speakers in proximity of the bar.

While waiting for his drink, Brian continues to fumble with his phone, pretending to look busy and trying to avoid looking over his shoulder at Ashima and her friends.

"Shima, isn't that the guy that came to Fahad's with your father on Sunday? Brian or something...?" Crystal asks, noticing Brian standing at the bar a few feet away.

"Yes, I believe it is..." Ashima confirms in a calmly perplexed tone. Although she recalls having a brief conversation with Brian Sunday about

151

the girls intended whereabouts this evening, she was a bit intrigued as to why she keeps running into him lately.

"Wow…perhaps I didn't notice it before, but he's a really attractive man. Don't you guys agree?" Naima, turns to ask the other ladies.

"Yes, I'd jump his bones if that's what you're asking?" Crystal boldly replies ahead of the others.

Ashima gasps astoundingly. "Crystal! I think that drink is getting the best of you."

"Yes Crys, you've definitely had too much to drink." Naima adds.

"What? All I said was that he was good looking. Is that a crime?" Crystal playfully denies.

The ladies suddenly burst into a loud female cackle at Crystal's humorous denial.

After paying for his drink, Brian turns to excuse himself through the crowd. But, his course was altered by a sudden tug at his wrist as he passed the women again.

"Excuse me! Aren't you the guy we met last Sunday that came with Amir…Brian, right?" Crystal shamelessly asks.

"Yeah, actually I am. Oh, I'm sorry I didn't even notice you were all here. How are y'all this evening?" Brian casually responds, carefully calculating his every reply.

"I told y'all it was him! Hi, I'm so glad you made it out!" Crystal cheerfully replies, giving him an inviting half hug.

Brian is taken aback by her enthusiastic reaction after the dry first encounter on Sunday. However, he obliges them by offering each of the women half hugs, to measure their reactions.

"Wow, I can't believe I didn't recognize y'all when I walked through the first time." Brian says trying to sell his apparent oversight of them.

"Oh, that's okay, I knew exactly who you were. I never forget a face. Besides, you said you would be here, so I knew to look out for you." Crystal explains.

"That's what's up, I'm glad you looked out. And…I don't believe we met on Sunday, I'm Brian." He says, introducing himself to Carolyn.

"Hi, I'm Carolyn." She responds leaning in for another hug.

"No, you're fine as hell is what you are! But, I'll call you Carolyn for now." Brian playfully says to himself as he moves on to Naima and then Ashima.

A chill raced up his back as it was Ashima's turn to be greeted. A chair stood between them from where she stood. So instead of creating an awkward moment, she extended her hand instead of embracing him with a half-hug.

"Hi, how are you this evening?" Brian asks with the most masculine, gentle voice.

"I'm well, thank you for asking, Brian from Apex." She replies pitching him a shy smile. Ashima replies in the most beautiful tone. Not only because of the way she naturally spoke, but his presence was comforting.

Immediately, Brian notices something different about the way she moved. The first time they shook hands, it was firm and business-like. But, this time there was a warm exchange of energy between them. Unlike Sunday, where she was visibly disturbed by her conflict with Fahad, tonight she appears more subtle and content. In the previous occasions she'd met Brian, she didn't think anymore of him than just another nice smile. But, tonight, in her feelings like a hopeless romantic, she quietly admires him, and found him easy on the eyes. She's curious of him and although not fully convinced, she feels compelled to know more about him. Meanwhile, Brian is simply enjoying her delicate touch and the softness of her hand. The greeting this time is noticeably more intimate than the others.

"So, did you come by yourself, or are your friends hiding from us?" Crystal curiously asks.

"Naw, actually I'm with those two cats down there at the bar looking up at us right now." Brian replies pointing his friends out for her.

"Okay, well we were just about to head up to the roof for more drinks and a change of atmosphere. You're more than welcome to come, if you'd like." Crystal implies.

"I'm sorry you said the rooftop?" Brian repeats to ensure he heard her correctly over the music.

"Yeah, up to the Stratus Lounge. You've never been up there?" Crystal asks in awe.

"Naw, this is the first I've ever heard of it." Brian replies

"Oh my God, you're going to love it! C'mon you're coming with us so you can see it firsthand. It's beautiful up there!" Crystal insists, interlocking her arm with his and leading the way with the others in tow.

153

The contrast in Crystal's behavior from Sunday clearly indicated that she's feeling whatever the bartender was serving her tonight; which prompted him to follow their lead and enjoy whichever way the night would take him. As Brian allows Crystal to lead him from the loft, he summons Marty and Cortez to follow him out with the ladies. Once the crew all gathers at the elevator and away from the crowd, Brian intends to introduce everyone.

"Hello Brian's friends! I hope you're as nice as he is." Crystal exclaims in a loud drunken slur.

"Haha…yeah, we're the good guys. This is Cortez and I'm Charles, but you can call me Marty." He replies in a soft charming voice, gently shaking her hand. His eyes are momentarily fixed on her abundant bust size, before lifting them to greet her.

"Marty huh? Well Marty, I'm Crystal, and these are my girls Naima, Ashima, and Carolyn." She replies, in a more subtle demeanor, after picking up Marty's vibe.

"Well, I was going to introduce all of us here, but thank you both for making my job a whole lot easier. Now that we got that out the way, it's a party!" Brian chimes in, stirring a laugh with everyone before walking on th

On the way, up to the rooftop lounge, the laughter is in abundance among the group as they amicably intermingle. When the doors of the elevator open, they step off into a stylish and sexy crowd dominated by upscale potential. The ambiance is more than what the fellas expected, and was nothing short of brilliant. The first thing that noticeably captured their attention, is the long island-like fireplace that burned vibrantly on the open terrace of the rooftop they could see from the indoor lounge area. Then there were the illuminated shelves of top-shelf liquor behind the bar, accented by a white wavy wall pattern that accentuated the classy décor. The illuminated bar made of a rock slab only added to the level of sexy they discovered 11 stories above the city. There were ethnicities of all kinds that graced the venue as they move about the interior of the bar to the outdoor patio area. The tall, trendy heat lamps situated on the patio, kept the air temp tolerable on the crisp autumn night. The women with the high heels, cleavage on display, and their freak'em dresses on were commanding attention tonight. On any other night, Brian would have been prowling the venue like a dog in heat with his tongue dangling out of his mouth. But, tonight, he found Ashima, and she was the only woman he could see in the building.

"Well Ladies, I know we just met and all, but I'm headed to the bar and I would love for you to join us for drinks." Marty requests in the joy of the moment.

"Aaw, that's so sweet of you! But, we actually reserved a table for bottle service. You're more than welcome to join us if you'd like." Crystal counters with an offer of her own. Taken aback by the lady's sudden surprise, the fellas didn't quite know how to respond.

"Naw, no disrespect, but we can't..." Brian starts before being abruptly interrupted.

"What? You can't swallow a pill of humility and let four attractive women have you to their table for drinks? I thought we were having fun?" Crystal asks, challenging the men to let down their ego. The fellas pause and give each other a befuddled look before someone finally answers.

"Umm…yeah. Well, since you put it that way, we wouldn't want to make it seem like we weren't enjoying ourselves, so…" Brian modestly replies with a gratifying grin of pleasure confirming his acceptance.

And enjoy themselves is exactly what they did. After being seated by their exclusive bartender at a table surrounded by a comfy couch and lounge chairs, the fellas found themselves comfortably lounging on a rooftop. Tapas, exclusive tableside cocktail service at their disposal and the most beautiful women in the venue playing host wasn't exactly what the fellas anticipated, but a night like this trumps a night at *The Fox* any day. There's an array of bottles of vodka, tequila, and wine lined up like they were having a tasting of some sort. The entire evening was unorthodox and unfamiliar to the men, who's used to buying the time of a woman versus being catered to, as these women insisted. As the camaraderie and comfort grew among the group, the spirits surely kept flowing. Before long, the venue shifts to a more upbeat tempo, and with it, so did the crowd.

"♪*Get up out your seat, you can have my drink, let me see you dance…♪*" The DJ spins as the crowd transforms from subtle socializing to fist pumps and excitement.

"Go…! Go…! Go…! Go…! Turn up! Turn up! Turn up!" Is all you heard from Naima and Crystal as they were certainly having a good time, and Marty is right there in good company cheering them on as they carry on like the ring leaders of a circus. Carolyn, on the other hand had no trouble being entertained by Cortez with their couch side conversation.

Ashima however, is enjoying herself a bit more conservatively; keeping it classy with glasses of white wine, champagne, and an occasional shot of tequila with rest of the gang. But, not in an arrogant sense; more like shy and reserved, as if she doesn't get out much. At one point, the women entertained themselves and each other with an Egyptian hand weaving dance they really seemed to enjoy. Ashima would occasionally join in, but only from her seat and for a very short while.

Brian plays it cool as well, trying to not be too assertive as everyone else interacts. While Marty and Cortez playfully joins in with the lady's dance moves, Brian watches from the sideline studying Ashima and her friend's mannerisms like a lion watching the pride, waiting for the right moment to make his move. Every now and then he'd throw her a compliment or passively make small talk to keep it social and avoid any awkward monotony. But, what really made his night, was sitting across

156

from her and quietly lusting after her features. Everything spells class about her as she sits with an elegant posture. Shoulders and back straight with her legs crossed and not a single hair follicle to be found on them. Even the way she held a glass and sipped from it while clearing the curly bangs from her face was nothing short of arousing for Brian.

To no avail, Brian wasn't certain that a night out with Ashima and her friends enjoying tableside bottle service was convincing enough that she would be receptive to his approach. This is a very uncharacteristic trait of Brian's confidence. Typically, he'd already be on to the next few women by now. But, Brian has never been challenged by this level of sophistication before. Ashima's refinement made it difficult for Brian to read her. So, while everyone was in the moment, Brian sips slowly and ponders his next move.

"What if I'm really not her type? What if she's really into that cornball she's engaged to? Dude ain't even into her like that and she might not even know it. Whatever, no matter how much I may doubt whether she's feeling me, it's killing me! I've got to do something about this, no matter how much I may doubt this. C'mon Brian, get it together! I'm Mojo, the one-night stand running man! I've got to show her how I move." Brian fights with his conscience, trying to convince himself to get over this embarrassing bashfulness he's experiencing. As the crowd dances to the rhythm of an upbeat moment, Marty comes over to check on Brian.

"What's up man...everything good?" Marty asks concern of Brian's chill mannerism.

"Yeah, man, I'm good! It's been love all night, right?" Brian responds as Marty places an arm around Brian's neck.

"Oh, it's definitely been on the love! Ever since we linked up with these girls, I've been trying to figure out exactly what is it I've done to deserve such a blessing; so, I can do it over and over and over again, ya' feel me?" Marty says as they laugh together.

"And your girl over there...what's her name? Umm...Crystal? My goodness, that womans got some skyscrapers! And you know 'I'ma' milkman! As a matter of fact, I wouldn't mind both of them fulfilling my 'minaj' fantasy, ya dig!" Marty implies, explaining his lustful desires of Crystal and Naima. Brian just shakes his head at his drunken friend, tolerating the intoxicating fumes from Marty's breath, strong enough to be eighty-proof.

157

"I see you over there trying to be some kind of gettin' over Casanova." Brian teases.

"Actually, that's ya' boy Cortez over there. Acting like he's about to walk out with that tonight. Knowing damn well Brandy will snap his neck. Look at him, sittin' over there probably boring her to death. Talking about immigration reform and Latin inequality, he ain't even Mexican!" Marty clowns.

"Ha! I see Tez over there. But, I see you over there too. And ole girl is definitely feeling you and that bald head of yours." Brian replies putting Marty on notice.

"Man, we've said some pretty crazy things about Arab women and all, but all bomb jokes aside, these girls are a lot of fun and sexy as hell! Every time I'm out there dancing and clowning with them, I'm not saying 'oh yeah, oh yeah...!' I'm trying to convince myself, 'I love my wife! I love my wife! I love my wife!' But, enough about me and my drunken indiscretions, what's up with you getting' at ole' girl?" Marty questions, shifting his focus back to Brian.

"What you mean, Marty? I'm chillin'!" Brian nonchalantly replies.

"C'mon, 'B'! I know your trying to play it cool and all, but this ain't the Mojo I know. The Mojo I know would have been all in her ear, hittin' her with the Germantown brown, makin' plans to give her the one-night stand running man by now! That's all I'm saying. I mean, that's the whole reason why we're here tonight, right?" Marty reminds him.

"I can't front Marty, you know I stands 'em up and knocks 'em down like bowling pins. But, truth is, I've never come at an Arab woman before. And you know how they do...their parents ain't settling for their kids to be anything less than doctors, lawyers, and engineers. And the Arab women don't just want 'any' doctors, lawyers, and engineers...they want successful ones, ya dig!" Brian shamefully admits.

"Yeah, I hear you. But, I'm starting to wonder if I had you figured all wrong. 'Cause I thought your playbook had no boundaries, playa? I mean, don't get me wrong, shorty is without a doubt the headliner for the evening, her and her crew. But, I ain't ever known you to take a back seat to a challenge, playboy!" Marty struggles to understand.

"C'mon now, have faith in ya' boy. I never said the mission was impossible. I just feel like I need to get her away from her friends, so I can

158

really figure out her vibe without all the interference." Brian explains, shedding light on Marty's confusion.

"Okay, well here's your chance. She's on your six as we speak and it looks like she's heading to the lady's room to tinkle. Ayo, just be yourself, man! Aight...do you!" Marty alerts him, observing Ashima's movement on Brian's blindside.

"Bet! You find out about the food and 'I'ma' go handle my handle, aight...how I look?" Brian asks as he playfully arches his eyebrows with his fingers and strokes his Goat-T.

"What?! Get outta here!" Marty demands as Brian scurries off.

Patiently, Brian maneuvers his way through the crowd, giving Ashima enough time to exit the restroom in an attempt to make running into her seem incidental. But, before executing his plan, he's suddenly interrupted by his phone vibrating with a text notification.

(Text)
Mallory: *"Hey sexy, u comin' though 2nite?"*

"Hmph..." Brian gestures, humoring himself over the message.
Brian: *"Might be late when I get there, but I can manage that."*
Mallory: *"That's ok. I just finished a bottle of wine and I could use some attention tonight."* ☺
Brian: *"Aight, I'll see you then."*

Brian responds. But, before he could put his phone away, he receives another random text message.
Pumpkin: *"Hey stranger!"*

Wow, these chicks must have their radars up tonight or something? He thinks to himself, amazed by the timing of the messages. But, this text will go unanswered, as he spots Ashima on the move and he didn't want to risk the opportunity to engage her alone. With his drink in his left hand and his phone in his right, Brian studies his phone like an important distraction, while moving towards Ashima to intercept her. Although he'd made up his mind that she was way to fly for him, he was committed to making his move.

"Oh hey...!" Brian nervously greets as he fakes a slight incidental nudge.

"Hi!" She pleasantly smiles, delightfully looking up at Brian as the pair nervously face-off amid the busy venue.

"Going in for another round of Martini's, huh?" Brian asks, measuring her level of interest.

"I'm sorry, I didn't hear you." Ashima responds, because she couldn't hear him over the music.

"I said, going in for another Martini?" Brian leans in and repeats in a subtle tone.

"Oh-no! I'm not a big drinker. My friends are so crazy…they've been giving me drinks since I got here. As much as I've enjoyed them, I couldn't possibly have another." Ashima modestly explains leaning closer to Brian's ear. The glassy look of her eyes supports her claim as she clearly appears tipsy at this point.

"Yeah, I can respect that. Speaking of friends, I just want to thank y'all again for being great hosts tonight. I think my boys are still in shock about what's happened tonight. It's not often that four beautiful women are adamant about having three strange guys join them for drinks." Brian gracefully states.

"Well, I'm glad you're having fun. My friends and I get tired of all the creeps that try to talk to us with their silly cat calls and disrespect when we go out. We'd rather hang out with people we know. Besides, you're not a stranger. I know who you are and I know where you work." Ashima voices pleasurably.

"That's good to know. I hope me and the fellas have given y'all a better impression than what you're used to?" While conversing with her, he feels like he was standing center stage in the crowded room. Men and women alike were passively cueing side stares as deliberate signs of envy. Brian ate it up, embracing every glare like he was the man.

"Trust me, you guys are the reason we're even here past eight o'clock. If you were the typical type, we would already be at another venue, or anywhere but here!" Ashima shamelessly admits.

"Well, I hope a compliment wouldn't be typical at this point, but you're really wearing that dress." Brian confidently confesses.

"Thank you and I appreciate you being a gentleman." She gracefully replies as she looks at him fondly.

Until this moment, Ashima didn't think much of Brian. Every moment beforehand, she either looked him off with no regard, or engaged him

160

passively. The idea of taking it there with someone not relative to her upbringing was not an idea she was willing to consider. However, tonight would prove to be different. In spite of her inebriated influence and the bitter emotions of her nauseating life, Brian's laid-back demeanor and handsome appeal made her want to open up and find out a bit more about Brian Jones from *Apex*.

"Well, a gentleman can only live up to his name by the way he treats a woman. My grandmother used to always tell me that." Brian profoundly explains.

"Your grandmother sounds like a wonderful woman." Ashima politely replies.

"Yeah, she's a sweetheart!" Brian agrees.

"I'm sure she is. Well, it looks like my friends are ready to wrap it up for the evening, so I guess I better join them and figure out how to get them home in one piece." Ashima replies taking notice to her friends all standing with their purses in hand.

"Oh, no doubt! I don't want to hold you up. I mean, that's probably my cue too. But, umm…before you go, I noticed from Sunday that you have a situation and all, but I was wondering if there was any chance that we could…I mean, we had a really good time tonight and I was hoping that we could possibly be friends, that's all." Brian nervously pleads his case.

"Hmm…well perhaps you should get to know me a bit better, because my situation may not be a situation at all. Perhaps, more like a misunderstanding." She cleverly replies as she hands him her cell phone. Although amazed that he actually pulled it off, he plays it cool and confidently enters his information. Ashima on the other hand, found his shyness and perfectly aligned smile endearing and felt content with her decision to establish a friendship with him. After returning to the table to leave with their friends, Marty seeks out Brian for a side conversation.

"Yo, let me holla at you real quick, dawg!" Marty calls out over the music and crowd noise.

Just as Brian and Ashima are able to have a comfortable exchange and put their emotions at ease to enjoy themselves, the evening is short lived after Crystal and Naima decides to call it a night at a respectable time. Although Ashima and Carolyn would have preferred to stay a bit longer, out of respect for their married friends, they all decide to leave as a group.

"Ayo Dawg, we got a situation!" Marty announces in a cheery and intoxicated as he places his arm around Brian with a drink in hand.

"What's up? What I miss?" Brian asks prepared to hear his friend's drunken confession.

"Well, as you can clearly see, none of us are in a position to drive tonight, and the girls made me promise them that we would all take cabs home. So, me and Tez will take a cab back out West. The girls agreed to share a cab all around the city and you get to ride home all by yourself." Marty explains, summarizing the strategy.

"Damn, I was hoping to convince them to stay longer." Brian replies, eager to extend the evening since having a moment with Ashima.

"Yeah, but Happy Hour can't last all night when you're dealing with married women. Besides, you wait to holla five minutes ago when we've been in here for hours. And one of them already called a cab or Uber anyway, so it's a rap for tonight!" Marty explains.

As Naima takes care of the bill and Ashima pitches in for the tip, Cortez also stood-by to talk at Brian.

"Yo, man, I just wanted to tell you I really had a good time tonight, 'B'. I mean, from the happy hour, to the rooftop, to the bottle service, and most importantly, the girls...I had a good damn time! Especially with that Asian sensation Carolyn over there! My Lord...yum, yum, dim-sum is right!" Cortez dramatically expresses his gratitude with his breath smelling three time the legal limit.

"Yeah, well you might want to go to the bathroom before heading home and get the stench of a 'good time' with another woman off your face before Brandy sees it. Remember, I live in a studio apartment. I ain't got room for extra bags and furniture." Brian replies as Cortez laughs off Brian's blunt warning.

"Hey, a man can flirt and dream, can't he? I don't see a crime in that." Cortez protests.

"Look, you ain't got to convince me Bruh, I'm just trying to look out for your domestic situation. But, never mind all that. They're ready to go, so let's be out!" Brian urges watching the mixologist return with the check booklet. Brian also observes Ashima reach into her clutch and drop three crisp one hundred-dollar bills in the booklet for a tip.

"Five letter shopping, huh...?" He ponders, reminded by Marty's forewarning about affluent women and their spending habits. But, without

investing in too much thought, he simply takes a mental note and exits the venues with the others.

They empty out onto Chestnut Street to a seasonal chill in the air, where three double parked black town cars are parked out front, instead of three taxi cabs the fellas were anticipating. The drivers were each standing by the rear doors waiting to open them for their arriving passengers.

"Damn, that ain't us, is it?" Cortez asks in awe. However, his astonishment fell on deaf ears as no one replies to his spontaneous query.

"Whew…it's chilly out here! We need to say these good-byes quick, so we can go!" Naima exclaims with her arms folded tightly to keep warm.

"Actually, Brian lives closer to Ashima than we do, and Carolyn said she lives in Brewery Town. So instead of us taking a ride all around the city, why doesn't he ride with Shima and Carolyn and y'all can drop Carolyn off along the way?" Crystal rationally suggests.

"I'm good with that as long as the ladies don't mind." Brian gladly agrees.

"Okay! Sounds good! It's cold! I'm getting in! Good night everyone!" Naima hastily concludes before climbing in the warm car.

"Okay…that's the move then!" Marty confirms as the fella's exchange hugs with each of the ladies.

"I was worried about you for a minute there. But, looks like my main man Mojo strikes again!" Marty patronizes embracing Brian's alter ego.

"Haha, no doubt. But, you should be worried about your man Tez, lookin' like 'Joe suck head' over there." Brian replies referring to Cortez's inebriated state.

"Tez get home, Boy!" Brian calls out.

"I'm already gone!" Cortez responds with a tired voice.

"Yeah, he's gone alright! Yo, 'B'. I'll call you, man!" Marty says, hurrying the sloshed Cortez to the car.

"Have a good night people!" Marty shouts to everyone as they all depart.

"Good evening folks, I'm Thomas and I'll be your driver this evening." The middle-aged, grey haired, Caucasian man greets after opening the door for them.

"Hi Thomas, actually we'll be going two places. Brewery Town first, and then East Falls please!" Carolyn requests, leaning forward as she sits between Brian and Ashima.

163

"Okay folks!" Thomas acknowledges before tuning in to his Frank Sinatra on the radio.

"So, Brian, did you enjoy yourself this evening? We didn't really get a chance to talk tonight because you were so quiet. Are you always this quiet?" Carolyn asks.

"Well, I'm usually a really social dude. But, I like to chill when I get a few drinks in me. I did enjoy y'all and I really appreciate what you ladies did tonight. Very classy!" Brian expresses with gratitude.

"I'm sorry, what did we do?" A bewildered Carolyn asks.

"You know…inviting us over for bottle service and being great hosts." Brian elaborates.

"Oh, actually I wasn't sure who was picking up the check. I just offered to help pay the bill. But, apparently Naima and Shima took care of everything." Carolyn explains.

"Lenny, you know I got you whenever we go out. I could never repay you enough for lending me your brain at Wharton." Ashima graciously replies.

"I know, I know. But, I just feel like such a deadbeat when I don't contribute something to our outings. I mean, I make pretty good money too, ya know!" Carolyn insists.

"Well, you can't put a price tag on friendship, right? Besides, if it means that much to you, I'll let you treat for our first night in Vegas next week, okay?" Ashima proposes.

"Hmm…Okay!" Carolyn agrees.

As Brian sits quietly listening to the women flatter each other, he couldn't help but be reminded of not only how beautiful Ashima is, but how sexy her Asian friend is as well. Of course, being the promiscuous prowler he is, he couldn't resist the urge of an inappropriate thought or two.

"Man, Cortez was right, you are sexy as hell! Brian lusts, suggesting what Cortez said earlier about the young Asian vision.

"Mmm…I'm sorry, but that is a really nice scent you're wearing. I'm surprised I didn't notice it before. If you don't mind me asking, what is that?" Carolyn asks, suddenly distracted by the pleasant scent Brian is wearing.

"Black Code, right?" Ashima interrupts.

"Yeah, actually it is…a favorite of yours?" Brian asks, impressed by Ashima's knowledge of the fragrance.

"It's one that I've certainly noticed recently. It's even better when a man knows how to wear it like your wearing it." Ashima explains as the two talk across Carolyn.

"How's that?" Brian inquires, trying to carry the conversation.

"Code is a soft, subtle fragrance. Men often overdo it, thinking it's not strong enough. But, it looks like you figured it out." Ashima elaborates.

"Well thank you. Hit the neck twice and once for the wrists is how the men in my family were taught." Brian replies.

"Hmph..." Ashima gestures, offering Brian a deliberate stare and a smile unconventional to her usual shyness.

The influence of desire and alcohol inspires Ashima to shed her passive interactions and channel her inner carefree, at least for one night. Brian reciprocates with a cunning smile of his own. The energy exchanged between them is no ordinary interaction, this was chemistry. However, Ashima's nonverbal reply opens the door to an awkward moment of silence.

"So, Brian, speaking of Vegas, you look like you're no stranger to the Sin City. What's your favorite spot on the strip?" Carolyn presumes to break up the monotony of the moment.

"Well, I'd love to tell you I have to impress you, but I'm more of an Atlantic City and *Parx Casino* guy myself." Brian modestly replies.

"Oh okay! Nothing wrong with that...you like to keep it close to home. Probably like you keep your poker hand, right?" Carolyn suggests with sarcasm.

"Actually, I've always been a fan of roulette when I gamble." Brian admits.

"Wow, sounds risky!" Carolyn replies.

"Not really...you see, if you stay loyal to your numbers, eventually it may become worth the risk. Now, how much you risk, determines whether it was worth the reward in the end." Brian subliminally explains.

"Hmm...good theory. I think I'm all set to play some roulette next week, Shima!" Carolyn replies, impressed by Brian's swagger and advice.

"Yeah, I think I'll lay a bet down with you." Ashima playfully agrees.

"Umm...left on 31st Street, 1307 please!" Carolyn requests of Thomas.

"Well Brian, it has been a pleasure to meet you. I had a lot of fun with you and your friends and uh...thanks for the gambling tip. I'll try to put it to good use next week." Carolyn states as the driver pulls to a slow stop in front of her address.

"Likewise, good times and best of luck next week!" Brian replies before Ashima opens the door to let Carolyn out.

"Dayum!" Brian says sizing up both women with a lustful glare out the corner of his eye they stand outside the car.

"So, are you going to be alright? I mean, we had a great time with him and his friends and all, but…I'm just saying, the world is full of crazies, and I don't want to read about you in the paper tomorrow." Carolyn appeals of her friend's decision.

"Who…him? Please…he's harmless! I'd be more fearful of Fahad stalking me than be worried about him." Ashima dismisses.

"But, Shima, how well do you know him?" Carolyn questions with concern.

"He delivers for Apex. He's been delivering at my house for years. I met him a few times recently and he's delivered to my work. Lenny trust me, he's one of the good guys." Ashima replies, vouching Brian's credibility.

"Well, he's really handsome and that cologne he's wearing is really nice!" Carolyn admits looking over Ashima's shoulder to take another look.

"Yeah, I know that fragrance all too well. I remember when Fahad tried to wear code, but it stunk on him!" Ashima reveals with an embarrassing smile.

"Ashima…!" Carolyn gasps in utter disbelief.

"Well, it's true. I've never smelled that fragrance so good on a man before." Ashima shamelessly admits.

"Is that right? Okay then, so how is that going to work…with Fahad, I mean?" A giddy Carolyn questions.

"Oh my God, Lenny! I said he smells good, I didn't say I was going to sleep with him?" Ashima denies with a devilish smirk.

"No, but you didn't say that you wouldn't neither, so there! Listen, all I'm saying is that I have a really handsome bed in my guestroom too…I'm just saying!" Carolyn teases sticking her tongue out.

"Oh, whatever Lenny! Speaking of handsome, what are your thoughts of his friend, Cortez? I saw you over there investing a lot of your time with him on the couch. It seemed pretty intimate to me." Ashima teases back as the pair cackle a bit.

166

"Well yeah, he was very nice, cute, and he had great conversation. But, I don't do married, Shima. Sorry!" Carolyn expresses with disappointment.

Ashima responds with a deep gasping sigh. "He told you he was married?"

"No, but there was a ring missing from his tanned finger." Carolyn replies.

"Wow Lenny, you're so observant!" Ashima replies, amazed at her friend's attention to detail.

"I graduated Cum Laude, remember?" Carolyn jokes as the ladies share a cackling moment yet again.

"Anyway, the meters running and Brian is waiting, so I'm not going to hold you. Besides you look really tired too, so..." Carolyn implies.

"Okay, I'll get going then. Love ya!"

"Love you too, be safe!" Carolyn replies as the two exchange smooches.

"Bye Brian!" Carolyn yells as Ashima opened the door to get in.

"Good night!" Brian responds with a casual wave. After waiting momentarily for Carolyn to open her front door safely, Thomas pulls off.

"Gypsy Lane, East Falls please!" Ashima requests of the driver.

"Interstate 76 or the drive Ma'am?" Thomas asks in case she had a preference.

"East River Drive is fine!" Ashima replies.

"Sorry to keep you waiting. My friend just wanted to make sure that I'll be safe." Ashima explains as she turns her attention to Brian and settles back into her seat.

"It's okay, I understand. You have great friends that care about you. That's a good friend to have." Brian modestly agrees, calculating his every reply to impress her.

"Awe that's so sweet of you. Lenny and I have been really close since we were roomies in college." She appreciates, embracing Brian's compassionate charm.

"So...are you safe?" Brian asks rhetorically.

"Yeah...I think I'm pretty safe." She responds in the most delicately accepting voice.

Her unwavering eye contact confirms the truth of her response. Brian is elated by her response, but is also a bit concerned about the glazed look over her face. Her eyes hung low as if she is very exhausted.

"Are you sure you're okay? You look really tired." Brian asks with a heightened sense of concern.

"Well, it has been a long day. Please forgive me if I look tired. I guess all work and play in one day has become a bit overwhelming." Ashima explains as Brian nods his head with a smile of understanding. But, his concern for her made him lost for words and the car goes awkwardly silent. Only the sound of Thomas' contemporary jazz tunes filled the void of conversation.

"So, and then there was two!" Brian re-opens the conversation.

"Yes...and then there was..." Ashima pauses to cover her mouth as she struggles to hold it together from a fierce and sudden nauseating gag.

"I'm sorry, driver could you please pull over!" She urgently requests with dire constraint.

"Are you okay?" Brian calmly asks looking over at her and noticing her face turning red.

"Yes, I'm fine!" Ashima quickly responds.

"Ma'am, I can get you to the house in about five minutes. Are you sure you don't want me to just take you home?" Thomas suggests, unaware of what's happening.

After allowing herself a moment to regain composure, she throws her purse on the seat between herself and Brian and clutches her stomach and mouth to suppress another threat of nausea.

"NO PLEASE! Right here is fine, please just stop the car!" She declares, barely able to hang on.

"Ayo, she's sick my man, pull over!" Brian implores the driver in reaction to her distressing gestures.

As the driver slows to a stop, Ashima opens the car door, leans outward and lets out a violent roar of vomit onto the street. Instinctively, Brian immediately slides over to her aid and rubs her back to comfort her, and to ensure she doesn't fall out the car as she continues to relieve herself onto the street. After a few agonizing heaves, she finally lifts herself back into the car and gathers herself.

"You aight?" Brian asks again, as he continues to gently rub her back and observes her trying to catch her breath.

168

"I'm so sorry…please give me a moment!" Ashima pleads as she tries to find comfort in a still position.

"Here you go…this might help." Thomas offers, passing Brian an unopened bottle of water.

"Thanks boss! I appreciate it!" Brian replies, opening the bottle and offering it to Ashima.

"Here ya' go, this might help…you can rinse your mouth out and take a few sips of this." Brian presents the bottle to her.

"Thank you." She replies pushing the hair from her face and sniffling as she lifts her head to acknowledge him. She takes the bottle and after swishing and rinsing a few times, she takes a few swallows for herself as Brian advised. She appears to be doing better afterwards.

"Feeling better?" Brian asks, noticing the color returning to her face. Still sitting close enough to comfort her, with his arm now comfortably atop of her headrest.

"Yes…thank you so much. Oh my God! I'm so embarrassed right now! I can't let my father see me like this. I'll never hear the end of it." She replies in a faint, sleepy voice as she takes another sip of water, then falls back into the seat. After reaching over Ashima to close the door, Thomas picks it up a bit to get her home as fast as the speed limit will allow.

"Naw, it's okay. I've been there before far too many times myself." Brian exaggerates to help her feel better about her unpleasant circumstance.

With one hand on her stomach and the other on her forehead, Ashima rests for a moment to let her stomach settle. Then, to Brian's surprise, as Thomas makes a turn, Ashima falls carelessly into the pit of his arm. Feeling comfortable and confident, Brian wraps his arm around Ashima to secure and comfort her like a gentleman.

"Wow, this just feels nice!" Brian says holding Ashima as if she belonged to him, if only for that moment. But, he couldn't under mind the fact that in her vulnerable state, he's only playing the role of a concerned friend for now.

Meanwhile, Thomas eventually takes onto Gypsy Lanes and heads up the hill to drop off Ashima. However, she hasn't uttered a word since her heaving episode.

"You need me to walk you to the door?" Brian asks as her head now lay relaxed on his chest. But, his question goes unanswered.

"Okay, here we are folks!" The driver announces as he prepares to pull into the driveway.

"Hey, hold up right here Thomas, before you pull into the driveway. I don't think she's ready yet." Brian requests, to allow time for Ashima to become coherent.

"You got it, boss!" Thomas replies.

"Ashima...Ashima your home. Are you going to be okay?" Brian gently nudges her to respond. She reacts with a heavy sigh of exhaustion.

Brian looks up and notices Thomas eyes fixed on them from the rearview mirror as he patiently waits.

"Thomas, what you think, man? She's back here sleepin'!" Brian asks facing the challenging decision to let her face her father in her embarrassing state, or take her with him and allow her to sober up.

"Well, I don't mean to pry in your business, but she did say she can't go home like that. And, you look like a guy who was raised right, so as long as you're not some kind of creep, I would let her sleep it off at your place." Thomas suggests as Brian nervously laughs.

"Haha...naw, I'm not weird, Thomas. I come from good stock." Brian replies.

"Alright, so where to young man?" Thomas asks awaiting an address.

"Wayne and Walnut Lane." Brian answers, hoping for the best with his decision as Thomas pulls off for the short drive to his apartment.

"So, is that your lady friend, or a friendly lady?" Thomas asks communicating through the rearview as he drives.

"Oh, she's just a friend...nothing serious." Brian replies in absolute truth in case she's not as sleepy as she appears.

"Well, she's a very pretty young lady, and you're not a bad looking young man. I think one day, you two will figure it out." Thomas implies observing her embedded in Brian's arm.

"Thanks Thomas. Maybe one day we will." Brian replies appreciating the comment. Thomas pulls into the parking lot of Brian's apartment building and parks in front to open Ashima's door.

"Hey, are you awake?" Brian nudges Ashima to help wake her.

"Yes, but I'm afraid to open my eyes...everything is spinning right now!" She faintly replies.

"Okay, I'm coming around to help you, aight? I got you!" Brian assures her before walking around the car to assist.

170

"Hey, thanks for everything Thomas. I really appreciate you helping me out with her. How much do I owe you for the water?" Brian modestly asks.

"Don't worry about it. Just take care of your lady friend, alright. Have a good night!" Thomas humbly declines.

"Thanks boss, I'll do just that. Stay safe!" Brian replies as he grabs he purse off the seat and takes Ashima by the hand to supports her to her feet, before closing the car door.

"Wait, where are we?" Ashima asks alarmingly, struggling to open her eyes and realizing her surroundings were not familiar.

"Well, I hope you don't mind, but I couldn't get you to wake up when the driver went to your place, so I brought you to my place so you can sober up and get some rest. Now, you can trust me to do this for you, or I can call a cab for you right now and we can wait for him out here on the steps. I promise I'm not weird and I won't be fresh or any nonsense like that!" Brian nervously explains with assurance.

"Okay, I trust you." She carelessly replies, as she's more concerned with shaking her intoxicated state than any distrust in Brian.

"Okay, here we go…" Brian replies as he reaches around her waist to support her up the stairs and she responds by doing the same, resting her head on his chest.

Brian enters his apartment and immediately sits Ashima down on his neatly made bed which is positioned next to the door of his humble studio apartment. Aware of how sensitive her eyes were, he is reluctant to switch on any bright lights until he reaches the kitchen area.

"May I use your restroom, please?" Ashima requests in a very delicate tone.

"Yes, it's to your left. Can I get you anything?" Brian offers in a caring effort.

"No thank you. I'll be fine." She replies as she heads towards the bathroom. Fortunately, Brian maintains a clean household and keeps it on point for unexpected female company.

However, he undermines her modesty and decides to prepare something for her anyway. As he rambles through his cabinet for what he needs, he starts to have a surreal moment. Taken aback by the idea of having this intimidating Goddess of a woman in his apartment, about to fall asleep in his bed is unbelievable.

171

"Dear God, thank you!" Brian whispers to himself, grateful for the opportunity to even get this far with her. Ashima quickly returns from the bathroom and immediately sits at the edge of his bed.

"You have a very quaint apartment, Brian. And a woman always appreciates a man who keeps a clean bathroom." Ashima compliments, despite still feeling uneasy.

"Well, thank you. I know it's not much, but I try to take pride in the little bit that I have." Brian replies with a slight insecurity about his humble home.

"So, I know you said you were okay, but I've actually tried this a few times and believe it or not, it actually helps. Would you like to try it?" Brian asks, holding a bottle of water in one hand, while holding a bottle of honey and a tablespoon in the other.

"Umm…sure, I'll take your word for it. How does it work?" She inquires.

"Well, you take a spoon of this…" Brian says as he squeezes honey onto the spoon and hands it to her.

"Okay…" Ashima complies, swallowing down the spoon of honey.

"…now, you drink as much water as you can." Brian continues handing her the bottled water and taking the spoon. "Take as much time as you need to finish it. 'I'ma' go back into the kitchen and knock out a few dishes really quick." Brian says excusing himself.

"Okay, thank you! I really hope this helps." Ashima replies.

He pauses momentarily to take in how beautiful Ashima really is before returning to the kitchen. The room fell silent, as neither one of them says another word. After loading the dishwasher and wiping the counter, Brian realizes that he hadn't heard any movement coming from the other side of the room. He peeks around the dividing wall into the common space and finds Ashima sleeping peacefully, curled up on his bed clutching one of his pillows. Her shoes were still on and a half the bottle of water standing on the floor. Brian shakes his head as he walks over to grab a blanket from the bottom of his closet and drapes it over her like a true gentleman. Then he removes her shoes before laying out a blanket across his futon for himself. He too, remained fully clothed to avoid any awkwardness in his boxers, which is how he would normally prepare for bed.

Before calling it a night he couldn't help but to send Marty a text to let him know he made it safe and to let him know he's not alone.

(Text)

Brian: *"Yo, I'm at the spot. Ole' girl came back with me. I'll hit you in the A.M..."* Send.

Just Imagine

The next morning, Brian sluggishly awakes to the sound of a.m. traffic and movement from his neighbors above. Groggy from the night before, he slowly opens his eyes and quickly realizes that his face is embedded in a puddle of slobbering drool. His eyes immediately spring open, realizing he didn't come home last night alone. His eyes strain to focus as his head pops up and looks over to his bed to ensure that last night's events wasn't a bizarre dream.

To his surprise, there was nothing more than a neatly made bed, with no sign of Ashima. Confused by her absence, he wipes the wet drool from his cheek, stands to his feet and looks around his studio in hopes of finding her either in the kitchen or the bathroom. After a quick check of the kitchen, he takes a diminished walk the bathroom before noticing the only evidence of her being there was a lonely note lying on his bed.

"Oh boy!" He says as he sits on the edge of his bed, skeptical of what he's about to read.

Brian,
Please forgive me for my very sloppy behavior last night. I can't put into words of how embarrassed I am. I could only imagine what you think of me this morning. I'm not even sure how I ended up at your apartment. But, I can't thank you enough for being such a gentleman. Thank you for giving me your bed and taking care of me. xoxo
-Ashima

BTW...your bed is very comfortable and I love your blanket! ☺

"Hmph…" A relieved Brian gestures with the biggest smile of relief on his face.

He falls back and lounges comfortably across his bed as snapshot images of last night flashes through his mind. Judging from how the night played out, and the hand-written note from this morning, Brian was somewhat convinced that he was in a good place with Ashima. Yearning for any other trace of her being there, he curiously reaches over and grabs his blanket to find her fragrance.

"Mmm..." he reacts after burying his face in the fabric as the scent of her perfume vividly reminds him of her. Still, the anxiety of uncertainty would grow as he lay stretched across his bed in a euphoric moment.

"So, what now?" He thinks to himself, as his brain races a mile a minute, pondering the 'what if's' and possibilities.

He thinks about the idea of calling, but remembers that when he put his number in her phone, he never called himself to lock her number in. However, across the room, Brian can see his phone blinking, indicating that he has missed messages. Without hesitation, he immediately dashes off the bed to investigate.

"14 new text messages? I guess I was Mr. Popular last night?" He opens his phone to see that six of the missed messages were from Mallory, a few messages from others, and one from a 610-area code he wasn't familiar with. He starts with Mallory's text messages before reading the rest.

(Text)
Mallory: *"Could you pick up a bottle of something on your way here? Vince really worked my nerves today. I really need some relief!"*
Mallory: *"Never mind. I had to run to the store before it got too late. Just cum! Lol."*
Mallory: *"How much longer before you get here? I'm so horny!"*
Mallory: *"Falling asleep...are you still coming?"*
Mallory: *"It's 2:30! You're not here???"*
Mallory: *"Goodnight! ☹"*

"Damn, I know she's mad. I've got to make that up to her." Brian *thinks remorsefully.*
Marty: *"You can't be serious! Hit me up tomorrow negro!"*
Tricia: *"Hey stranger, was wondering if you felt like having company this weekend? Call me."*

"Hmph, your man must be locked up again." Brian speculates. He met her and spent a lot of time with her when her boyfriend was serving time for grand larceny. Since his release, the only time he hears from her is when he's back in the slammer.

175

Erica: *"Hey you! You came across my mind and I just wanted to say hello. So, hello!"*

"C'mon man, I've got enough psychos' in my life...next!" Brian laughs.

Pumpkin: *"Hi Mojo!"*

"Yeah... 'I'ma' need you to come up with a better nickname and stop putting out on the first night...Man, I must have had the scent of a woman on me last night? Everybody's hittin' me up!" Brian says aloud, as he continues to thumb through to his messages.

Cortez: *"Yo, dawg hit me back when you get this. Just want to make sure that I'm not the only one feeling like crap this morning."*

"No, you're not the only one, Tez..." Brian empathizes, not feeling a hundred percent himself.

"Who is this from a 610-area code?" Brian wonders before reviewing the message.

Unknown: *"Hi, this is Ashima. I'm sure you're still sleeping, but I wanted to apologize again for last night. I've never done anything like that before, but I'm glad you weren't weird. I know I was a mess last night, but I hope I didn't leave a bad impression on you. I'm so embarrassed! But, I really enjoyed my time with you. If you feel up to it, give me a call later."*

Brian would love nothing more than to call Ashima and indulge her request. However, he places his eagerness on hold to avoid the perception looking thirsty. The unwritten man code dictates he wait three days before reaching out. But, this wasn't exactly a typical three-day situation, considering they've already enjoyed each other's company and she's already slept in his bed. So, he decided to hold off until this evening to reach out. Until then, he needed to wash his chef uniform and prepare for a night of hustle and bustle in the kitchen.

Later that evening, after a shaking off the effects of the night before, Brian gets his mind right for the kitchen. As usual, it was all business when it comes to the kitchen. Preparing everything from exotic reduction sauces to brazing lamb shanks, he excels in the kitchen and the staff at Chops absolutely loves him for it.

"BRIAN!" Orders in, brotha! The last one for the evening!" Dave, The Executive Chef calls out.

"Aight, what you got?" An exhausted yet, resiliently motivated Brian responds.

"I've got a Chilean sea bass and kale order here. But, instead of the pumpkin risotto that it comes with on the menu, the lady requested we serve it with your bacon infused, asiago and cheddar grits, Brian. You hear that brotha? You're getting special requests now!" Dave informs Brian with pride for the young apprentice.

"Aight, will do!" Brian acknowledges with all smiles.

After his third week of internship at Chops, Brian has quickly established himself as a cook who knows the kitchen. He introduced the restaurant to a few dishes he branded as his own as a requirement for class credit, and now his grits based dishes has become a hit at Chops after debuting it for a test trial.

"Yo, Brian, once we finish this up, I need to 'holla' at you in the courtyard real quick!" Rick, one of the head sous chefs, requests with importance.

"Aight, after we wrap up, I'll see you out there!" Brian agrees as he began searing the sea bass.

Since the first day of working at Chops, Brian has been under the watchful tutelage of Rick and Bryce, the most senior sous chefs of the restaurant. Ever since meeting them, Brian has established a really good relationship with his new Caucasian friends.

Once the night came to a close, and the woman who ordered the last meal gave her compliments to the Chef, Brian wraps up his station, tosses his apron over his shoulder, grabs a coke from the bar and heads outside to meet with Rick. To his surprise, Bryce who worked earlier this morning is also there in his street clothes to greet Brian.

"What's going on fellas? Bryce, what brings you back into work tonight?" Brian asks, happy to see Bryce, but was a bit curious as to why they needed to see him.

"You brotha, it's all about you tonight!" Bryce replies, as Brian gives both of them a pound.

"Okay then, what's on your mind?" Brian asks, peculiar of their motive, but resting his foot on a short concrete wall and sipping his soda as he listens.

"Well, it's no secret that you've been killing it in the kitchen ever since you got here. The management is happy and so are the customers, especially with adding the grits concept to the menu. So, I overheard Dave talking to the manager about you last week, and they want to hire you full term while you're still in school. Sounds good, right?" Rick explains breaking the good news to Brian.

"Yeah, I mean this is exactly what I wanted…a full-time gig, in center city, at a top-notch restaurant, working with guys like you and building my experience. What more could I ask for?" Brian replies with vigor.

"Well we don't like that idea. In fact, Rick and I have an even better idea." Bryce interjects.

"Okay…I'd be curious to know how much better it can get so, I'm all ears." Brian replies, curious to hearing them out.

"Well, Rick and I have been here since the old restaurant, and even back then we were already considering opening a place of our own. We felt confident enough that we've learned all of the tricks of the trade, and as you can clearly see, we run this kitchen. Since then, we've found a spot, saved up nearly enough cash, and we're just about ready to move on. Then you came along with this great grits idea, and we figured, 'hey, why not give our restaurant a theme that no one has ever seen before and become an instant hit with the customers? So, we sat down a few weeks ago and talked about it, crunched a few numbers, figured it would be an excellent opportunity for someone like you just starting out, and we decided we want to take you with us!" Bryce further elaborates as they both stare at Brian, awaiting an inspiring response. Instead, Brian looks at them both with a blank expression, then looks towards the ground to process what their proposing.

"The way we see it, they want to take you on full time making prep cook money. But, we think you're more valuable than that. We think you have much greater potential. So, we want to offer you the opportunity to build something from the ground up. We're talking a partnership, Brian, in exchange for giving 'our' business, the exclusive right to feature grits as the foundation of our business plan." Rick adds placing his arm around Brian.

"What do you think?" Bryce concludes, joining Rick in placing his arm around Brian on the other side. Brian pauses for a moment in thought, takes another sip of his soda, then looks at both of them and smiles.

"Hmph…well, I think I'd be a fool to say no to that!" Brian readily accepts shaking each of their hands with the upmost enthusiasm.

"Awesome man…that is awesome! We'll be glad to have you with us!" A delighted Bryce replies as he and Rick gladly shake Brian's hand and gives him a hug.

After agreeing to the proposal, Brian understood that the plan was still in the works and would require an undetermined amount of time to get done. So, until then, he carried on as usual and didn't want to get his hopes up too much. He decided to avoid discussing it with anyone else, until it was certain that it would actually happen. Yet, the joy he felt knowing that someone recognized his potential and was willing to grant him this type of opportunity is unprecedented.

Feeling pretty good about what just transpired, Brian remains in the courtyard while Rick and Bryce took off and decided to top off the evening by finally giving Ashima a call back. Assuming it wasn't too late at 10:43pm Brian pressed his luck and reached out anyway. To no avail, her phone immediately went to voicemail.

"Damn, that probably wasn't a good idea!" Brian assumes, now concerned that the time may have not been appropriate. So, he hangs up the phone to avoid leaving a voicemail, and decides to send her a text instead.

(Text)
Brian: *"Hey, how are you? I apologize for getting back to you so late. It's been a really busy day. Assuming you're not mad from me calling so late I hope to hear from you soon."* Brian sends.

Now leaving it up to her to respond, Brian decides he'll give it a few days before he reaches out to her again. To his surprise, after changing from his work clothes and heading out to his car, Brian receives a reply from Ashima.

(Text)
Ashima: *"Hi, I'm so glad you got my message. I actually left town for the evening to party with a friend in New York, before heading off to Vegas on Monday. Perhaps I can call you when I get settled in Vegas?"*
Brian: *"Sounds good. Enjoy your flight, good luck in Vegas, enjoy NYC and be careful up there. It's rough in those New York streets! lol"*
Ashima: *"Lol. Thank you!"*

179

The exchange of text messages left Brian with a remarkable smile as he stops in his tracks to point to the heavens, thanking a higher power for his good fortune. On the ride home, Brian couldn't help but wonder about all the potential good foreseeable in his future. With graduation just around the corner, the potential of being involved with someone like Ashima, the possibility of a pay raise and now a life changing career opportunity, it seems as if his life is preparing him for a path he'd never imagined.

As the weekend dwindled, Monday arrives for yet another weekly routine. Marty and Cortez who hadn't spoken to Brian the remainder of the weekend, and they also didn't get a chance to catch up with him during the busy day at work. For Brian, it was another typical delivery day at *Apex*. But, the day couldn't have ended fast enough for Brian. Not only was he awaiting Ashima's phone call once she settles in Vegas, he's also been avoiding Mallory all day knowing an unpleasant encounter with her is looming. Narrowly escaping her wrath this morning with nothing more than a scathing stare in passing and not a single text message from her since Saturday, Brian knew he was in for it the moment she caught up with him. When Brian returns to the warehouse after his shift, with no Mallory in sight, he tries to breakout as quickly as he could even avoiding Marty and Cortez to get to his car without detection.

Nonetheless, the moment he entered the parking lot, there was no need to avoid running from Mallory any further. She was already waiting for him at his car with a piercing look on her face sharp enough to cut glass. Brian smiles with a look of ominous fear on his face as he walks towards her.

"Who do you think you are thinking you can just blow me off like that?! I'm calling and texting you this weekend and you don't even have the decency to respond?" Mallory stomps in her working heels towards Brian, grilling him about his absence this weekend.

"Wait! Wait! Mal, hold on a minute! Don't blow up on me like that, bring it down. Listen, I really got busy on Friday and forgot to hit you back...my bad!" Brian replies trying to defuse the situation.

"Oh wow! You forgot to hit me back all weekend? You know, I don't recall you forgetting to hit me back when you want me to chew your little man!" Mallory replies with a demeaning comment.

"Whoa...first off, 'I'ma' need you to pause, because you know my man ain't little!" Brian defends from her humiliating jab.

"See, that's your problem. I said all that and all you heard was little man. You're an arrogant bastard that's smelling himself a little too much!" Mallory disdainfully replies.

"Wait, you're seriously going-in on me like this because I didn't call or text you back?" Brian replies with a look of confusion.

"No, I'm going-in on you because you stood here and deliberately lied to my face. I heard Marty and Cortez on the loading dock talking about you and what a great time y'all had Friday. How you were acting all shy for some skank at happy hour. Wow…I don't recall you ever being that shy for me. She must have been one good looking piece of ass, huh?" Mallory replies with asinine disgust.

"Wow, if I didn't know any better, it almost sounds like we were exclusive or something? I mean c'mon, we're grown. This little jealousy act you're 'puttin' on, confronting me at my car when your angry is cute and all. But, let's be mature about this!" Brian replies in a civil tone as he leans against his car to respond to a text message.

"Screw mature! How's that for mature?!" Mallory sounds off, jealously taking a swipe at Brian's phone, and knocking it to the ground.

"Wow, okay seriously! You just knock my phone out of my hand like that? You don't see me wilding out when you be coming up in here with them camel toe tights on like its hump day or something." Brian replies with fuming restraint.

"Yeah, Brian, seriously! You just pissed me the hell off! And what does wearing gym clothes have anything to do with what we're talking about right now?" Mallory asks with no regards Brian's allegations.

"It has nothing to do with this, but it has everything to do with being jealous if I really wanted to take it there!" Brian responds in an aggravated tone as he fetches his phone, the battery, and the pieces of his pride as well.

Mallory stands there tight lipped, with her arms folded and didn't utter another word. Initially Brian wanted to react to her reckless behavior. But, after noticing the sexy of her angry expression, it actually turned him on and prompted him to respond differently.

"Okay, you know what…I'm not trying to be at odds with you, 'aight'? Look, I'm sorry for whatever you want me to own up to. But, right now can we just take this to your office or anywhere but out here so we can bring resolve to this issue and talk like civil adults?" Brian asks trying to defuse the situation. He pauses in a void of silence waiting for her reply.

"C'mon Mal, let's be amicable about this. You know, most women can't pull it off, but you actually look good when you're mad." Brian flatters her as he caressed her arm in an attempt to soften her callous posture. Mallory stands firm, avoiding eye contact with him.

"C'mon, you know it's chilly out here with that tight skirt on!" Brian insists to persuade her stubbornness.

She responds initially by shrugging his hand off as an unwanted gesture. But, even in the wrathful moment, she couldn't stay mad at him for long and eventually concedes with a stubborn smirk.

"Sorry about your phone. I was just acting out of frustration." Mallory mutters, finally breaking her silence.

"It's cool. I needed an upgrade anyway." Brian replies in a forgiving tone. Brian could sense the remorse in her voice and he knew at that moment he had her.

"Look this isn't over!" Mallory quickly reminds him with a stern face.

"I know it isn't, but let's just take it out of the parking lot." Brian responds.

"Meet me in my office in five minutes." Mallory demands.

"Five minutes!" Brian echo's.

Brian locks his car and heads back towards the offices above the loading dock. On his way up, he spots Marty and Cortez with their backpacks in hand on their way out.

"You two…!" Brian exclaims as they walk towards him.

"What…what happened?! What was that all about in the parking lot?" Cortez asks as they gave each other a pound.

"Man, y'all just got me in trouble, talking about what happened on Friday in front of Mallory." Brian explains in frustration.

"Damn it! Marty, I told you she was ear hustling our conversation." Cortez declares with dismay.

"Yeah, but it was too late by then. My bad, 'B'…we were talking by the truck and your girl rolled up talking to Ben about putting a truck out of service. We didn't even know who they were talking to because she was hiding behind a stack of boxes we were loading for second shift. But, I knew something was up when I saw her gettin' at you in the lot a few minutes ago. Again, my bad, dawg!" Marty sincerely explains.

"Well, it doesn't matter now, it's already done. I'm on my way up to her office right now. I'll get at y'all later!" Brian rapidly responds.

"Aight then, let us know what happens." Marty answers with concern.

"No doubt! I'll see y'all tonight." Brian replies, dapping them both before taking off.

As he reaches the top of the stairwell to the executive suites, he notices all the closed administration doors on his way to Mallory's office at the end of the passageway. As he enters the office, Mallory is standing behind her desk wrapping up some last-minute work behind her duel monitors.

"So, what's up, corporate lady?" Brian says announcing his presence.

"Give me a minute and shut my door please!" Mallory requests as she continues to review something from her email.

Brian takes a seat at the edge of Mallory's desk as he waits, looking into Vincent's adjacent office. With a disdainful taste in his mouth for Vincent, Brian decides that this was the right moment to execute his plan to get even.

"Hey Mal..." Brian calls out.

"Yes." She answers.

"When was the last time you did something crazy and spontaneous?" Brian asks with naughty intentions.

"Umm...probably when you had me stretched across the hood of your car this summer at Belmont-Plateau in the rain." Mallory candidly reminds him.

"Oh c'mon, it was drizzling that night." Brian playfully replies.

"Drizzling, raining, whatever is was doing, I ruined a nice pair of suede heels that night. Anyway, what are you asking me? What's going on in that brain of yours now?" Mallory curiously asks turning her full attention to him as she watches him pace the office and tightly closing all the blinds to the outside corridor.

"Well you know me, always thinking of the next big thing!" Brian replies in a sneaky tone.

"Okay...what the hell are you doing, Brian?" Mallory abruptly questions.

"Come here, I want to show you something." Brian asks extending his hand across her desk to bring her closer to him.

"Okay, I didn't bring you up here for a Kumbaya moment, Brian. I brought you up here to talk about these trifling hoes you be dealing with." She makes clear, taking his hand anyway as he leads her around the desk.

183

"You know what I see when I look into this office?" Brian asks as he faces her towards the office and grabs her hand.

"What's that, Brian? What do you see?" She responds abrupt and to the point.

"I see an opportunity to be just as trifling and disrespectful as the person who occupies this office. The same person who propositions and disrespects you regularly, the same person who threatened your job if you told anyone about his inappropriate advances. I say…" Brian pauses as he stands behind her and kisses her on a bare part of her shoulder.

"…we do something…" Brian pulls one side of her hair back and kisses her exposed neck.

"…to get even." Brian attempts to kiss her for a third time, but Mallory pulls away and confronts him.

"Wait! Are you kidding me? Do you not remember where the hell we are right now? This is not some sleazy hotel on the Roosevelt Boulevard, and this is not the Belmont Plateau!" She whispers fervently.

"Shhhhh…" Brian hushes her continuing with no regards to her rebuttal. Pecking away at her neck, and pushing the knot in his pants against her backside.

"Brian, I am a manager. I can't…I can't be…I…I…ahhh…" Mallory can resist no longer as she completely relents to Brian's sexual advance.

Now in complete control, Brian takes her hand and leads her into Vincent's office. But, she suddenly stops him and spins him around.

"What's wrong?" He asks, alarmed by her sudden gesture.

"Nothing…I want you, now!" She murmurs with anxious desire. Initially Brian's rousing of her was only a bluff. He didn't expect her to go through with such a risqué act. To his surprise she calls his bluff.

"Right here?" He asks bewildered as they stand more than arms reach of anything in the room.

"Right now!" She utters, kneeling to his crouch in her heels to unzip him.

Brian just watches as she resumes. She didn't even bother to unbuckle his belt. She just reached in and pulls his rigid manhood from his pants. Staring face to face with what she desires, she proceeds to pleasure him. Brian simply stands with his hands on his hips and enjoys the view from above. Suddenly, she stops and pushes him into Vincent's leather office chair to finish him off.

184

Brian reclines with his hands behind his head as she continues to indulge him. But, after a few minutes, Mallory decides she wants to be satisfied. So, she stands up and pulls him from the chair, dictating her way with him.

"Hmm...what's next?" He asks, waiting for her next directive as she looks at him with endearing eyes.

"Now, it's my turn!" She replies leading him to the front of the desk to assume the position.

In the heat of the passionate moment, Brian obliges her, clearing Vincent's ink pens, papers, name plate and stapler to the floor, then grabs Mallory by both bottom cheeks and props her onto the desktop. Wildly they kiss as he grabs handfuls of her breast and buries his face in her exposed cleavage. She grabs him by the hoodie and unzips it off of him, so she can grab hold of his solid biceps exploding out of his tightly fitting shirt. Then she reaches down and grabs his thickness as he unfastens his belt to finish her off. He pulls her to the edge of the desk to insert her, but she stops him.

"No! I want it this way...!" She demands, hopping off the desk and turns her back to him. She reaches behind and grasps the back of his head, massaging his neck as he massaged her breasts.

Ensuring she's ready to receive him, Brian moistens his fingers, and reaches around and underneath her dress to arouse her. To no surprise, there were no panties to slide over to get to her moistness. And there was plenty of moistness to feel, as his hand quickly becomes messy from fondling her juicy wet lips, while the other hand caresses her D size breasts. Fearful of being heard, Mallory lets out a controlled, passionate sigh as she throws her head back, enduring his pleasurable foreplay. With his hand nearly dripping from secretions, Mallory grabs his hand and puts his wet fingers into her mouth. Overwhelmed with sexual energy, she leans across Vincent's desk ready for Brian to take her.

Brian obliges her by gently spreading her and filling every void of her walls until he bottoms out. Enduring his endowment, she lets out a loud initial squeal and bites her thumb trying to avoid any sound echoing beyond the office. Brian goes to work enjoying every moment of pleasuring Mallory in Vincent's office, knowing how much Vincent would rather be doing Mallory himself.

"Hurry...hurry up! Somebody might come!" Mallory urges trying to speak between every exhausting breathe as Brian continues to work her.

185

Responding to her demanding request, Brian grudgingly pumps faster to climax sooner. As he comes close and with no protection, he realizes that he has nowhere to release. He notices a box of tissue across the room but it was too far for him to reach and he certainly wasn't about to unload inside of her. So, he did the next best thing.

"Grrr...Ohhh..." He grunts as he pulls out and releases all over her backside and trickling on the carpet as well.

Barely able to stand and breathing heavy, he braces himself against the desk to give himself a moment to recover.

"Oh Shh...!" Brian suddenly outbursts.

"What?! What happened? Did you pull out in time? You didn't get it on my skirt, did you?" Mallory asks with concern.

"Yeah, I pulled out. But, I got it on you and I've got to clean Vincent's chair too. Stay right there I'll grab some tissue." Brian explains as he notices a few fresh droplets of something running down the headrest of Vincent's chair. Brian quickly takes up his pants to grab the tissue box.

"What?! Oh my God! Wow...the chair too? I can't believe you just talked me into doing that!" Mallory realizes as she remains limp across the desk while Brian wipes her off.

"Yeah, but aren't you glad I convinced you to kiss and make up?" Brian asks assured that she enjoyed every moment of it.

"Truthfully, you had me at 'I'm sexy when I'm mad'." Mallory admits, recalling Brian's cunning appeal. After wiping the mess he made on Mallory, he cleans up the chair and remaining evidence.

"Brian really? That's just wrong!" Mallory comments, while observing him shellacking his DNA into the headrest Vincent's chair.

"Sorry Vince. But, you can't say you didn't have it coming, no pun intended!" Brian says with a devilish grin as he works the droplets into the leather chair like polish.

"No, it was intended!" Mallory frowns in doubt.

"Yeah, you're right!" Brian smiles in agreement.

"Yeah, well, enough with getting even with Vincent. Now you've got to get out before some stray person comes up here knocking about their pay, knowing damn well the offices are closed." Mallory implores him as they both fix their clothes.

"Wow, that's how we do it? The old wham, bam, thank you Ma'am, huh?" Brian playfully replies.

"I'm sorry, the sex was great and all, but not worth losing my job over." Mallory explains with brutal honesty.

"Well, since you put it that way, I'll leave you to lock up, and I'll head out like I was about to do about twenty minutes ago before you got rude with me." Brian replies with a departing peck on her cheek as he heads for the office stairs.

Later that day, Brian wanders into *The Fox*, eager to catch up with his friends to recap the exciting recent events.

"Uh, oh…there he is! Just the man I've been waiting for!" Marty boisterously announces as Brian enters the venue.

"There 'ya' go Sir, a fresh cold one!" Cortez hands Brian a cold beer and a pool cue.

"Aight, Casanova Brown, let's hear it! What happened with you and ole girl at the gig earlier?" Marty probes, chalking his pool stick for a break.

"Well, no thanks to you two, I was ambushed by a woman scorned because she overheard y'all talking about what went down on Friday. So, as usual, I had to talk my out of another mess." Brian explains with displeasure.

"Yo, my bad man! But, like I said before, me and this man had no idea she was standing there ear hustling the conversation." Marty sincerely explains.

"Look, don't worry about it, y'all. Everything's cool, when I went up to the office we smoothed everything over…I blessed her, and we're good now." Brian nonchalantly replies.

"Wait, what do you mean you blessed her? What, you whipped out some Holy oil, and anointed her forehead or something? YOU'RE HEALED!" Cortez asks, animating the actions of a priest.

"Naw man, just trust me on this one. I took care of it!" Brian casually responds.

"Whoa…okay…now you've got my attention! So…what happened?" Marty asks with peaked interest.

"Haha…y'all really don't want me to tell all that." Brian attempts to dismiss the topic, masking his anxiousness to tell all.

"Oh, do tell! Do tell!" Marty insists standing behind his pool cue. Brian stands silent, looking at Marty first, then he looks over at Cortez with the most devilish grin.

"C'mon with it, Mojo!" Cortez impatiently blurts out.

"Aight. Y'all remember I told y'all that I was going to do something crazy to ya boy Vincent, right?" Brian reminds them.

"Yeah, when I told you to make sure it doesn't involve me getting fired, okay...I'm listening." Marty firmly recalls.

"Well, I don't know about anybody getting fired over it. But, I took her into Vincent's office and gave her the business." Brian proudly boasts taking a sip from his beer.

"You did what?!" Marty replies with a controlled outburst.

"Oh...! My main man Mo to the Joe strikes again! You're a wild boy, 'B'." Cortez adds, giving props to his friend toasting their bottles.

"Are you crazy?! How the hell did you pull that off?!" A dumbfounded Marty asks.

"Well, you know ain't nobody hangin' around the offices after quittin' time. So, once I drew those blinds and turned on that Mojo..." Brian confidently replies.

"You know what, something's wrong with you. I can't believe you actually went there." Marty replies in awe.

"Yup, and I had to wipe his chair, too." Brian adds.

"You know, there's a thin line between playa and stupidity and you just crossed it, right? I mean, you're my man and all, but you're dangerous! I just hope you at least put a patch on that third eye during your little impromptu sex session?" Marty sensibly cautions.

"Umm...yeah...I strapped up!" Brian replies with an unconvincing sneer as he hides behind another swig of his beer.

"Umm...yeah, ya didn't! I can see it all in your forehead wrinkles. You're slippin' with these man code violations, 'B'. You're slippin'!" Marty reprimands with disappointment as he makes a violent break of the balls. Brian smiles knowing he was just exposed by his friends.

"You know, on second thought I've got to agree with Marty on this one. You're are crazy, Bruh!" Cortez co-signs.

"Alright, alright...so maybe I slipped a little by going naked with Mallory. But, how you figure I'm violating so many codes? I'm a free agent, Baby! Single and free to mingle. Where's the violation in that?" A confused Brian tries to justify.

"Are you serious? Tez is he serious right now?" Appalled at Brian's rebuttal, Marty runs down several instances to which Brian has violated the man code.

"Sleeping with a co-worker…violation! Sex in the workplace…violation! Sex with a supervisor…violation! Sexing on the job, with a co-worker, who happens to be a supervisor and no lid on your soldier…now that's just plain stupid!" Marty summarizes, resolute in delivering his point.

"Okay, I get it! I live for the thrill of an intense moment! Yes, I get off not always placing the safe bet. Sometimes I like to gamble a bit. I know! I'm young! I get it! But, you've got to admit, serving Mallory in Vincent's office is worth some style points at least." Brian replies trying to make better of the situation as he leans over the table and lines up to take a shot.

"Yeah, yeah, yeah, five points for creativity and a hundred points for stupidity, whatever! What I really want to know is how things went with you and ole' girl Friday night since you never got back to me?" Marty inquires shifting the conversation.

"Well, there wasn't much else to tell. She got sick on the ride home, she decided she didn't want to go home nauseous, so she came to my spot to sleep it off." Brian casually explains as he takes a side pocket shot.

"Wait a minute! Are we talkin' about the same girl from the rooftop? She actually came to your crib that night?" A perplexed Cortez asks.

"Yeah, we' talkin' about the same girl from the rooftop. Boy Wonder over here pulled something from his gadget bag and somehow managed to get ole girl to stay the night at his apartment." Marty jealously explains.

"Wait, arguably the baddest chick in the building last week, and somehow you managed to get her back to the crib?" A stunned Cortez repeats.

"C'mon man, I'm clutch baby…corner pocket!" Brian replies with comical arrogance as he knocks in a bank shot.

"Clutch huh? Funny…I don't recall all this clutch confidence when you were trying to holla last week." Marty smiles with a candid reminder.

"True, true...but, you can't just come at somebody like her with your chest poked out like she's a typical chick in the club. You've 'gotta' come at a girl that on the humble. It 'ain't' always about confidence, sometimes you've got to have finesse." Brian explains.

"Aight, so what's the conversation been like? Does she seem like she's into the Mojo or what?" Cortez curiously asks.

"Honestly, I couldn't tell you. I haven't had a real conversation with her yet, and the last time I saw her was the night she stayed over. She hit me

189

up on Saturday, saying she was partying in New York with some friends." Brian explains.

"Oh, she's fancy, huh? Most of us head downtown to get our groove on, on a typical weekend. But, this girl sounds like she's doing big things." Cortez replies in a condescending tone.

"Hmph, I'll bet you that ain't the only friend she had to go see out there in the big apple. I'm sure she's got some five letter friends that live on 5th Ave. that she had to go visit, too!" Marty implies, teasing Brian.

"Oh, here you go with these five letter theories again." Brian replies.

"Wait, break it down for me again." Cortez laughs, getting a kick out of the Marty's high maintenance philosophy.

"Gucci, Louie, Fendi, Prada, Coach, Jimmy, or any other high dollar brand that has a five-letter name." Marty reiterates.

"Funny…you're real funny!" Brian laughs off.

"I know! I hope you've got at least a ten-thousand-dollar credit limit and a great interest rate on that credit card of yours." Marty warns mischievously.

"What credit card are you talking about?" Brian asks naive to Marty's point.

"The one you're about to apply for when she lets you taste that cookie. Speaking of cookie…how was it? I see you left that little detail, out." Marty probes, continuing to play the table.

"To be honest with you, I've got nothing to tell. I gave up my bed, slept on the futon and by morning she was gone." Brian replies.

"Wow. She hit you with the money on the night stand maneuver, huh?" Marty teases.

"Yeah, she did. Not even a long kiss good night. I felt so violated." Brian jokes.

"Now that's something you don't hear every day, a woman sleeping in your bed without leaving her drawls?" Cortez jokes taking swig of his beer.

"Actually, y'all would have been proud of me. She was really going through it, and I wasn't about to take advantage of a drunken situation. That's not how I move. So, I put on my best rendition of a gentleman that night." Brian proudly explains.

"Uh oh…tryin' to play the role of a playa and a gentleman, huh?" Cortez teases Brian.

190

"Well, you know…I've been known to turn it on a time or two." Brian charismatically replies. "But, since we're talking about five letter shopping and the finer things, maybe y'all can help me understand how a woman who has everything, has a need for something?" Brian asks trying to get clarity from his friends.

"Honestly, I couldn't tell you. But, the next time I'm dating a woman that can not only buy out the bar, but buy the whole damn building, I'll let you know." Cortez replies, not taking the question seriously.

"Tez I'm with you, brotha. I've got nothing. But, when I can give you a sensible answer, I'll let you know." Marty seconds as they casually stand around the table. "Could you imagine Mojo actually settling down and raising a family…slipping up and having a bunch of little Mulatto kids running around with Mallory?" Marty frivolously entertains as he leans in to take another shot.

"You mean gelato kids, right? Get it…gelato? Because she Italian…" Cortez laughs entertaining himself with corny humor.

"SHUT UP TEZ!!!" Marty and Brian simultaneously reply, not amused by Cortez's dry joke.

"Wow, tough crowd!" Cortez replies, deflated by his friend's reprimand.

"Seriously though…I think I really like this one." Brian says on a more serious note.

"Hmph…the one, huh?" Marty says looking over at Brian with unconvincing character.

"Yeah, man. It's something about her that's different than the others. I think I can be faithful to this one." Brian confidently confesses as the mere thought of being with Ashima takes him to a happy place.

"Faithful? You can't stay focused for five minutes when something nice enters the room and you talking 'bout faithful?" Marty says unconvinced of Brian's sudden good faith.

"C'mon man, don't judge me from my promiscuous past. All I'm saying is that if she gives me a chance, I'm all chips in on this one." Brian replies, adamant about his thoughts of Ashima.

"Well, being faithful is one thing, but you know as well as I do that it won't take long before you find something wrong with her too, and she'll be cut like the rest of them, right or wrong?" Cortez adds, speaking on Brian's track record.

"I mean…not really…" Brian replies, passively denying the truth about himself.

"Okay then…what happened to ole girl you bought the drinks for a while back?" Marty asks, calling Brian out.

"Who Cassandra? I mean, we went a few rounds." Brian bashfully admits.

"Okay, okay…and, how was it?" Marty asks demanding more explanation.

"It was good…really good!" Brian answers as if withholding more to say.

"Wait, I'm sensing a 'but' here! That answer was a little too short and a little too quiet." Marty replies, knowing the mannerism of his friend.

"But, what…?" Cortez says prompting Brian to spit out his answer.

"But, her titties had low self-esteem, man! I'm saying, I like cute, perky tits. Not the six-kid's flapjack variety." Brian explains trying to plead his case.

"Oh my God! Are you serious?" Cortez blurts out as they all laugh at Brian's explanation.

"See, my point exactly! Now, shorty was bad! And I'm sure her titties were fine to an average dude. But, not quite good enough for the likes of Brian Jones." The men laugh, as Marty proves his point.

"I'll tell you what I can't imagine, is seeing snow on the ground this weekend." Marty says altering the topic.

"Yeah, I saw that this morning. It's 'kinda' early for snow, right?" Brian replies in awe.

"Yeah, a little bit. Kerry's trying to have a game night Friday too. Y'all can slide through if y'all want." Marty informs the fellas.

"Game night this weekend? Word…I'm down!" Cortez quickly agrees.

"I'm down too! What do you need us to bring?" Brian asks with enthusiasm.

"Whatever, its game night! Bring whatever you're feeling." Marty carelessly answers.

"Cool!" Brian replies as he returns focus to the pool table.

As Brian enjoys another billiards night of beers, laughs, and life with his friends at *The Fox*, roughly ninety miles north of Philadelphia, in a modernly renovated Brownstone in Brooklyn Heights, New York, Ashima is at her friend Maloni's house hanging out. Carolyn, Crystal, and Naima also came along, preparing for a mid-morning flight out of LaGuardia, in route to Las Vegas. After relishing a day of carefree spending, the ladies are nestled on a cozy, espresso fabric couch, enjoying a night cap of hot chocolate infused with mocha liqueur and red velvet cake. A ceiling height bookshelf surrounds them, as they enjoy a backyard fire pit on the concrete patio. The towering glass doors provide a panoramic view to the backyard and separates them from the elements.

"Now, today was definitely my definition of 'a girl's days out'." A jubilant Crystal expresses, pouring more liqueur into her mug.

"Yasss! All my favorite places in one day...the spa, 5th Avenue, Pho for lunch, and bubble tea? Today was indeed a treat. I can't wait to touchdown in Vegas!" Naima adds recapping her pleasurable day.

"Oh yeah, that was definitely a good call on lunch today, Lenny. I'm still full from all that seafood soup and spicy calamari." Maloni adds.

"Yes, and I'm glad we were able to walk it off. They must definitely get the Hermes store closer to 5th Avenue." Ashima playfully complains as the lady's cackle about the haughty inconvenience.

"Oh Shima, stop it. We only made it about seven blocks before you wanted to wave down a cab." Crystal chimes in as the ladies laugh at everything silly.

"Yasss! Fortunately, a girl can still wave down a cab by showing a little leg." Maloni jokes as the laughter continues.

"Shima, I absolutely have to agree! I mean, heaven knows what would have happened if you weren't able to shop for another ten thousand-dollar Birkin bag? I'm so jealous..." Naima pokes fun.

"Hey, a woman has needs, right?" Ashima casually responds, as the women cackle loudly at her nonchalant response.

"Well, I hope you girls saved some for Vegas, because you know they'll be plenty of shopping to do at the Grand Canal Shoppes when we get out there." Naima reminds the women.

"Yes, my absolute favorite place to shop! I can't wait to get out there! Speaking of which, how are the amenities going to be for the flight over? You know a girl can't fly without my sparkling glasses of champagne to keep it grown and sexy." Crystal pretentiously asks.

"Well, I chartered the jet from luxury charter as always, so there should definitely be plenty for us to sip on while in flight. I even made sure they added prime rib, lobster tails, and shrimp cocktails to the in-flight menu, so we can eat and be merry like true queens on the way over." Naima assures the ladies of their posh accommodations.

"See, that's why we leave you in charge of planning, Naima. You're always on top of it!" Crystal praises of her friend.

"Oh please, I used Shelton's card for the charter. So, it was nothing...but, you're welcome anyway!" Naima snobbishly replies as the lady's breakout into haughty laughter.

"Oh, I'm so jealous!" Carolyn utters amid the other girl's laughter.

"Okay ladies, I know we're having hot cocoa. But, now let's talk tea! So, what's going on girls? How's love these days? I mean, I wish I knew. But, unfortunately the only thing I love these days is my freedom from work and my cat. I'm such a hopeless romantic!" Maloni pitifully states as she takes another sip of her night cap.

Since graduating college with Ashima and Carolyn, and being fortunate enough to land a job at Goldman Sachs, Maloni hasn't had time for anything that doesn't involve investment advice and portfolios. So, she tries to live vicariously through the love life of her friends.

Breaking a short period of silence Crystal sighs heavily before she answers. "Well, the money is still good..."

"I second that!" Naima adds as the women engage in more senseless laughter.

"Wow, you're not even married yet and you feel the same way as Crystal?" Maloni seeks to understand addressing Naima.

"Well, if you know anything about affluent Muslim men, you know that they lose interest in women quickly. Money and leisure is what makes them happy...it's their priority! We are simply there to fulfill their sexual needs and bear their children." Naima explains nonchalantly eating a piece of red velvet cake.

"Wow...that must be tough to deal with." Maloni remorsefully replies.

"At times, yes. But, it's the way things are. It's all we know. Unfortunately, this is our normal." Naima answers with her eyes hung low in a sense of shame.

Naima replies with a sentiment much to the likes of hopelessness, yet making the best of her situation. Ashima and Crystal remains tight lipped as if they didn't want to even touch the subject. The room fell awkward to a

194

topic not frequently visited. Maloni's interest in her friends suddenly turns into the elephant in the room.

"How about you, Shima? Although I'm not a fan, how are things going with you and Fahad?" Maloni asks as she continues around the room.

"Hmm…I second that Maloni, not a fan!" Carolyn interjects, co-signing Maloni's opinion of Fahad.

"Well, I'd much rather talk about how delicious this cake is, than to even acknowledge that there's a relationship between Fahad and I." Ashima candidly replies.

"Wait…really?! A stunned Maloni responds, taken aback by the news.

"Yes really!" Ashima affirms.

"My goodness! And here I was thinking that life would be so much better if I could only trade places with you, Shima. I mean, I see the outbursts and the disagreements between you two. But, I thought of it to be no more than growing pains." Crystal speaks out.

"Listen, there are things you should know about Fahad and I that are left unsaid…troubling things. Things that would force you look at him differently if ever told you. But, you know that I'm a very private person and like to handle my own matters, my own way." Ashima explains with a sense of misery.

"Exactly, you've never shed light on any of your problems, which is why I never understood when you guys are openly at each other." Naima further elaborates.

"Well, if you must know…the arrangement between Fahad and I are mostly the doing of Fahad and my father. Years ago, my father found it to be a great idea for me to marry into the Gabr family through Fahad since we were the closest in age. And I admit, early on I thought Fahad was a nice looking young man that I wouldn't mind enjoying life with, because we grew up knowing each other and we would have everything at our disposal. But, darkness comes to light in time and once I found out what an obnoxiously spoiled creep he was, I was completely turned off. Everything Fahad does involve money as if he's constantly trying to impress me. I find it so repugnant. He has no imagination, he's never done anything for me that was genuinely romantic, and I'm a very modest person. I appreciate the simple things in life." Ashima explains, sincerely dropping the bombshell on her friends.

"My goodness, Ashima! Have you spoken to your father about how you feel?" A stunned Maloni interjects.

"No, even if I told him, he's so wrapped up in the idea of me marrying Fahad I don't think he would even care to listen. Despite my father's ambitions, I thought I could actually learn to love Fahad in time. But, all along I've only been kidding myself. Playing this foolish charade, and wearing this silly façade to appease my father, because he has such high hopes for this union. And I'd hate to disappoint him, but between us in this room this arrangement between Fahad and I will never happen. I don't even believe in arranged marriages. Honestly, I've hardly been intimate with Fahad for some time now. But, when we did, it would only last to his satisfaction. It was so disappointing to not feel much pleasure for five to ten minutes at a time. I'm not even sure if I even know what a true orgasm feels like." The sound in the room is so still, the only thing that could be heard aside from Ashima's depressing voice is the muffled crackle of the fire pit from outside and the clock ticking on the wall.

"I'm sorry, Shima, I don't mean to laugh at your circumstance. But, are you implying that Fahad is a preemie in bed?" Carolyn asks for clarification trying to hold back an outburst of comic relief, as were the others.

"What I'm saying is the reptile in his jeans is only a salamander." Ashima confirms with an embarrassing smirk on her face.

The ladies were all trying to hide their resistance to smile at first. But, once they see Ashima's grin, they couldn't hold it together any longer and the room erupts in amusement.

"Thank goodness you sampled the package, before committing to 'that' situation!" Naima exclaims over the roar of laughter.

"To add insult, I recently found out Fahad is sleeping with Aman's daughter." Ashima announces, dropping another bombshell on her friends.

The women gasp heavily in awe. "Oh my God, Nisa?! Ashima, are you sure of this?" Naima asks for clarification.

"Yes, one of my staff members informed me months ago that she saw him having an intimate dinner with someone at the Tashan restaurant downtown. She asked someone to take a picture of her and her husband with Fahad in the background to show me proof. Of course, I was mortified when I saw the picture of who he was with. Till this day he doesn't know that I know." Ashima irritably explains.

196

"Oh my God, Shima...I had no idea all of this was going on. I feel so badly for you." Crystal sympathizes for her friend.

"As surprising as this may be for all of you, this isn't the first time I've caught Fahad with his trifling infidelity. There were others before Nisa. But, he would always deny the truth. Including the one time I confronted him holding hands with some menacing groupie as he was stuck in traffic while I was on my way to a meeting with my assistant at three Logan Square." Ashima explains, divulging more appalling truth to the ladies.

"Wow...and what was his excuse?" Maloni asks, struggling to make sense of Ashima's story.

He claims it was innocent and he was being supportive because she was going through something. He thinks he's so clever. But, he's going to drown in his own arrogance. In spite of this, he wants me to convert to Islam and be his wife? For what, to be his toy? To be his slave? To be one of his faithful concubines willing to lay down with him to give him a son? I'm sorry, but I'm far too resilient for that!" Ashima rants in frustration as her voice begins to unravel.

Maloni comes over to console her as she becomes visibly upset. Nonetheless, Ashima sits resolute and holds back her grief, for she wanted no sadness associated with her plea.

"I'm sorry, but Shima I think you should be out looking for someone to make you feel special. I mean, is there no one in your profession that catches your eye, or anyone who has ever approached you?" Maloni inquires.

"No, even if I were looking for someone to fill the void, all of the good men at my job are taken. The men that are available just can't be taken seriously. Besides, I'm far too involved in my work to be focused on dating right now." Ashima regretfully explains.

"What about that guy that we took the cab home with, Brian? He was handsome, and very dark if you know what I mean?" Carolyn replies mischievously.

"Yes, he was very nice! I was checking him out at the venue myself. He had very nice build and very strong hands. But, anyway, he seemed to be very into you, Shima...I can tell." Crystal adds.

Maloni spills chocolate from the corner of her mouth trying to quickly respond. "I'm sorry, did I hear of a tall, dark..."

197

"…and handsome, man? Yes, Maloni that would be correct!" Crystal swiftly finishes.

Maloni gasps. "Shima, you never told me about this best kept secret! Who is he? What's his story?" Maloni ardently probes.

"Yeah, Shima, you guys have been holding out?" Crystal adds as she takes another sip of her night cap.

"Well, it's interesting that you've mentioned him. Because the night we shared the cab ride home, I didn't actually make it home." Ashima cautiously reveals, looking away from her friends.

The oxygen was entirely sucked from the room as the women all gasps at once at the stunning revelation. Carolyn's reaction is the loudest, considering she was not only Ashima's best friend, but the last person to see her that evening.

"Oh my God, Shima! What happened, and where did you end up?!" A disturbed Carolyn asks assuming the worst.

"It looks like this hot chocolate is turning into truth serum. Quick, someone get her a refill." Naima teases as the ladies enjoy another laugh.

"Well, everyone knows that I'm a lightweight when it comes to drinking alcohol. And if you can recall, I probably had a bit more than my usual that night. So, on the way home, although I hid it very well Lenny, I was quite tipsy that night. I tried to hold it together for as long as I could to avoid embarrassing myself. But, just short of getting to the house, my stomach turned on me and thank God the driver pulled over." Ashima explains.

"Okay, so if you didn't go home, where did you end up?" Maloni anxiously asks.

"Well, at this point, I couldn't go home in that condition. You know Amir is far too nosey and would have grilled me for hours about being responsible. So, I allowed him to take me to his place." Ashima replies shamelessly.

"My God Ashima, that was so reckless of you! He could have done something to you! You don't even know him to go home with him like that!" Carolyn chastises her, being critical of her friend's negligence.

"Listen, if I didn't trust him, I wouldn't have gone with him." Ashima calmly defends.

"So, what happened? Did he try anything?" Naima asks.

"No, actually he was a gentleman. He took care of me and helped me recover with no hangover." Ashima clarifies.

"Well, in that case, perhaps you should get to know more about him. What does he do?" Maloni asks biting another morsel of her red velvet cake.

"Well, I don't know much. He works for Apex and makes deliveries to my father, and I think he's studying to be a chef." Ashima apprehensively replies knowing that Brian's resume' was presumably unimpressive in contrast to the likes of Fahad.

As expected, the enthusiasm in the room quickly died down, as Ashima's friends were clearly unimpressed by the few details she knew about Brian.

"Hmph, he doesn't sound like the type that could afford to support a woman with an appetite for Hermes with that occupation." Crystal assumes with humorous intent. However, she stood alone on humor as the other women feed on Ashima's unenthused reaction.

"Actually, I'm not that particular about such materialistic things and I'm certainly not concerned about what a man could do for me. I'm quite capable of maintaining on my own. Some things are just far more important than material comfort. For me, that would-be happiness. For once, I'd like to just imagine that euphoric feeling of being happy." Ashima expresses with polite discord.

"Well, we all know that money doesn't equal happiness, and if you find him interesting then I say have some fun. I mean, it's not like you're going to marry him or anything. Just enjoy his company." Maloni condones.

"I agree. Happiness is what life is all about. Step out on faith and let fate have its way." Carolyn agrees, as the women begin to await the reaction of the others in the room.

"Well, he's not exactly royalty, but if there's nothing else to look forward to, then I say go for it. Go have some fun?" Crystal chimes in.

"Now wait a minute, ladies! I never said I was interested in him like that. I mean, yes, I stayed at his place to avoid my father and sleep off a few too many drinks. I didn't say I slept with him. Besides, I'm just like you Maloni. I'm far too busy for a companion right now!" Ashima attempts to deny.

"Shima cut it out! You've been blushing the moment we spoke his name. Everyone in this room can clearly see that there's definitely something there." Naima opposes.

199

Everyone stands by waiting for Ashima to come up with another clever reply of denial, but Ashima fails to appease them. Instead she sits slightly embarrassed not knowing that her friends were reading her.

"Well, in a strange way I think I like him." Ashima shamefully admits.

"See, I knew there was something there. It's written all over your face!" An excited Naima replies to the confession.

"Ashima I don't think there's any shame in being attracted to someone tall, dark, and handsome." Maloni adds as Ashima sits with an embarrassing smirk.

"I'll tell you what I'm looking forward to…I'm looking forward to landing in Vegas tomorrow and enjoying some balmy weather!" Lenny speaks out, redirecting everyone's focus from Ashima.

"I heard that! It was really chilly today. And did anyone else hear that we're coming back to our first snowfall this weekend?" Naima announces to the ladies.

"Oh yeah, it's supposed to start snowing on Friday. I hope you guys all packed jackets or something?" Maloni confirms.

"Hmm…well until then, here's to Vegas. Cheers ladies!" Crystal rallies the ladies for a toast.

"Cheers…!" The women follow, toasting their glasses.

Grateful for Lenny getting her off the hot seat, Ashima couldn't continue to hide the truth from her friends nor herself that there was definitely something she was feeling for Brian. Although she wasn't looking for anything, her friends co-signing on the idea of 'having fun' inspired her to consider differently about Brian Jones.

A Day Spent Falling in Love

CHAPTER ELEVEN

Thank God, it's Friday! It's been a week since Brian and Ashima cordially met at the Stratus Lounge and ended the night in utter surreal fashion. Despite being away on a Vegas vacation, the pair made great use of their distance apart. From the moment she left New York City, it was apparent that there was something about Brian that clearly made an impression on her. From the tedious four-hour flight over, to tossing dice across the craps table while enjoying a stress-free evening with her friends, it was obvious that there was something about this man that moved her. After a fun filled day of shopping, gambling, and frolicking with her friends, the dust finally settles on their first night in Vegas. Once settled into her luxury suite overlooking the Vegas Strip, stretched across her bed dressed in a sexy, black, one shoulder jumpsuit with her matching black heals kicked-off; an inebriated Ashima decides to reach out to Brian with a random text to see how he would respond.

(Text)
Ashima: *"Hello Brian from Apex!"*
Brian: *"Hello Ms. Batool. How's Vegas?"* Brian immediately responds with the new phone he purchased the day after Mallory smashed the old one.

That moment forward initiated a new chapter in both of their lives. The remainder of her time away was devoted to them getting to know each other. From sharing "good morning" sentiments each day at sun-up, to whispering sweet nothings eloquently throughout night, the two carried on like the bliss of a new relationship. Ashima's fondness of Brian grew so intently that her nightcaps would consist of a warm bubble bath in her hotel suite Jacuzzi, with a glass of red wine and late-night conversations with Brian. Not even a three-hour time zone difference would deter Brian from talking to Ashima for as long as needed. In fact, he slept with his phone in hand ready to answer every text notification and phone call from her even in the early A.M. hours, and there wasn't a night that passed that she didn't reach out. She was moved by his charismatic personality and grounded views on life and every moment she had alone she felt compelled to hear his voice again. She learned about Brian's rough upbringing, background, and ambitions, as Brian learned about her history, likes, and most importantly her displeasing relationship with Fahad.

She literally spoke to Fahad once the entire time she is away and that conversation ended in unpleasant bickering. From that point forward Ashima would send Fahad to voicemail and his text messages would go unanswered for the remainder of her trip. Needless to say, Ashima was fully invested in the interest of Brian and he was none the more grateful for it. As a naturally private person, Ashima didn't speak much of her circumstance to her friends. Although it was exciting for her, she wanted to steer clear of any ridicule from them. But, secretly she added a pleasurable dynamic to her trip; fun, vacation, relaxation, and Brian.

By Thursday, Ashima is exhausted from the Vegas experience and ready to come home. But, she's even more excited about the opportunity to engage Brian face to face. After explaining to Brian her plans to return home early to attend the Gala, Brian insists that Ashima give her driver the day off, so he could pick her up and seize the opportunity to have face time with her upon her arrival at Philly International. Ashima was adamant about Brian not seeing her travel face, but she wanted her return home to be a good impression on him. Eventually she agrees to allow him to pick her up from the airport. Since everything happened on short notice and he needed to be at the airport at 10:15am for her arrival time, Brian couldn't take the day off on such short notice unless he had someone to cover. So, despite it being Marty's off, he calls him anyway to ask if he could cover his route. Marty agrees, but only if Brian promised to bring Ashima by the house for game night. Brian not only agreed, but he promised to pick-up a bottle of Marty's favorite vodka along the way.

10:15am Ashima's flight lands at Philadelphia International Airport as Brian sits in his car eagerly awaiting her arrival. Meanwhile, he'd spent the last ten minutes explaining to Mallory why he wouldn't see her at work today because Mama Ruth's ride to her appointments fell through. When she asked if he was coming over at the end of the conversation, he knew that she was none the wiser to his cunning excuse. But, Brian wasn't focused on the interest of Mallory, this moment was reserved for Ashima. He opens his

Robert Glasper playlist to help him set the vibe and give her his best first impression.

At last, the moment he'd been waiting for had finally come. Ashima sends her "ready" text and awaits Brian to pick her up curbside at the arrivals terminal. Naturally Brian is a bit uneasy about seeing her after all of the intimate late-night conversations they've shared throughout the week. But, he counters the emotion with the confidence of knowing her better and turning on a bit of that Mojo. As he enters the D terminal he slows to a crawl looking for anyone who resembles Ashima. Eventually he spots a beautiful woman casually leaning against her tall standing black travel baggage, fumbling with her phone that undeniably fits her description. Wearing a thick open top cardigan sweater with a pair of jeans, and a pair of low cut leather boots, Ashima makes even that simple ensemble look extraordinary.

Brian pulls to the curb where Ashima stood with his hazard lights on and immediately gets out the car to assist her.

"Hello Ms. Batool." Brian charmingly greets her as she lifts her eyes from her phone.

"Oh, hello Brian from Apex!" She responds with a delightful smile as she eventually recognizes Brian as he approaches her.

"How was your flight?" Brian asks as he walks over to her and confidently exchanges a hug.

"It was very relaxing, but I'm glad to be home. Thanks for asking." She replies, suddenly becoming bashful in his presence.

"I'll take this…" Brian says as he reaches for her bag.

"Thank you!" Ashima, feeling a bit timid, immediately takes notice to Brian's considerate mannerism. As she places her phone in her purse, she's also reminded of how handsome Brian is up close. Although, this is the first time she'd seen him since the last time she was home, she felt safe.

Brian lifts the tailgate of his Magnum to carefully place the bulky black luggage in the back of his car. Before closing the tailgate, he quickly inspects the bag to see what brand of luggage Ashima was working with.

"Dayum…Louis, I knew it! This doesn't look like a Louis bag, though." Brian is baffled as the bag wasn't designed with the typical Louis patterns he was accustom to seeing all over.

He then walks over to the passenger side to open the door for her, assisting Ashima into the car like a delicate package. The car was probably the cleanest it's been in months inside and out and smelled as appealing as it looks.

"Hey, before we get going, I just wanted to say that I really appreciate you taking the time out of your day to pick me up. You really didn't have to do this." Ashima expresses with sincere gratitude.

"Awe...no need to thank me. I was looking forward to it! I'd do it again at any time in a heartbeat." Brian replies before closing the door and returning to the driver's side.

"Your car smells really nice, what did you scent it with?" Ashima asks as she looks around the interior of the car.

"Oh, that's just a morning fresh air freshener I keep in the car." Brian simply replies.

"Well, it smells really nice." Although it wasn't the luxury transportation she was used to, Ashima was honestly impartial to judgment.

"And so, do you..." Brian utters, as she dazzles him with another aromatic fragrance.

"Thanks. I purchased it while in Vegas." Ashima replies, appreciating the fact that he noticed.

"Well it was a great investment." Brian charms her as she smiles.

"Wow, it's really gloomy and cold out today. It's a big difference from Vegas this morning." Ashima notices as Brian takes the exit for I-95 north.

"Yeah, I guess we're supposed to get some snow showers later today." Brian informs her.

"Oh, yeah! I forgot about that. I actually had a conversation about it with my friends before we left. I guess you 'kinda' forget about crappy weather once you spend a few days out in the desert." Ashima explains.

"Speaking of Vegas, how was it? Did you break the craps table while you were out there?" Brian asks with amusement.

"Well, I'm not much of a gambler, but I did the tourist thing and had a great time with my adding money to the slots, throwing the dice, and spinning the money wheel. I only won something when we placed a bet together. Other than that, I really had a great time hanging out with my friends and enjoying the weather." Ashima explains.

"Wow, sounds like a lot of fun." Brian replies.

"Yes, it really was very enjoyable." Ashima agrees.

"Well, let's not allow a little overcast to ruin your homecoming. Are you hungry? Would you like to go somewhere to grab a bite to eat?" Brian asks to entice Ashima to have lunch with him.

"Hmm…well I wouldn't mind grabbing a bite. I never eat before a flight and the food they were serving on the plane really didn't look appetizing." Ashima explains.

"Okay cool! Well, I haven't had a chance to eat anything either. So, I'm open to whatever you're open to." Brian replies leaving Ashima the option to choose what to have for lunch, despite knowing that her choice in cuisine could be pricey.

"No, no, no…my life is so boring, I'm sure you venture out to far more diverse dining experiences." Ashima smiles as she insists on not being too imposing on Brian or his budget.

"Haha…yeah, I dabble a little. But, despite being a cook on a culinary level, I'm more of a greasy spoon kind of guy." Brian explains.

"I'm sorry…greasy spoon?" Ashima repeats with a confused look.

"Yeah, you know…Chinese food, cheese steaks and fries, meatball and sausage subs from the hotdog carts downtown…?" Brian further elaborates.

"Okay then…" Ashima simply replies as Brian looks over to notice her clever smile.

"Okay then…what? You want greasy food from a hotdog cart?" Brian asks with a look of uncertainty.

"Sure. I don't mind the humility of lunch from a hotdog cart. Besides, a meatball sandwich sounds pretty good right about now." Ashima responds to her growing appetite.

"Well, it wasn't exactly how I envisioned an appropriate lunch with you. But, I'll let you slum it with me for a day." Brian replies, playfully appeases her request.

After agreeing on a modest choice for lunch, Brian heads to his favorite street vendor at 16th and Arch at the edge of Benjamin Franklin Parkway. Parking is limited pulling up to the vendor's location, so he double-parks with his hazard lights.

"Wassup boss…lemme get a meatball sub with parmesan and a beef hot sausage with grilled onions, ketchup, spicy mustard, whiz, and 'kraut." Brian requests, ordering his usual.

"Wow, that's a really dressed sandwich." Ashima marvels as her idea of condiments would have simply been ketchup and mustard.

"Haha…yeah, I order it like this all the time." Brian simply replies.

"So, where do you eat street vendor food once you order it?" Ashima asks with genuine inquiry as the vendor prepares their food.

"Well, it depends on what you're doing at the time. Since it is a meal that you pick-up in passing, you can either eat it on the go, take it back to the office, take it home, or on a nice day, simply enjoy it on a park bench. I usually eat it on the go or take it home since I'm always working. So, what would you like to do?" Brian asks, once again leaving it to Ashima to decide.

"Well, you're the one who's got me into this mess, so I hold you responsible for picking a place and sharing this meal with me." Ashima playfully replies.

"Aight then…I've got you covered." Brian responds, mentally scrambling to come up with a good location to have lunch.

After grabbing the food and a few drinks, they return to the car and head down the Ben Franklin Pkwy.

"Mmm…that really smells good. I can't wait to try it!" Ashima suggests as the hunger of a few missed meals really begin to set in.

"I know! Most of the time when I get something from the hot dog cart, I'm usually pretty hungry and I just can't wait to dive in!" Brian concurs.

As he approaches the *Philadelphia Art Museum,* he favors the direction of Kelly Drive to park in the rear of the iconic structure where he quickly decided to enjoy lunch on a waterfront overlooking the Schuylkill River. Although, Brian planned on eating inside the car, Ashima has other plans once they arrived.

"Wow! I've never been back here before, it's beautiful! C'mon, let eat on the bench like those two are doing." Ashima suggests, wanting to enjoy a closer, intimate view of the scenic river's edge. A bit taken aback by Ashima's carefree spirit of the elements, Brian just rolls with it.

"Are you sure you don't mind eating out here on a cold bench?" Brian asks with uncertainty as they sit facing the currents southern flow of the Schuylkill River and the rapid movement of cars on the Schuylkill expressway across from them.

"It's not that cold out here. There's no wind blowing, and I actually feel quite comfortable. Besides, this just feels nice." Ashima replies, growing partial to Brian at every passing moment.

"Well, it's not too cold just yet, but the temperature is supposed to drop around noon so I wouldn't get too comfortable out here." Brian urges her.

"Well, if it gets too cold out, then I'll just have to steal your jacket away from you!" Ashima replies displaying a bit more of her playfully charismatic side.

"Touché, touché…but, you might want to open that sandwich before it cools off. I'm not taking the blame for a lukewarm, soggy sandwich." Brian counters, appreciating her jovial appeal as they both unravel their lunch.

"Wow…this looks and smells so amazing!" Ashima notes as she prepares to take her first bite.

"Well, here's to lunch…cheers!" Brian gestures holding his sandwich up to toast hers like champagne flutes.

"Cheers!" Ashima obliges before diving in for a bite.

"Mmm…this is really good! I mean, this is really, really good!" Ashima responds covering her mouth with a napkin as she spoke.

"Nice…I'm glad you're actually enjoying it. I was worried that this might be a little too urban for you." Brian teases watching her react with a delightful expression.

"No, it's not 'too urban' or 'too ghetto' at all for me. In fact, I find it quite exploring. It's delicious!" Ashima enthusiastically replies as they both smile about the comment.

"Haha…okay. I'm just checking. Personally, I would have preferred a seat next to a window in a warm cafe, but I guess this is nice too!" Brian explains trying to press upon his willingness to indulge her alleged premium lifestyle.

"Please…my life is saturated with posh dining experiences. It's not every day that I'm afforded the opportunity to venture out and explore the hidden gems Philadelphia has to offer." Ashima explains with shameless regret.

"Well, growing up in Philly, if it's one thing I know about this city, is hidden gems. But, it's nice to know that a woman of your sophistication is so down to earth that you can appreciate a modest meal." Brian compliments before taking another bite of his sandwich.

207

"Why thank you. One thing I've learned about myself long ago is that although I appreciate being blessed, I'm not typical of an affluent lifestyle." Ashima explains a bit more seriously.

"Fair enough…" Brian accepts with utter relief as the moment falls silent to a sense of thought between the two of them.

"This view is so beautiful and peaceful. I can't believe I've never been here before." Ashima points out as she marvels the view and tranquil sound of the Schuylkill River waterfall. Brian simply grins as he looks out to the water with her.

"Can I show you something?" Brian asks as the tone of his voice suggests that he had something more interesting for Ashima to see.

"Sure, what did you have in mind?" Ashima queries with interest.

"C'mon, let's go for short walk." After tossing the remainder of their food in a trash bin, Brian leads Ashima away from the riverfront and up a steep climbing hill where the Art Museum towers in front of them.

"So, Ms. Batool, we've learned quite a bit about each other over the past week. We obvious come from two different worlds. You're educated, witty, successful, and well-traveled, and I am the son of a goat herder…but, I want to know more. I want to know more about Ashima." Brian proclaims as Ashima places her hand over her mouth to hide her tickled reaction to Brian goat herding joke.

"I'm sorry, you're very charismatic. You make me laugh. I'll bet you make all women laugh." Ashima presumes considering Brian's attractive personality.

"Well yeah…I've been known to brighten a smile or two. One of my better traits, I guess. But, only the ones I like. How 'bout you? If I was to ask your friends what's it like to be friends with Ashima, what would they say?" Brian asks keeping the focus on getting to know her. Ashima shy's away from eye contact with a bashful grin.

"Well, my friends would probably say that I'm a spoiled material girl, because they seem to think I have an appetite for the extravagant. But, I'm really not. I have a lot of ordinary things to prove that I'm not material or high maintenance. I own nice things to keep up with the people in my social circle. But, I'm really a very simple woman. Unlike them, I actually appreciate the little things in life, like eating street food and sharing a cold park bench, versus wine and an entrée at a warm fine dining establishment." Ashima explains, winking at Brian as she sells her humility.

"I kinda got that about you when I picked you up from the airport." Brian reveals to her.

"Really…how so?" Ashima draws curiously.

"Well, when I put your luggage in the back, I noticed how nice it was. But, it wasn't until I took a closer look did I realize that it was surprisingly a Louis V bag. Now, it may not seem like a big deal to you, but to me it showed subtlety. Louis is usually undeniable because it always has the logo printed all over the bag for all to notice. But, you took the subtle approach. Your bag is black with a nice design but very unassuming. To me that to me says a lot about you." Brian profoundly explains.

"Hmph…that was very observant of you. I'm impressed!" Ashima replies, admiring Brian's attentiveness.

"Thanks." Brian says appreciating the comment with a smile. Eventually they find themselves along the front of the Art Museum to an open Downtown Philadelphia skyline, all the way up the Benjamin Franklin Parkway.

"Wow, the city looks so beautiful from here. You know, I've been to the Art Museum a few times. And I don't think I've ever stopped to really appreciate the splendor of the Philly skyline from this view. It's amazing what you miss when you're always on the go, and you don't take time out to see what life really has to offer. This is really gorgeous!" Ashima deeply expresses.

"I used to ride my bike up here with my friends all the time when I was little. We used to run up the stairs like Rocky just like these tourists are doing and we played in the water that runs on both sides of the stairs on some brutally hot days in the summer. The skyline has certainly changed since then." Brian reminisces as his eyes remains fixed on the scenic towering skyscrapers.

"I'm sure. The city is so beautiful from this view." Ashima concurs, admiring the downtown landscape. Even under the cover of an ominous sky the city maintained its inherent beauty.

"Really…? Well I think beauty is overrated." Brian spontaneously responds.

"Okay…why is that?" Ashima asks intrigued by the comment.

"Because beauty is something anyone can be. Now attraction…well, that's something different…and thankfully you're both to me." Brian explains, channeling his inner Mojo. The compliment left Ashima flattered and embarrassed and hiding behind her blushing smile.

"My goodness. I'm very touched by your kind words. You really do have a way with women, don't you?" Ashima asks, purely pleased to be in Brian's company. Meanwhile, Brian, hoping he's hitting all the right cords continues to attempt to charm her.

"Well, that's yet to be seen. I mean, I'm still not convinced that I've moved you yet." Brian cleverly responds.

"Hmph…is that right? So, what are you looking for to validate your certainty?" Ashima responds challenging his next move.

Without saying another word, Brian took a moment to evaluate the truth in her eyes before cautiously leaning in to deliver an endearing kiss on her cheek to check the pulse of her reaction. Ashima responds with a perplexed look that Brian didn't understand.

"I'm sorry, I probably shouldn't have done that…" Brian presumes from her reaction.

"No, actually…you missed." Ashima responds in a soft, subtle tone as she looks up at him directly in the eyes with resolute distinction.

Brian grins and grabs her by the hand, draws her in close, and follows-up with a slow passionate kiss on her lips that he's been yearning for since the day he first laid eyes on her. Ashima gracefully embraces his advance, by reaching behind his neck and pulling him in closer for a more intense passionate moment of intimacy.

From the moment Brian graces her soft lips, the ground vanishes beneath her feet and butterflies flutter her stomach and lifts her to an epic euphoria. The energy that bonds them at this moment was one that Brian wanted and Ashima needed. As they stand romantically intertwined atop of the famous Art Museum stares among a few tourists and onlookers, they were interrupted by the sudden sensation of something cold and wet landing directly on both of their noses.

"Oh my God, is it really snowing right now? This is amazing!" Ashima says marveling the timing of the moment as the sky and the ground around them are being cascaded by a flurry of snowflakes.

"Wow…right on time!" Brian thinks as he admires the wintery vista falling around them.

As promised, snow began to fall upon the city as the brilliant Philadelphia skyline is suddenly transformed into a giant picturesque snow globe. As Ashima melts away in Brian's arms in a moment that seems so surreal, it was almost as if it was rehearsed. She'd never experienced and wasn't prepared for this level of romantic bliss. Brian held her close and observed as she stood frozen in a daze, like she was in another place despite holding him ever so tight.

"Are you 'aight'?" Brian looks down to her from the height he stood as they continue to stand motionless. Her eyes remaining fixed down the Ben Franklin Parkway to the rise of the Philly Skyline.

"Yes, I'm okay. It's just so beautiful out here…" Ashima replies, expressing her thoughts openly and honest. But, the real honesty is that she's never felt anything like this in the arms of man before. The emotion she's feeling is almost scary and forces her to look up at him again to ensure that it was actually real.

As they gape into each other's blissful eyes, Brian initiates another series of pecks to her lips. There was something profound about the way she responded to him that led him to believe that this romantic engagement was special.

As he watches the warm air exit her every breath, he could tell she was delicately braving the cold. Her body shivers ever so slightly, but she remains undaunted. Ashima was enjoying his company and wants to continue getting to know him. Brian blows into his hands and rubs them together to warm them, before placing them on her neck, then rubbing her arms to comfort her. She responds to his gesture by wrapping her arms securely around his waist. Immediately, he could tell she was new to shivery. Embracing Ashima in his arms sent Brian above the overcast of clouds. She was like an angelic figure that stood before him with her angel wings stretched around him.

"I should probably get you out of this cold and to the house before it gets to bad out. You still have to unpack and get ready for this evening's festivities, right?" Brian asks rhetorically.

"Ugh…unfortunately! But, only if you'll force me to go." Ashima playfully replies as she loathed the idea of ending such a romantic outing for a function she'd much rather not attend.

"Well, as much as I would love to kidnap you and lock you away in my apartment forever, I actually like your dad and I wouldn't want him thinking something happened to his little princess. So how about we make this a 'to be continued' moment this time and I promise we can make it up later?" Brian offers, seeking her approval. She sighs in disappointment before answering.

"Hmm…okay…" She reluctantly agrees as she frowns with the cutest immature pout of disapproval.

As they walk back to the car, the joy of being in each other's company stimulated senseless playfulness. As the snowflakes showered down, turning the landscape around them into a glamor of white, Brian amuses Ashima by catching the snowflakes with his tongue. Suddenly, as they frolic down the steep trail, they come across a flock of Canadian goslings following their parents lead as they cross the path in front of Brian and Ashima.

"Awe…look at them. They're so adorable!" Ashima says as they stop to watch them parade by.

"Here goosy, goosy!" Brian calls out to the geese as he snaps his fingers at them. Suddenly, the gander of the flock, taking exception to Brian's harassment stands his ground and lets out a loud challenging hiss.

"Oh my God, Brian stop! These geese are aggressive." Ashima shouts as she fearfully pulls Brian in front of her for cover.

"What?! What?! You want some of this? You better fall back Air Canada, you're in Philly now, Bruh!" Brian challenges the gander as if he was preparing to spar with the bird.

"Brian! Oh my God, stop! He's going to bite us or something" Ashima pulls at Brian with amusement, laughing at him going at it with the fearless bird. Growing agitated, the gander hisses even louder. The mother goose even lets out a passive hiss, as she began to feel threatened.

"No, no…don't hold me back! Don't hold me back!" Brian exclaims, becoming more animated, playfully kicking and swinging at the geese. Fed-up with Brian's antics, the gander makes a daring charge at them both, letting them know he means business.

Ashima lets out a screeching cry as she runs from the gander with laughter, leaving Brian to fend for himself. Brian retreats along with her and concedes to the gander's fiery charge.

"My goodness Brian, you are so crazy. I can't believe you made that crazy goose go off like that!" Ashima declares in awe, trying to catch her breath.

"I know…he was coming for me like I stole one of his eggs for breakfast this morning or something." Brian replies.

"See, that's what you get for messing around with his family. I'd be pissed at you too!" Ashima exaggerates.

"Yeah well, 'I'ma' quit while I'm ahead, before the Park Service mess around and arrests me for harassment. Anyway, c'mon, I promise to leave the geese alone and you can hide behind me for protection." Brian assures her as he's ready to head to the car.

"I'm not going anywhere near that thing. I don't know what kind of rabies that thing has." Ashima firmly declines.

"Okay then, how 'bout you get on my back and I'll carry you to the car? This way he'll have to go through me to get to you?" Brian proposes.

"Umm...okay. But, you better not drop me!" Ashima warns, as she tentatively agrees his solution.

"I promise you'll be safe with me." He assures her.

"Okay then, just please be careful!" Ashima accepts as Brian crouches down and she nervously climbs onto his back.

"Don't worry, I got you!" Brian calmly consoles her. As he slowly paces his way around the frightened flock, the gander flares up with another threatening hiss.

"Oh my God, he looks so pissed!" Ashima says as she clutches Brian tighter around his neck.

"Look dawg, I mean goose. I don't want no trouble. Just go ahead with your little goose family and we can all have a good day out here, okay?" The gander aggressively hisses again as if he wants to square up with Brian while the rest of his flock continues on to safety. Ashima is amused, but gripping Brian tighter at every act of aggression from the angry bird.

"Look killa, you ain't no real angry bird! You better get out of here before I sell you to a restaurant in Chinatown! You ever heard of Peking duck?!" The gander's hisses grew more intently as the bird would charge a few paces with his wings flaring out to intimidate Brian. It was almost as if Brian and the gander were arguing with each other.

"You know what...you know what! You're 'gonna' need Aflac by the time I get done with you, Buddy. You're all beak and no action, Daffy. You and your little duck dynasty better get the hell on! Why don't you fly back to Canada! DO YOU EVEN HAVE A PASSPORT?! 'I'MA' CALL THE SPCA's IMMIGRATION DEPARTMENT ON YOU!!!" Brian exclaims as

213

he shouts louder, the further he retreats down the path from the agitated geese.

Ashima is riding Brian's back nearly in tears from the laughter as Brian playfully acted out. Despite the animated commotion Brian put on, passers-by's and museum tourists out enjoying the snowy day were highly amused and laughing at Brian's comical antics.

"Oh, my goodness...Brian! You are just too funny. I can't stop laughing." Ashima says enjoying every moment of Brian's silliness.

Likewise, Brian was having the best time with Ashima, and couldn't remember the last time he'd had such fun with a woman he went out with. Brian lowers Ashima to the ground and hides behind her as he continues his animated verbal assault.

"No, no! Don't hold me back! Don't hold me back!" Brian exclaims as Ashima plays along, embracing Brian by the waist to stop his playful charge at the bird.

"Okay! Okay! I think he's had enough." Ashima pleads trying to de-escalate the confrontation.

"That's why you need a pedicure with your webbed feet, punk! You better run!" Brian yells as he points his finger aggressively at the bird. Despite the twenty feet of distance between them, the gander still felt threatened and made another hostile charge at Brian with wings flailing about, hissing, and all.

"Oh my God, Brian that bird is going to kill you!" Ashima urges as they both retreat to the car.

"Yeah, I know. I don't think he cared for the webbed feet insult." Brian agrees as they hurry back to his car.

As they approached the car, Ashima slips and nearly falls to the ground. Fortunately, Brian right at her side and grabs her to break her fall.

"Whoa...! Oh my God, thank you!" Ashima graciously expresses as she grabs hold of his strong embracing arms.

"No worries. I got you!" Brian replies in a safe subtle tone.

Once she regains her balance, she didn't immediately let go, and neither did he. Knowing Ashima wasn't his to claim just yet, he selfishly holds her as if she were, if only for that moment. He knew the validity of her relationship with Fahad was unstable and eventually he would be granted the opportunity to set her free.

214

As Brian hustles to get Ashima home before the snowfall was too bad, they would leave this intimate, leisure moment knowing they were both emotionally invested. Although their day concluded early, the allure felt between them made them feel a sense of comfort and this was only the beginning.

6:13pm that evening, riding quietly in the back of a Bentley Mulsanne, Ashima is on her way to the Corporate Investors Gala with Fahad. Elegantly dressed in a black spaghetti strap, rosette ball gown and a pair of black Louboutin Kashou red bottom heels, Ashima sits reclined with her legs crossed in a defensive posture, clearly uninterested in attending the ball with Fahad. However, she didn't learn of the evening's itinerary until after Amir explained it to her once he came home. Amir specifically requested that Ashima attend the event to win over a few potential clients for future corporate endeavors.

Although, Ashima has quite the liberal tongue when it comes to righteous expression especially towards Amir and Fahad, she also quickly established herself as having a way with getting investors to open their wallets. To no avail, Ashima was not enthused about the arrangements of her date, and has been distant towards Fahad since he arrived. The ride in the cabin of the car was so quiet you could nearly hear a person think. As Fahad moves around his stocks on his phone, Ashima sits with an elated grin, as the snowfall pleasantly reminds her of how much fun she shared with Brian.

"So, Princess, how was your trip to sin city?" Fahad asks as he puts his phone away and turns his attention to Ashima to stimulate a conversation. The mere sound of his voice disturbed her thoughts.

"It was very enjoyable." Ashima replies nonchalantly as she looks out at the barely visible skyscrapers through the continuous snowfall.

"It must have been quite exciting considering I only heard from you once the entire time you were away." Fahad rousingly comments.

"Yes, well it was a lady's trip Fahad, so…" Ashima responds as she wasn't particularly interested in conversing with him.

"True, and as your significant other you should at least have the decency to pick-up when I call or respond to my text." Fahad boldly replies.

"Is that so…?" Ashima responds in short with a tone of denial.

"I'm sorry, did I say something wrong?" Fahad replies, growing annoyed of Ashima's disregard. Still weighing heavy on her conscience,

Ashima fights with every inch of temptation not to confront Fahad about his affair with Nisa.

"I just missed the part where anything between us was significant." Ashima smartly replies, alluding to her true feelings.

"Excuse me? Ashima, why do you reply to me with such an unsavory tone? I have not seen you in over a week, yet you look at me with such disgust." Fahad asks, trying to understand the root of her animosity.

"Perhaps you have forgotten, but I last remember you trying to scold me because I was trying to enjoy myself with my friends. It seems I can never have an amicable conversation with you. Every time we speak, there's always a disagreement or an altercation." Ashima calmly explains.

"Ashima, I don't wish to be at odds with you, that's why I go out of my way to do nice things for you. I mean, look around you. I try to provide you with nothing but the best. A Bentley for the Gala, a bottle of the finest wine in the chiller behind you, I even went out of my way to pick up something for you from jeweler's row." Fahad says as he reaches for a bag from the floor, and pulling a large box from the bag. He opens it for her and unveils a diamond and sapphire tiara choker necklace. Ashima passively looks at the necklace as if she's unimpressed.

"Here you are, a little something for the occasion." He says, removing it from the velvet lining and presenting it to her.

"It's very nice." She replies with a lack of enthusiasm.

"Good, I'm glad you like it. I bought it because I thought it would look good with your dress…although you don't seem to be enthused by my caring gesture." Fahad says, troubled by Ashima's mundane response.

"Forgive me, but I'm really not in the mood for diamonds tonight." A distant Ashima declines.

"Like you haven't been in the mood to wear the ten-karat engagement ring I bought you? Are you not grateful for the spoils of a queen that I try to provide for you?" Fahad explains with disappointment as he neatly places the necklace back on the velvet rest before closing the box and placing it back into the bag.

"Fahad, everything in life isn't about money. Yet, everything you do in life revolves around trying to impress people. You think this is impressive? This car, this necklace, all of these opulent things you throw at my feet? You think you're doing me a favor when you buy me gifts and take me to boring, snobbish restaurants? If this was your way of winning my favor, then you've been grossly misinformed. You can't buy my love, Fahad. You have to invest in knowing me for who I am in order to move me. Not trying to thrill me with unremarkable gifts." Ashima bluntly explains as they exit the highway into the downtown area.

"Unremarkable? There's nothing unremarkable about the seven hundred and fifty thousand dollars I spent for that ring or the hundred thousand dollars I spent on this necklace, Ashima. I just don't understand how you can be so ungrateful. I do my best to give you everything to make you happy. There are so many women out there that would literally throw themselves at the opportunity to live like this. Yet every day you take it for granted." Fahad bitterly speaks in response to Ashima's deflating comments.

"No, you take me for granted, Fahad! Ever since you and my father decided what's best for my future, you've taken me for granted at every turn. You speak and demand from me as if I am your wife already…a preview of being your Islamic slave perhaps, yes?!" Ashima challenges as Fahad avoids eye contact and nods in passive agreement.

"You really have me wrong if you think I'm going to submit to you and be your dog for a diamond leash and a promise of a life I already have." An irritated Ashima vents.

"Of course, somewhere along the way I obviously lost sight of what was important. I mean, how foolish of me to think that you could be bought with endless wealth. Private jets, million-dollar cars, unlimited spending, and a promise to be a part of the Gabr family royalty is all this life has to offer." Fahad is abruptly interrupted by Ashima.

"…Courtesy of your father of course! None of which you've done for yourself. You've never even had a job before, Fahad." Ashima rapidly fires back.

"Are you kidding me? I work nearly every day and I've made much of my own money! I…" Fahad contends as Ashima interrupts him yet again and he grows increasingly agitated.

"Fahad, you're a day trader who plays around with daddy's money all day! You don't punch a clock or run a business. Whether the market manages in your favor or not, you always win because there's plenty in the well to draw from, yes? You're just a spoiled little rich kid who thinks that everything in life has a price tag. Well guess what…not everything!" Ashima boldly reads Fahad as he sits frozen and speechless in his seat with wounded pride.

"Wow, is that what you think of me? Some low-life that plays around with daddy's money to impress you? Have you not forgotten that I've known you nearly all of your life? Have you forgotten that I'm an educated man who graduated at the top of his class in finance? I think you know me better to believe that I'm just some rich kid who strokes his ego by playing monopoly with the Sheik's money. Ashima, all I want to do is love you. You know you mean more to me than this affluent lifestyle." Fahad sympathizes with her as he gently strokes her hand while it lay on the armrest before she repulsively draws it back.

"Oh, I see…it's someone else, isn't it? Yes…indeed it is. I can see it in your eyes. You know the eyes never lie, Ashima. Who is he, hmm? Who is this person who grants you such intimate sanctuary, hmm? Someone at your work…? A colleague or friend of yours from college…? One of my friends perhaps, huh…who?" Fahad persistently accuses in a tirade of questions. Ashima doesn't even bother to interrupt his insecure rant.

"I don't know, but perhaps you can tell me since you're so adamant in your accusations." Ashima angrily replies.

"Sure…it all makes sense. I mean, why else would you deny me sex, huh? Why else would you distance yourself so sudden and speak to me with such disrespect, hmm?" Fahad questions as he allows his bitterness to grasp his emotions. Although Fahad's speculation couldn't be farther from the truth, it fueled her resentment of him prompting her to appreciate here fondness of Brian even more.

"Fahad, I refuse to dignify any of your accusations and I will not allow you to hamper my evening. It's bad enough I had to cut my vacation short to attend this function, only to have you accompany me with your false pretenses." Ashima replies as the driver slows to a stop in front of the *Loew's Hotel* entrance on Market Street, where greeters with black trench coats and top hats awaited curbside for guests to arrive. As Ashima prepares to exit, Fahad aggressively grabs her by the arm to get her attention.

"Ashima…!" He starts out with a fiery stare, but couldn't finish his discord to avoid embarrassment. Ashima looks back at Fahad with a degree of seriousness of her own before snatching her arm from his tight grip.

"Welcome to the *Loew's Hotel*, Ma'am." The greeter announces after opening her door to help her out of the car.

"Thank you." Ashima smiles. Disturbed by the aggressive encounter, Ashima doesn't bother to look back as she enters the hotel.

Fahad hastily trails behind her as she quickly paced to an open elevator in an effort to elude him. To no avail, as the elevator door began to close, Fahad reaches in to reopen it. Ashima stands among a few other formally dressed guests as Fahad enters the elevator with a sneaky smile on his face and stands next to Ashima. As the door close, Fahad looks over at Ashima as she stares straight ahead into the stainless-steel reflection of the elevator door trying to act as if he isn't there. Fahad prolongs his stare to gain her attention, but when his gesture goes unanswered, he grabs her hand with a firm grip. Struggling to hold her composure, Ashima reluctantly looks at him with a forged smile, then let's out a deep disappointing sigh as she glances back at an elder gentleman and his wife. He nods to her with a silent hello, and she responds with a simple smile.

After a short ride to the second floor, the elevator door opens to a bustling corridor filled with live jazz, servers with horsd'oeurves, ice sculptures, upscale executives, and accommodations to meet their every need. Ashima steps off the elevator and immediately snatches away from Fahad again after spotting her assistant Samantha socializing with a few other colleagues through the ballroom doors. Suppressing her anger, she quickly wears her professional façade to focus on her purpose for being there.

"Hi Sam! Hi everyone!" Ashima calls out as she approaches the group.

"Oh, hey Ms. Batool…"

"So glad you could make it…"

"How was your trip…?"

"Wow, you look great!" Various voices from the group respond.

"Thanks everyone! My vacation was very nice. I'm glad to see you're all enjoying yourselves this evening!" Ashima replies, standing as the center of attention.

"Always enjoyable when it's open bar!" One person cites as the group erupts in amusement.

"Has anyone seen my father?" Ashima asks, not only scanning the mass of people for her father, but also looking for Fahad who was nowhere in her view.

"Oh yeah, I just saw him over by the ice sculpture talking to Franklin and a Saudi Ambassador." Someone spoke out pointing to the area Amir was last seen.

"I can go get him if you'd like?" Samantha offers preparing to set her glass on a nearby table.

"Oh-no, Sam! Thanks, but you're not working tonight, you're enjoying yourself. Please, have fun everyone. I'll find him on my own, thanks! Please, excuse me everyone." Ashima pardons herself to find her father.

Sifting her way through the crowd, she runs into a few other professional associates, and briefly stops to chat to a few them as she makes her way to the other side of the room. Although there's plenty of seating in the enormous ballroom, it was standing room only as everyone in attendance was taking full advantage of the networking opportunity.

"Ashima! Ashima! Please come, Princess!" A voice rang out ahead of her as she could see Amir vigorously waving to get her attention.

"Hello Princess. You've finally arrived!" Amir says, as he greets her with a kiss on each cheek.

"Hello father...Franklin." She replies, noticing them dressed handsomely in their tuxedos, enjoying a glass of wine with another gentleman they were speaking to.

"Hello Ashima, you look stunning fresh off your vacation." Franklin compliments as he greets her with a single peck on the cheek.

"May I have the pleasure of introducing you to my lovely daughter, Ashima Batool. Ashima, this is Alkari Mohammed, a real estate developer of *Arab Emirates Commerce*." Amir gladly introduces his daughter to the Saudi Arabian businessman.

"Hello Ashima, it's a pleasure to meet you. I've heard so many great things." The heavy Middle-Eastern accented gentleman replies. The tuxedo dressed Mohammed takes her by the hand and greets her with a kiss on each cheek.

Amir's enthusiastic demeanor immediately suggested that this was the man she definitely needed establish a business rapport with. He was an older gentleman balding at the crown of his head with salt and pepper hair throughout his remaining hair and beard.

"الولايات في هنا إقامتك يستمتع أنت تكون كيف .محمّد ..مر, أيضا أنت يلتقي أن متعة"
"المتّحدة الأمريكيّة؟"

"Pleasure to meet you as well, Mr. Mohammed. How are you enjoying your stay here in the U.S.?" Ashima charmingly asks, sizing up his demeanor for a potential business arrangement later on. Taken aback by her fluent Arab tongue, he gladly indulges her.

"التزامات لعمل إلى الأمريكيّة المتّحدة الولايات إلى يأتي حبّ حالة أنا...ممتعة جدّا". وجبة شريحة جبن فيلّي على صفقة يغلق أن يمكن كان أنا وإلّا حيث .فيلادلفيا مدائن يحبّ ,خصوصا غداء؟"

"Very enjoyable...I love coming to the U.S. to for business engagements. Especially, cities like Philadelphia. Where else would I be able to close a deal over a Philly cheese steak lunch?" The Arab businessman comically replies as everyone is collectively amused by his humor. Franklin, who's completely bewildered by the Arabic exchange, simply laughs along anyway.

"Wow, well I'm certainly glad that you're impressed by what the city has to offer Mr. Mohammed." Ashima replies reverting back to English dialogue.

"Please, call me Al." Alkari politely insists.

"Well Al, what brings you to the city for such a lovely occasion?" Ashima asks, enticing him with her savvy business appeal.

"Well, my colleagues and I have been impressed with the business practices of many projects that U.S. investors have funded in recent times. Including the multi-billion-dollar construction project we cut the ribbon on just last year. Now we're already looking to add a half-billion-dollar extension to this project." Alkari explains.

"Oh...well in that case, I think you've already found what you've come to the states for then." Ashima confidently assures him as she looks him in the eyes with unwavering distinction and an appeasing smile.

"Please, allow me to get you a glass...let's talk!" Impressed by her beautiful grace and business posture, Alkari is interested in hearing more from the luminous young woman, speaking a language that he could identify with.

As he leads her away from Amir and Franklin, Amir winks at Ashima suggesting his approval of her "A" game. Doing what she does best, Ashima was able to convince Alkari to verbally commit to exclusive negotiations. Despite being bothered by the childish stunt Fahad pulled when they arrived, she still manages to put her best smile on display and vibrantly works the room, leaving an impression on nearly everyone in the venue, including Philly Finance and Trust competitors. One of the bank's corporate rivals brazenly offers Ashima a twenty-five percent salary increase and a

221

hefty signing bonus if she agrees to work for them. Although the offer was tempting, Ashima politely declines as she maintains her loyalty to Philadelphia Finance and Trust.

However, after being at the event for a few hours mingling with a few corporate heavy hitters, Ashima has already grown tired of the haughty party scene. Especially, after Fahad embarrasses her by interrupting a conversation she was having with a French Ambassador. Introducing himself as her fiancé, Fahad dominates the conversation which granted Ashima the opportunity she was seeking to excuse herself. On her last thread of patience with him, Ashima quickly walks away to ensure she loses Fahad in the thick of the crowd. Although she's preoccupied at the event with all things involving business, she couldn't help but wonder if it was too late to meet with Brian. Tucked away in a quiet corner, she opens her clutch to send Brian a text message. To her delight, she notices that she'd already received a text message from him not long ago.

(Text)
Brian: *"Hope ur enjoying your event. I wish you could have made it here with me."* Ashima reads as the bleak expression on her face is altered by a sudden pacifying smile.
Ashima: *"Hi. How's the game night going?"* She immediately responds.
Brian: *"Game nite is good, lots of fun. How's your event going?"* Brian answers.

Unprepared for the rapid reply, she moves to the massive ballroom ceiling to floor window view overlooking Market Street to avoid interruption as she responds to his messages.

(Text)
Ashima: *"It's very nice and very boring. I'm ready to go."*
Brian: *"The nite is still young. Ur more than welcome 2 join us 4 game nite if you'd like?"*
Ashima: *"I would love to, but I'm a bit over dressed for the occasion."*
Brian: *"U can come as u r. I promise you'll be surrounded by good people."*
Ashima: *"Well, no promises. But, just in case, may I have the address?"*

As she awaits his reply, she leans against the glass with her arms crossed in front of her; her clutch in one hand and her phone in the other. She stands in thought as she looks down at the traffic passing beneath her feet. Pondering her gleeful escape, she grows excited with every anticipating moment. However, her moment of elation is interrupted by a text from Fahad. But, just as he sent his message, she spots him in the ballroom among the crowd.

(Text)
Fahad: *"Where are you?"*

As she watches him texting her from a distance stalking the exit, she becomes a bit discouraged and needed a plan to lure him away.

(Text)
Ashima: *"Heading into the restroom. Do you need something?"*

She replies in an effort to make her escape. As predicted, rather than answer her, Fahad immediately makes his way towards the restrooms to corner her. Once he disappears from view, Ashima makes her way to the exit at a lively pace. She doesn't even bother to wait for an elevator. Instead, she picked up her dress and takes the stairs. As she exits the hotel, she looks out to the street to see if there were any passing cabs she could flag down.

"Taxi Ma'am?" The door man asks, taking notice to her urgent mannerism.

"Yes please!" She answers as she looks at her phone eagerly waiting for Brian's reply.

"TAXI!" The doorman hails as an approaching cab pulls to the curb in front of them. The doorman opens and closes the cab door for her before the cabbie drives off.

"Good evening Miss, where to?" The cab driver asks as she looks down at her phone to see if Brian has responded, which he did.

"Seven, six, two, four, Jay Place please! It's in Southwest Philadelphia." She replies with a sense of relief.

"Yes Ma'am." The cab driver replies plugging the address in his GPS.

(Text)

Ashima: *"On my way!"*

Ashima sends Brian as she comfortably enjoys the ride and checks her Facebook. However, barely a few yards from the venue, she began receiving text messages from Fahad as they wait on a red light at the corner of the hotel.

(Text)
Fahad: *"Where are you?"*
Fahad: *"Have you left the restroom? I'm looking for you."*

Ashima looks at the messages with utter disgust and with no regard, she ignores them. As she sits content in the back of the cab, anticipating her unconventional rendezvous with Brian, her delightful thoughts of him were jaded by a series of persistent phone calls and text messages from Fahad. His controlling, egotistical behavior is doing nothing but propelling her favor of Brian even more.

As the cabbie passes through the light, Ashima immediately notices the Mulsanne she arrived in parked ahead.

"Driver, could you hold up here please? I won't be a minute." She requests as they get closer.

"Not a problem, Miss. Take your time!" The driver obliges as he pulls alongside of the Bentley.

Once he comes to a stop, Ashima reaches into her purse and pulls out a red leather box carrying Fahad's ten karat diamond. She then hops out of the cab and taps on her driver's window to signal his attention.

"Yes, Ma'am?" He says after rolling down his window.

"Hi...! I need to toss something in the back that I no longer need!" Ashima asks urgently.

"Certainly Madam, by all means!" He replies unlocking the car doors.

Ashima opens the rear passenger door and quickly tosses the jewelry box onto the backseat before hoping back into the cab taking off. Not only did relinquishing the ring free her from its liability, in her mind it symbolized the end of a bane saga with Fahad.

Feeling such relief from the burden of Fahad lifted, for the remainder of the ride, she enjoys the night-lit scenic views of the city with a mild nervousness of her rendezvous with Brian.

"I'm here!" She texts as the cabby pulls in front of the address.

"That'll be thirty-one even, Ma'am." The driver requests as she stalls for a reply from Brian.

As she fumbles with her clutch for the money, Brian suddenly appears at her window and opens the door for her.

"Well hello Ms. Ashima." Brian says with a glowing smile.

"Hello, Brian from Apex. I was beginning to wonder what happened to you. I got no reply to my text messages." Ashima says as she continues to ramble, counting out the money for the cabby.

"Yeah, sorry about that, my phone died and no one's got an Android charger inside. So, I had to charge it in the car." Brian explains.

"Oh, well how'd you know I arrived?" She curiously asks.

"Excuse me for a minute…" Brian asks of her as he engages the driver.

"Excuse me Bruh, how much is that on the meter, thirty-one? Here ya' go Fam, here's forty. Keep the change, boss!" Brian settles up with the cabbie, handing him the money before helping Ashima out of the car.

"Awe…you're so sweet. You didn't have to do that!" Ashima replies, humbled by his generous gesture.

"Yeah, I did. It's only the gentleman thing to do, especially when you went out of your way to hang out with me and my friends from such a lovely event, I'm sure. And to answer your question, I watched for you from the window while you pulled up. I'm glad you made it though. You look more beautiful than I've ever seen you. I mean, you are really wearing that dress!" Brian flatters her with his honest assessment of her ensemble as he greets her with a peck on the cheek.

"Well thank you, I really appreciate that. It really meant a lot to me to just get out of that place. I'm still very tired from my vacation and would like to just relax." Ashima explains as Brian takes her by the hand and escorts her to the house.

"Well, we can leave anytime you're ready. I'm just glad that you were willing to even come out." Brian replies.

"Uh oh, there she is…" Marty belts out as Brian and Ashima walks inside.

"Hey everyone, this is Ashima! Ashima this is everyone!" Brian generally introduces, instead of naming each of the thirteen people in attendance.

"Hello everyone, I'm very pleased to meet you all!" Ashima replies with reserve shyness.

"Hi…! How you doin'…?" Various people in the room reply.

"Oh my God, you're gorgeous! Brian, she's gorgeous!" Marty's wife Kerry exclaims, frantically scampering over to greet Ashima with welcome hugs.

"Thank you, I'm flattered!" Ashima responds, completely taken aback and unsure of how to receive such admiration.

"I am in love with this dress, and those heels…oh my God! See Brian, a woman with class. I knew you could do it, boy! You go, boy!" Kerry carries on under the influence of a few glasses of wine. Ashima just smiles as everyone else in the room critiques her from a distance.

"Damn babe, give her some space. You act like you've never had company before!" Marty protests, urging his tipsy wife to calm down.

"She's not just company Charles, she's with Brian. That's better than company!" Kerry smiles, referring to Marty by his first name.

"Anyway, welcome to game night. Feel free to make yourself at home, we've got food, we've got drinks. But, you look like a glass of wine would work in your favor, girl…you classy!" Kerry assumes, judging Ashima by her apparent sophistication.

"Oh-no! Thank you very much. But, I had more than enough at the function I attended tonight." Ashima modestly declines.

"Yeah, she's had a really long day y'all. She just flew in this morning from Vegas, hung out with me earlier, then had to attend the event she just came from. I just had her come so she can meet everybody before taking her home." Brian explains.

"Oh, my God! You, poor girl. You must be a zombie by now! Are you sure you don't want to rest for a moment before you go?" Kerry asks with a hospitable plea.

"Oh…no thank you. Honestly, I'm fine. But, thank you anyway…I really appreciate your humble gesture." Ashima modestly declines.

"I like your tattoo art. If you don't mind me asking what exactly do they call that?" Kerry's best friend Ebony asks, admiring the designs on Ashima's hands.

"Oh, this is called mehndi. But, you may hear some people refer to it as henna." Ashima explains as she holds out her hand to allow all to see.

"Wow, that's nice!" Kerry comments as others gather to take a look.

226

"Yeah, it's so neat. Is it permanent?" Candace asks as she gently brushes her hand along the fine artwork.

"Thank you. No, it's very temporary." Ashima replies.

"How long does it take for something like that to get done?" Kerry's friend Yarnetta chimes in.

"Not very long, perhaps an hour or so..." Ashima answers.

"Well, as much as I'd like to keep spankin' y'all in Pictionary, she's had a long day and I know she wants to relax, so 'I'ma' get at y'all later." Brian interjects to save Ashima from being uncomfortable and bombarded with more questions.

"Spankin'? Boy bye, that stick figure on the board over there is the best thing you drew all night." Ebony jokingly speaks out.

"Uh-oh...shots fired! Man down! Man down!" Kerry blurts out as everyone laughs at her antics.

"Really...? You just gone put me out there like that, Eb?" Brian smiles with a hint of embarrassment.

"Really...? You just gone lie in front of your date like that?" Ebony mocks him. Brian has yet again fallen to the comic relief of the room.

Even Ashima is tickled by Ebony's mockery. Brian could only smile in the amusing moment with humility.

"You know what...on that note, I'm out! But, you might want to follow me to the car, Eb. I think I still got some grease in my gym bag so you can matte down those edges." Brian fires back.

"WHOA...!" The party erupts in laughter leaving Ebony speechless. Ebony responds with an extended middle finger as Brian sticks out his tongue.

"I'll get at you later, Marty." Brian yells over the noisy crowd as he scurries out the door before Ebony has a chance to say something else.

"Bye! Thanks for coming! Love you, Brian!" Ebony yells with good intent.

"Love you too, Eb!" Brian replies as he opens the front door for Ashima.

"Good night everyone!" Ashima exclaims addressing everyone in the room.

"Good night...! Nice meeting you!" Various people in the room reply as they exit the house.

"Wow, you have some great friends." Ashima mentions as they walk out to the cool of the night.

"Yeah, they're good people. I wouldn't trade them for the world. It's always love when I'm around them." Brian explains on their way to the car.

"Yes, and I can certainly tell they love you, too!" Ashima replies as Brian pushes his keyless remote to unlock his car.

After opening the door for her like a gentleman, Brian gets behind the wheel and notices frost accumulated on his windshield. The temperature dropped just as fast as he introduces Ashima to his friends. Although Brian is still trying to learn her, he can tell by the attitude of her body language that Ashima has become comfortable in his presence. The conversation is minimal on their way to East-Falls, but it's only because they were thinking of each other.

As Brian turns onto School House Lane from Ridge Avenue, Ashima realizes that she doesn't want to be bothered by her father and his million and one questions of where she's been, nor does she want to face the possibility of encountering Fahad and his foolishness. So, she makes up her mind not to stay. After a quick ride up the very steep hill of School House Lane, Brian pulls in front of her driveway.

"Here ya go, Ms. Batool...safe and sound as promised!" Brian says as he unbuckles his seat belt to get out and open her door.

"No wait! I'll be right back! Give me ten minutes." She says, placing her hand on his lap to gesture holding him in place.

"Okay...?" Brian replies with confusion as he places the car in park to wait for her return.

Completely unsure as to why he was waiting, Brian checks his social media page as he waits. While inside Ashima wastes no time packing a quick bag for her utility to avoid the possibly of Amir or Fahad showing up. Eleven minutes later, still dressed as before Ashima returns to the car with a duffle bag in hand.

"Okay, I'm ready!" She says with all smiles as after getting in the car.

"Umm...okay! I guess my place it is then!" Brian replies, caught off guard by her intentions, but excited nonetheless.

Once they arrive at his place, Brian walks in with her bag and quickly scans his humble abode to verify that everything is in good order before she walks in behind him. As usual, with the exception of a few scattered study materials and a folded bag of chips, everything appears to be good thanks to good housekeeping habits he inherited from Mama Ruth.

"Well, make yourself at home. You pretty much know where everything is so feel free to kick your off your shoes and relax." Brian explains to make her comfortable.

"Thanks, may I have some water please?" Ashima immediately asks, feeling a bit parch.

"Oh-no! First time you're a guest, second time you're at home. So, here's the remote, the fridge is that way…towels, linen, and soap is on the shelf over the toilet." Brian playfully informs her. Although confused, Ashima smiles at Brian's sudden change in hospitable demeanor.

"So, I know you ate at the event you were at, but are you sure I can't offer you something to eat?" Brian offers as she walks to the kitchen to grab a bottled water from the fridge.

"No, I'm sure. I'll be fine!" Ashima insists. Eager to showcase his culinary skills, Brian is determined to tempt her.

"Well, I'm in the mood for something sweet and I'd hate to eat it without you having a little for yourself." He suggests, enticing his guest to indulge.

"Hmm…okay! I could go for some dessert. What do you have in mind?" Ashima gives in, now a bit curious as to what Brian has to offer in the kitchen.

"Nothing in particular, but I'll check out the cabinets and see what I can whip up!" Brian explains as Ashima stands at the edge of the kitchen counter to watch him go to work.

Although Brian is in the mood for something sweet, he has no idea what he's going to prepare to impress her. So, he starts out in the fridge and ends up in the cabinets looking for something to throw together.

"Hmm…? A few scoops of chocolate ice cream, a can of whip cream, a few pieces of white chocolate truffle candy, a bag of banana nut mini muffins, a bag of chopped walnuts, and chocolate syrup…I think I can make this work!" Brian figures, as he allows his imagination to take over. Ashima sips from her bottled water and observes as Brian do what he does.

Now, fully engaged in chef mode, Brian takes two soup bowls from his cabinet and starts out with two table spoons of ice cream as the bottom layer for each dish. Then he sprays a whipped cream barrier around the ice cream. Next, he takes two muffins and semi-stack them on top of the ice

229

cream. Then he sprays a little whipped cream on top of the muffins, lightly drizzles chocolate syrup over the dessert and plate, and sprinkles a few pinches of walnuts atop the chocolate. Then he finishes his garnish with a small multi grater and grates white chocolate curls all over the dessert and plate.

"Voila! Dessert is served!" Brian presents her the dish with a teaspoon to enjoy in less than a few minutes.

"Bravo chef, this is dressed very well!" An impressed Ashima says, commemorating his efforts with applause!

Amazed at how quickly Brian put the restaurant quality, garnished dish together, Ashima takes a spoonful to finalize her approval.

"Wow! I just watched you grab some random items from your cabinetry and put this wonderfully garnished, delicious dessert together. This is really, really good for an impromptu preparation." Ashima compliments him, impressed by taste as well as the presentation.

"Hmph, it's amazing what you can do with a few items, a little time, and an imagination." Brian replies.

"Well, I'm going to finish this. But, if you don't mind, I'm going to hop in the shower and get out of this gown for the evening." Ashima says, aspiring to unwind after a long day.

"Be my guest! You know where everything is so take as much time as you need." Brian replies placing her bowl in the freezer.

As Ashima showers, and Brian's excitement of possibly getting lucky builds, Ashima's phone lying on the bed suddenly starts to vibrate over and over again. Brian tries to avoid the temptation of peeking at first. But, gets annoyed by the repeated vibration and grows curious as to who's blowing up her phone. As suspected, the name Fahad is showing as an incoming call. Brian smiles with a devilish grin as his quest to take Ashima from him has nearly come to fruition. As he waits for Ashima to finish so he can take his own shower, he strips down naked and sits at the edge of the bed with a towel wrapped around his waist, entertained by how many times Fahad calls her phone. He counts at least six before she opens the bathroom door.

"Dayum!!!" Brian mentally responds to the unexpected sight of Ashima wearing nothing more than a long, white, satin night gown, with lace and sheer in a v-cut from her chest to just below her belly button. Her hair is pinned up in a bun, and her bag in hand.

"Hi...!" A coy Ashima emerges from the bathroom.

The image of Brian's masculine, muscular figure at the edge of the bed is a soothing welcome sight for her longing eyes. However, Brian's eyes became luminous to the sight of Ashima's endearing one layer to nudity as well. Her bath scent is so elegant it nearly sends Brian to a state of arousal. But, neither of them were the wiser to each other's fondness at the moment.

"Hey, your phone has been blowing up ever since you got in the shower!" Brian informs her without prejudice as he stands to enter the bathroom.

"Oh okay. Did you happen to see who was calling?" Ashima asks innocently, but Brian not receiving it the same.

"Naw, I just heard it vibrating repeatedly for about twenty minutes." Although Brian knew Fahad was calling, he wasn't about to allow Ashima to believe that he's nosey or insecure.

While Ashima checks her phone, Brian disappears into the bathroom. Ashima

"Ashima, where the hell have you disappeared to? I've been looking for you for hours! ANSWER YOUR PHONE DAMN IT!!!" An enraged Fahad screams into the phone.

Ashima only needed to hear one of her nine messages and many text messages from Fahad to convince her to turn her phone completely off. The last thing she was concerned with at this point is drama from Fahad. After a quick shower, Brian steps out of the bathroom with only a towel, refreshed and ready to relax.

"Is everything good?" A sweaty Brian asks as steam wafts from the bathroom in his wake.

"Yes, everything is fine." She replies sitting Indian style on the bed checking her emails as Brian walks past her to on his way to the kitchen.

Brian grabs a water and joins her on the bed for a breather before changing into his night clothes.

"Thank you for allowing me to stay at your place. I could only imagine the interrogation my father would be putting me through tonight." Ashima says, grateful to escape the drama at home.

"You don't have to thank me. I'm just happy you're here. By the way, that scent you're wearing is amazing!" He makes a point to compliment.

"Thanks!" Ashima softly replies in a quaint voice.

Afterwards, the room becomes noticeably silent as if both of their minds were fixated on something other than conversation. As Ashima continues tinkering with her phone, Brian is sitting on the edge of the bed in thought holding his bottled water. Brian looks over to examine her sexy posture. Sensing his eyes on her, Ashima looks up and realizes Brian's eyes locked on her. The moment their eyes connect, an instant sense of chemistry takes hold and as the irresistible temptation of the moment takes over. Brian leans over towards her as she leans in to meet him and they kiss like this is what they've both been craving.

Instantly they explode into passionate intimacy, kissing and moaning fervently. Ashima tosses her phone across the bed and pulls Brian in to feel his intimate presence. Although very uncharacteristic of Ashima to initiate herself, especially with someone as new as Brian, she finds this exclusive attraction for another man intriguing and wants to explore it a whole lot more. Now with Brian atop of her in a commanding stance like a dog on all fours, Ashima she lays back and surrenders to his terms. Brian obliges her assertiveness appropriately, kissing every inch of her within his immediate reach, from her forehead, to her neck, to her shoulders. Ashima winds and squirms under his dark shadow as he pecks away at her moist, delicate skin.

Brian pauses briefly to kill the lighting in the room and set a better mood. And with his venetian blinds partially open, he receives an assist from beams of vibrant moonlight highlighting her picturesque body.

"Mmm…" She sighs as Brian attacks her neck and shoulders and sucks on her earlobes.

"Take me Brian…!" She moans ever so faint as her estrogen levels peak at his every sensual touch.

"Are you sure?" Brian asks to affirm that he's heard her correctly. She responds with a simply head nod as her mind had already been made up from the moment she'd left the Gala.

Unlike any of his previous sexual encounters, mentally he prepares to take care of her delicately and with dignity. He starts out with a simple endearing forehead kiss before sensually kissing his way down to the mesh of her nightwear. Then he lifts her gown to expose her everything to inundate her body with more kisses. Her breasts and areola so perfectly shaped. Her abdomen so beautifully toned down to her bikini line. He salutes her excellent canvas with a series of kisses to her tummy before working his way up to her delectable breasts. He rounds her left nipple with his tongue while caressing her right breast with a perfect handful.

232

She raises her arms and lifts herself so Brian can help her out of her gown. After tossing the gown to the floor the only garment that remained on her divine anatomy is the pair red laced panties concealing her privacy. Brian resumes with kisses to her soft lips and earlobes, before dragging his tongue from her neck, all the way down to her lower belly and grants her another series of kisses just above her panty line. He moves on with kisses to the interior of her thighs down to the balls of her feet before working his way back to the mid-section. Daringly, after dragging his tongue up her right thigh, he delivers a soft subtle kiss directly on her center. His meticulous love movements render her vulnerable as he toys with her senses.

He tugs at her red garment with his teeth before sliding them off with his fingertips, revealing her beautifully groomed landscape. Inhaling her fresh arousing scent only confirms his craze for her, making her that much more irresistible. Now prepared to pleasure her, he reaches for his nightstand, removes his towel and dons his contraception.

"Oh my God!" She contemplates, catching glimpse of his towel-less body and verifying that Brian is nearly twice Fahad's endowment. Now apprehensive, she nervously braces for his penetration.

As he rests between her legs, he kisses her as a distraction as he lines himself up to insert her. She tensely squeezes his firm biceps for leverage before he pushes inside. As Brian struggles to push in further past the tip, her face wrinkles in despair as the pressure from his size proves to be too much for her sexual experience.

"Are you ok?" He selflessly asks, cognizant of her lack of comfort.

"Mmm...hmm...!" She whimpers, as she tries to not disappoint him and grit through the intercourse.

But, as he attempts to go deeper, her facial expressions grow more anguished as she claws his back, digging her nails in like a cat clawing a piece of furniture. Once fitted inside her tightly wond walls, he manages about two half strokes. But, it didn't take long for Brian to realize that this was not pleasure for her and immediately backs away from his advances.

"What's wrong? Why did you stop?" Ashima asks, through heavy breathing.

"I'm sorry babe. But, you look like you're really struggling through this, and I don't want to hurt you. I want to make love to you." Brian sincerely explains, growing concerned for her.

"No, Brian I'm fine. It's just been a while. You didn't have to stop!" Ashima ardently attempts to convince him otherwise. She pretends to be okay through the ordeal, but Brian knows better. He realizes that she wasn't ready for a man of his experience. Although he mentally commends her for trying to be brave, what really convinces him to withdraw was a single tear that ran from the corner of her eye onto the bed sheet.

Without uttering another word, he redirects his focus to a more subtle, sexually gratifying approach. Trailing kisses from her neck, to her breasts, to her belly button, Brian slowly works his way further south until he finds himself kissing the fibers of her private area.

In a perplexed panic, Ashima reaches down to pull him up from whatever he is preparing to do, as if this sexual exploration was foreign to her.

"Wait! Brian, what are you doing?" She asks abruptly with a confused expression. Never being kissed there before, she wasn't prepared to be taken there at that very moment.

"Shhh…let me…" Brian softly insists as she's unable to overcome his persistence to continue.

"Wait!" She whimpers, grabbing his head and forcefully pushing him away. In the midst of this passionate moment, Ashima wasn't prepared to be taken there. She doesn't know what it's like to be orally pleasured and fearful of something she's never experienced.

"Do you trust me?" He whispers looking directly into her precious, intimidated eyes. She responds with a nod of consent and with that, she surrenders to the mercy of his sexual prowess.

As he resumes with several kisses to her inner thighs, he pauses for a moment to admire the most beautifully trimmed 'V' he'd ever seen with a scent as clean and refreshing as a meadow of flowers before landing a kiss directly on her money spot. Her body responds with apprehensive tension as she's never been kissed like this before. After a series of pecks to prep her for pleasure, Brian indulges her with his tongue for a taste.

"Mmm…" He moans as her nectar is sweet like honey dew. Ashima places one hand on his shoulder and the other on his head as he goes to work.

He maneuvers his tongue with big circles, little circles, up and down, and in between the juices of her rose. Confused and enthralled in sensual bliss, she glances down to investigate what's happening to her. However,

234

just as she thought the blissful sensation between her legs had reached its peak, Brian French kisses her sweet spot and gives her the best pulsating experience of her life. It doesn't take long before the effects of the pleasureful experience to overtake her.

"OH MY...OH MY...AHHHHHHHH...MY GOODNESS...YASSSSSSSS!!!" She gasps heavily, clinging to the bedsheets as the eruption of an exploding orgasm consumes her.

The ecstasy is so overwhelming, her trembling legs clamp together like a vice and she can hardly breathe as she experiences her first explosive orgasm. As the tension of negative energy, stress, and sexual deprivation releases, every tense muscle in her body starts to relax and Ashima feels free, her body feels liberated. Unable to quantify the feeling she'd just experienced, she lies silent as her heart rate and breathing settle to a tranquil calm. Brian simply rests his head on her thigh like a pillow with a gratifying smile as she falls into a deep coma-like sleep. Learning more about herself in this moment, she realizes that this wasn't something she wanted as much as it being something emotionally and physically needed.

Enough

The next morning, Brian silences his six o'clock alarm and found himself once again waking to a vacant bed where Ashima slept the night before. In spite of this, Brian lay face down and content with a sheet covering his lower half as he reflects on how wonderful it was to sleep with her nestled tightly in his arms all night. Although last night didn't flow as well as it normally should, Brian was excited about the idea of Ashima not being as sexually versed as the other women he's been with. But, last night wasn't about fulfilling his sexual conquest. In fact, last night wasn't about having sex with Ashima at all. Last night was about the fact that Ashima could have been anywhere she wanted. But, she chose to be with him and he appreciated that as he rips the covers from his naked body and motivates himself out of bed to prepare for another day at *Apex* shipping. In doing so, he notices a few tiny specs of what appears to be blood evidence of last night's sexual encounter. He rolls the sheets up for wash and smells them as the scent of her presence still lingered. Her scent made him reminiscent about last night before tossing the sheets in a hamper and hopping in the shower.

Meanwhile, sitting comfortably in her office with her legs crossed in an elegant grey suit and skirt, Ashima sits quietly in her office reviewing a financial report left for her by Franklin. However, a task that would routinely take her less than an hour to review was taking her nearly three hours to get through. The impression Brian left on her the night before, leaves her romanticizing and helplessly unable to focus this morning after. Growing frustrated from her lack of concentration, she pushes away from her desk and looks out at the elevate view above the city from her fifty-second story window. As she gazes out at the scattered clouds moving above the surrounding buildings and rooftops, Ashima smiles as she can still feel the residual ache of a few intolerable strokes between her thighs. Thinking in hindsight, she ponders that perhaps should have endured the pleasurable pain of Brian's penetration a bit more. Suddenly she's interrupted by a rap at her office door.

"Yes…" Ashima says as the door swings opens and Samantha peeks her head in.

"Hey, I know it's close to your lunch hour, but you have a signature delivery that just came in waiting for you in the main lobby." Samantha informs her.

"Oh, no worries…I'll just sign for it on my way out to lunch. Would you like for me to get you something while I'm out?" Ashima offers, since Samantha now has stay behind to answer phones because there aren't enough people in the office since the recent layoffs.

"No thank you. I brought in some leftover Chinese food from dinner last night. But, thank you!" Samantha kindly declines.

"Okay then, I'm off to lunch. Give me a call if you need me for anything." Ashima replies as she heads down to routinely sign for another package.

Mulling over what to have for lunch, she steps off the elevator reading off the list of local restaurants on her phone.

"Hmm…Capital Grill, McCormack and Schmicks, Davio's…" She reads, scrolling through the endless list of restaurants. Suddenly her thoughts are interrupted as she looks toward the main reception area, and is taken aback by a familiar face, in a familiar uniform waiting in the building lobby.

"Oh my God! Brian, what are you doing here?" Ashima calls out with an uplifting smile. Her recent blissful thoughts of him were suddenly rekindled by his unexpected presence. Brian responds with a pleasant smile as she approaches.

"Umm…I have a package here for an Amir Batool of Philadelphia Finance and Trust!" Brian humorously replies maintaining his professional composure as he hands her the envelope.

"Oh, is that so…" Ashima replies with a doubtful snare. "Okay, so why are you really here?" Ashima asks with a sly grin.

"I couldn't stay away. After last night, I had to come down here to make sure you were okay. So, now I owe a friend a favor for switching routes with me today." Brian confesses looking her in the face with tender, honest eyes.

237

Ashima's knees began to weaken for every endearing moment she stood before him. His voice, his tone, his swag, and his shiny dark complexion were exactly the details she yearned for all morning. She suddenly realizes that Brian's presence is the calm that sooths her anxiety. In spite of this, as a true consummate professional, she remains steadfast and carries herself appropriately.

"Well, it was very nice of you to check on me. It feels good to be thought of every now and then. But, you could have sent me a text." Ashima humbly replies.

"I know, but that's not quite my style. Besides, how would you feel if I told you that I can't stop thinking about you?" Brian candidly asks with a charming stare.

"Oh my God!" Ashima responds with as her moment of elation is suddenly cut short by an unwanted sight walking through the entrance of the building. Brian looks behind him to investigate the reason for her sudden puzzled look.

"Wow! I don't need this right now. Umm...call me later?" Ashima asks as she tries to quickly dismiss Brian, but is already too late.

"Well, looks like I got here just in time for the afternoon deliveries. Brian, how are you my friend? I had no idea you were working this route." Fahad asks with deceit in his tone as he shakes Brian's hand before looking over at Ashima intently. Sensing Fahad's condescending greeting, Brian responds accordingly.

"Well, every now and then I get the privilege of coming down to high society to deliver packages to the finest folks in the city, such as yourself." Brian replies firing back a sly remark of his own.

"Definitely no shame in that...I mean, someone has to deliver the mail, right?" Fahad responds with a conniving smirk, as he glances over to Ashima.

"Right...Ms. Batool if you could sign right here for me, I'll be on my way." Struggling to maintain his professionalism, Brian acknowledges the comment with a glaring stare at Fahad, before turning his attention to Ashima. Embarrassed for Brian, Ashima avoids eye contact with him as she signs the electronic signature pad he presents her.

"Thank you. Enjoy the rest of your day Ms. Batool...Fahad!" Brian departs the lobby shaking his head in mockery of Fahad.

"Fahad, what are you doing here?" Ashima asks with a hard-line expression.

"Not that it's of any concern, but I have business with Amir at noon." Fahad rolls his eyes as he looks down at his watch to as if to say his time was valuable.

"Oh, well he's in his office. I'm sure he's waiting on you." As she attempts to walk-off with no interest in engaging Fahad any further.

"I'm sorry. Excuse me! Hello? Ashima do you not see me here?!" An agitated Fahad asks as he gently grabs her by the wrist to thwart her escape.

"I'm sorry, Fahad. I have lots to do, and I'm off to lunch at the moment. Plus, you're going to be late for your appointment with my father. So, if you will excuse me…" Ashima calmly responds in the busy lobby, despite his brazen unwanted touch.

"Well, you know we haven't really spoken since you returned from Vegas. And I was hoping to take you to lunch after my meeting so we can do a little catching up." Fahad explains in a relaxed civil tone.

"I'm flattered, but I'm famished, and I need to have something now before I get light headed." Ashima replies trying to remove herself from his presence at all cost.

"Sounds like you need to have something on the go. Ordering a salad from the food court inside Liberty One perhaps?" Fahad implies referring to one of Ashima's typical on the go food choices.

"No, actually I was considering having something from one of these street venders, like a meatball sub, or beef sausage or something?" She replies with a semi-sassy flare. Fahad pauses for a moment in confused thought, before laughing off the aberrant reply.

"Wow, I never figured you to be the roach coach, street vendor type, dirty water dogs and all? I've always known you to be a knife and fork type of girl. Perhaps I don't know you as well as I thought?" Fahad replies, taken aback by her interest in street food.

"That's because I'm never the center of your focus, Fahad. Sometimes the easiest way to find an answer to your questions is to just take a moment to look. But, it's hard to do that when you're blinded by your own self-indulgence isn't it?" Ashima bluntly replies. Not taking kind to her mannerism, Fahad's eyes lower to a piercing stare as he struggles to make sense of her contrary tone.

239

"Ashima, what's happened to you? Why are you so guarded lately? Since when do you act like this?" A frantically concerned Fahad asks as he tightens his controlling grip on her wrist for a moment.

"Act like what, Fahad? Really?! You want to do this here? And please lower your voice in my place of work." Ashima urges him to be calm as she looks around to verify anyone taking notice.

"You don't..." Fahad pauses to calm his initial frustrating outburst.

"...you don't stay over at the house anymore. You don't wear the ring I bought that signifies my love for you. Lately, whenever I'm around you seem so disenchanted and don't want to be bothered. We haven't had sex in a period longer than I care to remember. You know, I'm really struggling to understand what's the meaning of all this?" Fahad angrily grunts under his breath.

"And I'm struggling to understand the root to your ignorance? Aside from the rude offhanded comments you made to Brian, you walk around acting as if everything is okay, as if I never caught you in the act with her. Like everything is supposed to be okay because you buy me expensive jewelry, take me out to fancy dinners, and offer your lame apologies? Well, you're right, you really don't know who I am, Fahad." Ashima ridicules him while trying to maintain her composure.

"Ashima, I don't know what else to say. I've given you my best apology and that's still not good enough!" Fahad pleads.

"And it may never be good enough! I'm not interested in playing your silly game of Polygamy because Islamic Jurisprudence allows it. This is America, and I will live my life the American way." Ashima passionately replies.

"Ashima, you have me all wrong. I love only you. I do not love her!" Fahad declares as he releases her wrist and runs his hand up her arm to console her.

"Whether you love her or not, the bottom line is there should be no 'her' to speak of! And I will not make amends simply because it's what you prefer. I'll do it on my terms!" Ashima vehemently demands.

"Very well then, Ashima...fair enough! In that case, I guess you'd rather have lunch alone...or perhaps you'd rather have lunch with the delivery boy, since you are so concerned of his well-being and you find me so revolting, yes? I'm sure someone as domesticated as Brian can provide better for you." Fahad exaggerates, deliberately provoking negative feedback from her. Her eyes quickly narrow in disgust as if her tolerance of him had just reached its peak.

"Goodbye Fahad! Enjoy your meeting, I'm in no mood for your childish insults." Ashima insists as she dismisses Fahad before walking away in utter repugnance. As she leaves Fahad standing in place with a dumbfounded look, she pauses in stride to leave him with one final notion.

"Oh, and just so you know, you could probably learn a thing or two from that man you call a delivery boy." She subliminally testifies to how Brian handled her just the night before.

"And what's that supposed to mean?!" Fahad asks as Ashima marches off.

"Have a great lunch!" She sounds off, as she ignores his question and turns her back to him like a 'mic-drop' moment.

"Ashima, Ashima!" Fahad calls out with controlled anger.

Ashima walks away with about as much tolerance she could stomach of Fahad for one day. The more she interacted with him, the more she found it impossible to understand how she allowed herself to fall vulnerable to the likes of such a man. Perhaps it was the unwavering level of loyal and respect she had for her father's wishes to marry Fahad, or the promise of being an heiress to the Gabr family wealth.

To no avail, after experiencing what it's like to be intimately touched by a man for what seemed like the very first time, it was more than confirming that she was ready for the start of something new. As she exits the building a smile of liberation graces her face, as her mind becomes inundated with promising thoughts of Brian. She immediately calls him to appease her exciting thoughts, and to do damage control for Fahad's offensive behavior.

"Ugh...voicemail!" Ashima mutters before leaving her message.

"Hi Brian, its Ashima, please give me a call when you can." She leaves on his voicemail.

After grabbing a meatball sub prepared exactly the way she had it the first time, with a diet soda, and chips, Ashima heads back to the office to eat at her desk while scouring over work. Suddenly her phone rings inside her purse. She smiles anticipating Brian's call back.

"Oh gosh, what now?!" She says aloud, annoyed by Amir calling instead. Compelled to answer, she sighs heavily before picking up.

"Yes father..." She answers in a reluctant tone.

"Ashima, how long will you be out for lunch? I just hung up from a conference call abroad and I need you back at the office." Amir promptly informs her.

"I'm on my way back now. Is there something wrong?" Ashima replies with concern.

"No, just hurry back when you can." Amir urges her.

"Okay then…" Ashima hurries intently, interested in knowing the importance of Amir's urgency.

After getting back to the 52th floor, Ashima drapes her coat, purse, and lunch on her desk before briskly heading to the conference room down the hall. As she draws closer to conference room down the glass partitioned corridor, she grows nervously anxious as she notices the bank's CEO and Chairman Greg Norman, the COO Jeff Fisher in the room as well as Amir, Franklin, and Amy Callaway of the Asset Investment Department.

"Hello everyone, sorry I'm late!" She announces as she enters the room timidly and shy, like a dog with its tail tucked between its legs.

"No, no…you're fine, Ashima. Please be seated, we were just getting started." The elder, well-seasoned Greg Norman replies sitting at the head of the table in a three-piece tailored suit like a true gentleman's, gentleman. Although Mr. Norman heads Philadelphia Finance and trust like a wise, consummate professional, he's often look upon as a father figure by his chain of staff.

"First off, I hope everyone had a wonderful lunch. Secondly, I won't keep you too long because I haven't had my lunch yet, so I'll be brief." Mr. Norman explains in an elder business-like voice as the others at the table chuckle at his dry sense of humor.

"I'd like to start by expressing my gratitude to you Amir, for deciding to step in as the Lobbying Director until we can get a permanent replacement for our recently departed Mark Shuman. I'm sure you're ready to start enjoying your own retirement, but I wish we could convince you to consider otherwise." Mr. Norman proposes with his best smile.

"Well thank you, and although I appreciate your kind words Greg, I'm not withdrawing my decision on retirement. Not even for that fifty-thousand-dollar box of cigars I wanted so badly on your desk." Amir answers as everyone in the room cackles at Amir's reply.

"Fair enough, Amir. Oh, and by the way, I happen to love my stockpile of fifty thousand-dollar cigars." The room once again indulges in subtle laughter as they appeased the humor of Mr. Norman yet again.

"Okay, now that we've gotten that out the way, let's get on to the real reason why we're here. We're all aware that the Arab real-estate powerhouse investor Alkari Mohammed attended the Gala last week. And aside from the opulent accommodations he enjoyed while overlooking the city from the top floor of his Ritz Carlton suite, I hope he was equally impressed by the conversation he'd shared with our young and beautiful deal closing prodigy, Ashima Batool. She seems to have learned quite a bit from her father about this business, and has a knack for reeling in top notch investors." Ashima grins with humility as everyone in the room momentarily turn their attention to her with all smiles. Amy clutches her hand as a gesture of 'job well done' as Mr. Norman continues.

"With that said, this morning I received a call from one of Mr. Mohammed's advisers halfway across the world and she informed me that he's in fact willing discuss a tentative deal on the new twin Al Kazahri building project in Dubai. The estimated cost of this project is expected to be in the neighborhood of 1.2 to 1.8 billion dollars. Needless to say, with our last quarter earnings looking meager at best, this could be one of the biggest deals this company has ever seen. So, I ask that Franklin, Amy, and Ashima enjoy the spoils of Dubai on my expense, and secure this deal for Philadelphia Finance and Trust. You do this for me, and I promise that Greg Norman will truly introduce you to the good life. Now, Jeff, Amir, and I have to remain stateside to finish brokering the Manhattan project. But, we'll be there in time to ink the deal and break ground at the end." As the longwinded Mr. Norman finally pauses, visible smiles stretch across the table as everyone looks to each other with affirmation and contentment.

"Thank you, Mr. Norman. I appreciate you giving me the opportunity to be a part of closing on such a lucrative deal. But, looking at the calendar, and I notice that the meeting is only a week after I'm scheduled to meet in London at the Gherkin and..." Ashima replies before being interrupted by Mr. Norman.

"Yes, I'm fully aware that Fashion Week Haute Couture in Paris falls between the London and Dubai meetings, Ashima. I know how important it is for you to be in attendance stage side at the *Louvre Museum* watching chic models rip the runway in the finest designer wear. In fact, I negotiated

243

that date with Alkari for that very reason. This way, if it's ok with you, you get to spend an extra week abroad rather than flying back to the states and have to deal with another monotonous nineteen-hour flight to Dubai at a later date. Certainly, you agree with this, right?" Mr. Norman asks, anticipating Ashima's approval.

"I'm absolutely fine with your decision Mr. Norman. I just wanted to make sure you were willing to approve another week of perdiem." Ashima replies with sarcasm as everyone snickers before erupting in laughter yet again.

"Perdiem...hmph...well, you certainly have your father's sense of humor, don't you!" Mr. Norman maintains looking over at Amir.

"Yes, she certainly has something!" Amir agrees, adding to the moment of humor before Jeff speaks on a more serious note, returning the room to business-like candor.

"There's no doubt that we have the team in this room to close on this deal. We have the brawn, the beauty, and the brains to get this corporation back to its rightful place among the top of this city's financial elites. With that said, lets continue to be the best at what we do moving forward and let's knock this one out the park!" Jeff concludes as he stands to his feet, firing everyone up in the room before the meeting concluded.

"Ashima, wait for me in your office, okay. I'll be right there!" Amir requests as he stays behind to speak to Mr. Norman and Jeff Fisher.

"Very well father, I'll see you then." She responds. Excited about the results of the meeting, she immediately sends a text Carolyn to share the good news.

(Text)
Ashima: *Hey Lenny, crazy news! Call me when you get a chance.*
Carolyn: *Really? I'll call you when I get through the security check point.*
Ashima: *Ok...*☺

Ashima returns to her office and awaits her father as she checks her email standing unsettled at her desk. She always found it difficult to relax whenever Amir requests to meet with her because of his overbearing work ethics. She could also tell what kind of mood he was in if he called her Princess or Ashima. If he calls her Ashima, her guard will naturally be up.

"Knock! Knock! Hello Princess, how are you feeling today?" Amir asks as he enters her office and lands a kiss on her cheek.

"Thank God!" She silently prays.

"I'm well father, thank you. What's wrong?" Ashima asks, stills bit guarded.

"Nothing…nothing Princess! I just wanted to tell you how proud we were of you. I'd hate to say it, but Alkari probably wouldn't have been willing to proceed with negotiations if it weren't for you. We literally stole him from brokering a deal with *Emirates Financial.* For that, I am grateful and proud to be your father. Thank you for validating me as your mentor." Amir humbly concludes.

"Thank you, father. I'm glad that I could make you and mommy so proud!" Amir smiles with a vacant expression, but doesn't utter a word. As if there was something more he needed to say.

"You know I met with Fahad today." Amir cautiously discloses.

"Yes, I'm aware!" Ashima replies in an apathetic tone.

"Is everything okay between you two? I don't mean to pry, I'm just simply asking." Amir curiously asks.

"Everything is fine father. Why do you ask, or are you about to tell me?" Ashima candidly asks.

"Ashima, Fahad has come to me with concerns about what's going on between you two. He tells me that you've been very distant towards him lately. Says you've suddenly become very unaffectionate and boldly disrespectful. I just want to make sure my daughter is okay, that's all." Amir expresses with concern.

"Hmph…and I'm sure he failed to mention his little role in all of this." Ashima subliminally counters.

"Actually, I already knew he was sleeping with Nisa. I just didn't know it was recent. I thought she was ancient history, until he told me he screwed up today." Amir openly admits.

"Are you kidding me? Even my own father knew how sleazy Fahad is and you don't tell me anything? What kind of father are you?" Ashima's anguish filled voice questions.

"Ashima, I didn't want to worry you with that nonsense, Princess. I knew about it and I took care of it then. I haven't heard anything about it since then until today." Amir defends.

245

"And you're okay with this? I mean, you don't seem to be too upset about the idea of him sleeping around on your own daughter." Ashima asks, growing annoyed by her father's lack of concern.

"Ashima, he came to me like a man and he confessed to me his mistakes. I can only respect him for doing so. Now, I don't condone Fahad's infidelity, especially when it comes to my only daughter. But, I do believe in forgiveness and I know I've raised you to be the same. Besides, I know he loves you very much, and he wants nothing more than to give you the very best in life." Amir sincerely pleads.

"Father, I appreciate your concern. But, I think that your judgment maybe just a bit jaded by that very notion. What he can do for me, rather than what he means to me. This life with Fahad is something that you've always wanted. Never did I sign up for this." Ashima passionately explains.

"لماذا أنت أشيما؟ لماذا أنت تحبّ محادثة هذا؟ ماذا قد حصل داخل أنت؟ أشيما, هناك شيء جدّا
مختلفة حول أنت حديثا ويذهب أنا أن يحصل إلى القعر من ذاه."

"Ashima, why do you talk like this? What has gotten into you? There's something very different about you lately and I'm going to get to the bottom of this." Amir sternly replies with piercing eyes, speaking heavily in Arabic dialect as he grows increasingly frustrated.

Ashima sits at her desk and sighs in her own frustration, before removing the contents of her brown bag lunch and placing them onto her desk.

"هذا وجبت؟ غداءك ماذا؟ يكون هذا؟ لا ينظر هو بالتّأكيد مثل يوفي من أيّ إقامة محترمة أنا
أكون مدركة من."

"This is your lunch? What is this? It certainly doesn't look like carry out from any respectable establishment I'm aware of." Amir questions, appalled by the brown bag items Ashima calls lunch.

"Father relax, it's just a meatball sub from a vender on 16th Street. You should try it sometimes. It's really good!" Ashima suggests, unwilling to entertain any Arabic dialogue.

"يكون؟ أنت تأكل شارع فندر طعام الآن؟ أنت تستمتع طعام مقرفة من بعض
صخرة عربة؟"

"Are you kidding me? You're eating street vender food now? You're enjoying nasty food from some roach coach?" A disappointed Amir replies.

"يستمتع الناس هذا نوع الطعام لوجبة غداء يوميّة. لما سوفت نحن كنت هكذا مختلفة؟"

246

"People enjoy this type of food for lunch every day. Why should we be so different?" Ashima challenges in Arabic, provoked by her father's annoying ridicule.

"نكون نحن الذي ليس أنّ لأنّ⋯!"

"Because that's not who we are…!" Amir shakes his head and walks out in utter frustration.

No longer in the mood for lunch, Ashima throws her sandwich in the trash. She then turns to her window overlooking the city. Staring down at the moving traffic beneath her feet, a single tear emerges from the corner of her eye and down her cheek. Bothered by the idea of her father knowing of Fahad's infidelity and hurt by their alliance, she decides at this very moment enough is enough. From here on out, she decides to confide in the comfort of her own happiness. No longer will she live for the sake of making others happy. Today, she decides to reclaim her life.

Suddenly her phone vibrates from an incoming call. Elated by the renewed oath to herself, she'd hoped that it was Brian returning her call. But, instead she realizes its Carolyn calling which is nearly just as good.

"Hey Lenny…" She answers enthusiastically as she quickly cleans up her somber mood and takes a reclining seat at her desk.

"Hey Shima. Sorry I didn't text you back earlier. I was going through the TSA checkpoint. I'm sorry, but first-class passengers should have exclusive check-in. I'm just saying…" Lenny replies as she puts her shoes and bangle bracelets back on.

"TSA?! What happened to the charter jet? A confused Ashima asks.

"Well, from what we were told, the plane needed unexpected maintenance and won't be ready until tomorrow." Carolyn explains.

"Wow, I'm sure that was inconvenient to the other girls. Where are they now?" Ashima wonders as she types an email response.

"They're doing the TSA shake down right now. But, never mind what we're doing, what's so exciting over there at Philly Finance?" Lenny replies.

"Well, at the Gala I attended last night…" Ashima is swiftly interrupted.

"Wait! You mean the Gala that you chose to go to with Fahad rather than your bestie?" Lenny teases.

"Lenny, please don't flatter him, it was already an unpleasant evening. Anyway, I met a Saudi investor there that the bosses apparently wanted me to meet to convince him to broker this new billion-dollar development project in Dubai. So, I just left this meeting with the top brass and my father of course, and the investor is not only interested in brokering the deal with us, they want me to shadow the deal in Dubai. Isn't that crazy?" A jovial Ashima explains.

"Dubai? Oh my God, Shima! I'm so jealous! Are you taking me with you?" An ecstatic Carolyn replies.

"If you can take another week off from your job to stay with me from London to Dubai, that would be awesome! You know you're more than welcome." Ashima gladly agrees.

"Absolutely! I've always wanted to travel to Dubai. I'm so excited, I'm about to check the calendar right now!" An ecstatic Carolyn, replies.

"Okay then, check your calendar and let me know. I'm about to head home for the day. I've had about all I can stand of Amir for one day." She explains in an aggravated tone.

"Uh-oh, what has daddy done to piss off his little girl this time?" Carolyn asks, familiar with Ashima's dissatisfaction of her father.

"Lenny, too much too tell you right now! We'll talk some other time." Ashima replies with an exhausting sigh.

"Okay, chat with you later then, smooches!" Carolyn concludes before they hang up.

CHAPTER THIRTEEN

A few days later, after smoothing things over with Brian, the off handed comments of Fahad have only drawn the pair even closer. They've been investing much of their time getting to learn each other, and noticeably Ashima hasn't been home for Amir to harass her. However, Brian finds himself traveling west on I-76 towards the Gulph Mills Golf Club on a late Saturday morning for an outing with Amir after an unexpected invitation. Unsure of why Amir chose such a brisk and dreary day in November for a golf outing, Brian just took it in stride and dressed accordingly. As he passes through the entrance of the Golf Club, he's nearly broadsided by a fast-moving red Ferrari exiting the parking lot. The middle-aged Caucasian driver who appears to look like a former professional athlete pardons himself by passively waving at Brian. Then he takes off in a thunderous acceleration. This is his initial impression of the club, which is followed by an elegant fleet of luxury cars in nearly every parking space on the lot.

After stepping out of his car, Brian is once again reminded of how dismal the day is, feeling the chill in the air with a light wind. Fortunately, he came dressed with a long sleeve shirt underneath his short sleeve Polo Shirt, Khaki pants, and casual low-cut shoes.

"Man, I feel so out of place..." He mutters to himself parking his Dodge between a Bentley GT and an Audi R8.

As he walks into the club house, he notices that there weren't many people in the venue. The people who were there were too busy to even notice he'd walked in the door. Just past the entryway of the club, he immediately enters a room that opened up to a gaping area with round tables dressed with white table clothes on hardwood floors, and wood beam ceilings.

"Brian...!" A voice rang out as he looks to his left and notices Amir standing from a table situated in a corner of the window surrounding dining area.

"I'm so glad you could make it, my friend. I like the way you dressed for the occasion. You look like…Tiger Hood, my friend!" Amir jokes as he greets Brian while wiping his mouth with a cloth napkin from his lap.

"Yeah, thanks for having me. I appreciate the invite." Brian replies as he shakes Amir's hand and observes the delicious mid-morning spread he was feasting on.

"Please, my friend, have some of this delicious brunch I've been enjoying. We've got Eggs Benedict, Wagyu beef, savory potatoes, Lox, mimosas, anything you want. C'mon, enjoy!" Amir generously insists.

"Naw, I appreciate it. But, I just had a leftover cheese steak for lunch." Brian politely declines.

"Awe, that's too bad. You would have really enjoyed it, it was delicious. But, anyway our golf cart is ready, so perhaps we can get going now, yes?" Amir prompts Brian as he leads him out to the golf cart trail.

"Sounds good to me. I've never been golfing before, but I'm always up for a new experience." Brian replies as he follows Amir's lead.

"Yes, yes! You should always get out and explore more, Brian. See the world and experience new things, my friend. There's a whole world outside of North Philadelphia." Amir encourages as he loads one set of clubs into the back of the cart.

"Oh, by the way, I have an appointment today around noon so unfortunately we'll only be able to play the back nine. But, we'll start at the 9th hole." Amir informs Brian before they head out.

Brian wasn't much of a golfer and didn't know exactly what the back nine meant, but he did find it strange that a wealthy Amir was only taking one set of golf clubs to share in the middle of the golf course. The men arrive on the green of the 9th hole and Brian is ready to take a swing at his first golf ball.

"Okay my friend, now it's time to have an honest moment like true men, yes?" Amir says to Brian as the men exit the cart. Amir steps to the rear of the cart as if he's about to set up.

"Aight Amir, just lead the way!" An excited Brian replies, open off the idea of taking his first swing. But, it appears as if Amir has something else in mind.

"You ever heard of Sabrage or Sabering, Brian?" Amir randomly asks.

"Sabrage? Naw, what's that, some type of imported cheese or something?" Brian aimlessly guesses.

"Hmph, not exactly…" Amir replies in a conniving tone. Instead of reaching for golf clubs and a tee, Amir opens a basket on the back of the golf cart and pulls out two champagne flutes and a bottle of Portuguese sparkling rose brut.

Brian stands bewildered as a speechless Amir busily moves about. Placing the Champagne and glasses on the seat of the cart, then opening a long-decorated box and pulling out a twenty-inch stainless sword, stenciled 'Sabrage' on the blade.

"Oh, that's Sabrage…!" Brian realizes, reading the font on the blade.

"Not exactly my friend, hold this." Amir asks handing Brian a glass.

Amir then holds the bottle of brut upwards at a forty-five-degree angle with his left hand and with his right hand he swiftly runs the blade up the bottle and lances off the top of the bottle with a loud pop as the champagne spills on the green.

"Ha! Now, that's sabering my friend!" Amir bolsters as he pours Brian's glass before pouring his own.

"Wow, so that's how they open bottles where you're from, huh? Personally, I'd prefer to open the bottle with an American corkscrew, or pushing out the cork, but that's just me." Brian pokes with humor as Amir takes a sip from his glass before responding.

"The tradition is actually French. The American way is boring. I prefer the French way when I need to have a drink and relieve my tension…cheers!" Amir, replies in a more sinister tone as he toasts Brian's glass.

As Brian looks up at the sky and notices an ominous sky moving in, he struggles to understand why Amir dragged him out to the ninth hole of the Gulph Mills Golf club on such an ominous day.

"Kind of a strange day to be out here on the golf course Amir, don't you think?" Brian asks as they watch the 9th hole flag flapping in the breeze.

"Not really. I chose a day like today because I knew there would be few people out and no interference. My friend…I didn't bring you out here to hit balls down the fairway." Amir reveals as the conversation shifts to a mood more serious.

"Okay, sooo…why are we really out here?" Brian asks with alarming concern.

"Brian, I brought you here to urge you to stop sleeping with my daughter. This foolishness has been going on long enough. She's not cut out for your kind and I want it to stop!" Amir demands in an abrupt tone.

"What do you mean by your kind?" Brian challenges.

"Please, don't try pulling that race card B.S. with me. This has nothing to do with race. It has everything to do with cultural difference...a culture that you couldn't possibly understand." Amir firmly replies.

"Listen, Amir I'm sorry, but..." Brian humbly starts out before being abruptly interrupted.

"Don't even think about patronizing me with your lies Brian Rodney Jones from Allegheny Avenue. I know about you...I know about the dates and your late-night trips to the cinema with Ashima. My daughter having interest in you is clearly some type of strange parody and I don't know how it's managed to go this long. Now, in case you were not listening when I told you before, Fahad will be Ashima's husband and I fully support this. So, I apologize if you feel as if you've been misled. But, this frolicking has got to stop and it ends today! My daughter is Egyptian royalty. She's a princess, not a peasant! Am I making myself clear?!" Amir speaks to him with reprimand.

Brian hands the glass of champagne back to Amir with a disparaging look. Despite the anger building within from Amir's scorn, Brian manages his calm and decides to gracefully tolerate Amir's bold aggression. But, not before leaving Amir with one final thought.

"By the way Mr. Batool, with all due respect...your daughter chose me." Brian cleverly responds before walking away. The comment didn't bode well with Amir, and he wasn't prepared to respond to such a sly remark.

"I'd be very careful who you talk to with such a slick tongue Mr. Brian Jones. You have no idea who I know in Philadelphia." Amir spitefully pitches to Brian in frustration as he walks off. Brian turns in stride and sneers with no reply.

Amir angrily throws the champagne from the glass onto the green in frustration as he watches Brian walk back towards the clubhouse.

After returning to his car, Brian sat for a moment fuming over his scolding by Amir. He had every intension on calling Ashima to vent about the encounter. But, after taking a moment to reflect on the reprimand, he decides to idol his emotions and watch how the situation plays out.

Meanwhile, Ashima is at home stretched across her bed in pink pajamas with her laptop in front of her, web-browsing the latest in fashion. When suddenly, she hears Amir enter the house and loudly drops his keys.

"Ashima! Ashima!" He calls out into the hollows of the vast foyer.

"Yes, father!" She replies.

"Come down to the kitchen please. I need to speak with you!" Amir requests as she can hear him rambling dishes in the kitchen.

"Okay, I'll be right down!" Ashima she answers, saving her last web-search to her favorites, before slipping into her large furry monster slippers to head downstairs.

"Yes, father." She says, observing Amir eat an apple with a paring knife as she enters the kitchen.

"Ashima, you know I've really gone out of my way to stay out of your affairs with Fahad. You're a big girl and you have lots of growing up to do. But, I cannot sit back and allow you to carry on this silly charade with Brian any longer. This has carried on long enough and I want it to stop, okay? It ends today!" Amir firmly explains.

"Father, what charade do you speak of? What is it exactly do you think you know about what's going on between Brian and I." Ashima calmly contests standing opposite of the kitchen island of Amir.

"Ashima don't try to play me for foolish! You know very well what I'm speaking of. I am fully informed of how you've been prancing all over the city with this man…this opportunist! Acting out with him as if there's really something you can invest with him." Amir replies growing agitated.

"So, that's what you think of him? He's an opportunist now? I must have clearly gotten the wrong impression, because I thought he was your friend? After all, it was you who brought him to Fahad's home to show off, right?" Ashima argues with sassiness.

"Friend…ha! He's an associate who delivers work to our home. Bringing him to Fahad's was a humanitarian gesture, and nothing more. But, that's not of your concern. You on the other hand, you are disgracing your peers and you've disgraced your family with this foolishness."

"So, that's what this whole golfing invitation was about? So, you could tell Brian to stay away from me?" Ashima angrily questions.

"Ashima, he doesn't blend with our kind. He's not of your affluent pedigree." Amir pleads.

"Pedigree?! What am I, a dog now? I don't care about status or wealth or any of this snobby, pretentious crap! All I care about is being happy as if that even matters to you!" Ashima replies, taking exception to the comment as the two wrangles with each other.

"هذا من أنمور أنا يتسامح ولن ,أسفل إلى قدمي أضع أنا !محاكاة هذا من بكفاية أشيما"

"أتَمَت أنا ,حسنة ···يّأخلاق لا فورنيكأيشن!"

"Ashima enough of this parody! I am putting my foot down, and I will not tolerate any more of this immoral fornication…okay, I'm done!" Amir adamantly demands smashing the apple to the counter and slamming the paring knife through it.

"أيضا أنا أتَمَت ,جيّدة!"

"Good, I'm done too!" Ashima replies as she storms off to her room.

"أنت إلى أنا يتحدّث ,أشيما !أشيما ?يعني أن يفترض أنّ يكون وماذا!"

"And what is that supposed to mean? Ashima! Ashima, I am talking to you!" A fiery Amir walks from around the counter, as he watches as she tramples up the stairs.

"أن يذهب لا يكون الذي ,مستقلّة إمرأة ,يربّى كلية ,ولد-ير وعشرون ثلاثة ينمى أنا هو يعني"
هذا ,الأمام إلى عزم هذا من !يعني هو ماذا أنّ .حياة في إختبار من ما أتلقّى أنا مثل عاملت يكون
"إسأكون أنا الذي وهذا ,أكون أنا ذيال"

"It means I'm a grown twenty-three-year-old, college educated, independent woman, who's not going to be treated like I have no choices in life. That's what it means! From this moment forward, this is who I am, and this is who I will be!" She exclaims before slamming her bedroom door behind her.

Silenced by Ashima's ardent rebuttal, Amir didn't utter another word. He simply stands at the foot of the stairs in frustration.

"Okay then…" He softly speaks with his eyes narrowed to a rigid look of deceit.

As the feud simmers to a calm at the Batool household, Brian decided to go for a run along the East River Drive to blow off some anger of his own, despite the autumn cool weather. Ashima has been hopelessly trying to reach Brian ever since her upsetting encounter with her father, calling and texting him several times at minutes apart. To no avail, locked into his run with his ear buds inserted, Brian ignores every attempt he received from Ashima. Concerned about what Ashima may have to say, he was in no mood to hear anything more impactful than Amir's threatening words. But, after running several miles in a steady moderate stride from the Falls Bridge to the Girard Avenue Bridge he decides to take a breather to answer a call from Marty, where paced around explaining what happened earlier today.

"So, wait, he swung a knife at you…missed, and cut the top of a champagne bottle off?" Marty asks, ensuring he heard Brian's recap correctly.

"Naw man, he didn't swing at me, he held the bottle in his hand and intentionally sliced the top of the bottle off with the knife." Brian clarifies.

"Well either way, it sounds like he meant business, and I wouldn't take his threats lightly, 'B'. I mean, I'm not trying to tell you to back down from a challenge. But, you're trying to smash his daughter and technically he did pull a knife on you." He rationalizes with Brian.

"Yeah, now that I think about it, he did seem a bit threatening with that blade. But, the way I feel about this situation between me and Ashima, he's gonna have to cut me deep to keep me away." Brian strongly avows.

"Hmph…well I ain't never heard you speak of a woman like this before, so she must be some kinda wow." Marty explains.

"Yeah, man…" Brian simply replies.

"Mmm-hmm…Cupid's got his foot in your ass, don't he?" Marty bluntly implies.

"Yeah, man…" Brian replies with an elated grin.

"Mmm-hmm…you love her, don't you?" Marty persistently questions him. Brian pauses for a moment to consider his reply, then smiles with an expression of guilt.

"Yeah, man. I think I do." Brian apprehensively replies, astonished by his true taboo confessions to Marty.

"Wow, the 'L' word has spoken, huh? In that case, you might want to put concerns about her pops on the back burner." Marty advises.

"Why is that?" Brian asks with raised eye-brows.

"Because love is about to deal you a far better ass whoopin'!" Marty candidly replies as they both laugh at his comedic warning.

"Well then Cupid better lace up, 'cause she's certainly worth fighting for." Brian resolutely replies.

"Aight brotha, don't hurt nobody out here." Marty cautions.

"Naw, I ain't trying to catch a case out here, Marty. I'm too busy trying to be a lover and…hold on a minute she's calling again. In fact, let me hit you back, Bruh." Brian says before answering the call.

"Go ahead and handle your biz, Bruh!" Marty replies before Brian clicks over. After his conversation with Marty, Brian finally musters the courage to answer Ashima's call.

"Hey...!" Brian answers in his normally thrilled voice.

"Hey, is everything okay? I've been trying to reach you for hours now." Ashima responds in an urgently concerned voice.

"Yeah, babe I just went out for a run. I didn't know you were calling. Is everything okay?" Brian asks, alarmed by her tone of urgency.

"Yes, I'm fine. I just haven't heard from you. I was getting so worried, Brian. I need to speak with you as soon as humanly possible!" Ashima insists.

"Okay. Do you need to talk right now?" Brian asks as he rests on a park bench.

"No, it must be face to face!" Ashima insists.

"Okay, Well I should be back at my apartment in about forty-five minutes to get showered and dressed. Do you want to meet afterwards?" Brian proposes.

"Yes, let's meet then!" She agrees.

Already at his anxieties peak, Brian runs anxiously back to the car to meet with Ashima as soon as he could. After finding a place to park in the front lot of his building, he wastes no time sprinting up the stairs to get a quick shower. After opening the vestibule door to the hallway of his apartment, to his surprise, there she stands in front of his apartment holding a conversation with T.J. the neighbor across the hall.

"My God, this woman can dress." Brian marvels as he gives her a once over as he walks down the hall.

Ashima is well dressed and smelling lovely as ever in a pair of brown peep toe wedges, black jeans, open neck striped blouse, an autumn pullover jacket, and loose-fitting scarf, with her shades on, bangle accessories, purse and phone in hand.

"Here he comes now!" T.J. announces as he spots Brian coming down the hall from his own doorway.

"Well, isn't this a pleasant surprise. It's not often that I get a beauty waiting at my door step." Brian says as he approaches her.

"Hey, I hope you don't mind. But, I really needed to see you." She quickly apologizes.

"Not at all...in fact I'm very happy to see you. I would give you a hug, but I'm all sweaty and smelly." Brian replies, leaning in to kiss her on the cheek.

"What up, 'B'. How you, Fam?" T.J. asks as Brian comes over to give him a pound.

"What up, 'T'? Keeping my company safe till I got home, huh?" Brian asks with speculation, knowing T.J. was probably more interested in talking her over to his place than looking out for him.

"Yeah, you know I always look out, Fam." T.J. assures Brian like a good neighbor.

"No doubt, I appreciate you looking out." Brian expresses with gratitude.

"No worries, Fam. You know I got you! Hey man, she got any sisters?" T.J. quickly asks Brian enters his apartment.

"Sorry, I'm the only child." Ashima responds for Brian with a flattering smile.

"Okay that's cool! Well umm...'I'ma' get back to this kitchen though, before I burn down the building, ya mean?" T.J. announces.

"Yeah, please do, Bruh! I don't feel like evacuating tonight. And thanks again for lookin' out, 'T'." Brian gratefully replies.

"Aight, y'all have a good night!" T.J. replies before dashing back into his apartment.

"You want something to drink? I've got some stuff in the fridge. You're more than welcome to help yourself to while I hop in the shower real quick!" Brian offers as he flicks on his studio lights.

"Sure, I'll take some water." Ashima quickly requests as she makes herself comfortable on Brian's neatly made bed.

"Okay, well..." Brian looks in the direction of the kitchen implying to help herself.

"I'm sorry, Babe. You know the rules...first time you're a guest, second time you're at home." Ashima can only smile at Brian's charming hospitality as he reminds her again.

"Umm...okay!" She replies as she leaves her designer handbag and phone on the bed and walks to the kitchen.

Meanwhile, Brian walks into the bathroom and runs the shower before returning to the bedroom to his dresser to grab his undergarments and change of clothes.

"Brian, you're so neat with your things. Even things in your refrigerator are neatly placed." Ashima admires.

"Well, with the place being so small, I try to keep an organized home so I can find everything I need. But, on a different note, what was so important that you came all the way over here to tell me?" Brian digresses to address her urgency.

"Well, I came over because I couldn't tolerate another moment at home with my father. I had a fall out with my Amir today after he told me about your golf outing with him. I understand that it wasn't exactly a friendly invitation and I want to apologize for his ignorance." Ashima replies in a serious demeanor, as she walks from the kitchen with water in hand.

"Yeah, I should have known something was up when he dragged me out to the ninth hole in the middle of nowhere on this perfectly whack day. But, your father spoke his peace. And in so many words, he told me that Fahad reserves the rights to be with you and if I don't fall back, it could get dangerous for me. Then he subliminally threatened me with a sword by shearing off the top of a champagne bottle and had the audacity to offer me a drink?" Brian explains as he shakes his head in disbelief.

"Are you kidding me? He used Sabering to threaten you? He's not even good at it!" Ashima replies in amazement.

"Yeah, well he must have been practicing, because he didn't have any problem with trying to get his point across." Brian informs her as he moves his things to the bathroom while they continue to talk.

"So, how do you feel about my father's cautionary words?" Ashima curiously asks, trying to determine if her father's threats have deterred his interest in her.

"Well, I can't say that I wasn't disappointed. But, I don't take kind to threats…" Brian pauses as he takes off his sweat dampened athletic shirt, before resuming. "…and if I want something bad enough, I'm more than willing to fight for it. I mean, no disrespect to your pops, but his threat means no more to me than caution to the wind. But, I was actually more interested in knowing how you felt about your father's crazy demands?" Brian asks as he purposely steps out of the bathroom to acknowledge Ashima, bare from the waste up.

258

Caught off guard by the sudden lustfully masculine frame before her, she struggles to retain her composure as she maintains a neutral expression. But, her mind helplessly says, *"Oh...my goodness!"*

"You know...my father has raised me well over the years, since my mother was forced to go back to Egypt to care for my Nana. But, he's tried to control every aspect of my life since I was a little girl...until now. I'm not going to allow my father to tamper with my personal life any longer. From now on, I'm doing what's best for me. So, you have nothing to worry about." Ashima avows as she walks over to give Brian a simple, teasing kiss, then turns to walk away. Brian stands motionless in awe with a smile of content, grateful for her reply.

"Hmph, well I'm glad you've made that decision. I'll be back in a minute." Brian simply replies, as he takes one lasting lustful look at her rear image before closing the door to shower up.

Brian steps into the shower with all smiles knowing Ashima won't be coerced by her father. Although he left her with a lasting impression, Ashima knew better than to allow herself to show signs of sexual vulnerability towards a man. But, it was something about Brian and his masculine bravado that forces her mind to wonder beyond the boundaries of etiquette.

As Brian starts his shower, Ashima looks around the modest apartment and admires how neatly decorated the dwelling is. She appreciates how much pride he took in attention to detail, from his tiny bookshelf to his clothes hanging in his partially opened closet. She couldn't quite put a finger on it. But, in a short period of knowing him, she recognized relatively fast that there was something special about the type of man he is that has definitely left an impression, and so far, it's been refreshing. Given the caring and unselfish type of woman she is, she wanted more for him.

Suddenly her phone is blowing up from a rash of calls. She ignored at least a half dozen phone calls from Fahad and one from her Amir. Fearing that something may be wrong, she picks up for Fahad when he calls again.

"Hello...?" She answers.

"Ashima, where have you been? I've been calling all over the city for you." An agitated Fahad questions.

"I'm out Fahad. Is there something important you needed?" Ashima passively answers.

"I spoke with Amir today and he told me what happened. Ashima, where are you? I want to talk to you!" Fahad aggressively demands.

"Fahad, I'm in no mood for your ridicule. Furthermore, what part of 'done' don't you understand? We have no more dealings and I will not tolerate your irrelevant questioning. Now, I have to go, okay? Good day!" An irritated Ashima reprimands Fahad, quickly hanging up after she hears the running water stop and the curtain pull back in the bathroom.

"Did you have dinner yet?" Brian asks after opening the bathroom door as he dries off.

"No. But, I had a very big lunch today and couldn't possibly stomach another bite. But, thanks for asking." She replies.

"'Phew'...! I need some water!" Brian says as he emerges from the bathroom with nothing more than a towel wrapped around his waist, and a pair of sport slippers as steam from the shower billows from the bathroom.

Barely able to bear the sight of his alluring, rigid frame, she bashfully turns away as he walks to the kitchen.

"Are you sure I can't make something for you? It wouldn't be a problem." Brian offers as he returns from the kitchen refreshed by his own bottle of water.

"No, I'm sure. Thank you." Ashima replies.

"Okay...I make a mean bowl of ramen noodles, though. I'm just saying..." Brian teases as he sits down beside her.

"Ramen noodles...?" She laughs, playfully mocking Brian.

Rapidly getting spun up by his arousing sculpture-like frame, Ashima holds the bottled water to her mouth to mask any obvious signs of lustful expression. Her eyes helplessly gawking a hormone intense stare when Brian looks away. As he looks towards her, she takes a few sips of water, not to refresh her pallet, but to cool down her libido.

"No really...fresh chopped scallions, pork or beef tenderloin, a little Shichimi pepper, with a parsley or cilantro garnish? You'll never look at ramen the same, again." Just as Brian finishes his ramen noodle pitch, Ashima's phone rings again as it sits on the bed between them. They both look at the phone and notice the name Fahad on the screen. Ashima sucks her teeth in disgust.

"You need to get that?" Brian asks in calm, condescending tone.

"Never mind that..." Ashima shakes her head as she silences the ringer before throwing the phone in her purse.

"Are you sure?" Brian ensures as he attentively studies her mannerism.

"I'm sure..." She responds, wrapping both of her hands around his bicep and resting her head on his shoulder.

Brian pauses in a moment of thought, before taking another sip of his water. Then he places his hand over hers before looking down at her face and kissing her on the forehead.

"Can I tell you something?" He asks softly as he begins to caress her hand.

"You can tell me anything." Ashima replies in the comfort of his presence.

"Look, I know I'm not what you're used to. I know I can't give you the world. I can't give you what Fahad can give you, and I may not even be the best fit for you. But, what I do know is that you being here, sitting in my tiny apartment isn't a coincidence, and whatever it is I'm feeling for you, I've never felt for any woman before...and I want to know how you feel about that?" Brian shamelessly admits staring unwaveringly into her bold luminous eyes as she looks up at him.

"Well, I think that you're right. I think there is a reason why I'm sitting here in your apartment and it's not because I need you to give me the world. I'm not looking for a man to sell me a dream. If I did I'd be with Fahad. I like you because of you. Not because of what you can do to impress me. There are some things in life that are far more important than material and money. Some women have other needs." Ashima honestly explains.

"What does a woman who seems to have everything possibly have a need for?" Brian asks with genuine confusion.

"Happiness, love, romance...these are the things that women really need. Money is nothing more than a pleasant distraction that makes life easier. But, it isn't everything." She explains.

"Hmm...so what is it about me you find so likeable?" Brian asks, curious of her interest in him.

"Oh, I don't know? Maybe it's your smile, or maybe it's you're touch, or maybe it's your soft kiss that's sweeter than anything out there?" Ashima playfully appeases Brian's Ego.

"You mean, like this?" Brian says as he lifts her by the chin and graces her with a tender kiss.

261

The gesture stimulates even more passionate intimacy as their tender lips engage. They lay back onto the bed caressing and touching each other before Ashima suddenly stops.

"I'm sorry, I don't mean to rush you into anything?" Brian considerately withdraws.

"No, it's nothing that you've done. It's just bad timing." Ashima replies with disappointment.

"Bad timing?" Brian replies with raised eyebrows.

"Yes, mother nature has come for me. I'm sorry." Ashima regretfully explains.

"Oh…well I guess it really is bad timing!" Brian laughs, understanding her situation.

"Yeah, I'm so sorry, Brian. I didn't mean to disappoint you. But, I promise this won't be the only opportunity." Ashima assures him with a cunning smile.

"Ashima, you don't have to apologize. You don't owe me anything. When the time is right, we'll have our moment." Brian expresses with empathy.

"You're so sweet, you know that? And you're right…when the timing is right we will have our moment." Ashima says as she sits up on the bed to give him a reassuring kiss before preparing to leave.

"Wait, you're not leaving, are you?" A puzzled Brian asks as she stands to her feet.

"Yeah, I should probably get going now? I just wanted to stop by to make sure you were okay." She caringly replies.

"No, wait, babe…it's still early. Why don't you stay?" Brian stands with her and pulls her in closely by the waist.

"I would love too, I really would. But, I do not feel fresh, Brian." Ashima pleads, referring to her feminine situation.

"Are you sure you don't want to just freshen up right here? I'm sorry, I just want to be close to you right now, that's all." Brian pouts in disappointment.

"Awe…I'll come by tomorrow so we can spend more time, okay?" Ashima replies, playfully pacifying his charming immaturity.

"Aight, well let me at least put some clothes on so I can walk you to the car, babe." Brian persists as they move towards the door. Ashima stops and gently grabs Brian by the face to give him a kiss.

"It's okay. Carlos is waiting outside. I'll call you when I get home." Ashima assures him with a kiss before leaving the apartment.

"Be careful!" Brian yells down the hall in Ashima's wake.

Saddened by Ashima's departure, Brian takes a moment to tidy up a bit before getting dressed. He walks to the kitchen to put away the unfinished bottles of water they drank, then peaks into the refrigerator spawn a dinner idea when he suddenly hears an unexpected rap at the door. His mood instantly lights up as he stands at the refrigerator door cheesing from ear to ear.

"I knew it...!" Brian confidently remarks to himself, anticipating Ashima's change of heart.

"I KNEW YOU COULDN'T STAY AWAY! HOLD ON A MINUTE, BABE!" Brian shouts as he scrambles from the kitchen to answer the door. Brian opens the door with a gratifying smile.

"Hello Babe!" Suddenly Brian becomes overwhelmed in state of confusion when he found himself face to face with three expressionless men standing at his door. To his surprise, there stood Fahad with a glaring, ominous stare along with his friends Manny and Shelton.

"Oh, I'm sorry. Is that something that you and Ashima share exclusively, or can I call you Babe, too? You know, on second thought that probably wouldn't be appropriate, now would it? I mean, you being dressed in nothing more than a towel and all." Fahad expresses with sarcasm. Brian is frozen in awe and doesn't quite know how to respond. But, one thing was for certain, he knew they didn't show up uninvited at his door step to be social.

"Actually, you standing at my door right now isn't appropriate. But, since you're here, 'I'ma' give you a minute to get whatever it is you need to get off your chest." Brian expresses in a not so amusing tone with adrenaline racing through his veins anticipating something about to happen.

Fahad lets out a sigh, and then he drops his head and smiles in disbelief. The reality of his speculation ended with the reality of truth standing before him.

"So, it is you whom I've suspected all along. You are the guy who's supposed to be man enough to replace me, yes? You know, my friend Manny here told me you would be trouble when you came to my home. But, I didn't see much of a threat. I guess I was just a poor judge of character."

Fahad and his friends chuckle at the sly remark undermining Brian. Unfazed by the comment, Brian snickers as well with disregard.

"Yeah, well, listen Arab, Akbar, Aladdin, Abu-Dhabi..." Brian slights Fahad before he interrupts him.

"...It's Fahad!" He interjects growing annoyed of Brian's name butchering.

"Okay then, Fahad! I don't know what you call yourself doing coming here with your camel jockey henchmen. But, you sound like you're in your feelings right now. So, 'I'ma' give you a pass. But, do yourself a favor and don't ever call yourself showing up on my doorstep like you 'bout that life, unless you're willing to go all the way with it, ya mean?" Brian warns with clenched fists.

"And let me remind you, you're not about this life, my friend! So, you should probably stop trying to sip champagne on forty-ounce money. You know what I mean, Money?" Fahad mocks Brian as he pushes up his sleeves and reveals a glistening diamond encrusted bracelet, diamond studded watch, and chunky diamond laced pinky ring.

"Okay and...what's that supposed to mean? You're trying to go home without it?" Brian bluntly implies with an indirect threat.

"I don't think so, my friend. But, perhaps you didn't quite understand the warning Amir stressed to you earlier on the golf course. Ashima is forbidden fruit my friend and it would be wise for you to back off. I mean, you honestly think you can keep up with the demands of a woman like Ashima, hmm...? You're a delivery boy who punches a clock for eight hours of pitiful wages. I hire guys like you to wash my cars while I'm on the phone making million-dollar deals. I mean, what did you think? You thought you were going to just cook your way into her life? You think salmon croquettes and asparagus spears will keep her happy, Iron Chef? I think we both know better than that, don't we?" Fahad asks as his eyes narrow to the coldest, disheartening stare. But, Brian doesn't back down as he stands fearlessly in the doorway with an intrepid look on his face.

"I'm sorry, I must have missed the part about Ashima being forbidden fruit. But, umm...you're at my door, uninvited with a lot of disrespect. Now, don't get it confused, the only reason why I haven't choked you out yet is because I'm wrapped in this towel. Now, 'I'ma' tell you like I told Amir, your chick chose me, regardless of what kind of money you have. Obviously, she's looking for something better, so if you got a problem, I suggest you take it up with her, ya dig!" Brian firmly suggests with no regard to Manny or Shelton standing behind Fahad.

"Are you kidding me? You think Ashima interested in the likes of you is better? I could best you on any day, for anything, okay! You see where I live. You see what I'm driving. The tires on my car will cost you two months' salary, my friend! Need I say more?" Fahad responds in an aggravated outburst.

Suddenly, the apartment door behind the three men swings open and a rough looking T.J. emerges, wearing a white-tee, a sagging pair of jeans, a pair of wheat Timbs, a ball cap cocked to the side, and a bag of trash in hand.

"Yo, what up B...you good over there?" T.J. asks, suspicious of the men loitering in his hallway. Taking note of T.J.'s thuggishly, disheveled look, Shelton immediately recognizes that this could possibly get dangerous.

"Yeah, I'm good, 'T'. These fellas were just about to be on their way, right?" Brian replies as Fahad gives him a hard, callous stare.

"You sure? 'Cause you know I keep my thing off safe at all times!" T.J. subliminally informs Brian as he notices the ring and jewelry Fahad is wearing.

"Fahad, another day. Fahad...let's go!" A nervous Shelton leans in and whispers, fearing the situation may escalate now with T.J. looming in the background. Deaf to Shelton's caveat, Fahad remains staring at Brian with an ominous snarl.

"C'mon B, let me get that from ya' man. It's too easy!" T.J. anxiously preys on the men as he awaits Brian to give him the word.

"Yo, be easy T, leave it!" Brian insists of T.J. to defuse his eager conspiracy.

"You're making a deal with Satin, my friend. I urge you to stay away from Ashima or so help me Allah...you have no idea." Fahad threatens in a thick Arabic accent as Shelton pulls him along. Brian simply stares at Fahad with his lips pressed in a dubious expression as Fahad carries on.

"Proceed with caution my friend. I'll see you soon!" Fahad calmly assures Brian with a cold stare leaving with the others.

"Yeah, aight...!" As the men walked away, Brian slams his door, then leans against the door in fury and frustration.

He couldn't believe that Fahad came for him at his own apartment as he immediately, reaches for his phone and dials Ashima.

"Hi…" Ashima answers excited to hear from Brian.

"Listen, I don't know how this clown got my address, but your Punjabi friends just left my apartment with a threat about me seeing you!" Brian explains out of ignorance in an upset adrenaline filled voice.

"What?! My goodness, Brian what happened?! Are you okay?!" Ashima frantically replies.

"Yeah, I'm good! But, shortly after you left, I heard a knock at the door. Thinking it was you, I answered the door in my towel, and I see Fahad and his cronies standing at my door. You didn't see them when you left here?" Brian angrily asks, wanting answers.

"No, I saw no one when I left. Surely, I would have warned you if I did. Oh my God, Brian! I am so sorry you had to go through that. I'm shocked and appalled that he showed up on your doorstep. I have no idea what his problem is." Ashima remorsefully replies.

"Well now he's got a new problem! As I said before, I don't take kind to threats." Brian cautions Ashima, venting his frustration.

"Brian no, I will handle this!" Ashima firmly urges him.

"Look, I'm not going to…" Ashima cuts him off.

"Brian…no! I will handle this!" She adamantly insists in an unwavering response.

CHAPTER FOURTEEN

The next morning on the loading dock of *Apex Shipping*, Brian, Marty, and Cortez are engaged in conversation while taking inventory on their trucks.

"Man, you've been missing in action lately. I miss whoopin' you on the pool table, Bruh. Where you been?" Cortez taunts Brian as they stand at his delivery truck.

"I know man. But, I've been trying to give a lot of my time to ole' girl, lately." Brian explains.

"Uh, huh…shorty done put that Egyptian musk on you, didn't she?" Cortez teases while Brian struggles to keep a straight face.

"Haha…yeah, she did! Look at him, can't even look up and face the truth." Marty adds to the comedy.

"Yo, 'B', just promise me you're not going to pull a prison conversion on me in the next few weeks. Next thing you know, you'll be leaving Apex to sling bowties and bean pies." Cortez jokes as all the men humor each other.

"Whoa…you remember what Red Fox said, 'She must be some mean nookie to make a Negro change God's'!" Marty adds. Brian shakes his head trying to hold back his laughter.

"C'mon man, I happen to like bean pies…so disrespectful! Both of y'all have no home training." Brian replies, shrugging off the playful insults.

"Hey, but on a serious note, what's up with you and Mal, man? What did you do to her?" Marty asks on a more important note.

"I don't know? We haven't seen each other in a while. But, I ain't do anything to her. Why, what going on?" Brian curiously replies as he scans another package.

"Is that right? So how does that feel?" Cortez implies.

"What's that?" A bufuddled Brian answers.

"Sleeping in your own bed?" Cortez laughs, finishing his punch line and amusing himself.

"Naw, seriously! I don't know what's up with her. But, she's been walking around here pissed the hell off lately…snappin' on folks and everything." Marty further explains.

"That's probably because I haven't been staying at her place for a few weeks. She hasn't been answering my calls and she hasn't been speaking to me at work, so it is what it is, I guess. Why, is she all up in Victor's face now?" Brian curiously asks.

"Well, I don't know about all that, but whatever it is going on between y'all two, you need to fix it! 'Cause ain't nothing worse than working around here with a pissed off, Mallory." Marty urges Brian. "But, hey speaking of Vince, I overheard him talking about you in his office this morning." Marty informs Brian.

"Uh-oh…this should be good!" Brian braces himself.

"No, actually it was good. He was on the phone talking to somebody about all of the great customer reviews you get and how great an asset you were to the company. Maybe there's a promotion or a raise in your future, Brotha?" Marty optimistically speculates.

"Well, we have been talking about raises lately. But, who knows with that guy. Hell, he probably wants me to clean his office and take out his trash." Brian exaggerates.

"Yeah, well you owe him at least that much for that little sexual misconduct you pulled." The fellas break out into a roar of laughter over Brian's unsavory stunt.

"Aight, y'all! I'll get up you later." Brian replies starting his truck and heading out on route.

Later that afternoon, after a string of text messages, Ashima agrees to meet with Jasmine and Crystal for lunch to catch up on some girl-talk. Eventually she would meet with the women after leaving work for a short walk to the Market-East side of City Hall, shortly after the other women arrive.

"Burrr…oh my, God! I can't believe I decided to brave the cold and walk down here!" Ashima says as she enters the vestibule were the other women awaited her arrival.

"You…walked? Where in the world is Carlos?" Crystal asks as Ashima exchange cheek smooches with all the women.

"It would have been such a waste of time to call him for such a short trip. Besides, a little fresh air and exercise is good for a girl sometimes." Ashima attests.

"Oh please, Shima you're a corporate girl. You know that walking more than four blocks in a pair of heels is not a good look for a corporate girl." Jasmine counters with a sense of amusement.

"I'm not that boujee!" Ashima replies with a straight face.

"Right this way ladies…" The waitress says as she leads them to their table.

The ladies sit for a reservation at their favorite fondue restaurant and order drinks and appetizers before ordering entrées.

"Good afternoon ladies, may I start you out with something to drink?" The waitress asks as the women settle at their table, hanging their purses and coats on the chair backs.

Jasmine orders a glass of Cabernet and a lobster fondue appetizer for the table, Crystal orders a sparkling Moscato, and Ashima orders her favorite Riesling.

"So, ladies, how is everyone? I don't think we've really been together since Vegas, right?" Crystal asks before sipping from her glass.

"Please…! Don't remind me of how much fun y'all had in Sin City while I was stuck here in Filth Adelphia!" Jasmine replies, expressing her displeasure.

"Awe…its okay, Jaz. But, Vegas was so awesome!" Crystal replies, taunting her friend.

"Anyway, aside from dealing with two nagging kids worried about Christmas gifts already, I've been great!" Jasmine replies.

"I know, the holidays are coming up so fast. Thanksgiving is next week. Before you know it, it'll be New Year's Day." Crystal adds.

"Wait! Why are we talking about the holidays? You guys are not celebrating Christmas!" Ashima chimes in as she enjoys a sip from her glass.

"Yeah, I know. But, we still buy the kids gifts around this time of year so they don't feel left out. They're just kids, you know? But, you're right. We don't do trees and decorations or anything resembling a traditional holiday setting. Jimmy would kill me if I even tried." Jasmine replies, explaining her position on the matter.

"I've got that same problem Jasmine, even though I converted to Islam a few years ago, that's one tradition I can't seem to shake. I don't think my children would forgive me if I ever denied them during the holidays. But, it is a challenging conflict to say the least." Crystal clarifies, adding light to the conflict of interest.

"Shima, looks like you'll be in a bit of a holiday dilemma yourself if you and Fahad manage to figure it out." Jasmine candidly implies.

"How so...?" Ashima curiously responds.

"Well, what I mean is, if you and Fahad have kids, are you going to buy them gifts for the holidays?" Jasmine further elaborates on her statement.

The room suddenly becomes a bit harder to breathe as the ladies all look at each other with their legs crossed and glasses in hand like an elephant just entered the room. Ashima, not the least bit amused, holds her reply as the waitress returns with their order.

"Here you go ladies, one lobster fondue. Please be careful it's very hot!" The waitress cautions the women as she sets the fondue warmer center table.

"Yasss! Lobster fondue is my weakness!" Crystal proclaims lifting her nose to the wafting aroma.

"Are you ladies ready to order?" The waitress asks. The ladies look over at each other, none of which has even opened a menu.

"No, we're just going to just enjoy the fondue for now." Jasmine replies for the group as the others silently agree.

"Okay, take your time ladies, I'll check on you later." The waitress replies. After the waitress departs, Ashima breaks the awkward silence.

"Now, to answer your question, Crystal, I don't see any chance of having a holiday dilemma with any children of my future, considering I don't have a future with Fahad." Ashima bluntly discloses.

"Wow, so that's still your stance on Fahad?" Jasmine chimes in as the women begin to awkwardly fumble with the fondue forks.

"Yes, and I intend to keep it that way. Have you heard different?" She replies, responding a bit more irritably to the conversation.

"Okay...let's just get this out in the open. We're all grown here and I think it's time to address the elephant in the room. Shima, I know Fahad isn't exactly high on your favorites list, and I'll be the first to condemn his infidelity with Nisa. But, this thing that you've got going on with this other

270

guy, umm…Brian, is it? I mean, c'mon Shima, what are you doing?" Jasmine asks as Crystal remains silent, awaiting Ashima's reply.

"Well, what I'm doing is taking charge of my life. For once I'm doing what's best for me and what makes me happy. And that doesn't include Fahad!" Ashima firmly responds.

"Wait, Shima you're not falling for this guy, are you?" An astounded Crystal asks.

"What does it matter? Before Vegas you were all applauding the idea of me seeing Brian. Encouraging me to have fun with him and enjoy his company. But, now that I'm maintaining my disdain for Fahad there's a problem?" Ashima defensively replies.

"Yes Shima, have fun! Not run around the city with him like you're exclusive with him or something. I mean, c'mon…he's a delivery guy. How could you ever really consider taking someone serious to the likes of him?" Crystal struggles to understand.

"Listen, I don't think it's appropriate that I have to sit here and defend myself about my personal affairs. What you chose to do with your life is your business and what I do with my life is mine!" Ashima fires back as the conversation becomes hotly contested.

"And I don't find it appropriate that you…a young, affluent, Wharton educated, and successful 'Egyptian' woman is wasting your time running around with some delivery, hood-thug from North Philadelphia. I don't care how big his penis may be." Crystal responds in a humble tone.

"What do you know, hmm? What do you know about him? What, he's not rich? He's not Muslim? What do you know, huh? You know nothing about him and you know nothing about my relationship with him!" Ashima replies with anger growing at every rebuttal.

"Shima, we weren't trying to offend you. We only wanted to talk to you because we care. Not to belittle you. But, to reach out to you to give you some truth. And the truth is, no self-respecting woman of our opulence would be content with fraternizing with such a man." Jasmine calmly explains trying to defuse the tension at the table.

"Yeah, Shima, he doesn't compliment you is all we're saying. You're better than this!" Crystal adds.

"Is that it? Is that what this is about? Protecting me from my own poor judgment? Saving me from making a mockery of myself? You call yourselves bringing me to lunch so you can read me? Spill tea about my life

271

and throw shade? I find that humoring, considering I've never judged any of you for any moment that we've been friends. Not even when you confessed to me that you married Jimmy only because he rescued you from the slums of Mumbai and gave you a better life…" Ashima divulges, addressing Jasmine.

"That's not fair Shima, I love Jimmy. He's a great husband and a great father!" Jasmine swiftly defends.

"And a great provider…let's not forget the real reason why you love him. You're not in love with him. You're in love with what he does for you. And based on how unhappy you've been over the last few years, you'd have to ask yourself, are you in love or are you in loyal? No matter what the truth may be, I'm not in a position to judge. Yet you elect to turn judgment on me!" Although Ashima is obviously affected by her friend's nonsupport, she refuses to back down and continues to defend her position with Brian.

"Ashima, we're not trying to upset you. We're only trying to help you understand your worth." Jasmine sympathizes with Ashima.

"How? By judging me about who I see? By judging my personal life? No, I will not sit here and allow you to criticize me about my personal life." Ashima rants as she stands from the table and grabs her purse and coat.

"Wait…Shima, don't leave. You haven't ordered your entry yet!" Crystal pleads as a visibly upset Ashima takes a hundred-dollar bill from her purse, and places it underneath her wine glass.

"Sorry I ruined your lunch ladies. Enjoy the rest of your day!" A disappointed Ashima mutters.

"Shima, please!" Jasmine begs as Ashima breezes past her toward the exit.

As she exits the restaurant, she notices a cab in front of the restaurant dropping of a couple on their way in. As the man holds the door for the woman to exit, Ashima assumes control of the door like a rehearsed hand-off and hops in back of the cab.

"Hi, 18th and Market please!" She requests, throwing her purse on the seat next to her with her phone in hand.

Ashima sits in the rear of the cab appalled and disappointed by the scrutiny of her friends. But, the annoyance of her mid-day drama didn't end there. Ashima's phone rings, just as she arrives back at work and pays the cabbie his fare. Optimistic that it could be Brian, she pulls out her phone and reads 'unknown caller' on the screen. Typically, she would ignore this type of call, but for some reason this time she answers.

"Hello...?" She answers.

"Ashima, please don't hang up!" Fahad quickly pleads. Ashima rolls her eyes and lets out a sigh of disgust, as she forces herself to tolerate him. Although she hasn't had a chance to address Fahad about showing up on Brian's doorstep, she still had unfinished business to take care of.

"What is it Fahad? And why are you calling me with your number blocked?" An irritated Ashima asks. Anticipating a lengthy phone call, Ashima puts on her gloves, bundles her coat, and leisurely walks down the street to avoid bringing drama into the building lobby.

"Because I knew you wouldn't answer my call if you saw my number." Fahad replies in a humble tone.

"You're right! I don't have any use for a conversation with you. But, now that I've answered, what do you want?" Ashima asks with no interest in the conversation.

"Ashima, what have I done? What have I done to deserve this despicable way you're treating me?" Fahad asks in a somber tone.

"Oh...! So now you're the victim? Now you're the one being treated despicably? After you've treated me lower than a dog for years? Forgive me if I don't shed a tear of sympathy for you, Fahad." Ashima carelessly replies.

"Ashima quit exaggerating. I gave you everything you ever wanted and whatever I didn't give you was only because you didn't accept it." Fahad tries to rationalize with Ashima.

"That's exactly my point! When will you ever understand that you can't buy my happiness? When will you get it through your head that you can't buy me? The only reason why you think you were good to me is because you tried to buy me everything. But, never did you take the time to know the real me." Ashima helps him to realize.

"Ashima, I can fix this, okay! Please, let me show you how much better I can be to you. Just give me that chance!" Fahad begs as the desperation grows in his voice.

"I'm sorry, Fahad. But, I don't have any interest in you anymore." Ashima firmly replies.

"But, you're interested in him?" Fahad, jealously responds.

"Why? Why does it even matter, Fahad? Suddenly you're so interested in me? Never have you cared before…never have I received any sense of reverence from you. Yet, you want to claim me as your wife. Why, to be your slave? To have Nisa and I both share your bed? Never! Never will I be a slave to you, and never will I be a slave to Islam!" Ashima passionately declares.

"So, you'd rather humiliate yourself for this black heathen? This pitiful excuse for a provider? We'll see how much he can provide without his pathetic wages!" Fahad rants as Ashima's remarks start to agitate him.

"What's that supposed to mean?" Ashima confronts his comment.

"It means that you're unbelievable! This is who you whore for? You whore for him…a charity case?!" An irate Fahad questions, becoming completely unraveled as he yells into the phone.

"Good-bye Fahad, it's too cold for this." She concludes, returning back to the building.

"Ashima this isn't over! Do you hear me?! ASHIMA!!!"

Later in the day, as Brian wraps up his deliveries, he receives a text message from Cortez who's already back at the warehouse.

(Text)
Cortez: *Vince needs to see you as soon as when you get back. He said don't worry about inventory.*
Brian: *Aight…*

Brian responds, curious of what Vincent has to talk about and excited that it may possibly be about the raise they recently discussed. Once Brian arrives back at the warehouse, as he backs his truck up to the loading bay, he sees Marty and Cortez walking towards the break room to clock out.

"On your way up to them executive suites, huh? Go ahead and get that paper, boy!" Marty yells as they see Brian exit the truck.

"We going out to *The Fox* tonight, you coming out?" Cortez asks as Brian reaches the base of the stairs.

"Yeah, 'I'ma' come out." Brian replies, looking forward to getting back on the pool table with his friends.

"Aight then. Let us know what happened when you get there." Marty suggests as he and Cortez walk into the break room.

"Aight!" Brian agrees as he heads up the stairs to Vincent's office.

274

Once at the top of the stairs his eyes spring open as the Mallory closes her door and heads out for the day.

"Hey Mal…" Brian nervously greets her as she strides right past him without even batting an eyelash.

Brian grins and shakes his head as he simply keeps it moving. Brian taps twice on Vincent's open door before entering.

"What's up Vince, you needed to see me?" Brian asks with a smirk of optimism on his face. However, Vincent's facial expression did not resemble the same.

"Jones, I don't know what you've done? But, I got off the phone this morning with a rep from corporate and they informed me about you getting into a verbal altercation with one of our proverbial clients yesterday?" Vincent informs Brian with a straight face. Brian demeanor immediately changes, realizing this wasn't a conversation in his favor.

"Altercation? I've never had a problem with a client ever since I've been here." Brian replies, stunned by the accusation.

"Yeah, Jones, I figured as much, and I tried to vouch for your character as much as he would listen. But, whoever filed this complaint must have knew someone in corporate, because they told me to terminate you immediately after your truck hit the loading dock." Vincent regretfully explains.

"Are you sure you don't have me mistaken for someone else? I mean, this is crazy. I really feel like I'm being punked right now!" Brian replies in dismay.

"I'm sorry, Jones. But, this is an action that was ordered from corporate. I'll need your badge and you could throw your uniform in the cleaning bin when you get changed out." Vincent calmly instructs him.

"Wow, just the other day we were sitting here having a discussion about a possible raise, and now you're telling me I'm fired." A baffled Brian replies.

"Sorry Jones, I hate to lose you. But, this one was way over my head." Vincent explains barely able to make eye contact with Brian.

"Aight cool!" Brian snatched his I.D. badge off his uniform, placed it on Vincent's desk and walked out without uttering another word.

After leaving the *Apex* warehouse and in dire need of a drink, Brian meets up with fellas at *The Fox* where he describes his meeting with Vincent.

"Fired?! Are you serious? What the hell did you do?!" Marty asks in utter disbelief as they sit at the bar enjoying beers and fried pickles.

"I don't know. Vince claims that corporate called him accusing me of having a verbal altercation with a client. He couldn't tell me with whom or give me specifics. But, with that he said, he had no choice. They forced his hand." Brian solemnly explains, still bewildered by the situation.

"Forced his hand...? You've got to be kidding me! I can't believe that clown came up with that weak excuse to get you 'outta' there. That's a shady dude y'all...shady! I know you're not going to take this layin' down, 'B'?" Marty rants in a hail of protests.

"Naw, Marty. I saw it in that man's eyes. I think he was telling the truth on this one." Brian surprisingly defends.

"I don't know about that one, 'B'. You know that cat has had it out for you for a minute now." Cortez suggests otherwise.

"I'd be very careful who you talk to with a slick tongue Mr. Brian Jones. You have no idea who I know in Philadelphia." Brian ponders as Amir's warning suddenly plays back in his mind.

"Naw Tez, I think I've got a pretty good idea of who's behind the complaint, the phone call, and everything." Brian replies with a clear reason of suspicion.

"Wait, you think ole girl's father had something to do with this?" Marty also questions with reasonable suspicion.

"He told me on the golf course that, 'I should be careful because I have no idea who he knows in Philly.' Now in some weird coincidence Vince gets a call from corporate about some wild story of me having a verbal altercation. What y'all think?" Brian asks as he swigs his beer after pleading his case.

"Sounds like a duck to me!" Cortez replies looking over at Marty.

"Well, at this point, what does it matter anyway? You've already lost your job, and with no gig, looks like you're about to lose the girl too. But, that's the least of your worries. You know the rental office don't care about domestic disputes and lost wages. They want their check on the first of every month, with a ten-day grace period if you're lucky. So, how are you going to address that problem?" Marty candidly explains before stabbing a few fried pickles from the basket.

"I'll be cool for a few months. I've been putting away money for those rims, so that should hold me over."

"Cool! Well, you know you're my man. So, if you need to grab some couch for a while, you know I got you, and you're more than welcome to come to the crib for Thanksgiving. You know wifey can burn so don't be a stranger." Marty assures his friend.

"Thanks man, I appreciate that." Brian gratefully replies.

"Yeah, same here...if you need a place to crash for a while, you know I got you." Cortez generously offers.

"Uh, thanks, Tez. But, hell naw, I'm not coming to your spot to crash! Brandy is crazier than a pack of Pop Rocks!" Brian playfully replies as the fellas share a laugh.

"But, seriously though, I really appreciate both of y'all being there for ya boy." Brian graciously appreciates his friends as they toast their bottles before Brian finishes his beer. He then stands from his bar stool to put on his jacket."

"Uh oh, there he goes, running from another butt kickin' on the table." Cortez taunts Brian trying to guilt him to stay.

"Naw Bruh, I've got to get to the crib and figure some things out." Brian replies as he counts out some cash to pay for his drinks.

"Wait, Wait! What are you doing with that?" Marty questions, while grabbing Brian's hand as he attempts to place the money on the bar.

"What do you mean? I'm paying my part of the bill." Brian replies.

"C'mon man, there's only two people employed over here and one of them ain't you, okay! Take that money and put some gas in your tank or something." Marty insists forcing Brian to put the money away.

"Thanks, Bruh. I'll get up with y'all later." Brian replies giving both his friends dap and a hug before leaving.

On his way home, Brian mulls over the reality of being fired, and when would be the right time to tell Ashima. More importantly, tell her about her father's suspected involvement. It didn't take long for him to realize that he needed to have that talk sooner than later. However, still apprehensive about reaching out to her, he sends her a text from his car once he parks in front of his apartment.

(Text)
Brian: *Hey u.*
Ashima: *Hey, how are you?*
Brian: *Can u talk?*

Instead of replying to the text, Ashima calls him right away.

"Hey, is everything okay?" A concerned Ashima immediately starts out.

"Yeah, I will be." Brian replies in a discouraging tone.

"How so? What's wrong? You don't sound like yourself." Ashima asks, alarmed by Brian's response.

"Well, not that you should worry or anything. But, I was fired from my job today at Apex." Brian regretfully informs her.

"Oh, no! Brian, what happened?" Ashima shockingly replies. Completely caught off guard by the news.

"I'm not sure. One minute my boss was discussing giving me a raise, and the next minute I'm fired over an accusation from a client." Brian struggles to understand.

"My goodness, who would do such a terrible thing?" Ashima asks, appalled by the news.

"Well, I have to be completely honest with you, Ashima. I've tried to make sense of this whole situation, and I can't look past the fact that your dad may have made good on a threat he made to me on the golf course." Brian explains.

"Oh no…what did he say?" Ashima frantically asks.

"He told me to be careful because I don't know who he knows in Philly. Now, I'm not one for speculating, but he could have made good on his warning." Brian considers.

"My God Brian, Fahad mentioned something alarming to me as well. He said something about seeing how much you can provide with lost wages. Brian, I am so sorry. I do believe Fahad and my father had something to do with you losing your job." Ashima sincerely apologizes.

"You don't have to apologize. You're not the one who's declaring war." Brian calmly replies as he boils with anger about Fahad and Amir.

"Yes, I do. This is my fault. If it wasn't for me being so difficult and obvious, there wouldn't be so much attention. I have to fix this." She replies upset and shouldering the blame.

"No, you don't, it's okay! Look, I have a couple dollars saved up to get me through the next few months, and I still have my internship down at the restaurant. They recently offered me a position there anyway. So, don't worry about me, I'll be fine, okay?" Brian ensures her.

"Okay..." She replies feeling a bit more secure about Brian's stability.

"Once I accept a position down there, maybe you could come down and I could cook for you? Would you like that?" Brian asks to further pacify her emotions.

"Yes, that sounds great." She gladly accepts.

"Aight great! In the meantime, how does lunch sound tomorrow, it's on me?" Brian offers.

"Well, I'll probably be busy at work as usual. But, sure. I'll make time." Ashima pleasantly replies.

"Okay then. I'll see you tomorrow." Brian concludes as they hang up.

Despite being fired today, Brian hangs up the phone with a renewed optimism and a positive outlook on his future.

Meanwhile, Ashima has been home locked in her room and away from any communication with her father. Sitting Indian style on her bed, in front of her laptop in a pair of white loose-fitting shorts and a tee-shirt, Ashima is still bothered by her confrontational lunch with her friends. Sipping from a glass of wine on the nightstand at her bedside, Ashima places her phone on the bed and stretches after venting her frustration to Carolyn for nearly an hour. Suddenly her phone rings again. The caller is showing unknown. But, Ashima has pretty good idea of who it is.

"So, this is how you do me? After all the years I've known you...since the sandbox, this is the respect I get from you?" A distraught Fahad appeals when she answers his call.

"Fahad what do you mean?" Ashima carelessly replies in a calm, cavalier manner.

"What do I mean? What do I mean?! You leave me at the Gala and I haven't heard from you since. I return to the car and your engagement ring is sitting on the seat. You don't answer my calls, you don't answer my text! You're never home! God only knows where you be! You give me no explanation as to why you've become so distant towards me, AND I WANT ANSWERS!!!" Fahad exclaims, exploding with anger.

"I'm over it Fahad, okay?! I'm over everything about this twisted scenario. I'm sick of your lies, I'm sick of your arrogance, your attitude, your chauvinism. I'm over you always knocking something down, simply because it's standing. You have no humility. You have no shame. No class..."

"…and he does?! This broke, ghetto, delivery boy you choose to be with has more class than me? He probably couldn't spell class, let alone show me up as a gentleman. He could never have you the way I have you!" Fahad jealously interjects.

"Have me? Understand this Fahad, you may have given me an expensive ring to claim me as property. But, my love can't be bought, okay! You don't have me until you have all of me, and you've never had me! Now, I'm done with wearing this façade, I'm done with this charade and I'm done with you, Fahad!" Ashima angrily rectifies his comment.

"Does he make you laugh…hmph?" Fahad questions with bias curiosity.

"He doesn't make me cry." She simply replies before hanging up.

The next day, with no job to go to, Brian spends the morning on the phone with Rick, the sous chef at Chops and Dave the restaurants head chef, about getting some paid hours on staff in lieu of his employment situation. They were both more than willing to consider and asked Brian to come down for lunch to discuss it further. This worked out favorably for Brian, since he'd already made plans to take Ashima out to lunch today. After hanging up with them, he sends a text to Ashima to see if she would be willing to have lunch with him at Chops. She happily accepted, considering Chops is one of the few restaurants she's never been to in the downtown area.

Along the way, Brian decides to stop at an ATM to grab some cash for the lunch bill and to leave a generous tip. Probably for one of the staffer's he often talks to when he's working. After withdrawing a few hundred dollars from his checking account, he checks his printed statement balance and comes across a startling discovery.

"WHAT THE F…?!" He blurts out loudly. Adjusting his eyes to a clear focus he checks the receipt again to make sure what he saw was actually real. "Twenty-two thousand, nine hundred and seventy-eight dollars?!"

"Oh sh…twenty-two thousand, nine hundred and seventy-two dollars!" He grunts again under his breath in disbelief. Realizing that this is obviously some type of banking error, he calms down and decides to deal with it later. However, he couldn't ignore the tingle of excitement running up his spine.

Brian and Ashima meet in front of the restaurant entrance after Ashima walks a few short blocks from her building, allowing Brian time to find a place to park. They greet each other with gracious smiles and immediately embracing with a hug and a kiss, before heading into the restaurant.

281

"So glad you could make it!" Brian says, elevating his voice over the ambient sound of downtown traffic.

"I told you I would come." She replies as Brian opens the door for her.

"Hi Brian!" The blond, attractive Caucasian hostess greets him as they walk into the venue.

"Hey Misty, this is my lunch date, Ashima." Brian proudly announces as the ladies engage.

"Hi Ashima, welcome to Chops. Is this your first-time dining with us?" Misty asks with her strong perky personality.

"Shamefully yes. I work in the Mellon building just around the corner and despite plenty of opportunities, this is my first time." Ashima smiles with embarrassment.

"Well, hopefully this won't be your last time dining with us. You're very pretty by the way." Misty compliments her as she grabs a few menus.

"I'm flattered, thank you." Ashima replies.

"Misty when you get a chance, can you tell Rick or Dave that I'm here." Brian asks before she walks away.

"Sure, let me seat you guys and I'll see if I can track either of them down for you." Misty replies as she escorts them to their table in the moderately occupied dining room. Brian pulls Ashima's chair from the table as the hostess places their food and wine menus on the table.

"John will be with you shortly, okay. Enjoy!" Hostess says before scampering off. After being seated, someone quickly comes over to wait their table.

"Hi, my name is John, I'll be your waiter today. How are you fine folks this afternoon?" The middle-aged waiter asks turning their glasses over and filling them with the pitcher of water he brought with him.

"We're good. Thanks for asking, John." Brian replies to the unfamiliar dayworker.

"Great, can I start you off with a glass of something from our excellent wine selection?" Brian looks at Ashima and waits for her to choose first.

"Umm, I'll take a glass of Riesling, please!" Ashima requests before looking over at Brian.

"I'll have the same, thank you!" Brian follows.

"Okay, two Rieslings coming up. Feel free to look over our delicious menu selection while I return with your drinks." The waiter replies before leaving the table.

"So, how's work today?" Brian asks as they both look over the menu options.

"Work is fine. As long as my father either stays home or in his office, I'll have a great day every day. As Ashima responds, she notices that Brian's focus is not at the table.

"Are you okay, today?" Ashima asks with a confused, discerning look.

"Yeah, I'm good. Why do you ask?" Brian answers looking down at his phone.

"I don't know. You seem a bit disconnected today." Ashima responds.

"Wow. You've already learned me that much to identify a problem? That's cool!" Brian replies, impressed by Ashima's attentiveness.

"In case you haven't noticed by now, I'm very attentive. I have to be in my profession." Ashima explains. Brian smiles at her crafty response.

"Well, to answer your question, I need to make a phone call to the bank as soon as possible to figure out a huge banking error I found this morning." Brian informs her.

"What type of banking problem? Perhaps I could help, since you bank with us." Ashima inquires as the waiter returns with their wine glasses.

"And here we go…two Rieslings. Are we ready to order, or do you still need more time?" The waiter asks ready for their orders. Brian looks over at Ashima for consensus.

"Umm…give us a few more minutes, John, aight? Thanks!" Brian kindly replies.

"Okay then, just give me a nod when you're ready." The waiter replies.

"So, on the way here I went to the ATM and when I looked at my bank statement, there was twenty-thousand extra dollars in my checking account, crazy right?" Brian explains with mild enthusiasm.

"Oh, yeah, wow!" Ashima utters in amazement.

"Yeah, I know. Now, obviously I don't know where the money came from…I wish I did. But, I'm not trying to go to jail over a banking error today." Brian earnestly replies before taking a sip from his glass.

"Yes, that does sounds like a lot of extra money in your account. I could run a check on your transactions when I get back to the office if you'd like." Ashima offers.

"Well, as much as I need it, I just want to return the money to the bank. That's just a headache I don't need right now." Brian replies, feeling uneasy about the situation.

"Yes, it's a shame that you have to turn that money in. I'm sure you could have used it for your bills and your leisure." Ashima implies.

"Yeah...especially after losing my job yesterday. It's almost like an evil joke is being played on me or something?" Brian replies with disappointment. Suddenly, without merit Ashima snickers at Brian's anguish.

"I'm sorry. I don't mean to laugh. But, I can certainly help explain your money problem." Ashima replies, offering clarification to the misunderstanding.

"Well, I hope it involves me keeping it." Brian jokingly replies as he lifts his glass to take another sip.

"Brian...I'm the reason behind the money." Ashima says with a straight face. Brian immediately brings his glass back down in a state of awe.

"Say what...?!" Brian's facial expression suddenly goes from silly to serious.

"Yes, I transferred the funds into your account this morning. Now, before you reprimand me for crossing the line, let me explain." Ashima defends before Brian could reply.

"Okay, I'm listening." Brian replies awaiting her explanation with raised eyebrows.

"Brian, I'm not some crazy, strung out over love woman who would do anything to please a man. I did this for you because you were wronged by my father and Fahad. I guess you can call it restitution. I also did this because I care about you, Brian. I realize that you and I have something special and I don't want to do anything to compromise that. But, if you would like for me to undo the transaction, I'll take care of it when I get back to the office." Ashima sincerely explains.

"Well, I guess I should start out by saying that I'm not mad at you. Furthermore, I think that sticking up for me like that really says a lot about you. I appreciate that. Now, I can't say that I'm thrilled about the way you

284

went about doing it, going into my account without my consent and all. But, I appreciate you having my back. As far as crazy is concerned, the court is still holding a ruling on that one." They both chuckle at the humor before he continues. "But, seriously, I'm not exactly comfortable with the idea of you carrying me financially. I've been more than capable of taking care of myself." He proudly explains.

"I'm really, truly sorry for going behind your back and tampering with your account, Brian. But, I knew you would have never taken the money if I would have openly asked you. Sometimes it's better to ask for forgiveness than to ask for permission. That's why I did what I did." Ashima explains with minimal regret.

"True…you make a good point. But, now that I know that you're capable of this I have to ask…" Suddenly, Brian interrupted by Dave who approaches him from his blindside.

"Hey Brian, what's up man! Sorry about the wait, but you know how it is in the kitchen. But, man I'm so glad you could come down. And I see you've brought a lovely young lady with you." Dave says with his usual raspy voice and his lively personality as he comes out dressed in his Chef whites to greet Brian. Brian stands to his feet and greets Dave with a strong pound and bear hug in return.

"Dave I'd like you to meet my lunch date Ashima. Ashima this is Dave the head chef." Brian introduces.

"Such a pleasure to meet you, Ashima. And I understand that this is your first-time dining with us. So, are you comfortable so far? Do you need anything? Is he treating you right? You want me to get on him?" Dave asks in a playful barrage of questions as he shakes her hand, pushing his glasses up on his nose.

"No, he's just fine, and yes I'm very pleased to dine at your establishment. The service is great and I've been enjoying the atmosphere." Ashima replies in a gracious tone.

"Awe…thank you! God bless you sweetheart. Well, hey I just wanted to come out here and personally make sure you're doing okay. If there's anything I can do for you kids, anything at all, please don't hesitate. Order whatever, lunch is on this guy. I'll just take it out of his first check. Just kidding Brian. No seriously lunch is on me! Order whatever you want. Ashima, it's been a pleasure! I have to get back to the kitchen. Enjoy your lunch!" Dave says as he hurries back to the kitchen.

"Thanks Dave!" Brian exclaims he and Ashima settle back into their chairs. Meanwhile, John has returned to take their orders.

"So, are we ready to order or do you still need more time?" John patiently asks.

"Yes, I'll have the shrimp cocktail." Ashima quickly orders.

"And I'll go with the Calamari…and please take your time." Brian requests to allot more time to share with Ashima.

"Okay, I'll take my time getting this out to you." The waiter assures them before wrapping up their order.

"So, where was I?" Brian tries to recall.

"You were about to ask me something." Ashima reminds him.

"Oh yeah, so I was saying that now that I've learned something a little radical and spontaneous about you, what else is there to know about Ashima Batool?" Brian asks taking advantage of an opportunity to tap into her personal story. Ashima smiles before she responds.

"On the outside, I'm perceived as a privileged and affluent twenty-something, who's never had a want for anything and has the world at my disposal. But inside, I'm really a simple woman, who wishes I led a simple and normal life. I can't apologize for being born and raised the way I am. That was God's will, not any fault of my own. But, that doesn't mean I have to live my life pretentiously. I can't even drive a car for crying out loud, because my father forbids it and insists that I have a driver. There are subways and buses that run all throughout this city, and I couldn't tell you the first thing about public transportation. Not even to commute like a normal person. But, recently I decided that it was time for change. It was time for me to stop living in the shadows of my father and come into my own. So, the questions I have for you is, 'are you willing to embark on this journey with me, or are you afraid you can't handle something new'?" Ashima challenges Brian with a smile as she sits back in her chair and takes a sip of wine.

"Hmph…well, since you put it that way, I'm up for a magic carpet ride. No pun intended!" Brian accepts as he picks up his glass and they toast to their newly established romantic bond.

Over the next several months, Ashima and Brian make good on their toast, and despite Amir and Fahad's idol threats, the allure between Ashima and Brian grew stronger. What took years for some couples to build, they were able to establish in a matter of months. Although Brian was willing to bring Ashima around family for the holidays, they both agreed that it might be better to pace their relationship a little slower and not put a title on their status as of yet.

In spite of this, the holidays were still festive between them. Brian invited Ashima down to Chops for a gourmet Thanksgiving feast prepared exclusively by the staff for their families. When Christmas came around, in the spirit of giving, Ashima has Brian bring his car to the rims store to have the Gianelle rims Brian always wanted installed on his car. Then she bought Brian a brand-new bottle of another scent of cologne she admired. Although she enjoyed the familiar fragrance on Brian, she wanted nothing about him to remind her of the bitterness of Fahad. Meanwhile, Ashima wanted nothing to do with a lavish gift in return. In fact, she didn't want a gift at all. In spite of this, there was one thing she wanted more than anything from Brian that he wasn't quite ready to part ways with. She wanted the emblematic key around Brian's neck because she knew what it meant to him. To no avail, Brian was able to get away with buying her a pair of shoes she admired another woman wearing during one of their outings.

When the holiday season came to a close, Ashima couldn't imagine ringing in the New Year without Brian. So, she invited Brian to enjoy the celebration as she has over the past few years. Every year Ashima is invited by her friend Maloni to join her at a suite party, hosted by Goldman and Sachs. Early New Year's Eve, Brian and Ashima drove to Times Square in a rental to enjoy a spectacular view of the ball drop from a forty-eighth floor suite of the *W Hotel*. The atmosphere was absolutely electric as he watched hundreds of thousands of people from all over the world converge on the world stage below, while rubbing elbows with top-notch executives, sampling premium finger food, and sipping the finest champagne.

As the New Year's celebration came and went, Brian and Ashima successfully kept their relationship discreet, and out of the prying eyes of Amir and Fahad. Despite many irresistible moments of temptation, Ashima also managed to withstand all urges of giving herself to Brian as well. Although it's been tough for months on end to resist him during their quality moments, Brian has been respectful and supportive of her desire for the right moment.

Now, time is winding down before Ashima's business trip to the UK, before heading to France for fashion week and finally business in Dubai. But, with only a few weeks left, Ashima receives the disappointing news that Carolyn won't be able to make the trip abroad, because Maloni got her an interview with the Goldman and Sachs' Philadelphia office. Unfortunately, the interview fell on the same week as her departure with Ashima. As her relationship with her other friends was still strained, Ashima wasn't as enthused about the trip because Europe may not be quite as fun without her friends. However, all was not yet lost to boring business meetings and death by power point.

"I still can't believe this brotha has only kissed the lips of one vagina, in the last three or four months. That my friend is amazing!" Marty expresses in the middle of a conversation he, Brian, and Cortez were having sitting at a booth at *The Fox*, after not seeing each other since before the holidays.

"Ha! I can't believe he finally got them rims put on his whip, and a trip to Times Square to watch the ball drop? You can't be mad at that!" Cortez adds as they toast their beer bottles. Suddenly, Brian's phone rings as it rests on the table.

"Hold on fellas, this is baby girl calling right here!" Brian interrupts them to answer.

"Hey babe, what's up?" Brian answers.

"Hi Brian, how are you? What are you up to?" Ashima asks in a cheerful voice.

"Nothing much, just hanging out with the fellas at *The Fox*. What's going on with you?" Brian asks with intrigue.

"Oh, I'm sorry to interrupt you. I'll call you when you get home."

"No, you're fine. I can talk. What's up, babe?"

"I just wanted to ask you what you were doing in the next few weeks." Ashima asks warming up to a much bigger request.

"Umm…nothing other than starting at the restaurant next week and going to school. Why, did you have something in mind?" Brian curiously replies.

"Well, I know its last minute and all, but I was just thinking how great it would be if you came to Europe with me in a few weeks. I mean, I know it's a big commitment, but I just think it would be great for both of us to travel to London. Especially, considering your job situation." Ashima explains, pleading her case. She also found it to be a great opportunity to get Brian away from Philadelphia with things being so volatile with Amir and Fahad.

"I mean, that sounds great. I would love to go with you overseas. But, babe I don't have a passport, I don't have any luggage…I mean, is this at all possible on such short notice?" Brian replies with shakiness in his voice.

"Absolutely! Luggage is a non-issue, and we can get you an emergency passport which you can have as quickly as twenty-four hours. So, what do you think?" Ashima explains. Brian takes a moment to weight the options before giving his reply.

"Wow, Europe, huh? Well, I guess I can do my assignments online, and as long as we can work out the passport situation then, yeah! Sure! I'm down to go!" Brian optimistically agrees.

"Yes, I'm so excited! We're going to have such a great time together. Okay, I won't take up any more of your time with your friends. Call me later so we can talk more about the trip, okay!" Ashima replies, anxiously enthused by Brian's acceptance.

"Okay then, later babe!" Brian hangs up the phone in disbelief as he turns to his friends and breaks the news.

"What's up man, everything cool?" Cortez asks as Brian returns with a befuddled look on his face.

"Umm…yeah, I'm good! I mean, considering Ashima just asked me to go to London with her just now…yeah, I'm good!" Brian replies, still in awe.

"Say what, now? She just asked you to go where? London? You can't be serious, man!" Cortez rambles in disbelief.

"Man, it just keeps gettin' better don't it? Look at you, livin' that champagne life!" Marty smiles like a proud dad admiring his son.

"What's the champagne life?" Brian asks with a perplexed look.

"You know, the champagne life…where trouble is a bubble in a champagne glass. Everything is lovely when you're living that champagne life!" Marty further elaborates.

"Champagne life…huh? Okay, I'm feelin' that. So, let's toast it up then, to the champagne life." Brian celebrates as they all raise their bottles for a toast.

"Champagne life…!" They toast together.

"Damn! I knew I should have hollered at shorty first." Cortez teases Brian, giving him a hug around his neck.

"Shut up Tez!" Marty and Brian yell at the same time.

"What?! A man can dream, can't he?" Cortez responds.

"Hey, hey, hold up y'all. Who's that girl working the bar?" Brian digresses after spotting a strangely familiar face working the bar.

"Uh-oh, there he goes!" Marty says as he tilts his bottle.

"Man, that didn't take long." Cortez adds.

"No, I'm serious, y'all! I think I've seen her before. How long she been working here?" Brian asks, intrigued by the woman's familiar appearance.

"I think shorty's been working here for about a month now. Probably one of your victims you can't quite remember, huh?" Marty jokingly assumes.

"Ha…! You got jokes!" Brian replies unamused.

"So far she's been a good look at the bar. All the cats that come in here are trying to holla. But, that shouldn't concern you though. You're about to meet the Queen of England with a certified Egyptian dime piece. I know you're not about to risk that over a bar tender." Cortez reminds him.

"Look, I'm not trying to holla. I just want to know where I know her from." Brian replies, as he back pedals away from his friends and makes his way towards the bar.

"Mmm…hmm…do you playa! I'll be watching the Mojo show from right here." Cortez dubiously replies as Brian shakes his head in denial.

Brian walks up to the bar and patiently waits for a drink like everyone else. As the young, attractive bartender prepares a drink for a customer her distraction doesn't prompt her to notice his unwavering stare, as he still struggles to remember where he's seen her before. Brian also couldn't help but notice how sexually attractive she is. Beautiful face, thin waist, medium bust, sizeable backside, all the ideal features Brian sought in a woman. But, contrary to his friend's disbelief, his curiosity is nothing more than a social inquiry. As the woman scans the bar for another patron to serve, she happens to establish eye contact with Brian. Brian holds up a twenty-dollar bill to signal her over from the other end of the bar. As she moves towards him, her eyes squint as if he suddenly looks familiar. Brian maintains a straight face as her body language certainly confirms that he's come across this woman before. As confirmation settles in for both of them, she approaches him with a smirk.

"Hi, how are you?" The woman asks as she lays a napkin down before him, to take his order.

"I good. How 'bout you...busy night?" Brian replies getting an up-close look at the beautiful woman. Meanwhile, she helplessly smiles as if she's holding back.

"Umm...it's been steady so far. What can I get you handsome?" The woman flirts as she stares at him with her dreamy eyes.

"Well, beautiful. I think I'll have a Johnny Appleseed on the rocks and an order of wings, please." Brian delightfully flirts back.

"A Johnny Appleseed, what's that?" The woman asks bewildered by the request.

"Oh, that's my own signature drink of Apple Crown and cranberry. You've never made one of those before?" Brian asks with a charming demeanor.

"Oh, you have a signature drink? Most people order something off the menu. But, you have a signature drink? So, I guess that makes you special, huh?" The woman asks, playfully mocking Brian.

"Well, I guess every now and then a man needs to feel special." Brian replies as she grabs the bottles to pour his drink.

"So, where do I know you from, sexy?" Brian asks in typical Mojo swagger as she leans towards him to scoop ice for his glass and gives Brian a close-up of her cleavage.

"I don't know, Mr. Magnum. Where do I know you from?" The woman replies with a sly smirk.

"Building 436! I thought you looked familiar. You're the one leaving the notes on my car?" Brian asks finally putting it all together.

"Hmm...maybe. Have you seen me somewhere before?" The woman asks interested in Brian's suspicion.

"I saw you leaving building 436 one day. You have a daughter, right?" Brian asks with certainty.

"Yeah, you might have seen me leaving with my little girl. So, where have you been? I haven't seen you at your little white friend's apartment lately." The woman boldly inquires.

"Well, I'm not rockin' with ole' girl like that anymore. So, what should I call you, Ms...?" He pauses for a response.

"Alexis. But, my friends call me Lexi...and you?" She answers.

"Lexi, that's pretty, I like that. Oh, and I go by Mo. That's short for Mojo." Brian replies in alter ego fashion.

"Mojo...? Well, here you go Mr. Signature drink. One Johnny Appleseed and your wings should be out soon." She smiles as she places his drink on the counter.

"Thank you." He pauses to take a sip. "Mmm...it tastes great! When the order comes out, I'll be at that table over there." Brian points out before placing the twenty on the counter as he turns to walk away from the bar.

"Thanks. So, I guess I'll see you around?" Lexi says somewhat confused by Brian's lack of engagement.

"Well, now that I know where to find you, I'll be in touch." Brian replies, giving her a wink before he turns and walks away.

The idea of walking away from a sure thing eats him up as he resiliently resists temptation. As hard as it was to walk away without exchanging information, with Ashima as the new woman in his life, Brian has no real interest in the likes of an around the way girl like Lexi.

"Wow! That was a whole lot of talking for only one drink." Cortez says as Brian rejoins them.

"Damn, all that time and you come back with one drink?" Marty adds.

"Look, I know what y'all thinkin', but I didn't even go there with her. In fact, it turns out I do know the girl." Brian explains as he sits down.

"Wow, that's not surprising..." Cortez replies with sarcasm.

"Naw for real y'all, that's the crazy chick that was leaving notes on my car at Mallory's crib." Brian explains as Marty and Cortez do a double take at the bar.

"Damn, that's her, huh?! She's fine as hell for a nut job!" Cortez responds in awe.

"Brotha' you ain't never lied, 'cause I would definitely knock her screws loose!" Marty adds with emphasis as he and Cortez toast their glasses in agreement.

"See...now you if the old Mojo was in the building, I'd be telling y'all whether she's bikini waxed or fuzzy by the morning. But, instead, I stuck to my loyalty and just walked away." Brian further elaborates to convince his friends.

"And how hard was that...?" Marty curiously asks.

"Well, let's just say, if I don't get the hell out of here soon, I'll be able to give y'all a status on that bikini wax after her lunch break." Brian replies as he stands to his feet.

"Damn, off on another adventure with ole girl, huh?" Cortez speaks out.

"Naw, actually I've got to stop by my school to see if I can do my assignments online while I'm gone." Brian explains.

"Oh okay. Well, look, if I don't see you by the time you go abroad, have a safe trip, take plenty of pictures, and get back here in one piece, aight?" Marty wishes Brian as he holds up his glass for another toast.

"Safe travels…?!" Marty exclaims as Brian and Cortez join in.

"Safe travels!" Everyone responds on one accord.

CHAPTER SIXTEEN

After being granted the okay from his college professors and a delayed start date for Chops, Brian and Ashima go down to the passport office on Market Street for his emergency credentials so he could be clear to travel abroad. His college professor even gave him an extra credit assignment to complete while on his trip. Brian wasn't exactly the traveling type, so he had to grab a few things for the trip, including luggage and toiletries.

Because of her father's disdain for Brian and his disapproval of their relationship, Ashima wasn't at liberty to share her intentions with her colleagues. So, rather than fly with them on the company's corporate jet, she decides to take a commercial flight ahead of them and made hotel arrangements across town so they wouldn't know she brought Brian along for the trip.

4:32a.m., it's the morning of their flight. Brian silences his alarm and wakes to the brightness of the bathroom light, running water, and the sound of a humming exhaust fan. He remains still and takes a moment to survey the room with his eyes, realizing that he's in a hotel with Ashima and this is the morning that will forever change his life. This is the morning he will board a plane for the first time and travel to a foreign country. Ashima walks across the room with nothing more than a pair of sexy pink and white lace panties that accentuates her perfectly round bottom and a matching bra. She grabs a few things from her bags in the corner of the room while Brian tries to avoid thinking about the potential of a sexual moment. Although they shared the same bed, and knowing Ashima wasn't quite ready for sexual intimacy, Brian refuses to spoon with her to avoid putting himself in a testicular situation. Her hair looked like it was under construction and her face was buried under what appeared to be a facial scrub as she moves about the room preparing for the flight.

"Hi sleepy head...its morning!" Ashima vibrantly announces as she walks to the bed and leans over to give him a kiss. Meanwhile, he was lusting for her as he anxiously waits for the moment she will break, and allow him to have his way with her.

"Morning! What time is our flight, again?" Brian asks in a deep groggy voice, knowing that he would eventually have to motivate out of bed. But, not until he calms down from his morning 'Jones' for her.

"Six o'clock, but there's no need to rush, we're already here." Ashima reminds him, since they checked into an airport hotel the night before.

Relieved that he didn't have to get up right away, Brian rolls over to relax a bit longer until Ashima is done with all of her prep. To no avail, feeling a bit apprehensive about his first flight, time seemed to accelerate and before he knew it, they were on their way out the door.

After checking out of their hotel room later than expected and checking in Ashima's many bags prior to getting their tickets, it was time to board their flight. Once they pass through the TSA international flights checkpoint, Brian's nerves were becoming unsettled as they walk briskly through corridor with their carry-on baggage all the way to the boarding gate. Brian has been nervously quiet all morning, prompting Ashima to be concerned.

"What's wrong, Brian? Are you okay?" Ashima asks, wiping his sweaty brow with her hand.

"Babe, I haven't been totally honest with you and I have to make this confession now because it's really starting to affect me." Brian says as he's suddenly overcome with anxiety.

"Okay...I'm listening." Ashima nervously replies, bracing for a bombshell.

"Babe, I've never flown on a plane before and I'm scared as hell right now." Brian shamefully admits with serious concern.

Barely able to contain herself, she covers her mouth as it was taking everything in her to keep from laughing at Brian's serious dilemma.

"Awe...Brian! Why didn't you tell me you've never flown before? I probably wouldn't have offered you to go." Ashima sympathetically responds.

"I didn't tell you because it's embarrassing being this old and never been on a plane before. I thought I could handle it once we got here. But, this anxiety is killing me right now!" Brian explains as they approach the boarding gate.

"Brian, I promise you'll be fine. I fly all the time. Just think of the take off as a really fast elevator. After that you should be fine, okay?" Ashima ensures him as she grabs his hand and gives him a kiss.

Ashima's words were encouraging, but it didn't help Brian's view of the massive British Airways A380 Airbus sitting at the gate they were preparing to board. The full double-decker plane is the biggest he'd ever seen. Although they'd missed the boarding call for first class passengers, they immediately walk to the front of the line and are immediately boarded.

"Hi, welcome to British Airways, you're all set. Have a great flight!" The flight attendant says after scanning their boarding passes.

Brian is all smiles as he plays it cool walking along side Ashima as they look at each other with excitement. But, it was all a façade. Brian's legs are tremble with anxiety the entire length of the gangway to the entrance of the airplane. His stomach is bunched into a ball of nerves.

"Hi, welcome to British Airways! May direct you to your seat?" Another flight attendant asks, welcoming them onboard with a heavy British accent.

"Sure, we're in first class." Ashima replies, handing the woman their boarding passes.

"Excellent! You're actually in our topside first-class seating area, which is straight down either aisle, to the stairwell, and to the front of the plane above us." The flight attendant directs them.

As they make their way towards the stairwell, Brian is amazed at how many seats there were inside the plane and all the screens on the back of each seat. The blue LED lighting is soft throughout the cabin and made for a relaxing atmosphere. After reaching the second floor they searched for their seats among the many privately enclosed suites in first class.

"Babe, this is crazy! This is how you fly every time you travel?" Brian asks as he marvels the lavish interior of the first-class area.

"No. I've never been on a plane this big before. I usually fly first class, but nothing like this. This plane is incredible!" Ashima replies in her own amazement.

"Suites 4C and 4D, right?" Brian says as they find their assigned seats, situated across from each other and not the adjoined center seats they'd booked.

"Wow! This is quite amazing. It's like the private jet experience on a commercial flight. Very profound..." Ashima replies as she peeks into her

296

suite and notices all the similar amenities of a private jet. From the wood finishes with brass trim, to the 27" monitor, mini bar, and reclining seats that lays down to a comfortable bed.

"This tiny suite on the plane looks better than my whole apartment." Brian says aloud as he and Ashima put away their carry bags.

"Welcome to the good life baby!" Ashima replies, as they hold hands in the isle and look into each other's eyes with contently.

"Yeah…too bad our suites aren't together though." Brian replies with mild disappointment.

"Hmph…that doesn't matter, the only thing that matters is that you're coming on this trip with me. Besides, you got the window seat!" Ashima teases before returning to her seat.

As the seatbelt light comes on and the flight attendants prepare for take-off, the captain makes his announcement. Once Brian and Ashima take their seats the reality becomes real for Brian.

"Wow, my first flight!" Brian nervously realizes as he looks out the window and watches the airport gangway pull away from the plane before looking over to Ashima. She smiles and winks back at him.

"Just think, in seven hours you'll be staring at Big Ben, eating fish and chips, and enjoying a pint of beer." Ashima says, excited for Brian's first flight and abroad experience. Brian grins and shakes his head in disbelief.

"…and you get to meet my mother later this week." Ashima adds with excitement. Brian raises his eyebrows and playfully presses the button to close the doors to his suite.

Ashima gasps. "Brian…!" An appalled Ashima exclaims.

"I'm just kidding. You know I can't wait to meet your Mama." Brian replies as he re-opens the doors to the suite. Ashima throws a napkin at him and smile back.

"Suddenly, the amusement ends for Brian after several thrusts from the engines indicates that the plane is taxiing and is ready for takeoff.

Brian's eyes are affixed out his window as the airplane starts to shutters from the thrust and sudden roar of the huge engines. He looks over at Ashima and notices how relaxed and calmly routine it is for her.

"You okay?" Ashima silently asks as Brian reads her lips over the engine noise.

"I'm good!" He responds, as he looks over to the window again and realizes how fast the plane is moving down the runway.

His heart rate speeds up as he anticipates the takeoff. As the nose of the plane lifts off the ground his heart sinks into his stomach and his fist clenches the armrest as he relents to the elevator effect Ashima told him about. Now, looking down at the city in the distance as the Philly skyline gets smaller, it suddenly disappears from view once the plane pushes into the overcast above. As the plane punches through the clouds, a new day comes into view as the light of the sun dawning from the horizon so bright like the most beautiful sight ever seen. The cloud layer is now beneath him like the topography of solid ground. The sight and feel of flying high above the clouds is unlike any feeling he'd ever felt before. To Brian it's heaven-like, which prompts him to think of his mother.

"Wow...hi mommy! Look at me...soaring high about the clouds like the angels in heaven. I know you're out there somewhere. May your angel wings hold me close and keep me safe at thirty thousand feet. I love you, mommy. Amen!" Brian daydreams with a smile on his face as he kisses his middle and index fingers, and presses them against the glass like an endearing kiss to his mother in the heavens.

From that point forward with the help of a few Apple Crown's on ice, and a gourmet lunch they serve him, Brian sleeps for most of the flight. Hours later, Brian finally wakes to the Captain's announcement flying over London and a rainy, forty-six-degree forecast.

"Welcome to London, baby!" Ashima says, noticing that Brian woke up.

"Thanks babe. This view is crazy!" Brian replies as he marvels the view of British soil as he stares at Big Ben and the London Eye from his window.

Immediately after they touchdown at London, Heathrow Airport, Brian is immediately reminded that he has officially arrived in the U.K. From the thick British accents of all the locals in the airport, to the British flag marked on nearly everything that came into focus, it was clear they were in the United Kingdom. Prior to leaving the airport Brian stops at a gift shop to buy his first souvenir.

"Hey babe, you mind if I stop at the gift shop and grab something real quick?" Brian asks as he spots some really nice umbrellas in a floor rack.

"Sure, I actually need to grab some pounds from the ATM next door." She replies as they kiss before parting ways.

"Hello Mate, what can I do for ya?" The man asks from behind the counter.

"How much for the British flag umbrella?" Brian asks, pulling a large umbrella from the rack.

"That one there will cost you twenty pounds, Mate." The clerk responds.

"Cool, I'll take it." He gladly accepts.

"Whereabouts you coming from, Mate?" The clerk inquires as he takes Brian's credit card and swipes it.

"I just flew in from the U.S." Brian proudly replies.

"The U.S., huh? Very nice! The U.S. is a very nice place. Is this your first time in the U.K.?" The clerk asks as the excitement in his voice grows.

"Yeah…actually this is my first time being out of the country." Brian replies still in a bit of awe.

"Well, welcome to London, Mate!" The shop clerk reacts with open arms and British exuberance.

"Thanks! I'm really looking forward to seeing what the U.K. has to offer." Brian replies with mild enthusiasm.

"Sausage rolls! You have to try the sausage rolls, Mate! The Market place in Camden is the best place to get them in all of London and they're bloody good!" The clerk suggests as he gives Brian his card back.

"Thanks for the tip!" Brian responds as he shakes the clerks hand before walking away.

"You're welcome, Mate. Enjoy London!" The clerk says as Brian walks off.

"Making friends already, huh?" Ashima says as she walks away from the ATM machine, in which Brian also happens to notice Ashima placing a black card back in her purse.

"Yeah, I guess so. He was real cool." Brian replies. As Ashima becomes sidetracked by a text message she's responding to, a man waiting to use the ATM behind Ashima draws Brian's attention.

"Pardon me, Mate! But, your wife left this in the bank machine, Lad." The man informs Brian handing him a banking statement.

"Thank you. I appreciate that." Brian replies. While Ashima is still distracted by the text, Brian curiously takes a glance at the statement the man gives him.

"Whoa…what the…?" He whispers to himself in amazement. Brian's eyes light up as he can hardly believe what he just saw on the statement. But, instead of handed it to her, he decides to keep the surprising revelation to himself and holds on to the receipt.

After getting their bags from the baggage claim carousel, Ashima is ready to check into the hotel and relax. Brian on the other hand got his second wind and is ready to see London. They exit the airport and Brian is immediately confused, forgetting that traffic drives in the opposite direction in England. Then he notices several men holding up signs with the names of passengers on it. One man is holding up a tablet with the name 'Batool' on it.

"Babe is that you?" Brian asks pointing to the properly dressed, suit and tie driver holding the tablet.

"Oh yes, that's our driver." She confirms, while walking over to the driver.

"Ms. Batool?" The short, dark, slender driver asks as she approaches him.

"Yes. *Park Plaza Hotel*?" She verifies.

"Yes, very good, my lady. My name is Cedric and I'll be driving you to your destination today. Right this way please!" The driver requests as he escorts them to a brand new, blacked out Denali, where he opens the door for them before taking care of their baggage.

"Babe, you didn't tell me you had a driver picking us up?" Brian states as they sit in back of the SUV.

"Brian, you didn't really think all of my things would fit in a cab, did you?" Ashima points out just as several of the iconic London cabs pass by.

"Oh yeah, I see your point." Brian replies, noticing the same. Meanwhile, Cedric returns to the driver's seat and prepares to drive off.

"Umm…Cedric, could you take the scenic route on your way to the hotel please?" Ashima requests as they leave the airport overhang.

"Very well, my lady. I know the perfect route." Cedric replies.

"Umm…babe? I know the flight was long and it's a little bit cloudy. But, why is it about to be dark again after it was barely daylight when we left?" Brian asks, completely thrown off by the time difference.

"Because London is five-time zones ahead of us and it was a seven-hour flight to get here. So, when you add the two together you get a twelve-hour difference. Which means your watch is twelve hours behind." Ashima wittingly explains.

"Hmph, beauty and brains...I like it!" Brian replies, impressed by her knowledgeable response.

"You ready...?" Ashima asks clutching Brian's hand with excitement. Brian looks at her with the brightest smile.

"Yeah, let's go see London!" He eagerly replies.

It's a long forty-minute drive down route 4A before Brian would get to see the city limits of London, but it was worth the wait. Along the way Cedric and Ashima spend much of the trip discussing what Brian had to look forward to as he looks out his window and takes in the sights. The many different European cars and trucks he'd never seen before; the landscapes and store fronts that were very similar to what he was use to in the U.S.

As they enter the city limits, before reaching the iconic landmarks and monuments, Brian notices all the American food chains, as well as all the double-decker buses riding around the city.

"Wow! This is really happening. I'm really here!" He thinks to himself in amazement.

As they drive deeper into the London metro area, Brian notices how different the buildings and architecture is from the U.S. He finally reaches his first iconic landmark as Cedric takes them down Constitution Hill, to ride by the iconic *Buckingham Palace* before heading to *The Mall to Central London*. From there they drive around *Trafalgar Square* to the famous *Piccadilly Circus*, which was bustling with shoppers and tourists as the electronic billboards light up the crossroads like *Times Square*. Brian rolls his window down to take in the sounds, the smells, and taste the air of foreign soil. After passing through the lively intersection, Cedric heads towards the *Plaza Hotel* so they can get situated. However, there were several other London icons within eye-shot of the hotel he drove by along the way. Just past *Westminster Abby* and *The House of Parliament*, Cedric makes a right onto Bridge Street as they pass the *Big Ben* clock towering above them. They cross the Westminster Bridge, crossing the Thames River with the hotel directly in front of them. The *London Eye* Ferris Wheel stands tall on the waterfront to their left. Brian is overwhelmed by the many inspiring sights of London he only imagined previously from his geography books.

After checking into the hotel, the staff wastes no time showing them up to their rooftop suite that opened up to a stunning panoramic, riverside view of the London Eye, House of Parliament, and Big Ben. The plush luxury suite, looks more like a lavish apartment laced with contemporary cherry wood furniture, stainless steel amenities, sliding glass doors that lead out to a furnished private outdoor patio, and a wooden spiral stair case that led to a second-floor bedroom. After a brief tour, Ashima plops on the heavenly soft bed face down as Brian plops on the bed next to her face up.

"So…how are you enjoying London so far?" Ashima asks kicking off her shoes as they both lay stretched across the bed.

"It still feels like a dream seeing it at night from a window. But, I'm really ready to get out there and feel it." Brian anxiously replies.

"Well, I do know a place that serves really good fish-n-chips if you're up for your first London food experience?" Ashima proposes.

"Sure, I could go for a taste of London right about now. I'm ready to hit the town!" Brian enthusiastically replies.

"Okay then, we can both take a quick shower and then we'll go." Ashima suggest with equal motivation.

"You mean, shower together?" Brian implies, hopeful of a quick, intimate moment.

"Hmph…nice try, Mr. Jones. But, we're not quite there yet. Besides, if that happened we'll never get out of here." Ashima kindly denies him.

"Yeah, you're probably right?" Brian agrees, but ready to address another troubling issue. "But, on a different note, babe, can I ask you about something?" Brian asks apprehensively as he sits up on the bed.

"Sure, we can talk about anything. Is everything okay?" Ashima replies as she sits up on the bed as well.

"Yeah, everything is fine, babe. But, while you were texting at the airport, some guy gave me this bank receipt you left at the ATM. Now, I wasn't trying to be in your business or anything like that. But, I happened to glance at it to make sure he was giving it to the right person and I was like 'whoa' when I saw all those digits nearly run off the paper. I mean, is this for real?" Brian explains as he hands her the statement.

"Yes, it's correct." Ashima nonchalantly replies after looking at the paper.

"But babe, the balance on that receipt is over six million dollars? I mean, when I glanced at it, there were so many digits on the statement I couldn't tell if it was a balance or an account number?" Brian struggles to understand.

"So, now you know...!" Ashima nonchalantly replies.

"So, now I know what? You're rich? I mean, I had an idea, but..." Brian replies seeking clarification.

"Well, it's not like I was going to just hand you the blue print details of my personal life the moment I met you. But yes, the affluence that surrounds me is real and everything that you've probably assumed about me is real. Nothing is different about me or the way I feel about you, except now you know what tax bracket I'm in..." Brian continues to listen as he looks on at her with blank yet compliant expression. "...Brian listen, I don't mean to sound cliché, but my personal life is privileged information. The only people privileged to that information are those that I trust, and the only reason why I'm comfortable talking about it is because I trust you. So, unless I'm wrong, let's get showered, get dressed, and get full off fish and chips and pints at a real English pub in London." Ashima candidly expresses holding back the details of her forty-two-million-dollar fortune. Brian takes a brief moment to mull before his reply.

"Well, in that case, how 'bout those drinks?!" Brian cheerfully replies leaning over to give Ashima a kiss.

After freshening up from a full day of travel, they later take a cab over to an English pub near *Piccadilly Circus* for dinner. As expected they share an order of fish and chips, served to them on newspaper in traditional English fashion. Ashima also introduces Brian to a potato, veggie, and egg breakfast dish called bubble and squeak. They chase the meal with a pint of dark and stormy and a few flavorful shots the bartender prepared for them on the house. The British hospitality proved to be a great start to the London experience. Once they stand to their feet to leave and realize how tipsy they were, the bartender hires a cab for them to make sure they left his pub safely.

After exiting the cab in front of the hotel, Brian takes Ashima by the hand and stops her from entering the sliding doors.

"Babe, hold on a minute. I just came up with a great idea?" Brian says with sudden enthusiasm.

"Okay, it's a little late. But, I'm listening." Ashima replies with a puzzled look.

"Let's go for a romantic walk." Brian suggests not quite ready to call it a night.

"Okay, where are we going?" Ashima asks curiously.

"C'mon. I know a place." He confidently replies. Ashima on the other hand is completely bewildered by Brian's intentions. But, the night was still young.

As the broken clouds move along the moon lit sky, Brian leads Ashima a few blocks away from the hotel, back towards the Thames River. The temperature remained chilly as the streets are still damp with puddles from the rain hours ago. Although traffic flows opposite in the U.K., Brian hasn't forgotten the right side of manners as he steps over to the curbside of Ashima to walk alongside her. Not sure of what to expect from an evening stroll in a country he's never been, Brian places his arm around her waist and holds her romantically close. As they casually stroll to the river's edge and turn onto *The Queen's Walk* promenade along the river's edge, the *London Eye* stands tall before them like an illuminated blue ring of inspiration.

"I knew this was where we were going. You want to go up on the Eye, don't you?" Ashima implies, as she wanted to do the same.

"Uh-oh, was I too predictable? We can go back to the room if you want. I mean, it's not too late." Brian suggests, toying with Ashima's reaction. She responds to him with a playful jab to his stomach.

"No! I think it's endearing and sweet that you would want to do something like this. You keep things interesting for me. Besides, I think it'll be good for my manic work depression." She jokingly smiles. Appreciating the moment, Brian stares out at the reflection of buildings and traffic on the other side of the river.

"Ever been up there before?" He asks pointing to the immense Ferris wheel.

"No, actually I've wanted to go many times before. But, I'm usually with my mother when I'm here and she's afraid of heights. Ashima explains as they approach the admissions booth.

"Excuse me. How much is it to go up?" Brian asks a man counting money in the booth.

"Twenty pounds each, Mate. But sorry, we're all done here this evening." The man replies speaking through the glass in a heavy British accent.

"Oh, my bad…I saw it moving, so I thought you were still open." Brian explains.

"Oh, out for an evening stroll, are you?" The man assumes as he looks over at Ashima.

"Yeah, we just got to London today and we're just trying to enjoy the atmosphere on the first day." Brian explains.

"Where from did you arrive? You sound American?" The man inquires as several people walk by them disembarking the Ferris wheel.

"Yeah, we're American. We flew in from Philadelphia. You ever heard of Philadelphia?" Brian asks.

"Philadelphia? Bloody hell Mate, of course I've heard of Philadelphia. Cheesesteaks and Rocky of course! So, what brings you two love birds to London?" The thrilled Ferris wheel operator asks.

"Well, we're here on business, but I come to London all the time and it's always a pleasure." Ashima responds.

"Well, I'm sure the Queen is pleased with your visits. But anyway, you two are all set, go ahead and grab yourselves a pod." The man generously reconsiders.

"Really? Are you sure it's okay?" Brian asks, taken aback by the man's change of heart.

"Absolutely, Lad. No charge! Enjoy your time in London." The man assures them.

"Thanks, we appreciate it, Mate!" Brian replies, mimicking the Englishman's slang.

"You nervous?" Brian asks as they wait for the next pod to line up with the platform.

"No, I'm excited! This is going to be great. I can't wait." Ashima replies, placing her arms around his waist, squeezing him with jubilation.

"Mind the gap please. Watch your step!" The attendant warns as they step into the continuously moving glass pod.

"Wow it's so spacious in here. You could fit like twenty people in here." Ashima says as the size of the pod astounds her.

"I know. It's much bigger up close." Brian agrees as he straddles the large bench in the middle pod facing the river view. He scoots back as Ashima sits between his legs and he holds her close in the most romantic gesture facing The Parliament and Big Ben.

"Mmm…this feels nice!" She utters as she lounges content in his arms under the warm glow of blue lighting.

"So…what do you think? Brian asks as they begin to ascend above the city.

"About?" Ashima asks as she reaches back and fondles with the key around his neck.

"About us…" Brian suggests.

"I think that life has been amazing since we met. I think I owe God a great deal of gratitude for bringing you into my life." She replies as she finds solace being in his arms.

"I agree, never in my life did I ever imagine that I'd be right here, high above the city of London with a woman as beautiful and perfect as you. If there's anyone feeling grateful right now, it should be me." Brian sincerely replies.

"Awe…you're so sweet, I appreciate you so much!" Ashima replies before turning to give him a kiss.

As the Ferris wheel climbs to its highest point and all of London stands beneath them, they look out to the multitude of city lights of the city from the panoramic glass view. Capturing the moment Ashima, pulls out her phone and snaps several selfies with *Big Ben* and the London skyline in the back drop. Then Ashima points out all the significant points of interest including the *Tower Bridge*, the pickle shaped *Gherkin building*, *Westminster Abbey*, and the *Waterloo Train Station* a few blocks away. As she points out and explains all the neat things about the city, Brian simply remained silent and takes it all in.

"Can I share something with you?" Brian asks, eventually breaking his silence.

"Sure, anything!" Ashima replies as she prepares to listen, caressing the key charm around his neck once again.

"Well, a few years ago I grew really close to someone who was very special to me. I honestly thought that we were inseparable because she loved me so much and unfortunately, I kinda took her for granted. In the end, I pushed her away and ended up losing her because I didn't have the courage to tell her three simple words. And now she's gone forever. Ashima, the reason why I'm telling you this is because I know that you've been waiting for the right moment for us, the right moment for you to share your love with me. But, I feel like my moment is now. Not to make love to you, but to tell you that I'm in love with you, Ashima Batool. I have been for a while now. I mean, hanging out with you makes me want to be a better man. Now, I'm not looking for you to express your feelings or anything like that. I want you to tell me how you truly feel when you feel it in your heart. But, this is my time. This is my moment." Brian sincerely and shamelessly admits.

"Thank you…thank you for having the humility to tell me how you truly feel. It's not often a woman will get that from a man." Ashima expresses with gratitude.

"How so?" Brian asks for clarification.

"Well, men often hide behind their feelings because they think it makes them look vulnerable and weak. But, to a woman, a man expressing his feelings takes courage. To me it's more masculine than any macho façade a man tries to impress." Ashima strongly affirms.

"Hmph…how's this for a façade?" Brian asks as he spontaneously lifts her chin for a passionate kiss.

Ashima absolutely melts in the moment. His unquenchable thirst for her love is intoxicating to her. The drinks at dinner and the height of the Ferris wheel couldn't lift her higher than the emotions she's feeling at this moment. In the midst of their intimate moment of bliss, they're suddenly interrupted by a random burst of fireworks.

"Oh, my Goodness, this is so cliché! Isn't it beautiful?" She asks as the vibrant illumination is so close, it appears to explode right before them.

"Yeah, it's like a scene from a movie. The timing couldn't have been any better." Brian agrees as the fireworks continue in rapid succession and they sit content watching the pyro lit sky inspire they're lives.

"It's perfect!" Ashima emphasizes as she sinks into his arms, savoring every moment of affectionate bliss.

As her head rests, comfortably on his chest and her hand interlaced with his, she tickles the palm of his hand with her index finger. Knowing the intimate significance of the gesture, Brian looks at her to validate her intentions. Ashima looks at him back with appealing eyes and confirms her gesture with another long passionate kiss.

After years of wasted time with Fahad, she finally found someone that makes her feel like a woman and she can finally exhale. The emotion she's experiencing at this very moment with Brian, is something she's never felt before. She was almost certain that this feels like true love. Life as she saw it at this very moment was perfect. But, there was an apprehensive side to her as well.

Obey

After returning to the hotel from an amazing first night out in London, it was time to wind down from a long eventful day. Tired and ready to settle in, they enter a night ready room admiring the soft atmosphere the hotel staff set for them.

"Wow, they really take care of you here!" Ashima notes as they walk in and she immediately notices the recess lighting and wall sconces, elegantly dimmed and the bed sheets turned down with chocolate mints left on each pillow.

"I guess so, look at what they left for us on the table." Brian adds as he also notices a black bottle of sparkling wine resting in an ice bucket on a sterling silver tray on a table in the great area with two flutes and a note attached to the bottle.

"Hmm…'bubbly compliments of the Park Plaza Hotel. We value all of our guests and we hope you enjoy your stay.' Maybe we can celebrate this later this week?" Brian reads from the card on the bottle. Ashima places her purse on the sofa table as she approaches the great area and walks directly up to Brian.

"Maybe we can celebrate it tonight?" Ashima suggests as she wraps her arms around his neck and looks up at him with beautiful endearing eyes. Brian, taken aback by her actions doesn't understand how to respond.

"What? Wait! What are you doing?" Brian asks with confused excitement as he embraces her around her lower waist. With the help of a lasting buzz from dinner, Ashima responds.

"Brian…make love to me." Ashima requests adorably with sincere conviction.

After a beautiful night, abroad and her affection restored, Ashima is finally ready to blossom for him. Stunned by her spontaneous request, Brian stands in disbelief and responds to her with a raised eyebrow.

"Are you sure?" Brian asks in a low uncertain voice.

"I'm sure!" She whispers confidently as she takes him by the hand and leads him to the bedroom.

309

In the dimly lit room, she kicks off her *Louboutin* heels and pecks his lips with a series of kisses before abandoning him by the bedside to retreat to the bathroom and start a shower. Along the way she grabs a medium sized Louis duffle bag from the floor and takes it with her, leaving the bathroom door partially open behind her. Brian stands dumbfounded as if he didn't know what to do next or what to prepare for. So, he removes his sports coat and shoes and opens his own travel bag to prepare for a shower.

Meanwhile, after starting the water in the contemporary stone and glass shower stall, Ashima stands in front of the vanity mirror and dresses down to an excellent bare petite frame, before draping a towel around her herself. To accentuate the mood, she lights a trio of candles on the shelf above the toilet to illuminate the room. She takes in a deep breath and exhales heavily in the mirror as she mentally prepares for a special moment of intimacy.

"Excuse me Mr. Jones, I think I'll need help washing my back." Ashima requests as she peeks out the doorway to lure him in.

"Umm, sure I can do that!" Brian happily replies.

As he enters the bathroom, with one hand on her hip and the other holding up her towel, Ashima's body language raves 'take me!' Brian obliges her silent request by walking over to her and satisfies his craving by softly grasping her by her lower cheeks, opening his foreplay session with a long sensual forehead kiss. From the moment, he met her Brian knew exactly what he would do to Ashima if ever given the chance, and now he's about to make good on that expectation.

"Mmm…" She exhales as her limbs instantly break out into goose bumps from his delicate touch and a sudden chill rips through her entire body. She places her arms around his neck and as they draw closer and Brian pecks her once on the nose. Then with their foreheads pressed together, he gives her a peck on her soft, hydrated lips, and another and another and another…

"Mmm…this feels nice!" She utters with her eyes closed as Brian continues to pecks away.

As the steam from the shower billows from the stall, Brian pulls off his snug fitted shirt and allows her a moment to admire his confident masculine bravado. Tantalized by his amazing upper body physique, she takes one hand and delicately runs her index finger down the center of his hairless chest, along the ripples of his chiseled abs, and down to his bikini

310

line. She pulls him in by grasping front of his pants for another kiss before her hormones compel her to unfasten his belt. Now, fully invested in the moment, as their emotions intertwine, Brian primes her for intimacy by moistening his middle and index fingers with his mouth, and placing them between her thighs.

"Huhhh…ahhh…" She pleasurably whimpers, clenching and squeezing his strong and firm biceps as he gently gyrates her spot.

The moistening and massaging of her lips arouses him so stiff he thought he'd grew several extra inches. Trapped in his pants he was nearly ready to rip through his jeans as his endowment began to stretch down his right pants leg. Unable to withstand another moment of foreplay Brian lifts her from the floor as she hugs his neck and wraps her legs around him. The intensity between them is so powerful they declare no time to deviate. With his pants now open and unzipped, he effortlessly walks her over to the shower. To her surprise and in true spontaneous and charismatic fashion, Brian opens the foggy glass door and with no regard to undress, carries her into the running shower with his jeans and socks on, and her towel still wrapped around her. The bold move is such a turn on they passionately kiss and barely come up for air. The water from the square, rain style shower fixture cascades on them like the love scene of a movie.

As one arm supports her, Brian reaches down and frees his manhood from the opening of his jeans as they continue to kiss. Then he looks her in the eyes and he prepares to make love to her.

"Do you trust me?" He asks clearing the hair from her water drenched face.

"Yes, I trust you." She utters in a soft whimper looking him in his eyes with unreserved trust. Confidently, she releases the soaked towel between them and it falls to the stone tiled floor.

Seeking added support, Brian pins her against the tiled shower wall and makes his adjustment. Reminding himself of how delicate she is from their last encounter, he uses his fingers to spread her moistness and slowly eases inside her as she anticipates his entry.

"Uhhhh…!" She gasps, squeezing him as tight as a constricting snake.

"You okay?" Brian whispers as he pauses to make sure he doesn't hurt her.

"Yes…" She whimpers as she initially struggles to take in all of him.

Brian eases inside her an inch at a time until he eventually bottoms out before he begins to stroke her delicately. It was evident she's never been handled like this before, so he patiently takes his time. Her walls were as tight as the innocence of a virgin as every stroke felt as smooth as tightly wound silk. The feeling is incredible to Brian, as if she was built different from any other woman he's ever been with. Her head rests on his shoulder as her eyes are clinched so tight from the pressure. But, as the secretions of her walls lubricate his motions, the painful sensation evolves into sensual pleasure.

Moaning at every stroke, Ashima's apprehension soon turns into painful delight as he patiently handles her just right. Although this was not her first moment of intimacy, with Brian, it felt like she was being touched for the very first time.

As she comfortably adapts to Brian's copious size and energy, he decides to seize the opportunity to have his way with her and give her the best sex she's ever experienced. As he eases her to the floor to change positions, they smile at each other with zeal. He kisses her again as she looks at him with consent as if to say 'I'm all in.' As she timidly stands before him, he takes a moment to admire her beautiful, goddess like build before palming a handful of her perfect cup size breasts. He then turns her away from him and lifts her hair to expose the back of her neck, before tonguing her ear and dragging his tongue down the side of her neck. The works of her inner thighs pulses and her legs tremble as Brian goes to work. As he continues to map kisses from her neck, shoulders, and upper back, Ashima daringly reaches behind her shoulder and grabs the back of Brian's head, as the other hand reaches to grab his manhood.

"Mercy…!" She softly calls out as she runs her hand along his length and grips him firmly.

Brian takes her by the hand, places her middle and index fingers between her legs and makes her fondle her secretion soaked lips. Then he takes her hand from her privacy and places her fingers into his mouth.

"Mmm…" Brian hums in a deep baritone moan as Ashima's knees weaken and nearly buckle from the ecstasy. He lowers himself slightly to get underneath her short stance and with a hand around her mid-section he carefully inserts her from behind.

"Oh my…Brian…!" She shrieks as she bites her lip to endure his penetration.

With one hand in his mouth and the other palming the back of his neck, Ashima holds on as Brian's six-foot stance dominates her petite five-foot frame. The sounds of love movements echo the room as he finesses her from behind in a passionate rhythm. Ashima throws her head back and over his shoulder as Brian licks and sucks every part of her neck and earlobe as the water droplets pelts her face. His simultaneous work of her ear, neck, stroke, reach around, and free hand massaging her breast relentlessly overwhelms her stimulation and drives her senses crazy.

"Yes…! Yes…! Yes…! Oh my…oh my…uhhhhhhh…!!!" She screams as she climaxes to an unusual extreme.

Her body tenses fiercely as she releases all over him. Her legs quiver intensely before they give way and she nearly collapses to the floor if it weren't for Brian supporting her. Brian feels the vibration from her trembling body as he bears her weight and she remains slumped in his arms. As she struggles to recover, Brian supports her to the shower floor and sits with her cradled in his arms under the cascade of the shower.

"You okay?" He softly asks, then kisses the back of her head as she calms from an elevated heart rate.

"Yes…just give me a moment." She breathlessly pleads as she sits content in his embrace, trying to quantify the level of love making she'd just experienced.

Then suddenly, after a few passing moments, her body erupts into an intense shiver followed by a few intermediate jolts as if she were convulsing from a seizure. Nervously confused by her erratic behavior, Brian is momentarily frozen with alarm and confusion.

"Babe, are you okay? Ashima?! Babe?!" He calls out to urgently nudging her and desperate for a response. After about ten unnerving seconds, Ashima finally settles to a relaxing calm.

"Mmmm…" Ashima reacts, letting out a long, deep sigh of elation as Brian feels her body decompress.

"That…was amazing!" Ashima gleefully expresses with an embarrassing smile after another unexpected, unprovoked orgasm.

Taken aback by her reaction, Brian immediately thinks of Marty's aftershock theory to define logic. It was exactly how Marty explained it and it was just as scary as it was thrilling knowing he was capable of having that type of effect on a woman.

313

As for Ashima, she is riding an emotional high insurmountable by any feeling she'd ever felt before. Her first time with Brian, being handled by him, able to endure him, partially clothed on the floor of a candle-lit running shower in London, was better than any script she'd ever envisioned, it was ecstasy.

After a few moments of sitting, Brian helps her from the floor and finally sheds his shower soaked jeans, underwear, and socks as they prepare to lather each other with shower gel. Brian foams her loofah and meticulously applies soap to nearly every part of her body. Irresistibly, he couldn't live down an opportunity of romance. So, he kisses her suds coated body as he applies more soap to her lower back and backside. Ashima simply couldn't get enough. She enjoys Brian's pleasureful pampering like the spoils of a sexual spa day.

Then it was Ashima's turn to return the favor. Ashima grasps and massages his manhood and attempts to squat to show her gratitude. But, Brian has other plans and asks her to meet him in the bedroom while he finishes up in the shower instead. With a toothbrush wedged in her mouth, her hair wrapped in one towel and another from her chest down, she leaves the bathroom and prepares for bed. Once Brian finishes his shower and hangs his jeans, socks, and underwear to dry, he emerges for the bathroom as well.

With a towel barely wrapped around the dips of his lower abs, a refreshed Brian walks out of the bathroom. As Ashima stands at a mirror to adjust the towel on her head, he stops to give her a kiss on the neck before heading to the kitchen for a bottle of water.

Although Brian had every intention of picking up where they left off, Ashima surprises him with a little surprise of her own, engaging him first with naughty intentions.

"So, how about that bubbly?" Ashima asks with her index finger provocatively lodged between her teeth and poised for round two.

Despite having a business meeting in the A.M., watching the clock is not a priority for her at the moment. After an incredible and intense sample of real love making, with no regard to her schedule she yearns for more.

"How 'bout that bubbly...?" He replies, gladly accepting her bedroom invitation.

First, he walks over to the black bottle of sparkling Chardonnay, unfastens the muselet wire cage, and pops the cork. Ashima jumps as she's startled by the sound of the cork firing off somewhere into the kitchenette area. After pouring Ashima a glass, he pours himself a taste and joins her bringing the bottle with him. Now with their glasses in hand, Brian walks to over to her and with an endearing expression, he deliberately backs her towards the bedroom. Ashima adheres to his advances, retreating all the way into the master suite until the back of her legs contact the tall standing bed. With nowhere else to go, they gracefully stare into each other's eyes as she ponders his next move.

As the lustful chemistry between then persists, Ashima timidly takes a sip from her glass while reading Brian's eager facial expressions. Brian's energy for her at this point is so intense he swallows down the remaining contents of his champagne flute, tosses the glass to the floor, and sinfully prepares to engage her. Her towel wrapped body is so arousing, he grabs hold of it and tugs it loose from her grasp until it falls to the floor, revealing nothing more than a gold belly chain draped around her petite waist with a teddy bear hanging from the bitter end.

"You were hiding that under your towel, weren't you?" Brian asks, taken aback by Ashima's sudden sexy transformation.

"Mmm...maybe?" She cunningly replies.

Instantly, Brian is stimulated by her nude, as he's never encountered the likes of a belly chain that's highlighted a woman's figure and made her that much more enticing. He immediately takes the glass away from her, aggressively lifts her off the floor and tosses her onto the bed in sexually barbaric fashion. He leans onto the bed and randomly marks her body with kisses as he climbs on top of her.

"Don't move!" He demands, as he suddenly stops and leaves the room, leaving Ashima bewildered of his intentions. Taken aback by his request, she finds his demands seductively arousing while submissively awaiting his return.

Brian re-enters the room with the burning candles from the bathroom and stages it on the nightstand next to the bed to set the mood. After dimming the lights in the room to a candle-lit darkness he returns to Ashima to resume love making.

Conceding to his sexual assertiveness, she lays quaint as he initiates his opening act with a trail of kisses from her lips, to her neck, to her breasts, to the belly ring at her naval. He consumes the diamond encrusted teddy pendant and chain into his mouth, then slowly pulls away link by link

315

until the pendant drops from his mouth. Then he proceeds to use his tongue like a paintbrush to canvas her body as he runs it from her stomach, to her neck, to the bottom of her chin.

"Mmmmm…" She squirms and moans with one hand around the back of his neck and the other clutching her pillow as he gyrates his tongue around her areolas, before tantalizing her erect nipples.

Ashima's role in this foreplay session is to render her total compliance, in which Brian demands full autonomy in order for him to perform. So, he grabs both of her wrists and locks them down above her head, rendering her vulnerable and defenseless to his control.

"Brian…" She softly whimpers as he affectionately has his way with her, trailing kissing and placing his tongue where he randomly pleases.

Eventually, he kisses and tongues his way back to her abdomen, and licks around her belly ring before sinking further down below her bikini line. Ashima's body tenses as Brian loiters around her private domain, reminiscent of a pleasurable feeling that felt all too familiar. But, he doesn't rush to deliver a kiss to her lower lips just yet. He teasingly pecks around her mid-section and drags his tongue along her inner thighs, driving her hormones to the brink of lunacy. She grabs Brian's head with both hands trying to control her emotions, while Brian persistently toys with her erotic sensory.

After feeling the tremble of her weakened knees, he goes in for a sensual kiss and takes her there. One simple kiss turns up her already heightened sense of pleasure, then another, and another he indulges until he finds himself immersed in her secretions.

"Yesss…!" She exhales with an exhilarating moan of elation as Brian parts her lips and intensely stimulates her sensory with his tongue.

The last time he was afforded the opportunity, he was seeking to compensate her for their difficult first sexual encounter. This time, he elects to take it slow and overwhelm her with his patience and prowess. Immersed between her legs, he indulges in her new guilty pleasure, only coming up for air to blow on her delicately like soft cotton.

"Oh my…Oh my…Brian…Yes…Yesss…!" She bellows exhaustingly as his oral tactics get the best of her and she climaxes yet again. She clenches any part of his body she can grasp to get through the intensity of the moment.

As she lay stretched across the bed jovial and content, Brian reaches over to the dresser to drink from the champagne bottle like a Viking, before resuming his assault on her erotic senses. As Ashima sits up to take a sip from her glass, Brian stands in front of her with his man in full salute under his towel. Yearning for more, Ashima gawks at him sinfully as she takes another sip from her glass before placing it on the floor and pulling his towel from his waist.

"My goodness…!" She thinks, as she marvels his endowment.

As he stands before her exposed and sexy, she's enticed to reach for his manhood to perhaps try again to pleasure him orally. But, Brian intercepts her reach, kissing her hand and shaking his head 'no' instead.

"Just relax baby, this is your moment." Brian informs her, as he kisses the palm of her hand before kissing the back.

"But, I want to…" She faintly pleads looking up at him with remarkably convincing eyes. But, Brian shakes his head no, not to deny her, only to hold out for what he has in store.

"The only thing I want you to do is relax, enjoy, and obey." He requests with a kiss between each word, before placing her index finger in his mouth then seductively sucking it as he slowly pulls it from his mouth. He approaches this next round of intercourse like a teacher schooling a novice, and class is now in session.

"Where do you want me?" She asks as she lay beautiful for him.

"Here…" Brian answers kissing the right side of her neck.

"And here…" kissing the center of her chest.

"And here…" kissing her just above her naval.

"And here…" As he leans in and delivers a prolong French kiss between her legs.

Grateful for his generous kiss at her center, Ashima simply let's go as he turns her over lie on her stomach so he can focus his attention on finessing her backside. Brian climbs onto the bed and immediately marks her neck and her back with more sensual kisses. As she lays content and moans from kisses to her lower back, her backside, and down the back of her thighs, he channels his inner Mojo and reaches for the black bottle again for another sip. This time, with a sudden spontaneous urge, he pours champagne down the middle of her back. As the champagne pools in the small of her back, Brian slurps the puddle and licks her vertebrae all the way up to her neck. His profound creativity excites her, sending a chill up her

317

spine and a shockwave of pleasure to her privacy. After sipping all of the first puddle, Brian spills a little more, mopping up all the residual with his tongue. Ashima finds his delicate touch and soft lips therapeutic to her sexual eagerness.

As his strong, masculine hands grasp her hips and stands her up to her knees, he seductively pulls her by the hair and attacks her neck with tongue kisses. He then reaches down and guides himself into her sexy from behind, this time with less resistance as she conforms to him.

"Uhhhhh…" She sighs heavily as Brian slowly inserts her until she feels all of him inside.

His sex on top of hers, she helplessly she whimpers intimate love tones as Brian graces her. His love is patient as he sinks every inch of himself into her on every stroke; savoring every moment as if he's making love to her for the last time. She reaches back with both hands and massages his head as he conquers her with his best sex yet. Between his passionate strokes and his fondling hands, his simultaneous acts of stimulation send her hormones into a raging sensory overload. Fueled by their allure for one another, they're kindred souls make more than love under the flicker of the open flame, they make beautiful.

Seconds turn to minutes, and minutes turn to what seems like endless hours as hot wax bleeds off the side of the sweet aromatic candle. Seamlessly, there's no end to Brian Jones' love session as Ashima wonders if there's ever an end to his sex drive. Addicted to her femininity, he's focused and determined to give her his best with intention and purpose. As the sounds of love making echo's the walls, time just continues to elapse as his sex is intoxicating and she couldn't get enough.

12a.m., 1a.m., they tussle under the brightness of an orange moon. 2a.m. she climaxes for a sixth time and Brian is still not done making this the single most memorable sexual experience of her life. His love is intoxicating and renders her helpless to his dominance. Every motion he imposes and every kiss leaving its mark forces her body to obey; from her lips, to her neck, to her earlobes, obey…her shoulders, her breasts, her belly, obey…her hips, her thighs, her privacy, obey…her back, her front, her middle, obey…her body craves him as the love affair carries on throughout the night.

As she lay with one leg up, he watches her make beautiful love faces from their missionary position. As he takes his time inside her like a lazy

318

river, Ashima is pleasantly fulfilled as her body prepares to let go from yet another orgasm. As Brian continues to perform, her moans grow louder and louder to her excitement.

"Uhhh…! Yes…! Mmm…! Yessss…!" She whines louder and louder as her hormones are wildly stimulated again.

Her energy excites him as they breathe heavy and kiss with feverish intensity. Brian pushes harder and faster, filling her up on every stroke until the sensation of climatic elation begins takes hold of her for a seventh time. Panting, moaning, and now sweating, Brian is finally primed and ready for a much-anticipated orgasmic finish as well.

"Oh my…yes! Oh my…ohhhhhhh…!!!" They collectively sigh as their bodies tense ever so tightly before climaxing in tandem.

Ashima clutches Brian like a constrictor as her body shutters. Brian grasps the bed sheets as he releases with such intensity. Paralyzed from the energy released he lays limb as he pulsates inside her. After hours of intense love making they eventually settle to a tranquil calm, as he touched every inch of her body from her hair follicles to her perfectly manicured toe nails. As he rests silent and still with his head between her breasts, he listens to the sound of their hearts beating in perfect time. After an incredible evening of romance, the night is finally capped with Ashima nestled in Brian's arms, fast asleep as they spoon. For Ashima, the night couldn't have been scripted any better. She experiences the single most intimate love affair she could have ever imagined. As for Brian, so endeth the lesson.

Last Train to Paris

6:11a.m., Brian stands naked at the window with his head leaning on his hand pressed against the glass, as he enjoys a glass of orange juice and an amazing iconic vista of London before him as the light of morning breaks the horizon. *The Parliament* and *Westminster Bridge* are within eye-shot of the 12th story view, while the top of Big Ben and the London Eye hide within the cloud ceiling of a dense London fog. He looks down at the passing traffic and realizes just how far away from home he really is. Cars driving on the opposite side of the street, double-decker buses, and the iconically unique taxi cabs moving beneath his feet seemed more like a wild journey in his ninth-grade geography book than real life. Regardless of it all, this is the world outside his window and he was happy to be in the midst of it.

Suddenly, the rustle of bed sheets can be heard behind him, reminding him of how he'd gotten to this very moment in the first place, and how lucky he truly is to be here. Without uttering a word and still half asleep, Ashima walks up to him with the bed sheet draped around her and presses against his back to embrace him from behind, giving his body the most sensual squeeze around his waist.

"Morning…is everything okay?" She asks in a groggy morning voice.

"Good morning beautiful. Yeah, everything's perfect." Brian assures her as he takes a sip from his glass, his eyes still stretched along the Westminster Bridge.

"In thought…?" Ashima inquires with her face pressed against his back.

"Yeah…I was just standing here zoning out to this beautiful view thinking to myself, 'how in the world did I end up here'? And knowing as much as I know about you now, you could be anywhere else in the world if you wanted to. But, you chose to be here at this very moment with me…I appreciate that!" Brian replies, sincerely expressing his gratitude.

"Well, right now, at this very moment…I couldn't think of a better place I'd rather be." Ashima graciously responds.

"Hmph…and I appreciate that as well." Brian replies, grabbing her hand from his waist and kissing it before placing it over his heart.

"You know something else?" Ashima asks.

"What's that?" He asks awaiting another endearing sentiment.

"Yesterday I learned that there are over six million cameras throughout the United Kingdom, and if you don't get your naked self away from this window soon, Scotland Yard will be breaking down the door trying to arrest you for lewd exposure." Ashima sarcastically warns off-topic.

"I'm sorry babe I was just enjoying the view." Brian explains as he backs away from the glass laughing at her sarcasm.

"Yeah, well so was all of London!" Ashima cleverly answers as she turns Brian away from the window to face her. But, as he turns she notices something she hadn't noticed the night before.

"Oh, my God, Brian! Did I do that to your back?" Ashima frantically asks, noticing several claw marks to his upper back and shoulders.

"Oh yeah, I suffered a few battle wounds from the first time we tried back at my apartment. It's all good though, it's a good reminder." Brian replies, embracing his intimate scars.

"Oh, my goodness, Baby. I'm so sorry! I didn't even realize it. Does it hurt?" She asks as she touches the scabbed over wounds.

"Naw, it never hurt. I just happened to notice it was their one day." Brian nonchalantly explains.

"Well, I'm glad you're okay. I promise to be careful next time." She remorsefully replies.

"Okay, can we go back to bed now?" Brian trying to get some cover or find something to cover up with.

"Yes, we have an exciting day ahead of us." Ashima replies with one hand behind her back securing the sheet and the other hand around his neck.

"That's right, big day in London today, tomorrow I get to meet your mother, and then it's off to Paris on the fastest thing moving out of London after that." Brian replies as he places his hands on the small of her back.

"Hmm…you seem pretty excited about going to Paris. Have you not enjoyed London, so far?" Ashima asks senselessly.

"Are you serious? I love London. I love everything about London. This city is amazing! I was just excited about the train ride." Brian explains in a spirited tone.

"Is that so? So, what's your favorite part about London so far?" Ashima asks in a rousing tone as she raises to her tippy-toes to kiss him.

"Hmm, well I can show you better than I can tell you." He proposes, initiating another kiss.

"Okay, then show me." She softly accepts.

Brian slides his hands down to her bottom, lifts her off her feet and they kiss as he carries her back to the bed to soil the sheets again.

Later in the day, as the clock winds down to the 4 o'clock hour, it's been nearly five hours since Ashima sat at the negotiation table at The Gherkin building in the heart of London's financial district with her colleagues to close on a nearly one hundred-million-dollar expansion deal with associated banks in the United Kingdom region. Although, the meeting was already a prospering success with contracts, plans, and agreements being signed across the table, Ashima often found herself not even in the same room as the meeting because she couldn't help from being distracted by the events that took place the night before and the morning after.

Still throbbing from the residual effects of intercourse, Ashima spent nearly the entire afternoon romanticizing about Brian. Thoughts of last night's intimate euphoria often caused her to sit restless at the table during the many periods of boring discussion. She wasn't use to being handled by a man like that before and yet again, wasn't prepared to be taken there orally either. The sexual chemistry, intensity, and longevity sent her estrogen levels to a peak much less familiar. Unlike Fahad, who she laid lame and emotionless for, Ashima performed for Brian trying to keep up with her thriving libido; matching his passion and sexual rhythm at every unpredictable moment.

Longing for his embrace at every passing moment, she sits at the meeting distracted and impatient. She tries her best to take notes and keep up with the meeting, but can't even hold a pen straight. Vivid visions of the way he touched her has her turned-on, right at the conference table. She watches the clock trying to accelerate time with eager anticipation.

"It's unfair! He can't be that good all the time!" She questions trying to rationalize her thoughts.

Thinking of last night's intimacy causes her to be visible restless at the table during the many periods of boring discussion as the business dressed British executive delivers his presentation. She didn't want to seem intrusive by excusing herself from the meeting. But, she was in desperate need of a cold splash of water to the face to calm her anxiety and the longwinded presenter wasn't helping.

She looks around the room to see if anyone's taking notice as she struggles to hold it together in her hot and bothered state. In her mind, she can think so clearly about all the things she wants to do to Brian at that moment. And right now, all she wants to do is relive moments of uh…uh…uh…with him.

Nervously, she fumbles with her pen and restlessly pivots back and forth in her swivel chair as if she was focused, but actually trying avoid being noticeable. To no avail, Amy looks over and recognizes Ashima's fidgety movements.

"You okay?" She lip sync's to Ashima from across the table. Ashima responds with an assuring head nod, then looks her off to return her focus to the meeting.

But, Ashima couldn't fool herself. She pours herself a glass of the chilled water trying to calm her hormones. But, the damaging effects of rapture have already taken its toll. The amazement of his masculine build, his spontaneous shower erotica, his tantalizing tongue, and sexual bravado gives her the thrill of an unexpected, sexually gratifying surprise.

"Mmm…! Oh, my goodness!" She silently raves as her hands clench the chairs armrests for leverage. She squirms ever so slightly, desperately trying to evade embarrassment as heat flashes over her body like an oven door, and her tight secretions let go like summer rain.

"Are you kidding me? Did that just really happen? Yes, you just had a private moment in front of a room full of people." She marvels to herself in disbelief, clearing her throat disruptively several times and pouring more water to get it together.

She looks across the table and notices Amy staring at her with the biggest *"what is wrong with you?"* expression. Ashima responds with an embarrassing smirk as she shakes her head in disbelief. Positioned nearly closest to the exit, she stands from the table attempting not to disturb the meeting.

"Is everything alright?" Mr. Naples Palmer of the Royal Amalgamated bank asks mid-presentation in a thick British accent as he notices Ashima rising to her feet.

"Pardon me! Yes, everything is fine. Please continue I'll catch up!" Ashima insists as she motivates towards the door.

"No! No! Please, my apologies. I tend to be a bit longwinded during these meetings at times. Frankly, in can go on forever, ha-ha... Please, how 'bout we all take five to stretch our legs and use the wash room, shall we?" Palmer asks as he amuses himself with dry humor.

As everyone else takes a moment to stretch, Ashima scurries ahead of everyone else to freshen up. After closing the bathroom door behind her, Ashima leans her back against the door and lets out an embarrassing sigh instead of a screaming outburst, still in disbelief of what occurred. She braces herself against the sink, looks into the mirror and giggles in astonishment before disappearing into a stall as others begin to enter. After using the stall to freshen up, she emerges and finds Amy standing at the mirror adjusting her make-up.

"Hey, are you okay? Amy expresses with concern.

"Oh-no, I'm fine! Just having some menstrual difficulties is all." Ashima dismisses concealing the truth of her orgasmic mishap.

"Oh okay. 'Cause you were squirming and fidgeting back there like you were having an orgasm or something." Amy empathizes.

"Hmph, would've been the most exciting part of this meeting." Ashima jokes as both ladies laugh it off.

Before returning to the meeting, Ashima sends Brian a text to satisfy her thoughts of him.

(Text)
Ashima: *Hi baby, just thinking about you. Really missing you* ☹. *What are you doing?* She sends him before exiting the bathroom.

But, as the meeting resumes, she couldn't sit idle awaiting his reply. Although it's killing her that she couldn't wait for a response, as a woman of her profession, especially in the midst of brokering a deal this big, it was imperative for her to maintain her professionalism.

It's now 6:15pm and all have stood from the table with handshakes and congrats as the deal is finally secured. The last hour of business included a video conference with the executive board in Philadelphia overseeing the final agreements. Once the final contracts were inked, the celebration is followed by a champagne toast in which Amir boasts his signature sabering technique to open the champagne bottle back in Philadelphia. Once again, Ashima receives high praise for her involvement

324

in deal, in spite of her not doing much at all during this business venture. However, her colleagues are even more intrigued by her distant behavior, which wasn't like her.

"So, Boss lady, where have you been?" Franklin asks, referring to her as Boss Lady, not with mockery, but out of respect.

"Yeah, we missed you on the flight over! Where are you staying?" Amy follows up as they stand in a group with champagne in hand.

"I know, I'm sorry I missed the flight with everyone, but I decided to fly ahead of you all to meet with my mother." Ashima casually explains.

"Oh, how is mom?" Franklin asks as he tilts his glass for a sip.

"She's well. Thank you for asking." Ashima replies in a mildly guarded tone.

"Well, perhaps we can all have dinner together to celebrate? I have a table reserved for us at *Rhodes* on the 24th floor so we can all do some catching up." Franklin proposes to everyone.

"I'm sorry guys, I would love to join you for dinner. But, I'm not exactly feeling my best today." Ashima regretfully declines as she's already reserved her time to be with Brian.

"Why, what's up? Is everything okay?" Franklin asks with genuine concern.

"She's got woman's problems Franklin, you wouldn't understand!" Amy quickly interjects.

"Sorry, I didn't mean to be intrusive. But, I certainly hope you feel better!" Franklin sincerely wishes her.

"No, it's okay Franklin and thanks for your concern. But, even if I were to suck it up and join you anyway, it would be short lived because Mother Nature has certainly been getting the best of me." Ashima regretfully replies.

"Nope, I totally understand. Well, actually I don't…but, I'm sure she does." Franklin sarcastically replies, pointing at Amy as they cackle at his sense of humor. "But, seriously, great job to all of you today. Now, I can't promise you that they'll be a fleet of luxury cars waiting for us when we get back to Philadelphia. But, I'm sure the brass will find a way to make us very happy when we get home." Franklin explains as he lifts his glass for a toast just as Ashima's phone starts to ring.

"Excuse me, I need to take this." Ashima interjects. "Hello?" She answers as she walks away from the others.

"Hey babe! How's the meeting going?" Brian asks as he pays to enter the turnstile of a subway entrance and ascends the long escalator ride down to the platform.

"Well, it's official. We have sealed the deal and it only took one day!" A relieved Ashima replies as she walks to a window view overlooking all of London along the Thames River.

"Nice! Congratulations, as if I ever had a doubt." He replies as he strolls along the subway platform.

"Thank you. I'm just excited we could get it done in one day." She expresses with relief.

"Did you get my text earlier today?" Ashima inquires.

"Yeah, actually I just saw it, Babe. Sorry I didn't hit you back. But, I've been so distracted by the sights and sounds of London, I forgot how long it's been since I checked my phone." Brian explains as he notices the light of an approaching train further down the tunnel.

"No, it's okay baby, I understand. London will do that to you. Where are you at now?" She inquires.

"Wait babe, hold on a minute. A train is coming into the station." He replies as he struggles to hear her over a train roaring into the station.

"Okay, what were you saying?" Brian asks once the noise settles.

"Where are you, right now?" Ashima asks at a higher tone over the sudden incoming noise.

"Well, I was walking around *Piccadilly Circus* for a while. But, right now I'm at Leicester Square Station on my way back to the hotel." Brian explains as 'door is ajar' and 'mind the gap' announcements are made over the train's PA system.

"Oh, baby that's perfect! Actually, there's a restaurant my mother and I frequent in *Leicester Square* called *Maharaja*. They have excellent Middle-Eastern cuisine. Perhaps you could meet me there for dinner?" Ashima proposes, eager to spend her evening with Brian.

"Yeah, sure babe. Sounds like a plan. How long will it take you to get here?" Brian asks as he backs away from the platform and walks towards the subway exit.

"It should take me no longer than twenty minutes to get there." Ashima replies as she walks away from the scenic view and heads towards the nearest elevator."

326

"Aight then, I'm sure by the time I find this place you should be close. So, I'll see you at Maharaja then." He replies.

"Okay baby, I can't wait to see you!" A zealous Ashima replies.

"Me too babe, I'll see you soon." Brian concludes before hanging up.

As Ashima hangs up and waits at the elevator, she receives another call unexpectedly from her mother.

"لالغد وأثار حزم جميعا أنت ,أم مرحبا؟"

"Hi mommy, are you all packed and excited for tomorrow?" Ashima gleefully answers the phone. But, as she listens to her mother speak, her elated demeanor quickly changes to a much darker emotion, sensing distress in her mother's voice.

"Oh-no...!" She responds with her hand over her mouth.

Meanwhile, prior to speaking to Ashima, Brian spent the last six hours getting to know his first ever destination abroad. Confidently, he scouted around London, riding the Tube subway and double decker buses taking in London's rich history, from *Buckingham Palace* to *St. Paul's Cathedral* and all points in between. When night fell, the bustling evening rush reminded him of typical night in an American big city. The vibrantly bright billboard energy of *Piccadilly Circus* reminded him much to the likes of *Times Square* in New York. Along the way, he couldn't help but notice some other similarities of the U.S., from the food chains, to the style of clothing, and the typical tendencies of people being people. Some of them on their cell phones, some of them shopping, and others just going about their way nearly made him feel like it was just another day in Philly, until a few iconic red phone booths and policemen wearing Bobby hats put him back in British perspective. Of course, in typical UK fashion, the streets were still damp from a light, passing drizzle that had just let up. But, the biggest distinction he'd noticed between the two countries aside from the heavy British accents and riding on opposite sides of the street, is the countless number of Range Rovers, Jaguars, and Mini Coopers dominating the roads. Aside from a few luxury imports here and there, the British built automobiles seemed like the only things moving at every turn.

Another detail he'd noticed was how beautiful the British women are. The many women he encountered during the course of the day were absolutely stunning in most cases, no matter which way they were dressed, color, race, or creed. Perhaps in a different time, Brian would've broken out his inner Mojo and taken advantage, but today his wondering eyes lusts for only one woman, who also happens to be his ticket home. Yet, he still couldn't resist the urge to engage at least one passing beautiful face for directions to the restaurant along the way. As he draws closer to the restaurant, he receives a phone call from Ashima.

"Hey baby, how far are you?" Ashima asks when he answers.

"I'm coming down the street right now. How far away are you?" He replies as the sign to the restaurant is now within eye shot.

"I'm pulling up in front right now." She answers.

"Okay then…" He hangs up as he notices a blacked-out Range Rover pull curbside in front of the restaurant ahead of him.

As the driver opens the door for her, Ashima steps out of the vehicle looking as sexy and sophisticated as ever in her knee length black dress and blazer business attire with a pair of red, designer Atwood pumps. She's all business as she exits the vehicle with her purse draped over her arm, and of course, her phone in hand. However, her stern business expression melts as she becomes giddy with all smiles once she establishes eye contact with Brian as he approaches.

"Hey beautiful! Looking lovely as always." He comments as he walks up to a beaming Ashima. She immediately wraps her arms around him with an exhausting sigh.

"Mmm…" She expresses with relief as she buries her face into his chest and gives him an urgent tight squeeze.

"Umm…hi babe! Long day?" Brian asks, awaiting her reply as he responds to her decompressing hug.

"I've been thinking about you all day, baby. I just miss you." She mumbles with her face pressed against him as they remain at pause in the middle of a damp London sidewalk.

"I missed you too, babe!" He replies as he plants a kiss to her temple.

"Okay, I'm ready now. Let's go in!" Ashima says, interlocking her arm around his as they walk into the restaurant.

"Welcome to Maharajah. Do you have a reservation with us this evening?" A young Arab hostess asks as they approach the reception counter.

"Yes, reservation for Batool, please." Ashima replies.

"Oh yes, right this way please." The hostess acknowledges, leading them to their table.

Once they are seated in the narrow seating area towards the back of the restaurant, they open their menus to overlook the restaurant options. Although Brian is no stranger to the kitchen, he is unfamiliar with Middle-Eastern cuisine and has no idea what he's looking at on this menu.

"Hmm…Tandoori King Prawns, Chicken Tikka Masala, Lamb Jalfrezi…babe I'm lost. What's good to order here?" Brian asks, struggling to understand the flavors of the menu.

"Well, my personal favorite is the Garlic Chili Chicken with Biryani Rice and my mother's favorite is the Tandoori Mixed Grill. But, all of the food here are good choices." Ashima explains as she points to each menu item.

"That Garlic Chili Chicken sounds pretty good. I think I'll have that." Brian settles for something he can identify.

"Good choice!" Ashima agrees.

"It smells really good in here. How did you find out about this place?" Brian asks as the succulent aroma of a passing plate wafts past his nose.

"My mother and I are foodies, especially when we come to London. Some of the Middle-Eastern food I've had in London is better than the food I've had in Egypt." Ashima explains.

"Is that right? Well, of course as an aspiring chef I'm forced to be a foodie. I really enjoy exploring new cultures on the palate as well." Brian replies as he relates to the foodie concept. Ashima responds to his comment with a smile as she finds their likeness comforting.

Once they're orders are placed, they blissfully sit at the table enjoying each other's company over glasses of wine.

"So, I have news." Ashima starts out.

"I'm listening." Brian replies.

"My mother informed me that my Nana has taken ill and she's canceled her trip to London to care for her." Ashima explains in a somber tone.

"Oh-no! Is she going to be okay?" Brian asks with concern.

"Yes, she'll be fine. My mother says that she has developed a slight infection and she needs to be cared for. She tells me not to worry." Ashima explains to Brian.

"Wow. I'm so sorry your mom had to cancel her trip. I was really looking forward to meeting her." Brian remorsefully replies.

"Yes, well, unfortunately my Nana lives in a village about 40 miles from the nearest town, where she raised my mother and her siblings. But, there are no cell phone signals or lines of communication where she lives. It's very primitive and a whole lot of living off the land out there, and the only way to communicate is to use the sat phone of the local mission." She explains as they sip from their wine bulbs and share a roti appetizer.

"Wow, I couldn't imagine. But, if you don't mind me asking, I'm just curious to know why not just move her to a place where she can be better cared for?" Brian curiously asks.

"Well, my Nana is the matriarch of the village and she made it clear long ago that the village is her home and her family and when she grows old, she would never abandon them, no matter how successful her children become. So, we just make sure we get the best care out to her." Ashima further elaborates.

"Are you okay? Do you need to be there for your grandmother?" Brian compassionately asks.

"Oh-no, I'm fine! When mommy tells me not to worry, then I know everything is okay." She replies with optimism.

"Well, I'm glad she's going to be okay, but at least we'll be able to spend the day running around London, together right?" Brian enthusiastically assumes.

"How about we run around Paris instead?" Ashima proposes to Brian's surprise.

"Paris? But babe, I was just getting warmed up right here in the UK!" Brian pleads taken aback by her suggestion.

"I know…but with securing the deal early and my mother not coming, I just figured I could get a head start on Fashion week. Now baby don't get me wrong, I love and enjoy London every time I come here. But, 'Pari'! Ohhh, how I love 'Pari'! Especially, on the eve of Fashion week! I actually get to enjoy the Cavalli party that I've missed the last two years because of work." Ashima exaggerates in animated fashion.

"So, what's special about the Cavalli Party?" He asks with peak interest, based off her fanatical explanation.

"The Cavalli Party is the unofficial event that kicks-off Fashion Week and everybody that's somebody is at this party. All the top designers, models, and celebrities like Paltrow, Diddy, Kim K. and Kanye, the

Beckhams...all the big names in Hollywood come to the Cavalli Party." A zealous Ashima explains.

"Well, in that case, what time are we leaving?" Brian replies chiming in on her enthusiasm.

"The last train to Paris leaves at 10:35 tonight!" Ashima rapidly responds before Brian is barely able to finish his sentence.

"Babe, that's only in a few hours. Are we going to make it? I mean, we still have to get back to the room to pack up and check out." Brian dubiously replies.

"Well, yes, but we'll make it just fine. We're only ten minutes from the hotel and another twenty minutes from the train station. So as long as you're not willing to have dessert, we'll be in good shape. Besides, I'd rather have dessert when we get back to the room anyway." Ashima subliminally implies as she reaches for his facedown hand resting on the table and tickles his palm for a second time during the trip.

"Yeah...?" His eyes suddenly perk up with an embarrassing grin as he acknowledges her gesture. Ashima responds to his embarrassment by biting her bottom lip in arousing fashion.

"I really missed you today." She seductively emphasizes again.

"Yeah...?" Brian simply responds.

"Mmm...hmm..." She softly whimpers, taking it a step further by stepping out one of her pumps and running her foot along his leg beneath the table.

"Can we get this to go?" Brian asks spurring another spontaneous moment.

"Mmm...hmm..." She shakes her head yes as they lean in for a blissful kiss across the table.

After leaving the restaurant and hiring a cab, they immediately return to the room to prepare to catch the last train to Paris at 10:35. However, with their hormones raging at its peaks, they couldn't manage to keep their hands off each other long enough to even slide the room key to the door. Once inside the room, Brian drops the bag carrying the entrees to the floor as they tussle all the way to the bedroom to satisfy their sexual appetite for each other. After 25 intense minutes of long awaited love making, an exhausted Brian lays limp atop of her partially clothed and sprawled across the bed as his Jones rests inside her.

331

"Oh my God, Brian we have to go!" Ashima suddenly realizes, losing track of time after being lost in the intimate moment.

"Damn babe, its 9:49! Are we going to make it?" Brian asks, amazed by how fast the time went.

"Yes, we can still make it. I'll take a quick shower while you gather all of our things and call the front desk for a cab." Ashima instructs him, undressing as she spoke.

As Ashima rushes into the shower, Brian complies with her request. He quickly freshens up at the sink before calling the front desk, packing their things, and ensuring they have their credentials. After dressing into a pair of comfortable sweats and giving the room a quick once over, Ashima and Brian bypass the hotel checkout counter and rush off in a waiting cab out front.

After a short ride along the Kingsway they arrive at the front entrance of the *St. Pancras International Railway Terminus*. Brian tosses the cabbie fifty pounds for the eighteen-pound fare before grabbing the bags from the boot and rushing into the terminal dragging luggage in both hands and a backpack on his back.

"Attention passengers, this is the final boarding call for Eurostar ninety-fourteen to Paris Gare Du Nord, departing on track four." The announcement resounds over the terminal's PA system as they enter the vast terminal.

"Oh my God, 10:29!" Ashima reads on the overhead information board as she walks briskly towards the nearest ticket booth with two travel bags trailing behind her as well.

"Two tickets to *Gare Du Nord* please!" Ashima promptly requests as she gasps for a breath.

"Paris?! Sorry, but there's no way that you'll make the train unless you've pre-checked your passports!" The granny-like booth attendant informs them with her glasses set at the edge of her nose.

"We're pre-checked! Our tickets were already purchased. We're just departing earlier than expected." Ashima explains as she slides their passports through the glass opening.

"Well, in that case, let's get you on your jolly 'ole' way!" The attendant replies as she quickly prints their boarding passes.

Fortunately, already at track four, Brian and Ashima immediately break for the sliding glass doors, just as the conductor turns to board the train.

"Wait! Wait! Hold up!" They shout as they run down the platform.

Just short of walking onboard, the conductor hears their frantic plea and holds the train from departure.

"Cutting it mighty close, aren't we?" The conductor yells as he waves them on.

"Thank you so much for waiting!" An out of breath Ashima says as they hand the conductor their boarding passes.

"You're very welcome my lady, and welcome aboard the last train to Paris this evening." The heavily accented Englishman greets them.

After the conductor leads them to their premium seats and puts away their luggage, Brian and Ashima rest with a sigh of relief. As the train pulls away from the station, Ashima enjoys the view of city lights from her window seat. A porter immediately comes over and offers a bottle of Veuve Clicquot Ponsardin French wine, which they gladly accepted from him. After the porter pours each of them a glass, Ashima raises hers for a toast.

"To Paris!" Ashima lifts her glass to celebrate her excitement of the trip.

"To Paris!" Brian touches her glass and seals the occasion with a kiss.

Bollywood, Paris

After closing his eyes to the darkness of the tunnel beneath the English Channel just over an hour prior, a small surge from the train slowing down awakens Brian from his slumber. His eyes suddenly open to a profound city-like view which he is not accustomed.

"Wow, so this is France...?" He thinks as he can't make out much under the cover of darkness. But, identifies with the illuminated American business signs atop of buildings like Panasonic and Siemens as the train snakes its way through the winding city route.

"Good evening passengers, welcome to Gare Du Nord Paris, France..." The PA announces first in English and again in French dialect.

Ashima yawns as she awakens to the announcement with a smile on her face as bright as the light of the moon, as she arrives at her favorite place in the world.

"Mmm...welcome to France! Are you ready?" Ashima asks as stretches with a beaming smile.

"Ready when you are...let's see Paris!" Brian replies, buying in to her positive spirit.

As they tote their luggage down the platform and into the main concourse, the reality of being in Paris sets in for Brian as advertisements and PA announcements resound in everything French. However, he wasn't expecting to see quite as many American food chains that surrounded him as they make their way through the station.

Ashima leads them to the "sortie" or train station exit where they find several men standing dressed in black suites, holding signs with the names of arriving passengers.

"Madam Batool...?!" A slender French gentleman exclaims among the others.

"Yes, I'm Miss Batool!" Ashima responds as she walks over to the man holding a tablet with her last name scribbled on it.

"Hello, Madam Batool, Monsieur...welcome to Paris. My name is Jean-Pierre, and I will be your driver during your stay at the *Shangri-La*

Hotel. I trust your ride from London was pleasant, yes?" The driver asks as he opens the door for Ashima before placing her bags in the open trunk of the black S class Mercedes.

"Yes, the ride was very comfortable Jean-Pierre, thank you for asking." Ashima replies.

"Monsieur, your bags please!" The driver asks as he reaches for Brian's bag. Brian hands him the luggage and allows the driver to close the door for Ashima before walking to the other side.

"Monsieur please!" Jean-Pierre interrupts Brian, preventing him from opening his own door.

Just short of being annoyed, Brian controls his impatience and realizes that the driver is just doing his job. Once Brian joins Ashima in the back seat, Jean-Pierre prepares to take-off.

"Jean-Pierre, l'itinéraire scénique svp. Je voudrais montrer à mon ami pourquoi j'aime Paris."

"Jean-Pierre, the scenic route please. I'd like to show my boyfriend why I love Paris." She requests, so excited to see Paris after being absent from Fashion Week the last few years. Meanwhile Brian smiles as he's flattered by the upgrade in status, but keeps it as a note to self.

"Très bien Madame Batool."

"Very well, Madam Batool." Pierre acknowledges.

Brian's ride through Paris already reminds him of London as he's once again awe-inspired riding through another iconic city abroad. Ashima explains to him the different landmarks and tourist attractions as they ride past *Notre Dame Cathedral* and the *Louvre Museum* where this year's Fashion Show will take place. As they ride down Avenue De La Grande, the trees that line the street on both sides are beautifully decorated with lights that stretch down the long Avenue like a runway for cars. Much like an everyday New York, Paris is lit up like a city of blinding lights, especially during Fashion Week.

Directly in front of them further down the Avenue, stands the massive landmark *Arc de Triomphe* monument where they circle around it to change direction and ride along Avenue de New York to get a bird's eye view of the *Eiffel Tower* across the Seine River. Brian can't believe what his eyes are seeing. It's as if he'd flipped to the French pages of his geography book and teleported into the page illustrations. Ashima clutches Brian's hand to share this defining moment of his life as the *Eiffel Tower* projects a beam of light across the Paris sky like the beacon of a lighthouse.

Then without warning, the massive structure transforms into a barrage of brilliant sparkling lights as if to say, "Welcome to Paris!"

"Whoa…! What's going on with the tower right now?" Brian asks as he marvels the fascinating show of lights.

"Some of us call it Champagne Hour. At night, the tower sparkles for about five minutes on every hour until midnight, showcasing its brilliance. Amazing, isn't it?" She asks as she too marvels the magical performance.

Finally, they arrive at their rooftop hotel suite just after 2a.m. Upon entry, they walk into a moon-lit, open curtain room with a grand view of the Eiffel Tower right off their terrace. However, in spite of the stunning view, they're too exhausted to enjoy it and doesn't waste any time turning down the sheets to turn in for the night.

The next day, after enjoying a French spread for breakfast which included French toast, Quiche, raspberry crepes, fresh fruit, and mimosas to wash it all down, the couple find themselves in the main lobby waiting on Jean-Pierre to arrive to take them shopping. But, before leaving the lavish suite, Ashima couldn't ignore a meaningful desire to make love to Brian in the city of love. This time Brian allows her to fulfill her naughty intention to pleasure him, to which Brian was certainly grateful. Jean-Pierre pulls to the front of the hotel as Brian and Ashima leave the comfortable lobby to a chilly forty-five-degree temperature outside.

"Bonjour Madam Batool…Monsieur! Where to…?" Jean-Pierre asks as he holds the door for them.

"Triangle d'Or Jean-Pierre." She replies before donning her large designer shades.

"Absolutely Madam!" Jean-Pierre obliges her request and takes them to the finest Haute Couture shopping district in the world.

After making her rounds of the many shops and boutiques, they enjoy beignets and sip crème Brule flavored café au latte on the sidewalk of a small café. Later she has Jean-Pierre take them to her favorite shopping destination, Hermes of Paris. Brian could only watch as Ashima spends money on items that could purchase a compact car. Although, Brian took a more frugal approach to spending in Paris, he did make one purchase at a small novelty shop that is perhaps most meaningful. However, her excitement to be in Paris is a bit dampened after finding out that the Cavalli

336

party she'd been anticipating all year has been canceled. But, she doesn't let the news keep her down for long. She simply shifts her focus and prepares for the *Louvre Fashion Show*.

It's now been a few days since Brian and Ashima arrived in Paris, and unlike London, with plenty of downtime to unwind, there's been nothing but quality time spent between them. From taking selfies atop the *Eiffel Tower* to enjoying a lazy afternoon cruise on the Seine River, they make the best of their time in Paris together. Ashima even introduces Brian to one of her favorite chefs, who allows Brian to dabble in the kitchen to learn a thing or two about French cuisine. In return, Brian trades secrets with the French chef, preparing him one of his signature grits dishes and the chef absolutely loved it. At the request of his culinary teacher, Brian also had a menu from the restaurant signed by the chef to take back for extra credit.

As night falls on the city of love, Brian and Ashima are preparing to hit the runway this evening. Ashima stands at the bathroom vanity applying eye-liner, while Brian steps out onto the terrace to record the brilliant view of the Eiffel Tower's thousands of sparkling bulbs illuminating the clear and crisp Paris sky.

"Hey baby, are you ready?" Ashima asks as she walks out onto the terrace.

"Yeah, babe I'm ready…just capturing the *Eiffel Tower* in rare form so I can share this with the fellas back home." Brian explains, documenting his Paris experience.

"That's a great idea. How about we capture this selfie moment together?" An ecstatic Ashima suggests as she takes Brian's camera and takes a selfie of them with the *Eiffel Tower* sparkling in the back drop.

Ready to hit the town, Ashima is dressed in a black poncho dress with jewelry draped to her waist, wrist bangles, and suede thigh high boots folded down at the knees, while Brian sports a black stripped button down with rolled sleeves, a black vest, jeans, white sneakers, and a gray scarf. As they take poses and make funny faces, there was something about her energy that convinced him that tonight is going to be a good night.

As they make their way to the *Louvre Museum*, Brian is a ball of nerves as he has no idea of what kind of atmosphere he's about to encounter. On the other hand, Ashima's demeanor is content and routine as if it was all familiar to her.

"Wow babe, you really look amazing! I mean, you always look amazing but tonight you're glowing!" Brian mentions as she sits neatly across from him, fashionable and fabulous like she was about the walk the runway herself.

"Thank you and you look very handsome as well. We look handsome together!" Ashima replies before they lean in to kiss.

As the iconic museum glass pyramid comes into view, the scene becomes organized chaos as the celebrity guests start to arrive and security maintains order at the checkpoints. Once inside the first checkpoint Jean-Pierre falls in line with the rest of the luxury celebrity carriages off-loading its passengers at the designated entrance.

"Are you ready for this?" Ashima asks grasping his hand as they inch closer to the red carpet.

"No, but I'm with you so I'm sure I'll be alright!" Brian assumes as he can see the mob of people, camera flashes, velvet ropes just ahead of him.

He wasn't exactly sure what's about to happen, but whatever it is, it was happening now. Once the celebrity ahead of them clears the red carpet, it becomes their turn to grace the red carpet.

"Here we go...!" Ashima smiles with eager anticipation, as Brian is suddenly hit with a rush of anxiety.

When Jean-Pierre opens the door, Brian and Ashima are immediately hit with camera flashes the moment their feet hit the red carpet as a mob of paparazzi and spectators roar and cheer, hoping to get a glimpse of another notable celebrity.

"WHO IS THAT, IDRIS...?! TAYE...?! IS THAT MORRIS...?! WAIT, WHO IS SHE?! HEY, LOOK AT ME!!!" The shouts ring out from the mob of paparazzi lining the velvet ropes.

"AWE, IT'S JUST SOME RRG?" One photographer dismisses.

"Babe, what's an RRG?" Brian asks Ashima as he escorts her along the carpet with their arms interlinked.

"Random, rich, guy...but, don't mind them. They're just celebrity whores starving for a photo." Ashima explains.

Following Ashima's lead, Brian casually walks to the entrance of the Museum. After a brief check-in at security, they make their way to the underground lobby beneath the glass pyramid, where cocktail hour is in full swing. As Brian looks around, it seems as if everyone from Hollywood 'A' listers to Runway Royalty is in the building. Klum, Campbell, Beckford,

Crawford, Banks, Teigen, Lee-Simmons, and Moss were just a few runway legends Ashima points out in the crowd, while celebrities like Paltrow, Samuel L, Tatum, Stefani, Hathaway, Statham, and Lawrence where a few among the many Hollywood 'A' listers in attendance.

The *Louvre Museum* venue is incredible as the decorators and caterers spared no expense on pampering their distinguished guests. There are food stations and bars throughout the museum and servers with cocktails and hors d'oeuvres at every turn. Ice sculptures of famous Paris landmarks and sheer drapes hanging from the ceiling with fancy lights passing through them made for an elegant touch to the décor. After taking a glass of champagne from a passing tuxedo dressed server, they walk around to take in some of the museum's notable art collection. The first thing he notices as he looks up is the famous Cy Twombly art painted on the Ceiling. As they tour a few of the other exhibits cordoned off by velvet ropes, Ashima points out some of the most famous artwork including the armless marble sculpture Venus de Milo and the original Mona Lisa painting. As they return to the ballroom just past the massive spiral staircase that stretched to the base of the glass pyramid, Brian takes into accord how much the celebrities in the room were actually worth.

"This is crazy! I don't think there's a vault big enough to account for the amount of money in this room." Brian ponders as he observes all the celebrities, designers, and models around him.

But, what's really confusing to Brian, is how many of these famous people are familiar with Ashima as they move around the vast room. She mingles and cackles with a few of them comfortably, as if she'd known them for years. There were a few notable faces Brian could identify, but there were others Ashima had to explain. Due to Ashima's ethnic background, it was almost as if Bollywood meets Hollywood in a sense. Despite being silently star struck, Brian does well maintaining his composure. As he shakes the hands of those whose clothes he's wearing on his back or seen on T.V., he simply smiles and tries not to engage them much, while bursting at the seams with jubilation inside. But, despite his cool approach, his inner groupie couldn't resist taking a few snapshots to text his friends and family back home and post them on social media.

"Hey there, Miss lady!" A voice shouts out from the busy crowd.

"Oh, my God, hi Ru! How are you?" Ashima replies as she embraces RuPaul with a hug and smooches on each cheek.

"Oh, magnifique Honey! You know I still gotta teach these models how to work it, girl! So how have you been? You look fabulous, Honey! And who is this young chocolate morsel?" An animated RuPaul asks sizing Brian up.

"Ru, this is Brian…Brian, RuPaul." Ashima introduces.

"Enchant'e, Brian! Mmm…he is scrumptious, Honey! But, don't let him out of your sight, Child! You know how these cougars have a sweet tooth for chocolate. Good seeing you, Honey! au revoir!" RuPaul playfully cautions, winking at Ashima before walking away.

"Who is this woman? How does she know so many people in this room?" Brian asks himself as Ashima stops and speaks to yet another celebrity.

Trying to make sense of it all, he also began to wonder whether he's really over his head as far as Ashima's status and why is she really interested in the likes of him. But, for now, he just goes with the flow and enjoys this unbelievable experience.

As guests start to filter into their seats preparing for the start of the show, Brian and Ashima grab another glass of sparkling wine from a passing server before making their way to their seats as well. As they excuse themselves to their second-row seats from the runway, Brian notices what appears to be a familiar face about to sit in front of him.

"Babe, isn't that…" Brian starts out.

"…Tom and Gisele? Yes, it is." Ashima finishes as she and Gisele wave hello to each other. Tom looks back and acknowledges Brian with a simple head nod.

"Hey, how's it going?" Tom asks standing about four inches taller than Brian and extending his arm for a handshake.

"I'm good man, just happy to be here. How are you?" Brian replies over the crowd noise as he tries to mentally block the idea that he's talking to a sports icon.

"I'm here with the wife, Bro. Happy wife, happy life!" He replies as he shakes Brian's hand with a huge Super Bowl ring clustered with diamonds sitting on his finger.

"Wow. That's a nice piece of hardware you got there, Sir." Brian compliments as he turns Tom's hand over to take a closer look.

"Yeah, it's the ring I won against Philadelphia in 2005. It's my favorite ring." Tom explains as Brian begins to grin with embarrassment.

"What? Were you there?" Tom asks reacting to Brian's spontaneous reaction.

"Naw, I wasn't there, but I'm from Philly." Brian uncomfortably admits.

"Oh…I'm sorry! Maybe next time Philly? Enjoy the show." Tom smiles as he takes his seat.

As surreal as it already is to be sitting behind Tom and Gisele along a Fashion Week runway in Paris, Brian looks around to see who else he could catch sight of in the crowd of onlookers. As he scans the crowd he spots Brad and Angelina, Will and Jada, and the Beckhams sitting directly across the runway from him in another awe-inspiring moment. As the lights of the venue come down, so does the voices of the runway crowd as they prepare to get the show started.

"LADIES AND GENTLEMEN…!" The M.C. announces as he welcomes everyone to Fashion Week Paris and introduces an opening act, who performed to kick off the event. Suddenly, pyrotechnics shoot up from the floor and rain down from above as the models rip the white, glowing runway.

There are so many blinding camera flashes and pyrotechnics that nearly everyone in the room were hiding behind a fashionable pair of designer shades. The venue is absolutely electric as each fashion brand presents a different runway effect. Some brands with laser lights, some with fog rolling along the runway, some even with contortionist hanging from the ceiling. They watch as models from every fashion designer imaginable showcase their pageantry down the runway in rotation from Laurent, de la Renta, McQueen, Wang, Jacobs, Lagerfeld, Cavalli, and many other flagship designers of the fashion industry. From the music, to the lighting, to the swag of the models striking a pose, the atmosphere is on fire figuratively and literally, as one of the decorative drapes catch fire from the shows explosive grand finale which was quickly extinguished.

Once the show ends, it's on to the after party where the entire social scene converges under one roof to kick it up another notch. The entire room is inundated with 'glamazons' and fashionistas at every turn with plenty of congratulations and admiration to share. Whether you were a movie star, an athlete, or a socialite, no matter what your affiliation, people were moving to the beat of the music and having a great time. Brian is really taken aback by how easy going many of the personalities in the room respond to him. They laugh and joke and touch him as if they'd known him for years. There is nothing pretentious or snobbish about them and with a good reason. It was evident that if you were here it wasn't by accident, and he could tell that they were comfortable partying among their prominently affluent peers. They were confident that there weren't any crazies in the room and for at least one moment, they were dying to just feel normal again, no matter how embarrassing. And embarrassing, enjoyable moments is exactly what you were getting from this crowd.

The DJ is killing the party all night as 'A' listers kick off their red bottom heels, hike up their dresses and off the shoulder gowns, loosen their neckties and rock out all night to the wee hours of the morning. And with a few drinks in him to loosen his spirit there was Brian in the midst of it all, having the euphoric time of his life; line dancing and rocking out with the wealthy as if he belonged. Not much of a dancer, Ashima cheers him on as she stands entertained from the sideline. Of course, there were those on the dance floor who could stand to take a few lessons in urban dance moves. But, surprisingly, some of the opulent came prepared with their best whip and nae nae, stanky leg, and Dougie moves as well. As the alcohol, hor'doeuvres, and music kept flowing, so did the party. Many of the party goers were in rare form and Brian was right there to witness it all. In Philly, he was Brian from *Apex*. But, with Ashima on his arm abroad, he celebrates Paris like he's as big as the celebrities that have him star struck.

"OH MY GOD...ASHIMA?!" A voice rang out from the crowd from another person recognizing her.

"VANISHA! MY GOODNESS, I HAD NO IDEA YOU WERE GOING TO BE HERE!" A jubilant Ashima replies as the women greet each other with hugs and cheek smooches.

"My God, how long have you been in Paris? How long are you staying? Where's Fahad?" The elegantly dressed Vanisha asks, bombarding Ashima with several questions.

"Well, I got in from London a few days ago and I'm leaving in a few days for Dubai. As far as Fahad, we're no longer seeing each other. So, he's off doing God knows what with God knows who?" Ashima carelessly replies. Vanisha's eyes spring open as she gasps heavily.

"Nooo! Ashima, what happened?! I was expecting an invitation to your wedding not news like this!" Vanisha replies, mortified by the news.

342

"Yes Vanisha, I'm afraid so. Fahad and I were just too different. It would have never worked and hasn't worked for a long time." Ashima explains as Brian approaches them.

"Awe...! I'm so sorry to hear that. I really thought you guys would make it." Vanisha remorsefully replies.

"No, it's quite okay. I'm with someone else now and I'm very happy." Ashima gleefully reveals as Brian walks towards them with perfect timing.

"Hey...!" Brian walks over with a drink and all smiles as he makes his presence felt.

"Hey! Umm...Brian this is Vanisha, Vanisha...Brian!" Ashima introduces.

"Hello Brian, it's a pleasure!" Vanisha says with curious eyes as she sizes him up and reads everything about him in that moment.

"Likewise!" Brian replies, as her presence commanded Brian's eyes like a Middle-Eastern bombshell femme-fatale.

"So, Ashima, did I hear you say you are flying to Dubai in a few days?" Vanisha digress back to Ashima.

"Yes, I have meetings for the Al Kazahri project with Sheik Mohammed, Sheik Al Aziz and the development board." Ashima explains.

"Oh wow, you're actually a part of that project? That's great! I'm actually flying to Dubai tomorrow. You can fly with me and a few of my friends if you'd like? There's plenty of room, unless you can't leave tomorrow?" Vanisha happily proposes.

"Umm...what do you think? Wanna see Dubai a day early?" Ashima turns to Brian for his opinion.

"I'm good babe. I don't have much to pack so, yeah!" Brian agrees before taking a sip of his drink.

"Awesome! We're taking off at nine tomorrow, so I'll send a car for you at eight." She informs them with excitement.

"Perfect! See you tomorrow!" Ashima concludes followed by cheek smooches.

"Babe, who was that?" Brian curiously asks as they walk away.

"That's my good friend from India." Ashima simply replies.

"Oh okay! Is she one of those Bollywood actresses or something?" Brian inquires as he suspects something regal about the way she moved.

"No, she's the heiress of a billionaire empire." Ashima casually explains as Brian stands dumbfounded.

"Billionaire heiress, huh...? This woman has too many rich friends!" Brian ponders as they walk away to enjoy the rest of the party.

As the party resumes, Brian and Ashima find themselves departing the event shortly after speaking with Vanisha so they can catch the early morning flight. However, with only hours remaining till their departure to Dubai, Brian couldn't leave Paris without sharing one specially planned moment. So, after leaving the event, he instructs Jean-Pierre to drive to the Pont Des Arts Bridge, which sits just behind the *Louvre Museum.*

"What are you up to?" Ashima asks, suspicious of Brian's intent.

"C'mon, I want to show you something." Brian answers as Jean-Pierre pulls up to the bridge crossing the Seine River.

Once Jean-Pierre opens the door for them, Ashima immediately recognizes where Brian has taken her. The famous 'lock bridge' is what the Pont Des Arts Bridge is most commonly known as because couples from all over the world come here to place a love lock on the bridge to symbolize their love for one another. Brian takes her by the hand and leads her across the bridge as Ashima simply follows, braces for the uncertainty that awaits her.

"Tonight, was a great night, wasn't it?" Brian asks with exuberance in his voice as they walk past the thousands of locks attached to the structure of the bridge.

"Yessss! Tonight, was beyond great. It was absolutely insane! Especially when everyone was dancing down that line of people, what do you call it again...?" She struggles to recall, trying to talk through her laughter.

"The Soul Train line!" Brian reminds her.

"Yassss! The Soul Train line! And they were 'boogie boarding' and 'pop rocking' and doing the robot to those old rap songs...it was hilarious!" Ashima laughs reliving the moments.

"Yes babe, 'B-boying' and 'Pop locking'? Yes, they were really having a good time out there. I didn't know rich white people could move like that." Brian corrects her all in good fun.

"Oh, whatever Brian! You know I was sheltered as a child!" Ashima disclaimers as they're both tickled by her misuse of urban lingo.

"Wow! Look at all of these locks! There must be a million of them on this bridge!" Ashima notes, embracing and resting her head on Brian's arm as they walk.

"Yeah, it's a lot more than I expected. It's like each lock has its own personality." Brian points out as they stroll along the bridge on a beautiful Paris night.

"God it's such a beautiful night!" Ashima says as she looks down river at a spectacular view of the vibrant moon hovering just above the *Eiffel Tower*.

"It is…which is why it's the perfect time for me to do this…" Brian stops and reaches into his pocket.

Unsure of what to expect, she nervously watches as Brian unveils a white box garnished with a red bow tied around it. Stunned and completely caught off guard, she pauses in awe and gasps for breath, covering her mouth to prevent an embarrassing spontaneous reaction.

"I figured since our plans changed a bit, this would be the only chance I'd get to capture this moment." He says before handing her the box. "Babe, I really just want to thank you for an already amazing journey. I know I can't give you the world, but, I hope you don't hold that against me, because you're the best thing that has ever happened to me and I just wanted you to know that." Brian sincerely explains.

"Oh my…! Brian, what is this?!" Ashima nervously mutters.

"It's okay, Babe. Just open it!" Brian laughingly assures her.

Apprehensive and nervous, she cautiously unties the bow and reveals a red heart shaped open lock, engraved Brian~n~Ashima and Brian's treasured key and chain to his heart resting in the red satin lining of the box. One look in the box and she's instantly reduced to tears as she looks at him with disbelief. Standing speechless and overwhelmed, she resorts to hugging his neck to find comfort.

"I know how much you love this key and you know how much it means to me. So, I figured tonight would be the perfect time to surrender my heart to you and lock the special bond we have right here on the Love Lock bridge." He says in the softest masculine tone.

"Thank you…" She whimpers as she continues her prolonged embrace.

"I had something engraved on the back of it too." He informs her as she delicately turns the lock over and reads the engraving on the back.

"Forever grateful to have you in my life…" She reads aloud as she picks her eyes up and struggles to fight back tears. The gesture is so romantically intimidating she refuses to lift her head to resist the temptation of crying. As she stands before him in a ball of emotions, Brian takes the key from the box and places it around her neck.

"So, you like it?" Brian nervously asks, although the elation of her face says it all.

"Yes…It's perfect! Yes…I love it!" She emotionally replies, reaching her arms around Brian's neck again, this time pulling him in for a long passionate kiss as if this moment were the highlight of her life.

Finally, Ashima is at a place in her life where she feels totally secure in her happiness. At last she's at a place where she's moved by something other than money, lavish gifts, and empty promises. After years of drowning in displeasure with Fahad, sharing this moment with Brian has lifted her so high she feels like she's flying. The most meaningful gift she'd ever received wasn't a diamond studded watch, it wasn't the keys to a new luxury car, and it wasn't a diamond necklace or a ten-karat ring. It was merely a simple term of endearment that moved her more than any extravagant gift she'd ever received.

After eventually finding a spot on the bridge to place their lock among the hundreds of thousands of others, Brian and Ashima symbolically lock the strength of their feelings for one another. Although the purpose of the bridge is to express love, Brian is careful to respect Ashima's apprehensive feelings about love, even though he knows what she feels in her heart.

In spite of this, her courage to tell Brian she loves him still falls short. Although she knows what's in her heart, the stigma of everything she's ever loved being tainted still weighs heavily on her, and she continues to remain guarded until she's undeniably sure.

At last, the evening ends back at the hotel with Brian an Ashima sharing a relaxing bath with champagne and gourmet strawberries at their side. As they sit partially submerged in the large, rustic cast iron tub enjoying an incredible view of the *Eiffel Tower*. Paris has certainly lived up to the prestige of another fascinating fashion week, and for Brian, the most impressive week of his life.

"Mmm…that was delicious. The strawberry was good too!" Brian says as they share the bite of a strawberry and finish it with a kiss.

"You know…I wish I could live in this moment forever. Never have I felt so alive and content the way I do when I'm with you. You make me feel like a woman, and that's all girl could ever ask for." Ashima admits as she stares at the ceiling with her head resting comfortably on his hairless, masculine chest. Brian gently strokes her hair like the most incredible scalp massage she's ever received.

"I don't care how much disdain my father feels about us. God willing, I promise I will never let you go." Ashima firmly promises as she graces the key pendant around her neck as if it represented Brian.

"And I will never leave you either." Brian assures her as she turns to him to seal the promise with another kiss.

Dubai, UAE

The next day, Brian and Ashima are five hours into a six-hour flight on the last leg of their trip to Dubai. As promised, Ashima's friend Vanisha sends a car for them to catch a ride to Dubai on her luxury Falcon jet. Once Brian overcame his nerves like he did on his flight to London, he finds himself resting comfortably in the lavishly laid out cabin that reminded him of the most luxurious living room he'd ever seen with round windows. As Ashima, Vanisha, and two other women who also happen to be connected to royalty, are recapping their visit to Paris in a mix of Arabic and English dialogue and sipping wine, Brian lounges comfortably on a sofa gazing out the window at thirty thousand feet. During the flight Brian takes a moment to reflect as they cruise at altitude above the clouds. Never did he imagine that he would be in the position he's been in the last few weeks, especially not as soon. Taking his first ever flight, in first class to London, hanging out and partying with celebrities in Paris, and now flying to Dubai on a billionaire heiress' private jet was not something he'd had in mind when he first encountered Ashima in his Apex uniform. He often wondered if this was too good to be true or things to come for his life with Ashima, but for now he would just live for the moment.

For as far as he can see, there is nothing but mountainous valleys and peaks and desert terrain as they streak through the sky. When the pilot makes his final descent, Brian watches as the coastline of the Persian Gulf comes into view. Then the view of the Palm Islands and the World Islands appears before him as the sight of the dazzling Dubai skyline comes into focus. After seeing nothing but sand and mountains for hours, the city truly presents itself like a bustling oasis from the sky above. As they fly above the buildings of the downtown area, Brian is truly stunned as the glare of the sun reflects off the tallest building in the world, the *Burj Kahlifa*. Being from Philadelphia, he's used to seeing sky scrapers as tall as the Comcast Building, but nothing could have prepared him for the epic size of this building, as it dwarfs even the tallest of buildings around it. The women also break from their conversation to line the windows for a glimpse of the massive modern marvel.

Once the plane touches down and taxis the runway, Brian immediately realizes that he has officially arrived in the Middle-East. He looks out one of the windows and notices four blacked out luxury vehicles lined up on the tarmac as the plane comes to a complete stop at a separate location away from the airport.

"Whoa..., now that's how you greet royalty!" he suggests to himself as the small fleet of vehicles consists of two Phantoms and two Escalades.

As the women prepare to exit the plane, all of them including Ashima place a Shayla scarf over their heads as a customary respect to Dubai's Arabic culture. Brian isn't sure if there's a customary way he should exit the plane, but Ashima doesn't mention anything to him so once again, he just went with it. When it was his turn to disembark from the plane, his eyes squints nearly closed from the brightness of the blinding sun as the desert heat instantly flashes over him. Avoiding the sun's reflection off the brilliant shine of the vehicles, he stares at the ground where four men dressed in pure white throbe garments and four others in black suits were waiting to greet them.

The men in white garb greet the women as if they were royalty, kissing each cheek and their hands in an obedient manner. The men in black suites on the other hand remained expressionless as hid behind their dark shades, and ear pieces appearing to be armed and ready.

"It's been a pleasure to meet you Brian. Ashima, I'll be in touch!" Vanisha says, giving Brian and Ashima kisses on the cheek before disappearing into her own car.

Once the men load the bags from the plane and seat everyone in their vehicles, the security detail in the SUV's moves in front and behind the cars to form a motorcade as they leave the grounds of the airport.

"Hey, are you okay?" Ashima asks caressing his hand as they lounge comfortably in the back of the Phantom.

"Yeah, babe I'm fine. Do I look any different?" Brian replies, concerned whether he's wearing an expression that differs from his mood.

"No. It's just that you haven't really said much since we boarded the flight." Ashima points out.

"Oh naw, I'm good now babe. You know that whole flying thing is still a new experience for me and my nerves were on edge for pretty much the whole flight. So, I just enjoyed the scenery while you girls chatted it up!" Brian explains.

"Awe…I'm sorry, baby. I almost forgot about that. I guess things did get a little bumpy after the takeoff, huh?" Ashima sympathizes.

"Yeah, I thought I was going to piss myself, but you were so relaxed I figured it was just routine turbulence." Brian shamefully admits.

"Well, nothing is ever routine about turbulence in my book, but I've been in far worse." She explains.

"But, then we go from jet noise and turbulence to riding in this and it's like a magic carpet ride of silence. I mean, you can hear a pin drop in here." Brian admires as he runs his hand along the leather and wood finish of the center console.

"I'm glad you're enjoying it. But, you haven't seen anything yet. Wait until you see what Dubai really has to offer." Ashima delightfully informs him.

As the convoy makes its way along the Ghweifat International Highway, to the *Jumeirah Beach Hotel*, Brian is in absolute amazement of the scenery Dubai has to offer. The ride through London and France was certainly profound in its rich heritage and historical landmarks. But, as this newer city establishing itself as a world class travel destination, Dubai is clearly on another level. The alley of buildings that stretch along the highway for miles on end looks like towering marvels of architecture as they present all different shapes and designs.

However, there's a different type of impression at ground level, as Brian realizes that he's completely surrounded by money. The drive from the airport alone he's never seen so many exotic and premium luxury vehicles in one day. In the U.S., the only way he'd see these many cars, of this value at once is at a car show. But, here in Dubai, they drive Beamer's and Benz's like domestic cars, and Bentley's like town cars. Along with the many luxury cars and SUV's around him, there are also many supercars on the road as well. It's evident that the rich have no problem with splurging their wealth in Dubai as Brian had never seen a Bugatti before, yet he's already seen three on the way to the hotel. Suddenly, as Brian continues to enjoy his ride through the desert metropolis, the motorcade is suddenly buzzed by a Lamborghini and Ferrari racing down the highway on either side of them.

"Wow, babe! Pardon the expression but it's like, Arab money for real out here!" Brian naturally reacts, as the adrenaline of the dueling cars get the best of him. The driver looks into his rearview at Brian after the comment with an interesting smile.

"Yes, this is definitely where the rich come to play, not only Arab citizens, but many from all over the world. But, your comment about Arabs does remind me that perhaps this is a good time to explain a few customs and courtesies that will keep us out of trouble and out of jail while we're here." Ashima is prompted before they reach the hotel.

"Jail?! Is it really that serious in Dubai?" Brian replies, alarmed by the warning.

"Yes, Brian. They will throw you in jail for the most insignificant things here." She earnestly confirms.

"Like...?" Brian asks with concerning interest.

"Like kissing in public, inappropriate language, blasphemy against Islam...those type things. But, you can also get in trouble for public intoxication, photographing people, public indecency, lewd behavior, homosexuality even the way you dress may cause you problems here in Dubai." Ashima explains in serious candor.

"You mean they have fashion police out here too?" Brian asks with sarcasm.

"Well, not that dramatic, but Dubai is a stylish cosmopolitan city and you should be dressed appropriately at all times." Ashima emphasizes.

"Okay, so keep it grown and sexy, watch my conduct, and don't grab another man's booty...got it!" Brian sarcastically sums up.

"Yes, and don't ever offer someone your left hand." Ashima candidly adds.

"Say what?!" A further confused Brian asks.

"Yes Brian, in Arab culture the left hand is reserved for hygiene and is considered extremely rude if you offer it to someone for anything, especially food." Ashima clarifies.

"Wow, this definitely isn't London or France!" He specifies, feeling uncomfortably restricted by the rules.

"Nope! It's just Dubai and they take their culture and their guests very serious." Ashima stresses to him.

As they continue down the highway, Brian is able to capture another view of the massive *Burj Kahlifa* building as it towers into the sky so tall it

351

disappears into the sunlight. Passing the next exit, the rest of the motorcade breaks off as the security detail intended for Vanisha and her friends escorts them to their destination. However, Brian bears little concern from the security departure after being distracted by another architectural spectacle.

"Babe what's that slanted, slope-like building over there?" Brian asks pointing to the structure.

"Oh, that's the *Mall of the Emirates*. It's the second largest mall in Dubai. I love shopping there." Ashima answers.

"Wow, that's a weird shape for a mall." Brian replies.

"Oh-no! The structure you're referring to is an indoor ski slope." Ashima explains.

"Huh…indoor skiing?!" A dumbfounded Brian replies.

"Yes baby, Dubai has its own indoor ski resort attached to the mall." She clarifies with humor in her voice.

"That's crazy! It's like a hundred degrees out here and they're skiing in the desert?" Brian replies in awe.

"Yes, they literally thought of everything during the development of this amazing city, and they're still building as you can see with all the cranes moving around. But, this mall is a puppy compared to the Dubai Mall. It's currently the largest mall in the world." Ashima replies.

"Man, what will they think of next?" He says, already impressed by Dubai's many first impressions.

Once they arrive at the hotel, Brian is anxiously prepared to see Dubai after Ashima tells him about all there is to do in the sprawling metropolis. When the driver opens the door, Brian once again steps out into the unfamiliar desert heat. But, just short of perspiring, he and Ashima are rushed by a gust of Arctic-like air as the sliding doors of the hotel lobby opens to the grand, six story atrium areas. The air of the lobby is so frigid, Brian catches goose bumps and gasps for breath from the extreme heat to the extreme cold change in temperature.

As they enter the lobby they are immediately greeted by three women standing by for guest arrivals. The first woman is holding a brass genie lamp-like dispenser for a hand wash solution, the second woman has neatly folded, angel white towels for wiping your hands, and the third woman holds a tray for placing the discarded towels. While Ashima checks in at the front desk, Brian is distracted by the massive and beautiful lobby, with its towering gold columns, fascinating décor, and extravagant art. As the sound of a man playing a grand piano resounds throughout the atrium, interestingly he notices that most of the staff and patrons weren't wearing the customary Arab garb of an Islamic country. Instead, he finds plenty of business and leisurely dressed Americans, Europeans, and others letting their hair down in the luxurious, resort-like hotel. Opening the door of their twenty fifth floor luxury suite unveils not only a lavish apartment style dwelling, but an amazing shore side view of the *Jumeirah Beach and Marina*, and the landmark *Burj Al Arab* as well. After settling in, and showering off the stench of travel, they dress in relaxed attire and enjoy a soothing sea breeze on the balcony outside their room.

"I absolutely love this!" Ashima expresses in a lively tone as they casually lean across the balcony admiring a beautiful view of the *Burj Al Arab hotel* adjacent to them, as the Arabian Sea sparkles under the bliss of a beautiful sunny blue sky.

"What's that...?" Brian inquires.

"You, me, this beautiful view overlooking the sea, this refreshing sea breeze on such a sultry day. There's no better place I'd rather be, right now." Ashima elaborates.

"Yeah, this breeze feels real nice compared to how hot it was when we walked in. Of course, enjoying anything with you is the highlight of my day." Brian replies as his eyes softly engages her.

"Awe...you're so sweet! You know, whenever we're together, I can't think of nothing but wonderful adjectives to describe me and you." Ashima smiles and leans in for a kiss.

"Is it me or is that hotel shaped like the sail of a boat?" Brian asks, marveling the vast *Burj Al Arab Hotel*.

"Yes, the Burj Al Arab is shaped like a sail and the architects designed the Jumeriah to look like a giant wave to complement the Burj Al Arab." Ashima explains.

"Wow...the oil rich spares no expense when it comes to the imagination. Palm shaped islands, indoor skiing, giant sail shaped hotels..." Brian replies in amazement.

"Yes, this is pretty much a playground for the mega rich. They have so much money they're bored. So, they pretty much build whatever they envision. Many of them are also young and ambitious and they love the ways of the west, so they mimic the flash and lifestyles of the young and rich in the United States, only better. That's why you see so many supercars on the roads out here. Even Fahad has a supercar he keeps out here to drive recklessly when he comes to visit his father." Ashima explains as they watch a helicopter land on the *Burj Al Arab* helipad.

"Wow, that's just crazy! So, this guy Fahad is like, super rich or something, huh?" Brian exaggerates.

"Well, not that he's earned his way to a wealthy lifestyle, but yes. The Gabr family is worth billions in wealth." Ashima nonchalantly replies.

"Hmph…well I'm sure this trip to Dubai will be an experience. But, I'm still sitting here thinking about how much fun we had in Paris. I mean, that was really a life changing experience, babe!" Brian admits as Paris plays back in his mind.

"You think that was life changing? Dubai is about to change your life again!" Ashima avows.

"Wait Babe, I just had the time of my life Paris, less than forty-eight hours ago. Are you telling me that you can show me a better time in Dubai than Paris?" Brian dubiously replies.

"C'mon…let me show you!" She replies with a devilish smile.

And so, it begins… Less than three hours later, Brian and Ashima begin their Dubai adventure dune bashing in luxury SUV's in the Dubai desert sands. After overlooking not only all of Dubai, but the entire Arabian gulf from the highest floor of the *Burj Khalifa*, they later get dressed and enjoy an intimate seafood dinner in front of a massive aquarium at the *Al Mahara* restaurant in *Jumeirah Beach Hotel*.

The next day, they find themselves helping each other off the snow after enjoy a day of skiing, zip lining, and indoor luge at the *Ski Dubai Resort* at the *Emirates Mall*. Later in the day, after enjoying a couple's massage at the Talise Spa, they have dinner at the *Uptown Bar* on the 24th Floor of the *Jumeirah Hotel,* and share a melon mint shisha to cap off the night.

The following morning, Ashima awakes to several text messages she'd missed from the night before. Trying not to disturb Brian, she sits up and pulls the sheet above her bare chest as she reviews her messages. The first message is from her colleagues letting her know they have arrived in Dubai, the second message is from Vanisha for a spa rendezvous, the third message is from her Godfather Sheik Gabr, notifying her that his yacht will arrive in Dubai at the Pavilion Marina by dawn and he wishes to see her when he pulls into port. But, the last message is an unexpected text from

Fahad that causes her anxiety. After not hearing from him for over a month, he sends her a random text which she finds disturbing.

(Text)
Fahad: *"So, I hear you're in Dubai. I trust you'll be seeing my father while you're there. Enjoy your stay."* She nervously reads, knowing that the message was far from innocent.

Although concerned, Ashima pays little regard to the text as she prepares for her Ten o'clock meeting with investors. The ensemble for today is black business dress attire, red heels, and all the accessories needed for a fashion savvy woman. Although she avoids waking Brian early on, the clack of her heels will surely wake him as she walks on the hardwood kitchen floor to pour a few glasses of grapefruit juice. She walks back to the bedroom and sits on the edge of the bed placing a glass on the nightstand for him. Meanwhile, she takes a sip of her own glass and contently watches Brian as he sleeps peacefully with a light snore. Watching him sleep gave her peace, knowing how much he cares for her and how lucky he made her feel to be in her life.

"Morning, sleepy head!" She says as Brian awakes sensing her presence.

"Morning…" He replies with a long stretch before settling back into the comfort of the soft quilted bed.

"Sleep well?" She asks as Brian looks up at her.

"Yeah, I slept great! This bed is like sleeping on a cloud. You look lovely this morning. All ready for your important meeting?" He asks while checking out her business ensemble.

"Yes. I'm all set." She replies a she hands him the glass of grapefruit juice.

"Everything okay, Babe? You look like something is up!" Brian asks as she appears to look troubled. Concerned for her, he sits up to talk.

"Umm…yeah, baby, everything is fine. I just got a text from my Godfather and he wants to see me today." Ashima explains, not realizing she was wearing signs of worry on her face.

"Oh okay. What time are you going to see him?" Brian inquires.

"I'll probably go visit him once I leave my henna appointment with Vanisha, around three or so…" She answers as she takes another sip from her glass.

"Well, that should be fun…hanging out with your billionaire Godfather and friends." Brian jealously replies as Ashima stands from the bed and walks to the window.

"Well, I'm not going to lie, it certainly has its perks. But, if it makes you feel better, I'd rather be with you!" Ashima replies as she peers out the window.

"Come here, I want to show you something." She asks as she looks out at the Marina below. Brian throws on his boxer briefs and joins her at the window.

"You see that silver yacht out there with dark tinted windows at the end of the pier." Ashima points out.

"Yeah, that is a really nice, big boat over there!" Brian replies.

"Well, that boat belongs to Sheik Gabr. He arrived early this morning from Qatar." Ashima informs him.

"That's your Godfather's yacht?!" Brian asks in amazement.

"Yes, he actually pulled in for only a few days to fuel his boat for a trip to the Monaco Grand Prix." Ashima explains.

"Wow…he's actually going to take his boat all the way to the Med for a race?" Brian asks in astonishment as he places his arm around her neck from behind and sips from his glass.

"Yeah, that's pretty much what billionaires do. He'll take his yacht to the big race and park it next to the other big yachts, until a bigger yacht comes along and crushes his ego. Then he'll meet with that yachts owner and they'll make their billion-dollar deals over a ten-thousand-dollar scotch and toast to being masters of the universe." Ashima tells Brian as she caresses his arm while they stand at the window enjoying each other's presence. Staring at the yacht with his arm around Ashima, Brian's curiosity starts to wonder.

"Wow! How much is this woman actually worth?" Brian asks in his conscious, but can't bring himself to ask her.

"And what did you have planned to do today while I'm gone?" Ashima asks as she moves away from the window to prepare to leave.

"Oh, I don't know. I figured I'd just catch up on some homework assignments, catch up with my peoples back home, and watch Abu Dhabi

356

play Bahrain in a cricket match, pretty exciting stuff!" An unenthused Brian replies.

"Hmm…are you sure you don't want to do something a little more exciting?" Ashima asks with a cunning smirk.

"Like what?" Brian asks curiously.

"Like this…" Ashima replies handing him a brochure.

"Whoa…babe, are you serious…a supercar excursion?! Babe, this is crazy!" Brian replies, ecstatic about the brochure.

"I told you that you were going to have a better time in Dubai than Paris. So what better way to enjoy yourself than to drive like a mad man with a bunch of other mad men in some really fast cars racing across the open desert like a Gumball Rally or something?" Ashima replies.

"A what? Gumball Rally?" A confused Brian asks.

"Yeah, it's basically a rally for the rich where they meet somewhere in the UK and go on a 3,000-mile international tour with their superfast exotic cars and take over the local streets and highways. I believe it starts in Dublin and ends in Las Vegas." Ashima explains.

"Are you serious? That's just crazy, thanks babe! You never cease to amaze me. So, what time do I need to be out there?" A keyed-up Brian asks.

"I think you need to be at *The Dubai Mall* by eleven, so you should probably get going. I need to get going too, so have a great time, and I'll see you when I get back." Ashima advises him as she prepares to leave.

"Okay, babe, good luck!" Brian replies, giving her a kiss before she heads out the door. When the door closes behind her, is so overwhelmed by the news he throws himself onto the bed in animated fashion and flops around like a kid home alone. Then he breaks out his suitcase to figure out what to properly wear for the occasion.

Once he arrives at the rendezvous point at *The Dubai Mall* in the Jumeirah Hotel's complimentary 760 BMW, Brian is absolutely amazed by the staging area. As the driver enters the parking lot, a line of Lamborghini's are parked to his left, and Ferrari's to his right in an array of colors and models. Brian can hardly contain his eager anticipation as he takes out his phone and records the insane display of exotic cars to share with the fellas back home.

After checking in at the registry and going through a brief tutorial with the instructors in the parking lot, Brian is assigned a driving assistant since it's his first time behind the wheel of a supercar. The instructor explains the six-hour trip to Abu Dhabi to meet at the *Yas Viceroy Hotel* for lunch before returning back to Dubai. After the details of the trip are explained, then came the moment he'd been waiting for. It was time to choose which car he would share this experience of a lifetime with. The drivers chose their cars according to when they booked their reservations. Brian ended up 21st of 24 drivers left to choose between a white Ferrari F430, a yellow Lamborghini Gallardo, a black Lamborghini Huracan, and a red Ferrari California which was also the only convertible left. Although Brian was partial to the Lamborghini's, he heeds the advice of his assistant Denny 'Ali' to go with the open top experience of the convertible. Brian looks at all the other drivers and doesn't feel like much of an outcast, as they too appear to be tourists from other countries.

As the driver's get into their cars to make the two-hour trek to Abu Dhabi, Brian nervously gets behind the wheel, anticipating the thrill of a lifetime. With the other cars starting up and the sound of raw horse power roaring around him, he sticks the key in and pushes the start button to the convertible. Brian smiles at the assistant as the vibration of 453 horsepower rumbles behind him. Once the fleet start to head out, Brian falls in line and follows them out on the balmy, sundrenched morning at 10am. As the cars spill out onto the street, onlookers everywhere take their phones out to record the exotic caravan of cars parading along the streets of Dubai. Never having this much power at his feet before, Brian is giddy after giving the engine a few revs to test the cars potential.

The assortment of colorful cars presents a slow and loud show for spectators as they navigate their way to open road. But, once the cars enter the onramp of the Ghweifat International Highway, the lead cars nearly burn the rubber off the rims as they open up on the freeway at full throttle. Brian nearly losses it in a fishtail trying to keep up as the adrenaline forces his foot to the floor. Suddenly the highway is transformed into the autobahn as the cars take off and take over the fast lane. Ali inspires Brian by tuning to a local radio station, and cranking the volume to a song by The Chemical Brothers featuring Q-Tip.

"Woooooooo...yeahhh...boyyyy...!" Brian shouts letting out an exhilarating breath of jubilation as he pushes the Ferrari from 80 to 140 kilometers in seconds.

"Go! Go! Go!" Ali exclaims, egging Brian on as he nudges his shoulder.

Although the barrage of cars demanded the respect of the road, there was too much traffic to allow the supercars to really open up. Not to mention the green and white Lamborghini police car monitoring traffic from the side of the road. However, once the cars left the city limits, the race was on to get to Abu Dhabi. The drive becomes absolutely incredible for Brian as he finds himself dueling in the desert with other Ferrari's and Lamborghini's jockeying for position in excess of 200 kilometers. The air rushing over of the open top of the convertible gives Brian a euphoric sense of freedom. It made him feel like he was flying.

Suddenly, the pack is interrupted and humbled by the flashing headlights of a Bugatti Veyron and a Bugatti Chiron overtaking them like they were standing still. A few of the cars tried to give chase, but had no chance of keeping up with 1100 horsepower. Nonetheless, Brian is having the time of his life.

Meanwhile, after wrapping up her meeting for the day at the Emirates Office Towers with Saudi investors, Ashima is on her way to her appointment with Vanisha. After engaging her father during the video conference with him at the meeting, she is barely out of the lobby when she suddenly receives a call from him.

"Hello, Princess. How are you?" Amir asks in a delightful voice.

"I'm well, father. How are things back home?" Ashima replies as the driver holds the door for her while she has a seat in back of an awaiting car.

"Things couldn't be better. I wish you would call your father more, but it's okay. You're living your life and making me proud every day! Especially, the way you handled yourself in the boardroom today. Sheik…and his board members had nothing but high praises for you and I think we might actually get this deal done. Speaking of living life how was Paris and fashion week?" Amir asks with guile in his voice.

"Excellent as always, it felt good to be back after missing last year." Ashima replies.

"That's great! So, who did you end up taking with you?" Amir asks, catching Ashima completely off guard.

"I'm sorry…?" Ashima replies, taken aback by his random inquiry.

"You know, the two tickets you bought for London, the two train tickets you bought to Paris? I figured one of your girlfriends, Carolyn or someone must have tagged along. That is, until I noticed the purchase of a men's watch in Paris on your statement. I'm sure you certainly didn't spend over forty-six thousand dollars on a watch for Fahad. So, tell me, what's going on?" Amir confronts her in a forthright demeanor.

"What's going on is you snooping in my private affairs and scrutinizing my motives. You have no right requesting inquiry into my accounts and dissecting my spending habits, especially without my consent. I'm not spending your money, so what business is it of yours?" Ashima angrily fires back in an aggravated tone.

"I have every right! I have every right, and I will not tolerate your tone! Ashima, don't let me find out you're traveling with that infidel Brian or so help me Allah, I will be on the next flight to Dubai and deal with him myself! I will not tolerate the manner in which you are conducting yourself with him. You will work things out with Fahad, and we will put this foolishness behind us. Do you understand?!" A fiery Amir stresses to her.

"No, I don't understand, and you're right, you don't have to tolerate my tone!" Ashima simply replies before hanging up to avoid embarrassing herself in front of her driver.

Now, upset and nervous about her father finding out about Brian, Ashima didn't want to seem visibly shaken around her friends. So, she postpones her appointment with Vanisha and tells her driver to take her back to the *Jumeirah Marina* so she could visit her Godfather instead. The driver takes her all the way down the pier where the largest of the other marina yachts are moored. As she exits the car, two casually dressed Arab men come off the boat to greet her and escort her onto the ship.

"بتوول. مس ,كسولة الواحة متن على رحّبت"

"Welcome aboard the Lazy Oasis, Ms. Batool." One of the men says as he kisses and gently takes her by the hand to assist her onboard

"أنت شكرت."

"Thank you." Ashima replies.

"Hello Princess, it's so good to see you!" The bald, salt and pepper bearded Sheik Gabr yells from the deck above as he observes her walking across the brow.

"Papa Gabr!" She replies as she heads up to the second deck to greet him.

As she walks through the lower saloon area across what appeared to be a white tiger Persian rug, she notices his fully stocked bar of spirits, ranging from several bottles of Louis 13th, Vintage bottles of Macallan scotch, and an array of other top shelf bottles he seems to collect. Every inch

360

of the boat is designed with cherry oak cabinetry and solid gold finishes. Even the ceiling is finished in gold trim with a chandelier dripping in Lilac Crystals.

"There's my baby! I've missed you so..." Sheik Gabr says in a deep Middle-Eastern accent as she walks up the glass stairs with a gold railing.

"I miss you too, Papa Gabr. What's on the menu? You know I must eat well whenever I come see you." She replies giving the bald, slender, fully bearded Gabr a lively hug and kiss on each cheek.

"Ha! I knew this! So, I told the chef, grilled lamb kabob, spiny lobster, cracked crab, biriyani with spices, and all the jumbo prawns you can eat!" He explains as they have a seat.

One of the men who escorted her onboard stands off to the side at the ready as Gabr sits on a leather sofa designed from albino alligator skin with a bottle of Patron en Lalique on the table before him and a tall standing Hookah pipe at his side.

"So, I understand today was the first day of negotiations for the Al Kazahri project. How did it go?" Sheik Gabr asks in a more business-like tone.

"It went very well. They loved the figures we presented and they're having their lawyers look over the contracts." Ashima replies.

"Excellent! Now see, your father was so nervous about me not being there, but I already had it arranged with the Saudi's, so that all you and your team needed to do is come to Dubai and close the deal. Your father, he never listens to me. That's why I'm headed to Monaco and he's getting grayer by the minute with business in Philadelphia." A delighted Gabr jokes as his leather strap Patek Philippe watch glistens in the periodic glare of the sun.

"I know Papa Gabr, it's unfortunate that my father is so passionate about everything." Ashima agrees.

"You know I spoke with your father a few days ago about something other than work." He says in a somber tone.

"Yes...?" Ashima simply replies, bracing for a less than thrilling conversation.

"He informed me of a few things going on with you and Fahad. Now, you know I don't care to meddle in your personal affairs. I've always maintained my silence when it comes to you and my son. But, who is this young man that I've been hearing about, and why? Princess, what are you doing? What of these antics, Ashima? This…frolicking with this young man?" Sheik Gabr bluntly addresses.

"Papa Gabr, there are no antics. I've found something that's been absent in my life that no man has been able to provide." Ashima replies.

"Which is…?" He curiously asks.

"…The intimate love of a man. I've learned to care for this man very much. He has been such an influence in my life and I'm proud of that!" Ashima passionately explains.

"But, Princess, what about Fahad? Has he not given you that intimacy? Has he not provided all that you need?" Sheik Gabr asks with confusion.

"Papa Gabr, I do not love Fahad intimately. I love Fahad like how we grew up as playful children. I know he's your son, but your son is a buffoon! A tyrant in love with himself and your money! He's not in love with me. He is in love with the traditions of Islam, to which I am not partial. I wasn't raised that way, despite my father constantly forcing upon me the teachings of the Quran. Obviously, I preferred to follow my mother's Coptic beliefs. Brian makes me happy, Papa Gabr. He makes me feel loved. He makes me feel like a woman, not a trophy. And I won't apologize for that!" Ashima passionately pleads as a server presents a tray of seafood fresh from the grill.

"So, what do you know of him, Princess? What does this Brian do? Is he a musician…an athlete?" Sheik Gabr asks being stereotypical of Brian's background.

"No Papa Gabr, he's actually a student." She replies laughing off his bias assumptions as she places several grilled prawn skewers on a square plate.

"A student? Is he in law school, med school, studying for his doctorate? Where is he enrolled? Is it Princeton, Yale, Harvard?" Sheik Gabr continues with a flurry of questions, expecting Brian to at least be educated at an Ivy League standard.

"No Papa Gabr, he's a culinary student, studying to be a chef." Ashima clarifies, nervously biting into the skewer awaiting his reply.

"Hmph…" is his initial, expressionless reaction as he pours another glass of something brown he'd been sipping on earlier. "Princess, you do realize that the people I hire to cook the food also sweep the floor, too. I'm not trying to sound insensitive, but what does this man know about you?"

He asks with a concerning vice as he pours another himself another shot of Patron.

"I know what you're asking me, and I can assure you he knows nothing about my financial status. Right now, we're simply enjoying each other's company and I don't care about how much he can provide. That is exactly the problem I have with Fahad. He believes that money can solve any problem. When all he needed to do was get to know who I really am, instead of trying to pacify me with everything I can very well do for myself." An emotionally disheartened Ashima explains.

"I'm sorry Princess, I didn't mean to pry and you're right. Despite being thrilled about the idea of welcoming you into the family through marriage, I know that you're too mature for Fahad. And I've tried to explain this to him when he comes with his problems. But, as you said, he simply thinks he can buy your love. But, knowing you since you come out of the womb, I know you can't be bought. So, don't worry about Fahad and don't worry about your father. I will have a talk with them both. Life is too short to be unhappy Princess, so enjoy yourself. Enjoy every moment of it. As for your friend Brian, I just want to be sure this man isn't deceiving you for his own financial gain. I have faith in you, Ashima. So, if you tell me he's worthy of your trust, then all I ask is that you be careful and be sure it is you that he is interested in, okay?" Sheik Gabr sincerely explains as he stands to give her a hug and kiss on each cheek.

"Yes, Papa Gabr, thank you for your support and understanding." Ashima replies with solace, knowing she has her Godfather's approval.

"Very good! Now let's eat! You look a bit thin since I last saw you!"

International Incident

After Brian returns from his race across the dessert, Ashima meets him at *The Dubai Mall* to enjoy the remainder of the day with a pleasant stroll around the largest mall in the world.

"So, where did you guys go when you made it to Abu Dhabi?" Ashima asks, as an ecstatic Brian explains the events of his day.

"We went to this crazy looking hotel called the *Yas Viceroy* for lunch. The hotel looked like it had a metal net over the top of it." Brian explains with excitement.

"Oh, wow! I love that hotel. I actually had a conference there once." She replies, familiar of the venue.

"Yeah, but the craziest thing I saw was a perfectly round building sticking out of the ground. It looked like a Frisbee or a plate or something. That was 'cray-cray'!" Brian explains, still baffled by the architectural marvel.

"The Aldar Building…yes, I'm familiar with that one too! I thought it was an eclipse when I first saw it, because it literally blocked out the sun from the view I was driving." Ashima explains, sharing his enthusiasm.

"Yeah, babe, the whole trip was crazy. I really wish you could have been there to experience that rush of being on the open road. I've never seen or experienced anything like that before in my life!" Brian gratefully explains.

"Uh huh, I knew you would enjoy all that manly car stuff. That watch looks really good on you, too!" Ashima mentions, noticing Brian is wearing the watch she bought him for the first time.

"Yeah, you really know how to make an impression, I appreciate that!" Brian leans in to kiss her before she stops him short.

"Wait, no PDA in Dubai, remember?" Ashima reminds him.

"My bad, babe! I almost forgot." Brian withdraws before turning his focus to the mall and the many people moving around him.

As they move through the mall's massive walkways, with so many American stores occupying the mall on each level, he could have very well been at a mall back home, most comparably to the King of Prussia Mall. However, you can find everything from everywhere in this mall, because next to every American store is a different store from all over the world. Most of the local stores consist of textile shops with rolls of draped Egyptian cotton of any style or print and novelty shops with everything Dubai. But, what really made the mall sparkle is the gold souk area of the mall. The store fronts were literally draped in all types of gold chains, medallions, and other unique gold pieces. From the marble floors to the massive dome skylight, the mall experience in Dubai is nothing like anything he'd experienced the U.S. He also found it interesting that never before has he seen so many beautiful Middle-Eastern women in his life. It was almost as if women were bread to be beautiful in Dubai. Even women who were under the cover of Niqab garment bear the most beautifully enchanting eyes. However, despite the number of locals in the mall, he's a bit taken aback by how many tourists shopping in the mall than Arab.

"So, babe, I'm still trying to understand some of the customs in this country. Can you help me understand a few things?" Brian asks, observing so many confusing customs in Dubai culture.

"Sure, such as...?" Ashima asks, prepared to enlighten Brian on Mid-Eastern culture.

"Such as women wearing garb, but buying jeans and regular clothes...I mean, what's the point?" Brian curiously asks.

"Well, the garb that you speak of is called a khaleeji, and the reason why women buy street clothes is because they wear it in the privacy of their home among family and other Islamic friends. The purpose behind wearing the garb is to conceal their shape and appear less lustful to men." Ashima briefly explains.

"Okay, how 'bout those towels that these men wear on their heads, what are those called?" Brian asks as several men walk in front of them with head garb.

"Those are called Ghutra's or Shemagh's. Traditionally, the garb was worn to protect their mouths and eyes from dust and sandstorms. Today they're mostly worn because of its tradition and heritage, and it keeps the sun off their neck." Ashima explains in a joking manner.

"Well, that's good to know 'cause I'm sure calling these guys towel heads all the way out here in the desert wouldn't be a good look!" Brian replies, appreciating the explanation.

"Brian…!" An appalled Ashima replies with laughter.

"What…? I'm just saying babe! But, seriously, I do have a question about something I noticed back in Philly that I've noticed here as well. I noticed that the first time I met your friends, they would avoid direct eye contact with me and I can tell some of the women out here are doing the same. So, what's that about?" Brian asks with intrigue about the gesture.

"We call it lowering our gaze. Its most commonly practiced among married women to hide their eyes in the presence of another man. A woman should only have eyes for her husband so it's a sign of respect and obedience. You see, unlike westernized Muslims women, women here are more submissive to men and have less rights. Women are not thought of as equals in Islam. They're not thought to be educated, they are taught never to walk with a man but behind him, they're not even allowed to ride in the front seat of a car with a man." Ashima clarifies as Brian nods in understanding. It's very sad, but it's Sharia Law." Ashima poignantly explains.

"Wow, it's amazing that in a country so beautiful and has so much potential, is still exercising inequality for women. It's sad!" Brian replies with disappointment.

"Yes, sadness indeed! Which is why I will never subject myself to such tyranny!" Ashima firmly avows.

After making a few stops around the mall at some of Ashima's favorite fashion stores, they head to a restaurant for some Indian Cuisine. With a few bags in hand, the blissful couple walks towards the restaurant entrance when unexpectedly a voice calls out from behind.

"ASHIMA!" A man shouts in the near distance.

They immediately turn around and to their startling surprise approaches Fahad, Manny, and Shelton casually strolling towards them. Ashima becomes terrified as the color in her face instantly fades, while adrenaline rushes through Brian's body like a freight train as he clenches his fists around the handles of the bags, anticipating the worst.

"Well, now, that's not happiness to see me is it, Ashima?" Fahad asks as they undeniably meet face to face nine thousand miles from Philadelphia. Although he found the sight of Brian and Ashima damaging to his ego,

Fahad stands relaxed in street clothing while Manny and Shelton stand behind him in full Ghutrah white Garb.

Fearful of Fahad's intentions, Ashima grasps Brian's arm and braces for the inevitable. The gesture plunges into Fahad's chest like a dagger as he stares at Brian with fury in his eyes. Brian responds by snarling his face with discontent and bad intentions as the men stare at him fiercely. The tension is so intense between them that something as simple as one word could set off a violent chain reaction.

"So, here we are… Halfway across the world and I finally catch up with you two together. What's wrong Ashima, no words? No sweet nothing to whisper in 'my' ear?" Fahad calmly asks in a menacing tone with his hands tucked in the pockets of his jeans.

"Fahad, why have you come here? What do you want?" A frightened Ashima asks.

"What do you mean, Ashima? It's a free country, right? I mean, was I not supposed to come here and find you and this infidel shopping on your dime? All I needed to see was the truth and I'm sure I just found it. Traveling halfway around the world to find you belittling yourself to fornicate with the help?" Fahad explains.

"I got your help, Punjabi!" Brian angrily sounds off trying to restrain his emotions.

"Oh, I'm sorry, did I anger you? I mean, how could a man in your position ever be angry, when you have a lady that's pampering you with the spoils of a king? For example, I take you into my home as a guest when you were wearing grandpa's hand me downs, and now you're dressed like you could almost pass for a baller. I mean, you're wearing a nice Hublot on your wrist, you're wearing nice shoes now. What are those Cavalli? Surely you can't afford these things on a delivery boy's salary right, my friend?" Fahad asks disparaging Brian as Shelton and Manny snicker at Fahad's mockery. Although Fahad's remarks are searing, Brian chooses not to give him the satisfaction of acting on emotion.

"Hmph, you know jealousy is a weak emotion, Fahad. You should try to overcome that." Brian simply replies with a condescending comment of his own.

"Jealous…of who, you? Haha…you're nothing more than a modern-day peasant that crawled out of a ditch on behalf of Ashima. My idea of you as a cook is suitable for a refugee camp at best. I wouldn't hire you clean my floors let alone prepare my meals. In fact, I don't even know why you're wasting your time. Surely this slum dog can't afford the likes of you right, Ashima?" Fahad rants as the war of words become more personal. Brian taunts Fahad by smiling instead of acting out embarrassingly.

"Fahad, you're so pathetic...always using money to compensate your ego. Why don't you put your energy into chasing Nisa instead of trying to salvage something we never had?" Ashima carelessly replies. The comment enrages Fahad as he starts to unravel.

"Are you kidding me? You choose this broken down, coward of a man over this...?!" Fahad passionately states, reaching into his pocket and holding up the ten-karat engagement ring he gave her. "...YOU CHOOSE HIM OVER ME?!" He roars, enraged by her resentment of him. Ashima stands motionless and silent, and could only stare poker face at Fahad's foolish temperament as pedestrians begin to take notice to the quarrel.

"Listen, everybody knows you got money, Akbar. Congratulations, you can afford to buy yourself a life. But, you're talkin' real greasy right now and I told you before you ain't about that life, aight! Your chick chose me! So, I suggest you pipe down with all that Chihuahua you're barking, clown before I embarrass you in front of your people!" Brian cautions, growing agitated by Fahad's constant slander.

"Haha...about what life? You don't have enough stamps in your passport to be about 'this' life, my friend. What kind of life could you possibly give her, huh? Ashima wants the finer things in life, my friend. She wants to live like a princess; not like a peasant! What could you possibly offer her you slum dog, huh? You don't know the first thing about class or anything that make her happy. You don't know anything about her. SO, STOP WASTING HER TIME!" Fahad angrily grits through his teeth with fury in his eyes.

"Are you done?" Brian heedlessly replies, undaunted by Fahad's vilifying remarks. Brian's nonchalant demeanor only fuels Fahad's anger even more since Brian is able to maintain his cool. Instead, Brian stands unchallenged and with Ashima still clinging to his arm he turns to walk away.

"AM I DONE?! AM I DONE?! I WILL NEVER BE DONE! ASHIMA...!" Fahad exclaims as he lunges at Ashima and grabs her by the wrist. Caught off guard by the aggressive act, Brian drops the bags and swiftly breaks away from Ashima's grip.

"BRIAN NO!!!" She cries out.

Now feeling threatened and no longer able to manage his restraint, Brian suddenly grows deaf to the noise around him and blacks out, punching Fahad with full force squarely in the face with a free hand, then rapidly again with the other, hitting his target flush with two solid punches. As he draws back to swing again, Ashima grabs him in desperation. In a nano second Brian reads Fahad's body language, realizing that his opponent's knees had buckled and he's falling forward. Fahad fell so quickly, instead of swinging again, Brian's natural reaction was to catch him and softly lay him to the marble flooring. The incident happens so fast, Manny and Shelton never has a chance to react.

"NOW YOU'RE DONE!" Brian erupts emotionally from the sudden adrenaline rush, before being yanked away by Ashima. The scene suddenly turns chaotic as people start to scream and run away from the horrific act they just witnessed.

"OH MY GOD! WHAT HAVE YOU DONE?! STOP THAT MAN! SOMEONE PLEASE, ARREST HIM!!! PLEASE ALLAH!!!" Manny frantically declares as he and Shelton come to the aid of their unresponsive friend.

"توقّفته, توقّفته !!!توقّفته !يساعدني ما أحد !اللل رجاء !مساعدة ما أحد"!!!

"SOMEONE HELP! PLEASE ALLAH! SOMEONE HELP ME! STOP HIM!!! STOP HIM!!!" Manny pleads yet again, this time resorting to Arabic, seeking help from the locals. At this point, Shelton is so frightened by Brian's violent behavior, he elects to get help in the opposite direction to avoid confrontation.

"LET'S GO! BRIAN PLEASE COME, BEFORE YOU GET ARRESTED! Ashima hysterically pleads as Brian reaches for the bags from the floor. Ashima tugs at Brian's shirt to hurry him off and away from the melee, as Brian continues to look back in case Manny or Shelton decides to suddenly get brave. Fortunately, Brian and Ashima were able to reach the mall exit nearby without incident. The couple immediately spots a BMW cab a man is stepping out of and quickly ducks into it with precision timing.

"إسريعا, رجاء ,فندق شاطئ جوميره ,سائقة"!

"DRIVER, JUMEIRAH HOTEL! PLEASE, QUICKLY!" Ashima frantically requests, barely able to catch her breath before turning her attention to Brian.

"BRIAN, WHAT HAVE YOU DONE?! WHY DID YOU DO THAT?! WHAT WERE YOU THINKING?! WHAT WERE YOU THINKING?!" She shouts with anger, reprimanding Brian for his actions.

"WHAT WAS I THINKING? I WAS PROTECTING YOU! THAT'S WHAT I WAS THINKING! HE PUT HIS HANDS ON YOU, SO I PUT MY HANDS ON HIM!" Brian remorselessly defends.

"BRIAN, I KNOW YOU'RE BIG AND TOUGH. BUT, VIOLENCE IS NOT ALWAYS THE ANSWER. THIS ISN'T NORTH PHILADELPHIA, BRIAN! THIS IS NOT THE U.S., YOU ARE IN DUBAI! WE COULD BE IN A LOT OF TROUBLE RIGHT NOW! DO YOU UNDERSTAND?!" Ashima passionately explains as a Dubai police car passes them with flashing lights.

Brian could read the fear in her face and at that moment, realized the severity of the situation. Nonetheless, Brian was convinced and maintained that he was within his right to defend her.

"SO, WHAT WAS I SUPPOSE TO DO? LET HIM PUT HIS HANDS ON YOU? LET HIM PUNK ME, HUH? IS THAT WHAT YOU WANTED?!" Brian answers with frustration, trying to justify his actions.

"BRIAN THIS IS NOT ABOUT BEING PUNKED! THIS IS ABOUT BEING SMART! YOU'RE ON FOREIGN SOIL!" Ashima declares as tears begin to dampen her face.

Brian's heart instantly dissolves at the sight of seeing Ashima upset for the first time. Observing her emotional state, Brian concedes to humility. His justification was no match for her vulnerability and he couldn't bear to see her hurt.

"I'm sorry babe, but had he raised his hand to you, how could I justify standing there and allowing that to happen? That's not the reaction of a man, that's the reaction of a coward." Brian calmly explains, trying to reason in her visibly shaken state.

She shakes her head in disappointment gazing out the window, reluctant to look in Brian's direction. He reaches over to embrace her hand as it lay on the seat. But, she quickly snatches it away and rolls her eyes in disgust. She reaches into her purse and puts on her shades to conceal her emotion.

"غلطة هذا كان..."

"This was a mistake…" She murmurs as she sniffles.

370

"What was that?" Brian asks, a bit agitated by her demeanor towards him.

"I said, this was a mistake, Brian. I should have never brought you out here!" She strongly reiterates.

"Oh, now this was a mistake…really?! We've been halfway around the world together, and had the time of our lives. Now all of a sudden you're talking about regret?" Brian questions, growing more annoyed of her attitude.

The rest of the ride to the hotel remained awkwardly silent. Ashima utilizes the time trying to devise a plan to get them out of Dubai without being thrown in jail. Suddenly she comes up with an idea and immediately dials her friend Vanisha for a favor.

"فنيشا, أليكوم سلم-أس".

"As-Salam Alaikum, Vanisha." Ashima says with a sniffle.

"خاطئة يكون ماذا .أشيما ,سلم أليكوم؟"

"Alaikum Salam, Ashima. What is wrong?" Vanisha asks sensing something wrong.

"كلّ يكون تناصداق من كبير المعروفة يتمنّي أن أنت أحتاج فقط أنا .لاشيء أه"

"Oh nothing. I just need you to do me the biggest favor of our friendship is all." Ashima says apprehensively.

"ماذا ؟أمن ؟عملة تحتاج أنت ؟حسنة شيء كلّ يكون ؟أنت يكدّر يكون ماذا أشيما !إلهتي أه ؟فوق يذهب يكون"

"Oh my God! Ashima what's troubling you? Is everything okay? Do you need currency? Security? What's going on?" Vanisha anxiously asks.

"أنت من يسأل أن ضخمة معروفة حقّا أنا يتلقّى أنّ غير .أنّ لاشيء ,رفض يحبّ"

"No, nothing like that. But, I really have a huge favor to ask of you." Ashima asks with urgency in her voice.

"أنا يستمع...".

"I'm listening…"

"الأمريكيّة المتّحدة الولايات تو بك يطير أن طائرة يقترض أن كلّم هو ماذا أنت أنت سيدفع فورا! أنا أعرف أنت يتلقّى أنت أسئلة, غير أنّ أنا أعد سيملأ أنت داخل ما إن أنا أحصل فرصة".

"I'll pay you whatever it cost to borrow a plane to fly back to the U.S. immediately! I know you have questions, but I promise will fill you in once I get an opportunity." Ashima pleads of her friend.

"زوّدت نويكو صيانة فقط 6غ ال وف ووت كم ,فكت إين .أشيما ,أنت ل شيء أيّ ,إطلاقا ضمن أنت ل يتأهّب طائرة طاقم يتلقّى أن وي-ريغت فون دعوة سأجعل أنا .نتكلّم نحن أنّ بما الساعة".

"Absolutely, anything for you, Ashima. In fact, the G6 just come out of maintenance and is being fueled as we speak. I'll make a phone call right away to have a flight crew ready for you within the hour." Vanisha assures her.

"أنت سددت وقت أيّ في أنا استطاع كيف !فنيشا !ليفسفر أنت, إلهتي؟"

"My God, you're a lifesaver, Vanisha! How could I ever repay you?" Ashima expresses with immense gratitude.

"نفس ال أتمّت أنت أنا يعرف ,ذلك عن فضلا .أحتاج أنا دفع ث ألّ صداقة أنت !إلا نتأ يتمّ ي ل."

"You don't! Your friendship is all the payment I need. Besides, I know you'd do the same for me." Vanisha strongly suggests of her friend.

"إطلاقا!"

"Absolutely!" Ashima concurs.

After arriving at the *Jumeirah Hotel*, Brian and Ashima frantically pack their luggage to meet the plane on the tarmac in exactly one hour.

"So, babe, what's the plan? Are we going to another hotel, or are we heading to the airport?" Brian nervously asks. Ashima hasn't said much since the incident and Brian has no idea what the conversation over the phone was about.

"No Brian, we're heading to the airport. I've already made flight arrangements, now we must leave Dubai at once!" An edgy Ashima replies as they scramble to round up their belongings. Brian doesn't want to agitate her any further so he refrains from asking any more questions.

Suddenly, Ashima's phone starts to ring as she packs the last of her things and prepare to vacate the hotel. She looks at her screen and notices Amir calling, and then Fahad calls shortly after.

"Okay, we have to go!" Ashima says in an exhausting panic as they rush to an awaiting car to take them to the airport.

Ignoring several calls from Amir and Fahad, Ashima grows more paranoid as a police car pulling over a speeding McLaren puts her even further on edge. However, with the hotel now in their rearview, her anxiety eases a bit knowing they're in route to the airport. As they both peer out the window, dusk rapidly falls on the desert city during the silent ride to the airport. Ashima looks over at Brian and feels remorse for her attitude towards him. She reaches across the seat and grasps his hand, extending an olive branch for her behavior. He responds to her gentle touch by looking back at her with accepting eyes. Although feeling a certain type of way about her attitude towards him, Brian accepts her term of endearment.

"I'm sorry. I shouldn't have blamed you for this." Ashima sincerely apologizes as a tear runs down her face. Brian pulls her to his side of the car and embraces her with a hug and a kiss.

"It's okay, babe. I'm sorry too. I should have never let him get to me like that." Brian humbly admits.

As she remains nestled in his arms for the remainder of the ride, Ashima is taken back to that blissful place of compassion with him if only for that moment, as she comfortably rubs the key charm around her neck. Just as the driver enters the exclusive gate to the tarmac, and pulls up to the private jet, Ashima receives another phone call. This time it's her mother.

"مرحبا أم!"

"Hello mother!" She answers. As her mother speaks, Ashima's mood suddenly changes again for the worst.

"أفهم أنا نعم ···أم, رفض أه! ارفض أه!"

"Oh-no! Oh-no, mommy…yes I understand!" Ashima replies, deeply disturbed by her mother's phone call.

As they exit the car to grab the bags from the trunk of the Mercedes, Brian realizes that Ashima no longer has a sense of urgency. After hanging up the phone, she lifelessly drops her hand and looks to the sky as if she needed to sob. Brian notices her hand trembling vibrantly as she holds her other hand over mouth and immediately comes to her aid.

"BABE, WHAT'S WRONG?" He yells over the ear-splitting jet noise, from the opposite side of the car, realizing that she's visibly shaken.

"BRIAN, I CAN'T LEAVE." She exclaims in a distressed, broken tone.

"WHAT?! WHAT DO YOU MEAN? THE PLANE IS HERE, BABE! C'MON, LET'S GO!" Brian replies over the jet noise. Before Ashima has a chance to reply, she notices two black cars off in the distance rapidly approaching behind Brian.

"LISTEN, WE DON'T HAVE MUCH TIME! I'LL EXPLAIN EVERYTHING TO YOU LATER WHEN YOU TOUCHDOWN BACK IN PHILLY, OKAY?!" Curious as to what Ashima is focused on over his shoulder, Brian looks back and sees the cars coming as well.

"BABE, ARE YOU SURE YOU'RE GOING TO BE OKAY?" Brian asks as she reaches to gently touch his face.

"YES, I'LL BE FINE!" She replies confidently as a single tear streams down her face. She pulls Brian in for a hug, before a prolonged passionate kiss.

"I LOVE YOU, ASHIMA!" Brian informs her, full of emotion.

"ME TOO…!" She responds staring him directly in his eyes. Brian's heart weakens to barely a beat after the reply. But, he wasn't surprised.

"I KNOW…!" He replies with a smile and then another desperate kiss.

"NOW HURRY!" She shouts with urgency as the cars draw closer.

Brian grabs his bags from the trunk and hands them to the flight attendant before he boards the jet with his carry-on. The flight crew wastes no time pulling the wheel chocks of the plane in preparation for take-off.

"Welcome aboard, Sir. Your destination is Philadelphia correct?" The co-pilot asks in a heavy British accent as Brian enters the plane.

"Yes!" Brian simply replies.

He walks to his window seat nearest to Ashima with no regard to the opulent interior of Dassault Falcon jet. Once the door is secured, Ashima takes the neck charm around her neck and kisses it before the plane starts to taxi. Brian smiles at the gesture before kissing his two fingers and pressing them against the glass right before the fast approaching cars finally arrive. Out of two Rolls Royce's jumps Fahad, Manny, and Shelton, and two other brawny looking men who realize it's already too late to stop the plane. For a brief moment, Brian and Fahad establish eye contact with fury raging between them. Then, as the plane turns opposite of them to taxi the runway, Brian gets up and looks through the window across from him to see what happens next. Fahad angrily engages Ashima as he points at the plane. As she pleads with him, pulling out her phone, Brian helplessly watches as an enraged Fahad rips it from her hand and slams it to the ground, shattering it into thousands of pieces. This would be his lasting image of Ashima before the plane lifts off and shuttles him back to the U.S.

Cupid's Broken Arrow

Back in Philadelphia, storm clouds roll in as large rain drops pelting the window has awakened Brian at 1am. Brian rests on his back as he lay in a bed staring at the ceiling in the darkness. It's been nearly three months since the international incident in Dubai, and he hasn't heard from Ashima since.

Unable to go back to sleep, he gets out of the bed and stands at the window in his boxers watching the raindrops roll down the glass like tear drops on his soul. Undoubtedly, the last three months have been the hardest that he can remember. He must have called Ashima dozens of times during the week he returned to Philadelphia, fearing something serious had happened to her. But, every call went straight to voicemail and his text messages were left unanswered. The lasting image of Fahad chastising Ashima like a child and breaking her phone often burdens him since he has no idea of what could have possibly happened afterwards.

Fearing the worst, he drove out to Fahad's house several times, waiting just outside his cul-de-sac to see if he could confront Fahad, but he never comes home. Brian does the same at Ashima's house to see if she would ever come home. But, all he found was Amir, carrying on like business as usual. With no apparent signs of Amir being upset, and no sign of Fahad, Brian wonders if Ashima was either forced or willingly submitted to being with Fahad, and has started a new life abroad. Knowing he couldn't go to Amir to ask about his daughter, Brian is only left to speculate. But, his heart is not willing to accept the senseless speculation. Filled with uncertainty, the reality of disappointment really takes hold as he's forced to wonder what tomorrow will bring.

"Hey, you coming to bed?" A tired voice calls out to him from across the room.

"Yeah, I'll be there in a minute!" Brian replies to Lexi as she awakens in his absence.

Although reeling from his emotional state, on this night while feeling down and lonely, Brian decided to pick himself up and make good on the phone number Lexi gave him at *The Fox* a while ago. In true Mojo fashion, Brian keeps it interesting by spending the night at Lexi's apartment directly across the street from Mallory's place, rather than his own. To no avail, although Lexi is very gratifying in the bedroom, mentally Brian was never there and genuinely didn't want to be there.

Since returning home, Brian has been somewhat of a recluse dealing with his depressing separation from Ashima. Aside from returning to school and work, Brian hasn't been in contact with much of anyone as he struggles to turn the page. Of the three months he's been home, he's visited Mama Ruth once, and hasn't been out with his friends at all. But, tonight, Cortez is celebrating his birthday ahead of the gathering Brandy has planned for him on Saturday. So, Brian decides to take a day off from studying and depression and joins Cortez, Marty, and Mark, another co-worker from *Apex*, for a night out with the fellas.

"HOLD UP! HOLD UP! HOLD UP! Before we break, Tez I know it's your birthday and all. But, I just want everybody to put your glasses up for my man Mojo, and celebrate him coming home after coming off his world tour! TO MY MAN, MO...?!" Marty exclaims, leading the salute to Brian. "TO MY MAN, MO!" Everyone toasts before tipping back their glasses.

"Man, I'm just glad that you're home. My boy is back!" An ecstatic Marty blurts out, tightly wrapping his arm around Brian's neck.

"It feels good to be home, Fam! I missed being here at *The Fox* running the table on y'all! But, I wish I could've taken y'all with me though. Especially, when I was whipping that Ferrari. It was like being in a real-life movie or something, man. It was crazy!" Brian explains to his friends, still in a bit of disbelief.

"Yeah, we got the pics dawg! Man...Big Ben, the Eiffel Tower, private jets, Ferrari's in Dubai...? Brother, did I ever tell you that you were my hero? I mean, look at you, dawg...fresh to 'def', looking like new money! Even that timepiece you're wearing looks European. What kind of watch is that anyway?" Cortez asks, critiquing Brian's swag.

"Man, I barely know anything about this watch. Ashima bought it for me in Paris. It's called a Hublot, but I've never heard of it." Brian nonchalantly replies, shrugging his shoulders as he reads the label off the watch face.

"A Hub what?" Cortez cluelessly replies.

"I heard of it. I saw Birdman or some celebrity buying one on WordStar. The one they had was crazy though!" Mark interjects.

"Let me check it out?" Cortez asks as Brian removes the watch and they pass it around to examine it further.

"Well, one thing we do know, messing around with ole' girl, it must have cost a couple dollars. I'll bet you know the meaning of five letter shopping now, don't you?" Marty presumes, taking a closer look at the gun metal watch with a black face.

"Yeah, well, it feels like a regular watch to me." A humble Brian replies, brushing off Marty's posh speculation.

Although, the others were excited about Brian's clothing, accessories, and his European expedition, the watch only served as a painful reminder of how things ended on such an inspiring moment in his life.

"So, what else is news? What's going on at the gig? How's Mallory, I haven't heard from her in a while?" Brian asks, seeking gossip from his friends as he changes the topic.

"Oh Mal, 'pssshhh...!' Man, Mal ain't worried about you, playa! Mal got herself a new boo thang, she good!" Cortez says, teasing his friend a bit.

"Brotha, I'm sorry to inform you, but your services are no longer needed!" Marty adds with a sneaky smirk.

"Oh, so she finally broke down and gave into Vince's B.S., huh?" Brian asks, with just a hint of jealousy.

"Vince...?! C'mon now, you should know better than that! Mal is on some next level type 'ish'!" Marty indirectly implies.

"Okay, so what we talking about then? What's good?" Brian replies, growing annoyed by his friend's apprehensive behavior as the others cackle at his irritation.

"Aight, aight...so, remember when I teased you about Mal cheating on you with a basketball player?" Marty starkly reminds him.

"Yeah, and...?" Brian replies.

"Well, sorry I put that on you brotha, 'cause your girl done messed around and got her some ball playin' brown sugar!" Marty reveals with a smirk.

"Uh-huh, a nice sexy two-guard from Temple." Cortez instigates.

"Is that right? She found herself a dude that plays ball, huh? Good for her, I'm glad that she's happy." Brian passively accepts as he leans in to make his break on the table.

"Oh, she's happy alright. There's no doubt about that!" Cortez says with laughter as the he and the other's share fist bumps and laugh as well. Distracted by his friend's amusement, he backs off from taking the shot.

"Wow, y'all acting real comical about seeing her with another dude. I mean, what's so damn funny about that?" An annoyed Brian tries to understand why his friends are geeked up about the situation.

"Dawg, I don't mean to laugh but...her friend isn't a dude...she's a dime piece! She's finer than Mallory is, and you should see the look on your face right now!" Marty struggles to explain to him, as he tries to catch his breath through his laughter of Brian's reaction. Brian stands in a haze of disbelief, dumbfounded by the breaking news.

"Well, damn! I never saw that coming? And her friend is bad like that, huh?" An intrigued Brian asks as Mark and Cortez shake their heads.

"Yeah, dawg she's your speed. I'm talkin' Skylar Diggins bad! And I heard she got game, too!" Cortez confirms as Brian stands in thought.

"Uh huh! Lick-her-license and all!" Marty instigates.

"Hmph...well, y'all know me. I don't discriminate. If she likes it, I love it! In fact, I might just love it a whole lot more now, ya dig?" Brian smiles, enjoying the idea of a threesome. On the same page as Brian, the men toast their glasses again.

"Uh-huh, sounds like a Mojoism to me." Cortez comments.

"Yo, Bruh, if you really don't care about that watch I'll be more than happy to take it off your hands." Cortez suddenly proposes.

"Why is that?" Brian asks as he looks at Cortez looking at his phone.

"Because according to what I'm looking at on my phone, that watch costs about forty-five thousand dollars." Cortez informs him as he shows

"What?! Let me see that!" Marty interjects grabbing the phone from Cortez. "Uh huh, see I knew it! Trips to Paris, London, and Dubai...ole girls got money longer that Broad Street." Marty candidly replies.

"Do you realize what you've done? You just restored hope for the fellas with a bus pass...that's what you've done!" An animated Marty explains as the fellas break out in laughter.

After a great night of catching up and celebrating good times with his friends, suddenly, in the midst of laughter and enjoyment, Marty notices Brian standing off to himself, appearing to be troubled in thought. With concern for his friend, as Cortez and Mark play the table, Marty sneaks away to investigate the worry of his friend.

"Well, it doesn't take rocket science to know what that look means. Love is kicking your ass, isn't it?" Marty assumes as Brian watches him walk over.

"Naw...I'm good man! I'm just happy to be back at *The Fox*, that's all, really!" Brian replies, denying his true feelings.

"Well, even if that were true, which clearly it isn't...then why are you standing over here like a five-year-old that just dropped his ice cream on a dirty rug?" Marty counters, challenging his friend's honesty.

"Naw, Marty I'm good, really! I'm just over here thinking about some assignments due before finals and graduation, that's all!" Brian answers while stirring his favorite Crown and cran with his finger before taking a sip.

"You can't even look me in my eyes and tell me that with a straight face. But, 'I'ma' let you breathe, 'cause I can see you're in your feelings right now. But, when the time is right, I'm sure you'll be willing to open up about it." Marty bluntly replies. Brian gasps in laughter.

"You're right! I'm going through some things, right now. But, I'm good Marty, aight! Your boy is good! I just need to figure some things out, that's all." Brian reluctantly confesses.

"Aight brotha, well listen, I'm about to give Tez an ass whoppin' on the table for his birthday, then I'ma smoke one of these Donnie Chulos with him and Mark, before I take my ass home." Marty explains.

"A Donnie who?" Brian asks with a confused look.

"Cigars man! Grown man business! My cousin sends these to me from Virginia. They're real smooth. Here, take one...this should really mellow you out." Marty explains, handing Brian one of several plastic wrapped cigars he takes from his pocket.

"Thanks! I never smoked a cigar before, but if I can smoke a hookah, then I guess this will be my first cigar." Brian replies.

"Anytime Brotha...let me know if you need anything. You know I'm here for you!" Marty assures him.

"Cool, I appreciate that, Bruh! Look umm...tell Tez and Mark 'I'ma' catch up with them later, aight! 'I'ma' head to the crib and try to figure some things out, man." Brian replies, showing obvious signs of his emotions.

"No doubt!" Marty complies, giving Brian a pound before he makes his exit. On his way out, Brian stops at the bar and settles the tab for his friends before his departure.

Later in the evening stretched across his bed with textbooks open, Brian listens to a soulful music playlist as he attempts to focus for his exams on Friday, scribbling dietary notes with his felt tip pen. However, his mood is too poignant to focus on his studies as episodes of his time with Ashima persistently haunt him. As hard as he tries to mask his emotions and memories of her, he knows she left a mark on him and he can't remove the lipstick from his soul. For the first time in his life, Brian realizes that his heart has beat for someone other than himself, and he may have lost the one person that was able to reach him that way, forever.

Feeling the need to digress, he gets out of bed, and walks to the bathroom sink to clear his thoughts. He tries to wash away the affliction from his face as he takes a lasting look at himself in the mirror. But, his mind is so despondent that he doesn't feel the connection to the face in the reflection he sees. So, instead of scribbling notes from his textbooks, he sits at the edge of his bed, takes a blank sheet of paper and spontaneously inks it with raw emotions. Uncertain of where to even begin, he takes in a deep sigh and writes…

Ashima,

Since the last time we spoke, my life has been nothing more than a meaningless empty shell of itself. It feels like an eternity since the last time I physically felt the soft caress of your touch. Words simply can't describe how sick I've been since leaving without you in Dubai. Where are you? How are you? Is life treating you kind? ~~Are you happier without me?~~ Are you happy? These are the healing questions I need answers to as I try to mend the broken pieces of my heart. I need to know, I need to trust that you're okay. I want to touch you. I want to feel you in my arms right now! I'm missing your love. Even though you never admitted it, I know you love me. I can barely make it through the day without my heartbeat falling flat a time or two. Every now and then I cry a little in the dark because I miss the only person I've ever truly ~~cared about~~ loved. And I'm not ashamed to admit that. The notion of you and I was never temporary for me. It was forever. I'm really ~~fuc'd up, scewed up,~~ messed up out here without you. Sorry, for the grammar and mistakes I keep making. The hand that writes this letter sweeps the paper clean from the many times I've erased my thoughts to try and get it right. But, there's no words I can put to paper that can truly capture how I truly feel. This written letter is a true testament of the worst nonphysical pain I've ever felt. Ashima, you're my air. I love you like I breathe, and I'm suffocating without you. I'm not mad that you're not here with me. I'm just struggling to understand why. Anyway, ~~I wish I hope~~ I pray that your life is going very well. I hope the pillow you rest your head on at night is the softest. I hope that the sun that kisses your face in the morning is the brightest. And every now and then, I hope pleasant thoughts of me, or pleasant thoughts of us come to mind every now and then. I hope...

Forever Love,

Brian

P.S. My graduation is on Friday. Just thought you should know...

381

And at the end of all the emotion and feelings poured into the letter, he realizes that it's all for nothing, as his sadness suddenly turns into rage. "F****CKKK!!!" He screams in frustration as he balls up the letter and pitches it across the room.

Even Still

Nearly a year later, Brian and all of his friends and family are gathered under one roof, in a dining room filled with well-wishers, laughter, and celebration, and there is plenty of reason to celebrate. Tonight, marks the grand opening of Brian's restaurant *Gritz Soul Bistro*, and the line to get in is wrapped around the corner.

As it turns out, between the money remaining in his account and turning a handsome profit from the watch Ashima bought him, Brian was not only able to put a nice down payment on a house in his favorite part of Philadelphia, Chestnut Hill, but he also secured himself as a full partner with Rick and Bryce as well. With the help of some old friends in the restaurant industry helping them along the way, they managed to acquire and renovate a 3,200 square-foot storefront at the corner of 4201 Main Street in the exclusive Manyunk section of the city. The location is brilliant and the concept is fitting for the affluent and eclectic patronage that Manyunk attracts.

The interior décor of the venue is much more contemporary than Brian had envisioned in contrast to its quaint exterior. The first thing that commands notice upon entering the modernly designed restaurant, is the massive wallscape images garnished dishes the three chefs prepared for large canvas photos covering the entire left wall. The dishes were all prepared on white square plates and one red plate which gave contrast to the other photos, accenting the bistre hue of the restaurant. Armless sofas of the same bistre hue line the walls of the dining area with rustic wood tables forward of them. Taupe colored lounge chairs sit opposite of the sofas, adding more contrast to the seating. Recessed and track lighting adds to the contemporary touch of the décor, but nothing was more commanding than the large gold spheres which hung from the ceiling, suspended over the bar. However, one of the best amenities the restaurant has to offer is the tall standing outside glass that ran nearly from ceiling to floor and served as a bi-fold opening for the warmer months, giving the customers an outdoor feel without actually being there. Brian was humbled and owed his friends a great deal of gratitude for what they've been able to accomplish.

The opening also drew the attention of local media, magazine writers, and a representative of the Zagat survey for the restaurants unique grits with everything dishes. Brian stands proudly with his partners in front of the custom *Gritz Bistro* backdrop, in a studio-lit corner of the restaurant taking photos with various guests and posing for the media. Tonight, he dressed unassuming with his relaxed jeans draped over his brown hard bottom shoes, crisp button-down shirt, sports jacket, loose fitting tie and a short-brimmed fedora to bring the assemble all together. With a slight variation in style, Rick and Bryce were modestly dressed the same way. This was undoubtedly the proudest moment of Brian's young adult life. After taking a moment to answer questions, entertain a few folks, and meet Rick and Bryce's family and friends, Brian manages to eventually break away to check on his own guests.

Easing his way through the thick crowd, he acknowledges the many congrats along the way. In the process of excusing himself, he takes a fleeting look out the window and notices all the customers in line waiting to get in. As he browses the line of patrons, he was forced to pause and do a double take, focusing on this one particularly beautiful young woman conversing among her two friends. She was a dark haired, small figured, beautiful Arab woman whose features were all too familiar. Her image was momentarily haunting, because Brian had almost mistaken her beauty for the likes of Ashima. But, after closer examination, he realizes that the light was hitting her just right and discovers that she was just another pretty face in the venue. However, his heart nearly sunk into the pit of his stomach from the mistaken identity. In spite of this, nothing would have been more gratifying than knowing that the woman in line was actually her. Nearly a year later and Brian is still trying to surpass the pain of losing perhaps the best thing that has ever happened to him.

He closes his eyes to a three count to bring his focus back into the restaurant in an attempt to elude any thoughts reminding him of Ashima. Any instance reminiscent of her would dampen the spirit of celebrating this festive occasion. And on this one night, he would rather enjoy the evening without the painful memories of his 'ex'.

"Yo, 'B', this venue is crazy son, for real! Congrats man! I'm really proud of you!" An excited Marty says boisterously over the music and crowd noise with Cortez at his side.

"Thanks fellas, it's much appreciated!" Brian replies greeting each of them with strong pounds and bear hugs.

Brian couldn't help but cheese from ear to ear, knowing that there was so much love and support in the room. The tingling feeling of success and relevance reverberated throughout his entire body. He had every reason to feel accomplished, and yet he couldn't feel complete because there was still a part of him that fell void.

As the room moves around him, Brian stands momentarily with his back to the bar, looking aimlessly out at the crowd. He takes in the ambient noise of clanging dishes in the kitchen, the sound of chatter as it resonates throughout the dining room, and the flash of photography capturing every moment. Suddenly, the woman from the window has finally made it inside and breezes past him, leaving the trail of an all too familiar scent in her wake.

"Wow! Moiselle Chanel?! That's an odd coincidence... first the resemblance, and now the exact same scent?" Brian ponders as the fragrance triggers his nostalgia. His eyes follow the young attractive woman sporting open toe heels and a classy red cocktail dress to the bar. Although she wasn't who he'd mistaken her for, at this point her presence has made it quite apparent that he must engage her.

"Hey, hold on a minute y'all. I'll be right back!" Brian says to his friends as he doubles back to investigate his intriguing interest. There was no genuine logic as to why Brian felt inclined to address the woman. But, his intuition led him to further inquiry. Eventually, he catches up to her at the bar and stands to her right as she places her order.

"Three appletinis', please!" The woman requests in the most delicate voice.

"Very well, Ma'am...and will you be having another Mr. Jones?" The bartender attentively asks, mindful of the presence of his boss.

"Umm...actually I'll just have what the lady is having. It sounds like a good choice. Oh, and uh...you can add her order to mine as well. It's on the house." He confidently replies, directing his attention towards her with the charming gesture.

"Moiselle right?" Brian implies as an icebreaker.

"I beg your pardon?" The woman replies in confusion.

"Your fragrance...Moiselle by Chanel, right?" He rephrases.

"Oh, yes...actually it is Mademoiselle. One of your favorites I take it?" She replies taken aback by his knowledge of the fragrance.

"Yeah, umm...it reminds me of someone very special I knew once. It's a beautiful fragrance." Brian details, admiring her beauty to the likes of Ashima.

"Why thank you so much Mr...?"

"Jones, Brian Jones." He swiftly answers her as he extends his hand.

"Pleased to meet you Brian, I'm Samiya." She says shaking his hand pleasurably.

"Samiya... that's pretty. I've never heard that name before." Replies with a charming smile.

"Well, thank you again. I appreciate your flattery." She starts to blush.

"So, what brings you out tonight? Did you hear about the grand opening or are you just passing through?" Brian asked trying to make good conversation while admiring her beautiful features and aromatic scent.

"Well, my friend's and I were just getting off from work at the boutique down the street and neither of us had dinner yet. So, we saw the line outside and decided to check out this place to see what it had to offer...maybe have a few drinks?" She explains.

"Okay, well I'm glad you came, and I hope you take full advantage of the menu selection. I'm sure you'll find all of the food on the menu good here." Brian subliminally replies to measure her reaction.

"Oh, do you work here or something?" She asks curiously.

"Well, actually I'm one of the owners." Brian reveals as he watches her stunned reaction.

"Oh, wow! Congratulations on the grand opening! I'm sure you'll do well here in Manyunk, most businesses do." She replies as the bartender places the three drinks in front of her, and then another for Brian.

"I sure hope so. Maybe you can stop by again during your lunch break and we could have lunch or something?" Brian proposes, trying to bait her interest.

"I'm sorry Brian, I'm married." Samiya politely declines with a pouty face.

"Damn, I knew it!" Brian thought as he suddenly takes notice to the nice cluster on the woman's ring figure.

"That's ok. You're more than welcome to come back at any time…and please, bring your husband." He responds trying to mask the utter disappointment.

"Okay then…maybe I will. It was nice meeting you, and thanks again for the drinks." She gratefully replies, handling the three drinks as she left the bar.

Stunned by her rebuttal and sudden departure, Brian couldn't muster a reply. He was so impacted by the reply that he even lost his charm for a moment. Not even offering to help her take the glasses to her friends. He simply raised his glass in salute fashion and grins. Although he wasn't expecting anything more than how the scenario played out, her unattainable status still managed to deliver a glancing blow to his ego.

His eyes follow her curvy red shape until she disappears into the crowd. Not only was her disclosure revealing, but sobering as well. Suddenly his elated mood was over shadowed by a cloud of disappointment. In his mind, living in this very moment of possibility, if the situation was different perhaps she would have been that one woman who could have shaped his heart all over again. The night was supposed to be reserved for him to celebrate his greatest accomplishment in life. Yet, a painful aura of anguish has claimed him once again.

"Yo, Bruh…what's good with you?" Cortez asks with concern as he and Marty suddenly emerge with beers in his hand, offering one to Brian.

"Yeah, I'm great…never better! Why, what's good?" Brian resiliently replies, accepting the bottle of brew and while trying to maintain a façade of happiness.

"I don't know, you tell us brotha. Tez said you're over here looking disconnected from the rest of the room, so we came over to see what's good? And…you're over here baby sittin' an apple martini? Dawg, I know you don't even rock like that." Marty adds with concern taking a swig from his bottle. Brian smiles and lowers his head with useless denial, before taking a swig from the beer they gave him.

"Hmph…you're right...BARTENDER! Let me get three shots of that Don tequila, please!" Brian exclaims over the crowd noise.

"…And what was up with shorty in the red dress? We saw you over here trying to holla!" Cortez adds exposing Brian's motive for going astray. Brian responds with a brief chuckle, and replies in a subtle tone.

"I mean, you seen her. She was a nice eye catcher, right?" Brian replies.

"Mmm...hmm...an eye catching jawn that just so happens to look like your old flame?" Marty implies as the shots were poured and lined up at the ready. Brian reaches for a shot, and holds it up among his friends before responding to Marty's inquisition.

"Yeah, well, that flame is extinguished and long forgotten, so...ON TO THE NEXT...?" Brian exclaimed with an exuberant smile awaiting his friends to bring their glasses up.

"...ON TO THE NEXT!" The fellas loudly concur, toasting the shots before throwing them back as they normally would.

Once the shot glasses came down and they tap the bar countertop, so did Brian's exuberance and energy. He chased the tequila with another swig of his beer, but a buzz simply wasn't enough to maintain an elated mood. Feeling a bit shallow, Brian could no longer match the enthusiasm in the room. The burden of Ashima has manifested itself, and Brian is slipping into that dark void yet again.

"Ayo man, I gotta break out." Brian mutters as the trio stands at the bar.

"Break out! What the hell you mean, break out? It's your grand opening and you're about to bounce?!" Cortez contests in confusion.

Suddenly, in a room full of people, Brian felt completely empty. He stood expressionless and stared directly ahead as if nothing was there. His mood swiftly declined from zero to sadness in a matter of one beautiful resemblance.

"Ayo, you good, 'B'?" Marty asked with concern.

"Yeah, man...I'm just a little lost right now. But, I'm cool." Brian assures Marty.

"Aight then..." Marty trusts, giving Brian a strong pound and warm embrace before he left the bar.

"What just happened...?!" Brian faintly hears Cortez asking as he walks off, leaving Cortez standing dumbfounded.

The fellas watch as Brian walks over to a few other people and a few tables, offering gratitude and apologies for his sudden departure. His body language spelled alarm among his friends and people were left with the impression of concern and disappointment. However, the immediate need to clear his thoughts and refocus was the only coping mechanism that he could muster at the time. The shades of Ashima were too vivid, and his heart has simply had enough.

As Brian maneuvers his way towards the exit through the thick of the crowd, he happens to notice Samiya and her radiant dress yet again. In a sense of slow motion, as he moves towards the door, his eyes helplessly lock onto her while she's distracted by conversation. As much as he tries to avoid the bane thoughts of Ashima, somehow, he manages to find a moment of bliss in staring at Samiya. Suddenly her eyes veer to his direction. Their eyes connect for only a nanosecond before Brian is forced to look her off, and then the moment was gone as Brian approaches the door.

"Wow!" Is the only thought that came to mind as he makes his exit.

At very cool forty-four degrees, Brian flips up the collar of his sports coat to brave the brisk chill in the air as he walked out to the curbside. With his beer still in hand and no regard for the law, he aimlessly ponders his next move.

"Damn! I've gotta get outta here!" He says as he looks back and realizes he's still in plain view of the patrons inside. As he took another swig from his bottle, Brian sees a cab dropping off passengers at the next corner.

"YO, TAXI!" He quickly hails trying to summons the driver with a waving gesture. But, to no avail, the service light on the cab goes dark as the driver zooms right past him. However, he sees another cab approaching from the opposite direction, with barely enough time to lower his hand.

"YO!" He summons as yet another taxi passes him by. Only this time the cabby was with passengers.

"Damn these cabs!" He grows frustrated trying to make a fast getaway.

So, he starts his pace down Main Street in search of another taxi as thoughts of Ashima begin to rush in. Unconscionably, Brian found himself in a place that he'd once again, much rather not be. He wanders aimlessly as flashbacks of their time together interrupts his psyche. Resiliently, he tried to escape memories of her. But, he couldn't avoid the obvious. In a not so distant place in his heart, Brian yearns and waits for her still; still looking for her to make her grand reappearance; still waiting for her to restore the love that was painfully lost; or with sheer disappointment, still trying to find closure to a very dark chapter of his life.

At one point, he casually drifts down the street in a haze of incoherence, wandering Main Street dazed and confused, and in a ball of perplexed thought. However, the sudden sensation of cold rain droplets ricocheting his face redirects his focus.

Brian tips his bottle to finish what was left of his beverage, when he notices another cab coming down the street. Brian quickly swallows the bottle down to the suds, tosses the bottle underneath a parked car and hails for the oncoming cab.

"YO, TAXI!" He aggressively yells to the passing cab. The cab driver acknowledges Brian and pulls to the side to wait for him.

"What's up brother, where to…?" The bearded Caucasian driver asks.

"Drive man… just, just drive." Was all Brian could manage, in the midst of frustration and despair. The driver complies and rushes off. Brian slouches in the back-seat thumbing through the many text messages blowing up his phone.

"Whatever's bothering you, you'll bounce back from it"

"Yo, where did u go?"

"Did I just see you just leave? Call me when you get a chance." The text messages read as he skims through a few of them.

Brian sits lazy in the back of the cab, melancholy with his head resting on the window and his eyes fixed to the ominous sky. Rain drops began to blur his window, which metaphorically could have been his own tears falling with patterns of sadness. As the cabbie takes East River Drive to the direction of downtown, Brian just happens to look up at the driver's rearview mirror and notices that the cabby's eyes are fixed on him. But, the cabby didn't shy away from Brian's sudden awareness. Periodically the driver's eyes would continue to alternate from the road to the rearview as if he wanted to engage Brian with a question.

"Excuse me, Buddy? I'm not sure exactly where you're headed. But, if you don't mind, I was headed downtown to meet up with some friends at the bus terminal for some coffee if that's alright with you?" The cabby politely asks.

"Naw cabby, I'm good with that. In fact, here…here's a twenty spot just in case you think I'm weird, or I'm looking for a free ride because I jumped in the back of your cab with no destination." Brian offers, ensuring the driver that his intentions were good.

"Trust me brother, whatever your story is I'm sure I've heard it all before." The cabby replies as he reaches for the money Brian hands to him.

Brian replies with a smirk as he sinks back into the seat with a sense of emotional exhaustion, listening to the jazz playing from the cabby's radio as it plays on. Overwhelmed with emotion, he opens his phone and reminisces as he flicks through his photos of him and Ashima, like the selfie they took in NYC on New Year's Eve. Then he flicks to the one they took in atop of the London Eye overlooking the London night sky. Laughing to himself, he's tickled about the one they took on the patio in Paris before leaving for the runway show. Finally, he smiles as he flicks his phone to the selfies they took on the Lock Bridge and Dubai.

"Damn... good times!"

Suddenly the cab goes silent as the songs playing on the radio ends with only the intermittent sound of wiper blades clearing the windshield. As he sits in thought, thumbing through more photos, another song began to play. The familiar solemn intro instantly threw him deeper into his feelings, as the song "Far away" by Marsha Ambrosius takes over his emotions. The irony of the song playing, seemed so cliché and empathetic to his mood.

Caught up in his feelings, he flips back to his favorite picture they took on the London Eye Ferris wheel with the beautiful image of Big Ben and all of Westminster. It reminded him of perhaps the single most surreal and blissful moment of his life. Brian expanded the image to get a good look at Ashima, which provokes a heavy tear to fall from his eye onto the screen of his phone.

"Damn Brian! How did you mess this up?" He struggles to comprehend.

As he flips to the picture of her standing in her favorite store, the Hermes flagship store in Paris, he remembers the glow she had that day and how she randomly said, *"Brian, Hermes and my French cappuccino... life couldn't be more fulfilling."* It was moments like that, that made him feel like they would last forever.

Brian looks out at the Schuylkill River to his right, and vividly envisions that euphoric day he carried Ashima on his back on the day it snowed at the Art Museum, while they amused each other like children at play.

"That goose got lucky that day!" He thinks, trying to find humor in the memories.

He sighs in sadness as he places his face in his right hand to hide himself from the hurt. But, to no avail, with the fear of not knowing and with no closure, he knew that he was in for an extensive healing process. The rain showers suddenly lift as the driver reaches a stop light just past Boat House Row at the rear of the Art Museum.

"Ayo, this is good right here, man." Brian alerts the driver as he eventually rounds the corner to the Art Museum stairs.

"Okay Buddy, we're good." The driver replies, even though his meter reads $22.35.

"Naw, here's another ten spot for a cup of coffee and a danish or something?" Brian counters, pressed on leaving the cabby a tip.

"Well, thanks, buddy. I certainly appreciate that. And uh, listen...I've seen that look in a man's face many times before. I know you're going through something and it's probably with your misses, I'm thinking? But, let me explain something to ya...if it's meant to happen, it will happen. But, it will happen on his time, not on your time. His time is always the right time. We're the ones that's always in a rush to choose our own destiny. But, the man upstairs is always in control, okay Buddy? Take care, and have a good night, and good luck with your situation." The cabby says offering his heartfelt advice as he gestures pointing to the heavens above. Brian acknowledges the cabby with several head nods as the man spoke.

"Aight man, thanks! I appreciate the advice." Brian replies as he closes the door and raps on the trunk twice.

Brian steps away from the cab, heeding the man's advice and runs with the possibility that he may actually be right. He looks to the top of the museum stairs and thought about the last time he was there; he was having an intimate conversation with Ashima and claiming her as his own. Tonight, perhaps he'll make the assent to the top once again, this time in search of the answers to restore that intimate feeling. Feeling the effects of the elements, he gives his collar a tug as he inhales a lung chilling breath of night air and let out a sigh of despair in the palms of his hands to warm them up before taking to the first tier of stairs.

"Wow... this seems like a whole lot more stairs when you're not doing a Rocky re-enactment." He thinks as he takes his time touching every stair on his way to the top.

Once he reaches the top of the stairs, He turns to face the beautifully lit Philadelphia skyline just as he did, with Ashima by his side the last time he was there. He stands humble in the same proverbial spot, with his hands in his pockets asking himself the unanswered question, "is she 'the one' that got away?" From there he zones out and listened to his conscience as so many questions riddle his head with thought:

"How in the hell did we get here? How did things ever come to this? How is it that the most significant night of my life, also be one of the saddest? I wonder... does she ever miss me? Does she think about me? Does she dream about me? Am I a fool, or just being foolish? How could I ever love again, after having my first run at it end like this? Maybe this is just payback for the many hearts I've stole? Lord, if you're listening, I could really use your help with this one!"

But, before he could get too far into his feelings, another cab pulls in front of the museum with its hazards flashing. Brian found it to be an odd distraction, despite getting out of a cab himself just minutes ago. He watches as the cab sits for a brief moment before the passenger emerges from it. Being a considerable distance away from the street, he couldn't see exactly who the person was. But, he immediately notices that the person is wearing the same sweater Marty wore tonight.

Brian stands stuck for a while trying to figure out who the person is as he made his way up the stairs towards him. The person never lifts his head until about a third of the way to the top, and then he says something.

"I knew your ass would end up here tonight!" Marty exclaims, walking up the final flight of stairs with an open bottle of champagne.

"Yeah, I must of forgot to turn off my GPS tracker. How in the hell did you know that I was here?" Brian asks, thrilled to see Marty coming to join him. Brian is exploding with elation, knowing that his friend left the grand opening to seek him. He knew Marty was good people, but his presence couldn't have been more valuable than now.

"Dude, I saw it all in your face...I knew something was up and I had a pretty good idea of what it was." Marty replies, giving Brian a pound and a hug, as he joins him at the top of the stairs.

"What about Kerry? Did you leave her at the party?" Brian asks with concern.

"Naw, she was ready to go because she's gotta work in the morning. She was in the cab too. I just told her if I saw you out here, to drop me off before she headed home. She said congrats, by the way. She loved the food, too." Marty replies chewing heavily on a piece of gum.

"That's what's up man! I really appreciate that!" Brian replies as Marty puts the champagne bottle down and has a seat atop of the stairs. As Brian joins him, the two sit silent for a moment, taking in the view of the city.

"She's beautiful, isn't she...?" Marty randomly mentions as the night skyline shines bright before them.

"Who Kerry? She aight, y'all look great together." Brian replies a bit confused by Marty's question.

"The city fool, I'm talking about the skyline." Marty clarifies, looking at Brian strangely.

"Ha! Oh yeah, Philly? Greatest city in the world, Man. I love this raggedy town." Brian replies like the proudest son of the city.

"Yeah, you would know Mr. Passport Stamps. How many are you up to, now?" Marty facetiously asks.

(Sigh) "Man, I don't even remember. But, Europe is definitely a trip through." Brian smiles as he reflects for a moment.

"Is that right...?" Marty replies waiting to hear more.

"Oh yeah, if the devil really wears Prada, it was definitely pleasure vacationing in hell." Brian jokes.

"Oh, is that right?" Marty replies as they laugh at about the silly comment.

"Yeah...that's right." Brian replies in a more solemn tone, as the reflection emotionally takes him back to where he was before Marty arrived.

"You miss her, don't you?" Marty asks taking notice to Brian's sudden mood swing.

"Best thing I ever had, Marty." Brian replies with no hesitation.

"Uh-huh...cupids got his foot all in your ass, don't he?" Marty teases.

"Humph" Brian smirks as he avoids eye contact.

"Mmm...Hmm...I told you! Life is good when you get to sex all these chicks with no feelings attached. But, the minute love drags its ass into it, the rules of engagement completely changes." Marty reminds Brian as his err of caution hits home.

"Yeah, you were right Marty. It's like...I'm feeling things I've never felt before, things I never knew I was capable of feeling. I mean, I'm still trying to figure out how a woman who claims to be that much in love can just up and bounce like that? Where's the love in that? Where did I go wrong? What could I have possibly done that could have made this woman just abandon everything we had?" Brian mulls over, putting himself at fault.

"Let me explain something to you brotha, if it was meant to happen, she would be here by God's design, and that's not to say that it won't ever happen. But, if it ever does, it's going to happen in God's time, not in ours. Just like this restaurant…God saw fit for this opportunity to happen for you right now. Not because you asked for it a year, two years ago. Do you know how many twenty and thirty-year experienced cooks that are out there still struggling to hold on to a sous chef position? There are guys out there that have been doing this all their life, that dream about what you've accomplished. Favor ain't fair Bruh, but it's damn sure shining on you right now…ya know? Think about how good life has treated you all the time…graduating from culinary school, owning your own restaurant at only twenty-nine years old, you're a handsome young man who's probably slept with damn near every woman in the city except for my wife…"

"C'mon man!" Brian interrupts taking exception to Marty's last comment.

"What…?" Marty smirks, trying to keep a straight face before continuing.

"Anyway, you're about to move into a really nice crib in Chestnut Hill of all places. You dated a beautiful and rich Middle Eastern woman, who gave you all the spoils of a King. You've been around the world Bruh, literally! I'm forty-three years old, and the only place I've been abroad is the Bahamas', St. Thomas, and Jamaica and that was on a cruise. I mean, you're blessed, brotha…be blessed!" Marty says as he gives Brian a fist bump.

"Hmph, you know it's that's funny, the cabby that dropped me off mentioned the same thing, about how things happen in God's time and not our time." Brian replies, sharing the odd coincidence.

"So, you were having taxi cab confessions on your way over here or what?" Marty jokingly replies.

"Naw, he could just tell that a brotha was going through a little something on the way over that's all. I just feel like somewhere along the way, we lost sight of loves true direction. I just need to restore that feeling, ya know?" Brian replies.

"Oh, I know! I knew you were broken a long time ago. You haven't been the same since you came back. I mean, you've definitely changed a bit, man. Honestly, I think she broke you, Bruh. She damaged your heart. You thought that you would never get bit by the bug and I told you, it's real when cupid catches up to you. But, you can't stay down, Bruh. You're like a butterfly, fresh out of the cocoon. This experience has made you struggle to fly. But, all you have to do is spread your wings and be new again, brotha. Besides, you're going to meet new women everyday over at your new place, and you'll have plenty of options to replace ole girl, successful ones too." Marty rationalizes.

"Hmm…you really like the spot, huh?" Brian curiously asks.

"C'mon, Bruh…you were built for this. It may not seem like it, but you're in your zone right now, enjoy the fruits." Marty optimistically suggests.

"I'm trying, but can you ever imagine things getting so bad between you and Kerry that she didn't even show up for your graduation from college? Dawg, she didn't come to my graduation…or hit me up for my birthday. Not even a text message? I mean, it's been nearly a year since we last spoke." A frustrated Brian expresses.

"I know it's hard, but what do you expect?" Marty replies with a realistic approach.

"At this point, the simple sound of her voice would be enough closure; enough to know that she was doing okay and life is treating her good, Bruh." Brian sorely replies.

"I hear you, and no doubt, that's crazy! I mean, I'm not gonna lie, that would have been hard for me to get past as well. But, from the womb till this very moment, from Kerry to my own mother, aunts, and grandmother, if it's one thing that I've learned about women, it's this; women are very complex creatures. They can be very hard to read at times and just when you think that you've got them figured out, they'll change on you like wind direction. Especially the ones like ole girl, the educated and independent ones who find more pleasure in fingering themselves than the interest of a man. Truthfully, she might be the mantis kind. The type that mates with the male then bites his head off, and guess what…you look like a fine meal, brotha!" Brian shakes his head in amusement of the analogy as Marty continues to grant him wisdom.

"Money entitles women like her to get what she wants when she wants it. I mean, let's face it, if you had that kind of money, you'd be the same way. Hell, you're as broke as me and you've been getting away with it for this long." Marty adds with sarcasm.

"True…and I was just sitting here thinking that I'm probably paying for all the women I've ever wronged." Brian openly admits.

"Yeah, well…karma's a bitch! But, that doesn't usually catch up to you until your first daughter is all grown up and she wants to go out on her first date, ya dig? Trust me, I keep my shotgun off safety for dudes just like you, looking for another notch on the ole belt, ya feel me?" Marty clowns, playfully grabbing Brian by the shoulder. Brian laughs along, despite not finding much humor in Marty's comic relief.

"Although I hate to admit it, all I think about is that conversation that we had at The Fox, and I remember you telling me how dangerous this love thing really is. But, obviously I wasn't trying to even go there at the time." Brian confesses.

"Listen, you got a taste of what love has to offer and you weren't prepared for that sweet taste to have a bitter side to it. But, the next time you bite into that fruit, you'll be more than prepared for what it has to offer, ya feel me?" Brian nods with acceptance to yet another profound analogy from his friend.

"So, now what, black man? What's next? You ready to start a new chapter in your life or what?" Marty bluntly inquires.

"That's exactly what I'm trying to figure out Marty. But, one thing's for certain, I'm glad you came out to find ya' boy and drop some wisdom on me brotha. You brought clarity to a lot of unanswered questions." Brian expresses with sincere gratitude as Marty takes a sip from the champagne bottle before passing Brian the bottle to offer him a taste.

"Hey, let me ask you a question, man." Brian suddenly asks as he's once again while captivated in thought.

"What's up?" Marty quickly replies.

"What is love?" Brian asks straightforward.

"What is love?! Seriously, you want my version of it?" Marty asks taken aback by the question.

"Yeah, you're a family man. I'm curious to know how you view it." Brian reiterates.

"Hmph…okay, do you want Webster's version, or you want the fifteen years married with two kid's version?" Marty sarcastically asks.

"Just come with it, man! Lay it on me!" Brian anxiously replies.

"Hmph…aight then. What is love? Well, I can assure you it's the most powerful energy in the universe if you believe in it. But, it's also the most misunderstood. Love is that strong mental desire that you have for someone or something that you just got to have. You gotta have your mind set on the right frequency, in order to understand this thang, we call love, ya dig? But, when experience it you have to be careful. 'Cause just as fast as love becomes your best friend, it can also become your worst enemy. Love makes people do the strangest things. People kill for love, people die for love. Love will make you do things you never knew you were capable of. And just when you think you've got it all figured out, love gives you a reality check and your world comes crashing down on you. Honestly, I'm still not sure what love really is. To me it's an anomaly, it's dangerous as hell, and it should only be used when you truly mean it and you're willing to deal with the consequences that go with it. That's what love is. That's what love does." Marty wholeheartedly explains.

"Yeah…that's about right." Brian agrees quantifying Marty's definition to his own life experience.

"Honestly Bruh, I know this whole Ashima thing is weighing heavy on you and all, but know this…the problem with that guy she was dealing with is the same thing that's wrong with every other athlete, movies star, rapper or whatever clown with money. Every woman wants them and at some point, success over shadows humility. That's why she chose you, Bruh. She wanted to be with someone who had an imagination, someone who still appreciates the simple things in life, someone with a personality who could make her happy without throwing a dollar sign in her face. That's how a dude with nothing can take a woman away from a man who has everything. That's a great quality to have, Brian. Don't ever lose that, Bruh!" Marty

"No doubt, man thanks! I appreciate that." Brian expresses with gratitude.

"C'mon man, let's get out of here!" Marty says as he stands to his feet. "You know we miss you at the gig. It hasn't been the same without you, Bruh." Marty regretfully expresses as they make their way down the stairs to flag down a cab.

"Well, if things just get too crazy over there at Apex, I'll be sure to save you a spot in the kitchen for you. Maybe you can bring some of that

Nawlin's flavor over there and expand the menu." Brian seriously offers, trying to bring his friend's spirits up.

"Oh, trust me, Gritz ain't ready for the Bayou, baby! I'll burn that place down with some real southern cookin!" Marty counters in his southern twang.

"Yeah, that's what I'm afraid of! How about a nice mop job, instead?" Brian jokes.

"Yeah, okay, mop job!" Marty replies with laughter.

"TAXI!"

As Fate Would Have It

CHAPTER TWENTY-FOUR

A few months after the grand opening, *Gritz Soul Bistro* has blossomed into an instant Manyunk main attraction. They're concept of pairing grits with everything delicious has become a hit among the locals. The restaurant has generated even more local media attention and the City of Philadelphia has been literally eating it up ever since. Today proves to be no different as the kitchen looks like controlled chaos from all the orders coming in from a packed dining room.

"ORDER UP!" Someone yells over the noise of an active kitchen as the entire staff scrambles to fill orders for another bustling lunch hour crowd.

"WHAT YOU GOT?" Rick yells back acknowledging the incoming order slip.

"I'VE GOT A SOUTHERN CATFISH, GOUDA GRITS AND COLLARDS, AND A CAJUN SHRIMP AND GRITS WITH ANDUOILLE." The man responds as everyone involved springs into action to prepare the order.

Hard at work in chef whites with the *Gritz* logo Rick and Bryce pitch in on the food prep and management, as Brian is plating the food and finishing the plates with fancy garnishments before sending it out to the dining. The success of the restaurant has been overwhelming for the business partners and Brian couldn't be any happier as his dreams of being a successful chef has come to fruition. As Brian, sends another plate out to the dining room, a hostess comes to the kitchen requesting his presence.

"Excuse me Mr. Jones, but someone I just seated has requested you personally." The attractive Caucasian hostess informs him as he takes a sip of soda to hydrate.

"Do you know who it is? Did they give you a name?" Brian curiously asks with arched eyebrows as the interruption wrecks his flow.

"No, she refused to say. But, I seated her in a back booth so you could have some privacy." The waitress replies in a heavy South Philadelphia Italian accent.

"Is she cute?" Brian asks with a devilish grin, unable to resist himself.

"Yeah, she's a cutie." The hostess responds as her cheeks glow to an embarrassing rosey red.

"Okay thanks, Tricia. I'll be out in a minute." Brian smiles as he starts plating another order.

"Go ahead, I got this Brian!" Bryce says stepping in as he overhears the conversation.

"Aight, thanks!" Brian appreciates, taking another refreshing sip from his cup before slinging a hand towel over the shoulder of his chef whites to investigate.

Considering he'd already sat down with former Mayor Nutter, Eagles owner Jeffrey Lurie, a few local news anchors and professional athletes of the Sixers and Phillies, this particular request didn't seem out of sorts to him.

As he enters the dining room, the hostess points out the table where the woman is seated. Although, this is becoming routine for him, Brian paces cautiously as the possibility of this woman being Ashima suddenly comes to mind, to which he is not prepared. As he drew closer his eyes squint in disbelief.

"Hey you, how are you?" She says with mild enthusiasm while standing to give him a hug. Brian's jaw instantly drops to the floor as he's completely taken aback to see the likes of Keena Brown in his presence.

"Wow, you can't be serious…Keena Brown is in the building!" Brian calmly replies as to not draw attention to this incredulous moment. He smiles nervously as he embraces her with a short tight squeeze and she does the same.

"Look at you…you look good! And what is all this? I didn't know you had all this going on? This place is beautiful!" She admires, looking around the stunning restaurant with amazement.

"Yeah, well, it has been about five years since I last saw you. But, this is pretty much what I envisioned after culinary school and here we are." Brian replies in a proud yet humble tone.

"And you've done very well for yourself." She replies with admiration.

"Thank you! You're looking very lovely by the way. I'm not sure if I said that, but I can see that you've been taking care of yourself out there in

Cali." Brian comments with respect to her sexy in the tightfitting jeans, blouse, and heels she's wearing.

"Thank you, I try to keep it together." She replies with a charming smile.

"So, what brings you to Philly after all these years?" Brian asks, curious of Keena's timing amid his success. Although, very surprised and happy to see her, there was still a bit of pain and resentment that resonates within him.

"Well, my sister is getting married and I'm in the wedding, so...I'm back! Plus, I miss Philly. My family always come to Cali to see me because they love the warm weather, but it was my turn to come back home after five years." Keena explains as a waitress brings her the Cabernet she ordered.

"Here you go! And, is there anything else I can get you?" The waitress asks, turning to both of them.

"No, I'm fine for now." Keena politely declines.

"I think we're good here, Tricia. Thank you!" Brian replies, anxious to catch up with his former girlfriend.

"So, how'd you find me?" He asks with scrutiny.

"Mama Ruth! You know I couldn't come to Philly without seeing my favorite grandma. And she caught me up on everything that's been going on over these last few years." Keena replies with a telling smile.

"Is that right? So, what do you know?" He asks, sizing up her level of interest in him.

"I know that you've really done well for yourself and that's all that's important. I'm very proud of you." She sums up in short.

"Hmm...okay. Well, thank you. I see you've done well yourself, too. Finishing school, got you a nice USC Law degree, a handsome family, a nice house in Malibu, right?" He asks to be sure.

"Actually, Thousand Oaks, but close enough!" She corrects him as he continues.

"Okay, well pretty much Malibu and...yeah, you're living the American dream!" Brian replies summarizing all he knew of her.

"So, how do you know all this about me? Are you keeping tabs on me or something?" She smiles, flattered by his interest in her.

"You'd be amazed of what people post on social media these days." Brian cleverly replies.

"Hmph, I guess I'll have to call social media tech support to inquire about their weak security settings." She jokes, winking at him before sipping from her glass.

"You know I wasn't quite sure how I would react whenever I saw you again, but I'm really glad to see you." Brian says in a humorless tone.

"It's really good to see you, too. You know I'm really sorry about what happened between us. Even though I moved on and have a family now, I still think about you all the time. About what life would have been like if we would have made it." She confesses, addressing the elephant in the room.

"Well, since we're sittin' here being honest, I have to admit, it took me a long time to get over losing you. But, things don't always turn out the way we want. So, life goes on, right?" Brian remorsefully replies.

"Yeah, God must have a sense of humor, because he was definitely laughing at our plans." She implies as they share a laugh. "You know, I probably shouldn't tell you this because it's a little embarrassing but, I was actually thinking about you when I was at the alter exchanging my vows, again thinking about the 'what if's' and all." Keena shamefully admits as she smiles while looking down at her wineglass and rims the glass with her finger.

"Wow, that's heavy!" Brian replies in awe.

"I mean, don't get me wrong, Reggie is a good husband and a great father to his kids. But, we got married because I got pregnant, not because I was in love with him." She further explains.

"Interesting…and here I thought you ran off to California and married your college sweetheart?" A condescending Brian suggests.

"Hmph, not at all. I actually met him one year at homecoming and dated him for a while. Then I got pregnant and here we are. So, how 'bout you? Any plans to complicate your life anytime soon?" She asks, subliminally curious of his love life.

Immediately he thinks of Ashima when she poses the question. But, after a quick mull of frustrating thought, he renders his reply.

"Naw, but maybe one day. But, as of now, I'm through with love and all its misery!" Brian answers with a bit of disappointment as he still clings to a glimmer of hope.

"Hmph, you know I know about her, don't you?" Keena informs him.

"If you spoke to Mama Ruth then I'm sure you do." He replies, certain of her suspicion.

"Well, listen, I know that it's my fault that we didn't make it and I'm so sorry for that. And even when I finished college I decided not to look back. But, Brian, even if things just seem a little lost for you right now doesn't mean you stop loving. If you have a nightmare, that doesn't mean you stop dreaming. Don't give up on love because of what we went through. I just hope you're okay, I really do." Keena remorsefully sympathizes becoming emotional. Brian simply nods his head in understanding.

"How 'bout you? Are you happy?" Brian counters with a question of his own before Keena's phone suddenly rings. She raises a finger suggesting one moment before answering.

"Hello...hi baby! What are you doing?" She answers in an adorable tone as she speaks to her three-year-old daughter. "Okay, love you, too!" She concludes after briefly speaking with her husband.

"Sorry, I had to answer that. That was my baby girl. So, what did you ask?" She tries to recall before the interruption.

"Nothing, I was just asking were you happy, but I think I just got my answer." Brian reiterates only this time based on the call she just took; the answer would seem obvious. She takes a profound moment to consider her reply, then realizing at that moment how blessed her life truly is.

"Yeah...I guess I am..." She answers with a teary-eyed smile.

In support of her response, Brian extends his hand across the table and clutches hers as he smiles with her. At that moment, they both realize that the possibility they once shared has been exhausted and what once was, will never be again. To them, this was more than just a moment to reconnect, it was closure.

"Well, I don't want to keep you from your work, so I guess I'll go." Keena says as she reaches for her purse preparing to leave.

"I know...your babies need you. But, you're right I probably should be getting back to the kitchen and be a team player. Looks like we're getting slammed!" Brian replies as he looks around and notices the *Gritz* dining room rapidly filling.

"Yeah, this is quite the place you have here. I'm so proud of you!" She pauses for a sigh before continuing. "You know it was really good seeing you again!" She says in the most endearing voice as they stand and embrace for perhaps the very last time.

"It's been great seeing you too. If you're ever back in town you're more than welcome to anything on the menu." Brian replies taking in a long admiring last look of his beautiful 'ex'.

"Thanks! And if you're ever on the West Coast, look me up." Keena replies, extending the invite back to him.

"Okay...I love you!" Brian blurts out, finally granting Keena the one thing she's always wanted to hear. She responds with a smile as she's nearly choked up before responding.

"Hmph...you've always had a way of making me smile inside. I love you too, Brian!" She replies, pushing away a running tear before walking away. As she makes her way to the exit, Brian couldn't help but to watch until she completely disappears from his view as he silently wishes her well.

Later in the evening, at the height of the dinner crowd, Brian and his colleagues are diligently working the kitchen, giving the Manyunk patrons great reason to accept them as the new kids on the block.

"HEY BRIAN, I THINK YOUR GIRL IS BACK. TRICIA JUST STOPPED ME AND SAID A GIRL IS WAITING FOR YOU OUT THERE." Bryce announces, yelling over the business of the kitchen.

"WHAT THE...? DID SHE FORGET SOMETHING?" A bewildered Brian asks, confused as to why Keena had returned.

"I DON'T KNOW, MAN. I DON'T EVEN KNOW WHAT SHE LOOKS LIKE." Bryce nonchalantly replies as Brian finishes the dish he was preparing before headed into the dining room.

Curious as to what Keena may have left behind or left unsaid, Brian quickly makes his way through the dining room. As he approaches Tricia standing at the seating podium, he quickly realizes from a distance that the person standing next to the podium is not wearing the same thing Keena was wearing. As he draws closer, his heart falls into his stomach and his knees nearly buckle as his suspicion confirms the surreal image of Ashima standing before him.

"Are kidding me?! Twice in one day?! Am I being punked?! This can't be happening!" Brian screams inside in utter disbelief. The significance of such an odd circumstance is so great, he has no clue of what to say or how to feel. His heart suddenly pounds as blood races through his veins from the anxiety of seeing Ashima for the first time since Dubai. As he nervously walks over to greet her, he approaches her with such trepidation his hands begin to tremble ever so slightly.

405

"Hi…" She timidly says standing beautifully in a classy black midi dress with spaghetti strap heels and long flowing hair. Upon seeing Brian, she immediately wants to hug him with the tightest squeeze. But, Brian's body language suggests otherwise to which she refrains.

"Hmph, wow!" Is all he can muster to say. The gravity of the moment is overwhelming as he becomes lost in a whirlwind of thoughts. Anger, frustration, and elation rushes him all at once as he stands paralyzed in the moment.

"Umm…would you like to talk?" Ashima asks feeling intimidated by Brian's lack of enthusiasm as they face-off in the awkward moment.

"Yeah, umm…Tricia could you seat us in the booth near the kitchen? Oh, and two glasses of wine, please. Thank you!" Brian requests as Tricia leads them to their seat.

"Yes, right this way!" A compliant Tricia replies.

Once seated, Brian nervously sits across from her, unable to look her in the face as he wallows in disappointment. Ashima is equally coy, but couldn't shy away from her purpose of being there. Although his reaction to not seeing her wasn't exactly the reception she was looking for, she couldn't abandon the moment without at least granting him closure. She at least owes him that much.

"So, I'm not even sure of where to begin, and judging from your body language, I can see that you're obviously very upset. But, I'm going to get it off my chest anyway." Brian looks up at her with a stone face expression as anger resonates within. The whites of his eyes darken to a matador red as she continues.

"I know it's been a long time since we've last seen each other and…it's important that you know that I've been missing you for every moment of that time we've been apart. But, what happened that day in Dubai was a perfect storm of things gone wrong when you took off." Ashima pauses as a server places their glasses of wine in front of them. After the interruption, she allows Brian a moment to interject before she continues. But, still in his felings, he remains silent and expressionless instead.

"So, the reason why I couldn't return with you to the States is because the phone call I took in the car was my mother telling me that my Nana was gravely ill and I needed to return to Egypt immediately. So, I chartered a plane to get me there as fast as I could. But, Nana was gone by the time I

406

reached the village. I was devastated by her loss, but my mother was hit hardest and fell ill herself afterwards. Mentally she couldn't manage the reality of losing her mother and I needed to be there to help her through that difficult time. But, I see this doesn't mean much to you so perhaps I should go." She sobs, observing his unforgiving demeanor towards her. As she reaches for her purse and prepares to stand, Brian finally speaks.

"Do you have any idea what I've been through?" He mutters, as she pauses to the sound of his voice.

"I'm sorry…?" She replies, not hearing him clearly.

"Do you have any clue of what life has been like for me, seriously? As we sit here, I'm struggling to understand how it's been nearly a year since you abandoned me on the runway in Dubai. I don't hear a word from you since then and now I have you randomly sitting in front of me with no forewarning, no advance notice, just…here you are! I tried to call you, you never called back, no answers to my text, you could have wrote me, email, carrier pigeon, something to at least let me know that you were okay, instead of leaving to assume that something happened to you." Brian rants in a reprimanding tone. Ashima rests back into her seat before giving her reply.

"Brian, I couldn't reach out to you because Fahad smashed my phone to pieces just as you were leaving and I couldn't remember your number by heart. On top of that, I'm in a village miles and miles away from any communication, isolated from the rest of the world. Then, when I finally get back to the States, I go to your old apartment and you don't live there anymore. I try to find you at the restaurant and they tell me you graduated school and moved on. I mean, I tried Brian. I really, really tried to reach you and I got nothing. Finally, by the grace of an article featured online, I was able to find you. Now I'm here!" An emotional Ashima explains.

"Ashima, I'm really sorry for the loss of your grandmother. But, the timing for all this to happen couldn't have been any worse and at a time when I needed you the most. My birthday was a little less special, because my only wish was for you to help me blow out the candles. My graduation was little less significant because you weren't there to help me celebrate. The grand opening to my greatest accomplishment in my life, you missed it all. But, even through the tough times, I'm a better man because of it…because it made me stronger." Brian explains with conviction.

"I'm sorry I missed the opening, I'm sorry I missed your graduation, I'm sorry I missed your birthday, I'm sorry about everything that's happened. But, I lost my Nana, and I had to take care of my family, too! Doesn't that account for anything, or is this really all about, Brian?" She weeps, rising to her feet to avoid the humiliation of sadness. Feeling guilty about his insensitive criticism, Brian quickly responds by gently taking her by the hand to stop her from leaving as the sight of seeing her upset was tearing him apart.

"Ashima, I'm sorry…! Please, I'm sorry! I didn't mean to upset you. Please...let's just talk, okay?" Brian pleads with glassy eyes of sorrow, fearful that she may walk away and never return to him again.

"I love you, Brian Jones. I've wanted to tell you that for a long time. And I've felt that way since that magical moment we shared on the London Eye. I'm sorry that I didn't have the courage to tell you that before. But, I was so foolishly afraid of being hurt by love that I didn't have the heart to tell you. After all this time apart, I thought I'd lost you forever. The time that we'd spent together was honestly the best time of my life. That's what life has taught me since Dubai. And now that I've found you, the only thing I want in my life is to have that magic back again." She admits with shameless humility, looking him directly in his eyes. "So, what now? Do we just throw this all away?" She asks fighting back tears as Brian still maintains a grasp of her hand. In a pensive posture, Brian takes his time before he responds.

"I don't know…" He's pauses. Unable to face the sorrow in her eyes, Brian hangs his head as he focuses on the wine glass before him to express his emotion. "Somewhere in my heart I'm stuck between healing and facing devastation again. Even though there was doubt at first because we come from two different worlds, I took a chance and opened my heart to you anyway, because of the situation you were in with Fahad. And to be honest, I fell in love with you the moment you gave me a chance. I mean, your love, your kiss, your humbleness, and your smile was sweeter than anything I've ever felt, and I never wanted to lose that. Now I have to find a way to remove that scar that took so long to heal? I'm sorry Ashima, I just don't think I have it in me to ever trust love again." He regretfully informs her, this time standing his ground against love.

His response absolutely devastates her. Ashima can no longer fight back the tears, as her spirit becomes broken. With his hand still stretched across the table holding hers, his hand is moistened from the tears falling from her face. As she struggles to find comfort in the moment, she gently massages the teardrops into his skin with her thumb like cocoa butter healing his wounded heart. The sentiment softens his callous posture and breaks down every questionable barrier Brian had left.

"In that case, before I forget, I'm sure you'll want this back." Ashima says as she reaches into her purse and places Brian's key necklace on the table. Although thrilled to see it, Brian simply looks at it as if he doesn't want it back.

While her heart bleeds heavy with sadness, she picks herself up emotionally and stands from the table with resilience as Brian is left speechless.

"Brian, I wasn't asking you to be with me. I was just asking you to focus on the interest of your heart. If that's not possible I totally understand. Just know that I still love you…no matter what." She mutters in a despondent tone as she leans over and kissed him, then wipes her trace off his cheek before tentatively walking away. Yet, through it all, he simply couldn't let her just walk away. This time he won't allow foolish pride to get in the way of the love in his heart.

"Hey…" Brian calls out to her as he stands to his feet. Ashima stops and turns as he approaches.

"…you missed!" Brian says with tears of forgiveness and the most endearing smile. Despite all the anger, frustration, and anguish he'd been through, his moral compass forces him to navigate back to her heart.

Ashima giggles a sigh of relief as her eyes welt from tearful joy. He walks over to her and with the necklace in hand and rightfully places it back around her neck. Then with both hands, he gently embraces her face. Pressing his forehead against hers, he wipes away her tears from her face with both of his thumbs and kisses her tear moistened lips. Ashima laughs, whimpers, and cries all at once before embracing Brian with the tightest hug her strength would allow. Brian returns the embrace with intentions on never letting her go again.

CHAPTER TWENTY-FIVE

Six months later, Children's Hospital…

"Yes, may I help you Sir?" A woman asks at the information desk as Brian walks in, on his way to meet Ashima for an appointment.

"Uh yeah, my wife and I have an appointment with Dr. Holman. She should be already here being seen by the doctor." He explains.

"Okay, what's her name?" The receptionist asks as she prepares to look up the information.

"Ashima Jones." Brian replies with a confident smile.

"Okay Sir, she's in observation room six, down the hall on your left." The receptionist confirms.

"Thank you." Brian replies as he makes his way down the hall with a fresh bouquet of flowers and a brown teddy bear in hand.

"Knock, Knock…" Brian announces before entering the room.

"Hey baby, you're just in time!" Ashima says lying on her back awaiting her examination.

"Mr. Jones…how are you doing, Sir? Are we ready to answer this million-dollar question?" The charismatic Dr. Holman asks.

"Yes, the moment of truth!" Brian replies, handing Ashima the flowers and teddy bear as he leans over to give her a kiss on the lips before giving another kiss to her already bare stomach.

"Awe, thank you baby, they're beautiful!" She says, smelling the flowers before setting them aside and clutching the teddy bear.

"I'm just hoping for a boy, to make all of the men in my life happy, especially my father!" Ashima optimistically desires as she rubs her belly with her left hand bearing the flawless two Karat wedding band on her ring finger.

"Yes, fingers crossed for a boy. Isn't it crazy how your father is suddenly so content since he found out you were expecting?" Brian asks regarding Amir's sudden change of heart towards him.

"Yes, it is very strange. But, I'm glad he's handling everything so well, lately." Ashima agrees, elated by her father's excitement about the pregnancy. "Oh Babe, take a look at what I saw on social media today, too funny!" Ashima says handing Brian her phone while the doctor prepares to get started.

"Billionaire heir Fahad Gabr marries real-estate mogul heiress Nisa Samra in a private ceremony in Dubai." Brian reads from the headline. "Wow…that really is funny. I guess he got the girl he wanted after all." Brian says with amusement.

"Yes, I needed a good laugh today" Ashima replies as Brian hands the phone back to her.

Dr. Holman starts his ultra sound procedure, applying the ointment and maneuvering the wand around Ashima's tiny pregnant belly.

"Okay, there's baby's head, there. And there's baby's hand waving at us, hi baby! And there's baby's sex right there...and uh-oh, looks like this little bundle of joy is going to be a girl! Congratulations folks, yayyy!" The Doctor reveals with dry humor as joyous tears stream from Ashima's eyes.

"Well, looks like there's going to be a new spoiled princess of the family." Brian says, before kissing Ashima's hand and forehead, then shaking the doctor's hand once again.

"Congratulations!"

End

Contact Vdor:

www.vdorauthor.com
www.vernarddorsey.com

Email: info@vdorauthor.com

CPSIA information can be obtained
at www.ICGtesting.com
Printed in the USA
FSHW021633151119
64148FS